Praise for

DAMAGE

"Powerful and explosive, an unforgettable journey the dark side of the human soul. Gilstrap is a master of action and drama. If you like Vince Flynn and Brad Thor, you'll love John Gilstrap."
—**Gayle Lynds**

"Rousing . . . Readers will anxiously await the next installment."
—*Publishers Weekly*

"It's easy to see why John Gilstrap is the go-to guy among thriller writers, when it comes to weapons, ammunition, and explosives. His expertise is uncontested."
—**John Ramsey Miller**

"If you haven't treated yourself to one of John Gilstrap's Jonathan Grave thrillers, you need not deprive yourself any longer. *Damage Control* is riveting, with enough explosions, death traps, and intrigue to fill three books."
—**Joe Hartlaub**, *Book Reporter*

"The best page-turning thriller I've grabbed in ages. Gilstrap is one of the very few writers who can position a set of characters in a situation, ramp up the tension, and yes, keep it there, all the way through. There is no place you can put this book down."
—**Beth Kanell**, Kingdom Books, Vermont

"A page-turning, near-perfect thriller, with engaging and believable characters . . . unputdownable! Warning—if you must be up early the next morning, don't start the book."
—*Top Mystery Novels*

"Takes you full force right away and doesn't let go until the very last page . . . has enough full-bore action to take your breath away, barely giving you time to inhale. The action is nonstop. Gilstrap knows his technology and weaponry. *Damage Control* will blow you away."
—*Suspense Magazine*

THREAT WARNING

"If you are a fan of thriller novels, I hope you've been reading John Gilstrap's Jonathan Grave series. *Threat Warning* is a character-driven work where the vehicle has four on the floor and horsepower to burn. From beginning to end, it is dripping with excitement."
—**Joe Hartlaub, *Book Reporter***

"If you like Vince Flynn–style action, with a strong, incorruptible hero, this series deserves to be in your reading diet. *Threat Warning* reconfirms Gilstrap as a master of jaw-dropping action and heart-squeezing suspense."
—**Austin Camacho, *The Big Thrill***

HOSTAGE ZERO

"Jonathan Grave, my favorite freelance peacemaker, problem-solver, and tough-guy hero, is back—and in particularly fine form. *Hostage Zero* is classic Gilstrap: the people are utterly real, the action's foot to the floor, and the writing's fluid as a well-oiled machine gun. A tour de force!"
—**Jeffery Deaver**

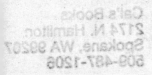

"This addictively readable thriller marries a breakneck pace to a complex, multilayered plot. . . . A roller-coaster ride of adrenaline-inducing plot twists leads to a riveting and highly satisfying conclusion. Exceptional characterization and an intricate, flawlessly crafted storyline make this an absolute must-read for thriller fans."
—*Publishers Weekly* (starred review)

NO MERCY

"*No Mercy* grabs hold of you on page one and doesn't let go. Gilstrap's new series is terrific. It will leave you breathless. I can't wait to see what Jonathan Grave is up to next."
—**Harlan Coben**

"The release of a new John Gilstrap novel is always worth celebrating, because he's one of the finest thriller writers on the planet. *No Mercy* showcases his work at its finest—taut, action-packed, and impossible to put down!"
—**Tess Gerritsen**

"A great hero, a pulse-pounding story—and the launch of a really exciting series."
—**Joseph Finder**

"An entertaining, fast-paced tale of violence and revenge."
—*Publishers Weekly*

"No other writer is better able to combine in a single novel both rocket-paced suspense and heartfelt looks at family and the human spirit. And what a pleasure to meet Jonathan Grave, a hero for our time . . . and for all time."
—**Jeffery Deaver**

JOHN GILSTRAP

HIGH TREASON

PINNACLE BOOKS

Kensington Publishing Corp.

www.kensingtonbooks.com

PINNACLE BOOKS are published by

Kensington Publishing Corp.
119 West 40th Street
New York, NY 10018

All Kensington titles, imprints, and distributed lines are available at special quantity discounts for bulk purchases for sales promotions, premiums, fund-raising, educational, or institutional use. Special book excerpts or customized printings can also be created to fit specific needs. For details, write or phone the office of the Kensington special sales manager: Kensington Publishing Corp., 119 West 40th Street, New York, NY 10018, attn: Special Sales Department; phone 1-800-221-2647.

This book is a work of fiction. Names, characters, businesses, organizations, places, events, and incidents either are the product of the author's imagination or are used fictitiously. Any resemblance to actual persons, living or dead, events, or locales is entirely coincidental.

ISBN-13: 978-0-7860-3019-4
ISBN-10: 0-7860-3019-4

First printing: August 2013

10 9 8 7 6 5 4 3 2 1

Printed in the United States of America

First electronic edition: August 2013

ISBN-13: 978-0-7860-3020-0
ISBN-10: 0-7860-3020-8

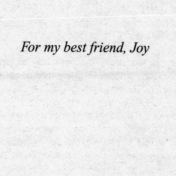

For my best friend, Joy

CHAPTER ONE

In all his seventeen years with the United States Secret Service, Special Agent Jason Knapp had never felt this out of place, this exposed. The January chill combined with his jumpy nerves to create a sense of dread that rendered every noise too loud, every odor too intense.

Rendered the night far too dark.

With his SIG Sauer P229 on his hip, and an MP5 submachine gun slung under his arm—not to mention his five teammates on Cowgirl's protection detail—he couldn't imagine a scenario that might get away from them, but sometimes you get that niggling voice in the back of your head that tells you that things aren't right. Years of experience had taught Knapp to listen to that voice when it spoke.

Oh, that Mrs. Darmond would learn to listen to her protection detail. Oh, that she would listen to *anyone*.

While he himself rarely visited the White House residence, stories abounded among his colleagues that Cowgirl and Champion fought like banshees once the doors were closed. She never seemed to get the fact that image mattered to presidents, and that First Ladies had a responsibility to show a certain decorum.

Clearly, she didn't care.

These late-night party jaunts were becoming more and more routine, and Knapp was getting sick of them. He understood that she rejected the traditional role of First Lady, and he got that despite her renown she wanted to have some semblance of a normal life, but the steadily increasing risks she took were flat-out irresponsible.

Tonight was the worst of the lot.

It was one thing to dash out to a bar on the spur of the moment with a reduced protection detail—first spouses and first children had done that for decades— but to insist on a place like the Wild Times bar in Southeast DC was a step too far. It was five steps too far.

Great disguise notwithstanding, Cowgirl was a white lady in very dark part of town. And it was nearly one in the morning. Throw in all those bodies floating in Lake Michigan from the as yet unresolved East-West Airlines explosion last week, and you had a recipe for disaster.

Knapp stood outside the main entrance to the club, shifting from foot to foot to ward away the cold. Charlie Robinson flanked the other side of the door, and together they looked like the plain-clothed version of the toy soldiers that welcomed children to the FAO Schwarz toy store in Manhattan. He felt at least that conspicuous.

Twenty feet away, Cowgirl's chariot, an armored Suburban, idled in the handicapped space at the curb, its tailpipe adding a cloud of condensation to the night.

Inside the chariot, Gene Tomkin sat behind the wheel, no doubt reveling in the warmth of the cab. Bill Lansing enjoyed similar bragging rights in the follow car that waited in the alley behind the bar.

Typical of OTR movements—off the record—the detail had chosen silver Suburbans instead of the black ones that were so ubiquitous to official Washington, in hopes of drawing less attention to themselves. They'd driven here just like any other traffic, obeying stoplights and using turn signals the whole way. On paper that meant that you remained unnoticed.

But a Suburban was a Suburban, and if you looked hard enough you could see the emergency lights behind the windows and the grille. Throw in the well-dressed white guys standing like toy soldiers, and they might as well have been holding flashing signs.

In these days of Twitter and Facebook, when rumors traveled at the speed of light, all it would take for this calm night to turn to shit would be for somebody to connect some very obvious dots. While the good citizens of the District of Columbia had more or less unanimously cast their votes to sweep Champion into office, they'd since turned against him. It didn't stretch Knapp's imagination even a little to envision a spontaneous protest.

Then again, Cowgirl was such a media magnet that he could just as easily envision a spontaneous *TMZ* feeding frenzy. Neither option was more attractive than the other in this neighborhood.

The Wild Times was doing a hell of a business. The main act on the stage was a rapper of considerable local fame—or maybe he was a hip-hopper (how do you tell the difference?)—and he was drawing hundreds of twentysomething kids. Within the last twenty minutes, the pace of arrivals had picked up—and almost nobody was leaving.

From a tactical perspective, the two agents inside with Cowgirl—Peter Campbell and Dusty Binks, the detail supervisor—must have been enduring the tortures of the damned. In an alternate world where the First Lady might have given a shit, no one would have been allowed to touch the protectee, but in a nightclub situation, where the headliner's fans paid good money to press closer to the stage, preventing personal contact became nearly impossible.

For the most part, the arriving revelers projected a pretty benign aura. It was the nature of young men to swagger in the presence of their girlfriends, and with that came a certain tough-guy gait, but over the years Knapp had learned to trust his ability to read the real thing from the imitation. Over the course of the past hour, his warning bells hadn't rung even once.

Until right now.

A clutch of four guys approached from the north, and everything about them screamed malevolence. It wasn't just the gangsta gait and the gangsta clothes. In the case of the leader in particular, it was the eyes. Knapp could see the glare from twenty feet away. This guy wanted people to be afraid of him.

"Do you see this?" he asked Robinson without moving his eyes from the threat.

Robinson took up a position on Knapp's right. "Handle it carefully," he warned. More than a few careers had been wrecked by YouTube videos of white cops challenging black citizens.

As the kids closed to within a dozen feet, Knapp

stepped forward. "Good evening, gentlemen," he said. "You know, it's pretty crowded inside."

"The hell outta my way," the leader said. He started to push past, but Knapp body-blocked him. No hands, no violence. He just physically blocked their path.

"Look at the vehicle," Knapp said, nodding to the Suburban. "Take a real close look."

Their heads turned in unison, and they seemed to get it at the same instant.

"If any of you are armed, this club is exactly the last place you want to be right now. Do you understand what I'm saying?"

"What?" the leader said. "Is it like the president or something?"

Knapp ignored the question. "Here are your choices, gentlemen. You can go someplace else, or you can submit to a search right here on the street. If I find a firearm on any of you, I'll arrest you all, and your mamas won't see their boys for about fifteen years. Which way do you want to go?"

Simple, respectful, and face-saving.

"Come on, Antoine," one of them said. "This place sucks anyway."

Antoine held Knapp's gaze for just long enough to communicate his lack of fear. Then he walked away, taking his friends with him.

"Nicely done, Agent Knapp," Robinson said.

They returned to their posts. "Every time we do one of these late-night OTRs, I'm amazed by the number of people who keep vampire hours. Don't these kids have jobs to wake up for?"

Robinson chuckled. "I figure they all drive buses or hazmat trucks."

With the Antoine non-confrontation behind them, Knapp told himself to relax, but in the world of gang-bangers, you always had to be on your toes for the retaliatory strike. He couldn't imagine that Antoine and his crew would be in the mood to take on federal agents, but you never knew.

He just wanted to get the hell out of here.

"Look left," Robinson said.

Half a block away, a scrawny, filthy little man was doing his best to navigate a shopping cart around the corner to join their little slice of the world. The cart overflowed with blankets and assorted stuff—the totality of his worldly possessions, Knapp imagined. Aged somewhere between thirty and eighty, this guy had the look of a man who'd been homeless for decades. There's a hunched movement to the chronically homeless that spoke of a departure of all hope. It would be heartbreaking if they didn't smell so bad.

"If Cowgirl sees him, you know she'll offer him a ride," Robinson quipped.

Knapp laughed. "And Champion will give him a job. Couldn't do worse than some of his other appointments." Knapp didn't share the first family's attraction to the downtrodden, but he admired it. It was the one passion of the president's that seemed to come from an honest place.

Knapp didn't want to take action against this wretched guy, but if he got too close, he'd have to do something. Though heroic to socialists and poets, the preponderance of homeless folks were, in Knapp's experience, nut jobs—harmless at the surface, but inherently unstable. They posed a hazard that needed to be managed.

He felt genuine relief when the guy parked himself on a sidewalk grate and started to set up camp.

Knapp's earpiece popped as somebody broke squelch on the radio. "Lansing, Binks. Bring the follow car to the front. Cowgirl's moving in about three."

"Thank God," Knapp said aloud but off the air. Finally.

He and Robinson shifted from their positions flanking the doors of the Wild Times to new positions flanking the doors to Cowgirl's chariot. He double-checked to make sure that his coat was open and his weapon available. A scan of the sidewalk showed more of what they'd been seeing all night.

When the follow car appeared from the end of the block and pulled in behind the chariot, Knapp brought his left hand to his mouth and pressed the button on his wrist mike. "Binks, Knapp," he said. "We're set outside."

"Cowgirl is moving now."

This was it, the moment of greatest vulnerability. Ask Squeaky Fromme, Sara Jane Moore, or John Hinckley. These few seconds when the protectee is exposed are the moments of opportunity for suicidal bad guys to take their best shot.

Robinson pulled open the Suburban's door and cheated his body forward to scan for threats from that end of the street, and Knapp cheated to the rear to scan the direction of the homeless guy and the real estate beyond him. He noted with some unease that the guy was paying attention in a way that he hadn't before. His eyes seemed somehow sharper.

Knapp's inner alarm clanged.

Ahead and to his left, the double doors swung out, revealing a clearly unhappy Cowgirl, who seemed to be resisting her departure. She wasn't quite yelling yet, but assuming that past was precedent, the yelling would come soon.

Movement to his right brought Knapp's attention back around to the homeless man, who suddenly looked less homeless as he shot to his feet and hurled something at the chariot.

Knapp fought the urge to intercept the throw, and instead drew his sidearm as he shouted, "Grenade!"

He'd just leveled his sights on the attacker when an explosion ripped the chariot apart from the inside, the pressure wave rattling his brain and shoving him face-first onto the concrete. He didn't know if he'd fired a shot, but if he had, it missed, because the homeless guy was still standing.

He'd produced a submachine gun from somewhere—a P90, Knapp thought, but he wasn't sure—and he was going to town, blasting the night on full-auto.

Behind him, he knew that Campbell and Binks would be shielding Cowgirl with their bodies as they hustled her toward the follow car. In his ear, he heard Lansing shouting, "Shots fired! Shots fired! Agents down!"

Once Knapp found his balance, he rolled to a knee and fired three bullets at the attacker's center of mass. The man remained unfazed and focused, shooting steadily at the First Lady.

Body armor, Knapp thought. He took aim at the attacker's head and fired three more times. The attacker collapsed.

But the shooting continued, seemingly from every

compass point. Had passersby joined the fight? What the hell—

Binks and Campbell were still ten feet from the follow car when head shots killed them both within a second of each other. They collapsed to the street, bringing Cowgirl with them. She curled into a fetal ball and started to scream.

Past her, and over her head, bullets raked the doors of the follow car. Going that way was no longer an option.

Keeping low, Knapp let his SIG drop to the pavement as he reached for his slung MP5. This wasn't time for aimed shots; it was time for covering fire. At this moment, the First Lady of the United States was far more important than any other innocents in the crowd. He held the weapon as a pistol in his left hand as he raked the direction he thought the new shots were coming from.

With his right hand, he grabbed Cowgirl by the neck of her coat and pulled. "Back into the club!" he commanded as he draped his body over hers.

To others it might have looked as though she was carrying him on her back as he hustled her toward the front doors of the club, past the burning chariot and around the body of Charlie Robinson, who'd been torn apart by the blast.

Knapp was still five steps away when searing heat tore through his midsection, driving the breath from his lungs and making him stagger.

He'd taken that bullet for Cowgirl. He'd done his job. Now he just had to finish it.

He had to get her inside.

The next two bullets took him in the hip and the elbow.

He was done, and he knew it.

"Inside!" he yelled as he pushed the First Lady as hard as he could.

He saw her step through the doors the instant before a bullet sheared his throat.

CHAPTER TWO

Jonathan Grave waited at the Learjet's door while the stairway deployed. When it was down and locked, he centered his rucksack between his shoulders with a shrug and hefted the two green duffels that contained rifles and electronic gear. He turned his head to the right, where he could see Boxers, his longtime friend and cohort, in the cockpit, shutting things down.

"Hey, Box, your ruck and the other duffels are here on the floor."

"Got it," Boxers said without looking. "Be sure to leave the heaviest ones for me. I don't want you hurting your little self."

Jonathan grinned. "I always do." And in fact, he always did. A couple of inches shy of seven feet tall with a girth that made linebackers look puny, Boxers was easily the strongest man Jonathan had ever known. Big Guy always did the heavy lifting.

As Jonathan made his way down the narrow stairs onto the tarmac, it occurred to him that this would be the first time in a long while that he wouldn't need to spend twelve hours after an 0300 mission cleaning weapons and replacing gun barrels and receivers. The mission had been a quick one, and surprisingly uncomplicated. They hadn't even fired a shot.

As a rule, the covert side of Security Solutions didn't get involved with recovering errant young people from the clutches of cults, but this case had had the feel of a kidnapping. At least, that's what the family had thought, though the FBI disagreed.

The kid's father—Daddy Lottabucks—contacted Jonathan through the usual combination of cutouts and fake e-mail addresses, and was anxious to pay the gate rate for Jonathan's services. In the end, when Jonathan and Boxers crashed the door to recover the PC—precious cargo—the cult leader just handed the kid over.

That fact alone—the absence of shooting—helped explain Boxers' fouler-than-usual mood. For the Big Guy, self-actualization had a lot to do with wreaking havoc. It wasn't that he was homicidal—not really—but rather that he enjoyed the . . . *efficiency* of solutions that created fire and noise.

Jonathan waited at the base of the stairs for Boxers. He had to laugh when the Big Guy's massive frame filled the doorway. With his ruck in place and the two duffels in his hands, squeezing through the door took on the elements of a high school physics calculation.

"There's some butter in the galley if you need to slather up," Jonathan quipped.

"My mama's womb had a bigger opening than this," Boxers grumped.

Jonathan let it go. No matter how close the friendship, jokes about men's mothers were eternally off-limits.

"I vote you tell Mannix we're done with his sardine

can," the Big Guy said when he joined his boss on the tarmac.

Austin Mannix had thrown in two years' access to his private plane when Jonathan negotiated the fee for this latest job. Given their line of work, it helped to have air service that was traceable to a third party. Commercial aviation options were out of the question. Between the two of them, they carried enough weapons, ammunition, and explosives to repel an invasion. You never knew what might go wrong on even the simplest of ops, so it always paid to be prepared. One man's preparation, though, was a TSA agent's heart attack.

But man this plane was tiny.

"We'll see," Jonathan said. "At least it's based in Fredericksburg." Other airplanes they'd negotiated for had been hangared in Dulles and Leesburg, easily an hour farther away from Jonathan's home in Fisherman's Cove.

"You say that like it's a good thing. It's still a long friggin' drive."

Again, Jonathan let it go. Jonathan knew how much money the Big Guy made for his contributions to Security Solutions, and there wasn't a community from Miami to New York City where he couldn't afford to live comfortably. *Very* comfortably. The fact that he'd chosen the hustle of Georgetown over bucolic Fisherman's Cove was his own problem.

Crossing in front of the civil aviation terminal building, Jonathan plotted a straight-line walking course toward the Batmobile, Boxers' pet name for Jonathan's customized and armored black Hummer H2. While not especially fast, the truck held its own on the highway, but it truly earned its keep off-road where, despite its weight, it could climb trees once you engaged the four-wheel drive.

He hadn't paid attention to the nearby vehicles until the doors of a black sedan opened in unison and disgorged two men in suits and sunglasses.

"At last," Boxers grumbled. "The day gets interesting. You thinking good guys or bad guys?"

"Feds," Jonathan said, knowing full well that he hadn't answered the Big Guy's question.

"Just so we're clear," Boxers said, "if they draw, I draw." He'd long been on the record that he would never tolerate any form of incarceration, whether at the hands of a foreigner or the local constabulary. Like anyone who had to deal with the meddling bullshit that doubled these days for due process, he had a particular hard-on for feds.

"Let's clear our hands, then," Jonathan said. He dropped his two duffels to the concrete, reducing his weight by one hundred pounds and clearing the way for him to draw the Colt 1911 .45 that always rode high on his right hip. Loaded with eight rounds, one hot in the chamber, that was six more bullets than he'd need if it came to a shoot-out.

Boxers likewise dropped his duffels to clear access to his holstered 9 millimeter Beretta.

They kept their gait steady as they approached the two men who'd clearly meant to intimidate them more than they had. You might even say they looked a little frightened themselves.

The guy on the driver's side lifted his hands to show that they were empty. "Whoa, whoa, whoa, guys," he said. "We mean no harm."

Jonathan shifted his eyes to the other one. "And you?" He stopped striding when good guys and bad guys were separated only by twenty feet and a door panel.

Mr. Passenger Side resisted joining the program. He took a hesitant step back, then stood his ground. His hands remained out of sight at his sides when he said, "We've done nothing to threaten you."

"It's more about *you* feeling threatened," Boxers said with a grin.

"Don't be an idiot, Kane," the driver said. Closing in on fifty, the driver had an easy twenty years on the younger man named Kane. One of the greatest gifts of maturity and experience was the ability to read the dynamics of a situation for what they were.

They were definitely feds, Jonathan decided, and the different degrees of swagger defined in his mind the difference between old school and new school. Since 9/11, federal law enforcers had been bestowed with remarkable power that they seemed oddly incapable of not overflexing.

"Let me guess," Jonathan said. "FBI." Actually, the matching high-and-tight hairstyles and attention to fashion spoke more of Secret Service, but he couldn't imagine how this could be their jurisdiction.

"Yes, sir," the driver said. "Special Agent Edward Shrom. This is Special Agent Carlton Kane. We both report out of headquarters in Washington. I'd be happy to show you my creds if you promise not to go Chuck Norris on me."

"Not necessary," Jonathan said. "I have every confidence that you have the skill to forge a set of creds if you were so inclined." He drilled Kane with his gaze.

"Son, if you don't show me an empty pair of hands right by God now, we're going to have an issue."

Somewhere north of eighteen and south of thirty-five, Kane had the look of a quarterback from a second-tier school. He had a lot of neck, but not much girth, and the kind of self-righteous smirk that Jonathan loved so dearly to wipe away.

"I am a federal officer, Mr. Grave. I'd be careful—"

"Oh, for God's sake," Shrom said. "Give it a rest. Either show him your hands or draw down on him. Just stop dancing."

Jonathan liked Shrom.

Grudgingly, Carlton Kane raised his palms so that Jonathan could see them.

"Thank you," Jonathan said. He felt tension drain from his shoulders. "So what's up, gentlemen?"

Shrom answered quickly, as if hurrying to get in before his young partner could screw things up. "I have orders from my boss's boss, Director Rivers—I believe you know her as Wolverine—to talk you into taking a ride in the car with us."

Boxers made a growling sound that perfectly reflected Jonathan's unease.

"Where would we be going and why?"

"That's need to know, sir," Shrom said. "I can't answer that."

"You want us to go with you to a place where we have no need to know where we're going?" Boxers asked with a derisive chuckle. "What are you Fibbies smoking these days?"

"We're the ones who don't have a need to know," Kane said.

Jonathan cocked his head and smiled at the illogic.

"And how are you going to drive us to a place you're not authorized to know?"

"I'm betting they drive blindfolded," Boxers quipped.

Shrom forced a smile that looked more like a wince. "We know the where, Mr. Van de Muelebroecke, although I suspect that it's only a first step. What we don't know is the why." The fact that he knew Boxers' real name was a card well played.

"Suppose we say no?" Jonathan asked.

Shrom seemed ready for that one. "When I asked the director that very same question, she guaranteed me that you would say yes if I told you she said it was important. The choice to come along or stay is entirely yours." He paused and shrugged. "That's it. That was the speech I was told to make."

Jonathan inhaled deeply through his nose and vigorously rubbed his chin. He'd known Irene Rivers for years—since long before she ran a field office, let alone been named director. He'd done the kind of work for her that the FBI officially never did, yet needed to do to protect the citizens of the United States. Her Wolverine code name had started as a joke nearly two decades ago, a quasi-insult that reflected her feisty personality. As so often happened in the unpredictable world of nicknames, it stuck as her handle within the tiny covert world of Security Solutions. The only way for these two Fibbies to know that the name even existed would be if Irene had shared it with them.

"Does this have anything to do with the East-West Airlines attack?" Nearly a week ago, an as yet unidentified bad guy had launched a Stinger antiaircraft missile into a fully loaded 747 as it climbed out of its takeoff from O'Hare International Airport. The perfect shot had scattered burning aircraft and human parts over a mile-long swath of Lake Michigan.

"We don't yet know that that was a terrorist attack," Kane said. That was the official line of the government to stave off panic, but insiders knew the reality. Whether Kane was too young to be among those insiders was a topic for the future.

"Okay," Jonathan announced. "We'll come with you."

Boxers' eyes popped. "We will?"

Jonathan shrugged. "If Director Rivers requests the pleasure of our company, it's only polite that we accept the invitation."

Boxers smiled and scowled. Simultaneously. It was an odd combination of expressions that was unique to him. Jonathan read it as a kind of amused tolerance—and perhaps a touch of anticipation that he might get to shoot something after all.

Before the smile could fully form on Shrom's face, Jonathan added, "But you come with us, not the other way around. In our vehicle."

"Absolutely not," Kane said.

Jonathan didn't drop a beat. "Then this conversation is over," he said. He turned on his heel and started walking back toward the bags they'd dropped.

Boxers followed.

"Wait," Shrom said.

Jonathan stopped, turned.

"What are you doing?" Kane asked, aghast. His ears turned red when he was upset. Jonathan found that amusing. Cute, even. Like he needed a hug and a teddy bear.

"We'll do it your way," Shrom conceded.

Kane's jaw dropped. "We will?"

Jonathan winked at the Big Guy. "Déjà vu," he mouthed.

Shrom said to his protégé, "I have orders from as high up as I can imagine. If you were Mr. Grave, would you climb into a car with us?"

"I would do what a federal agent told me to do," Kane said. Way to defend your position to the very end.

"Then you're an idiot," Shrom said.

Jonathan laughed. So did Boxers, and he was a much tougher audience. When Kane turned purple, it was as good as it got.

"Follow me," Jonathan said. He turned again, walked to the dropped duffels, and picked them up, Boxers with him every step. He led the four-man parade to the Batmobile and waited while Boxers thumbed the remote to unlock the doors. He called over his shoulder, "Don't get in until I tell you."

He didn't look back to confirm compliance because that would have telegraphed weakness. From this point on, the Fibbies needed to do exactly what he instructed them to do.

With the cargo bay doors open, Jonathan and Boxers heaved the heavy duffels onto the floor.

"Do I even want to know what's inside those bags?" Kane asked.

"I'm sure you do," Boxers said. "Which is sort of a shame."

When purple transitioned to grape, Jonathan actually started feeling sorry for the guy.

"Here's the deal," Jonathan said. "My friend will drive. Agent Shrom, you and Agent Kane will ride in the middle row of seats, and I will sit behind you."

Kane opened his mouth to say something, but Shrom put a hand on his arm. They all ended up in their assigned seats.

Jonathan boarded last, taking the spot behind everyone. He didn't really expect the agents to try to hijack the ride, but if they did, he'd nail them both. One could never be too careful.

"So," Boxers said, once the doors were all closed. "Where are we going?"

David Kirk never picked up his phone on the first ring. Or the third ring, for that matter. He was a fifth-ring guy. He figured that if someone really wanted to speak to him, they'd wait at least that long. On the sixth ring, the call would have gone to his voice mail.

"*Washington Enquirer*," he said as he snatched up the receiver. "This is David."

"Yo," a familiar voice said. "This is DeShawn. Have you got a few minutes?"

David rolled his eyes. DeShawn Lincoln was one of David's bar buddies. He was also a disgruntled rookie in the Metropolitan Police Department, which made him a reliable source for the kind of salacious news that city editors publicly decried yet secretly loved because it sold a hell of a lot of newspapers.

"Hi, Deeshy," David replied. "What's up, man? I've always got a few minutes for you."

The usual smile was missing from DeShawn's voice. "What's up is my bosses' heads. Completely up their own asses."

David's Spidey-sense tingled. "Are you calling because I'm a friend, or because I'm a reporter?"

"Can I choose both?"

"Absolutely." As he spoke, David donned his telephone headset and pushed the button to connect it. This way, David's hands were free to type notes. "Does this mean you have a lead for me?"

"Lead, no," DeShawn said. "Whole friggin' story, yes. It's not for the phone, though."

"Ooh," David said in his spooky voice. "Sounds scary." DeShawn's criticality sensor was dozens of degrees out of phase with David's.

"It *is* scary, David." Deeshy was rattled. David could hear it in his voice. "Do you want to meet with me or not?"

The elevated angst got his attention. He closed his e-mail screen to reduce distraction. "When and where?"

"You know where the merry-go-round is on the Mall?"

"Of course. And I believe they call it a carousel." Located outside the original Smithsonian Castle, it was also known by locals as one of the most sublime rip-offs in Washington.

"Whatever. Meet me there at eight o'clock tonight."

"Oh, Christ, Deeshy. It's cold and windy, and that's like the coldest and windiest spot in town."

"Don't be a pussy. See you there at eight?"

David groaned. The problem with DeShawn Lincoln was that he became a cop to break huge cases—the kind that only came up once or twice in a thirty-year career—or every week on network television. This was Deeshy's fourth imagined career-maker in eight months. When his bosses pushed back, Deeshy turned to his newspaper pal for support. Even in as corrupt a town as DC, sometimes the smoke you thought was a fire was really a cigar that was really a cigar.

"Give me a hint," David said. "You're talking about pulling me out of a warm apartment when I could be devoting my evening to Internet porn. What've you got?"

DeShawn hesitated. David imagined that he was checking his surroundings to determine if he could speak freely. Finally, he said, "What I've got is what Washington's best at: a cover-up."

David's neck hairs rose. "Of what?"

The answer came as a whisper. "Murder. I think the Secret Service is involved, and that means it goes to the very top."

David felt blood drain from his head. "Say that again."

"Did you hear about the shooting last night at the Wild Times?"

David prided himself at being a devoted reader of the newspaper that employed him. "Yeah. Secret Service was there. They lost a couple of people."

"And what is the Secret Service doing in force at a bar in the middle of the night?"

"Was the first family there?"

Deeshy paused. "I'll see you tonight." The line went dead.

David laid the receiver in its cradle, but his hand stayed in place for a long time.

"Are you all right?" The question came from Becky Beckeman, a fellow graduate of Radford University's journalism school, though she one year before he.

"I'm fine."

"You just got bad news on the phone," Becky pressed.

"No, really."

Becky's desk was directly opposite his, and when she stood, her untethered boobs swayed behind her blouse, threatening to drown out any sound she might make with her mouth. "Is it about the attack?" she asked. She was an earthy Birkenstock gal.

The directness and the accuracy of the question startled him until he realized that she was speaking of the East-West Airlines attack at O'Hare. One hundred seventy-three dead people.

David shook his head. "No, it has nothing to do with that."

But did it? He hadn't connected those particular dots, but if there was an unreported attempt on the first family's life last night, just a week after the airline attack, couldn't they be related?

"Kirk!" Charlie Baroli's voice boomed like a cannon across the vast expanse of the newsroom. "You! My office! Two minutes ago!"

Eighty pounds overweight, with an alcoholic's nose that looked like it might have been chewed by a dog, Baroli was certain to stroke out one day. David just prayed that he could be present when it happened.

David killed his monitor and pushed himself away from his workstation. As he stood, Becky gave him a look acknowledging the torture that lay in his future, and that she was on his side. Becky was always on David's side. He knew about the crush she had on him—everyone within twenty feet knew about it whenever they saw her look his way—but she wasn't his type. He preferred his women less . . . free-spirited. He'd tried not to encourage her. Except sometimes, when she had a tidbit of a source and wanted to get his attention with it. On those occasions, it maybe was possible that he gave her a mixed message. Or maybe a wrong message. Maybe.

David didn't dawdle on his way to the city editor's desk, but he didn't hurry, either. If you internalized Baroli's perpetual angst, you'd end up beating him to the grave.

Baroli's office was little more than a cube with real walls, and was decorated in Early Ceiling Collapse. Think hoarder. Think roaches. Think Taco Bell wrappers that were older than David. Baroli had already closed the door before David could arrive.

The door thing was a power play, a requirement to knock. David gave three quick raps with the knuckle of his forefinger.

Baroli made eye contact through the glass panel that ran the length of the door and motioned him in with his middle finger. His way of flipping off employees while maintaining plausible deniability.

David opened the door. "You needed me, sir?" In his mind, it was treacly irony, but he had every confidence that Baroli would miss it.

"Come in and close the door."

He did, in that moment thanking the Holy Things for the fact of the window and the witnesses it created. If the two guest chairs had not been stacked with meaningless crap, David might have sat down. As it was, he remained standing.

Baroli filled his seat with flesh to spare. He pushed

himself away from his desk and simulated crossing his arms across his ample man-boobs. "You know that if it was up to me we never would have hired you, right?"

"I believe that you might have mentioned it, sir. Sixty or seventy times in the last fifteen months. Sir."

"You're here because your father is a major share-holder."

"Again," David said. "Seventy-one times now." In reality, his father would have been more than delighted to see him crash and burn, but Baroli wouldn't care. David was supposed to be in law school now, on his way to a Wall Street job that would add to the Kirk family's billion-plus-dollar legacy. "But I disagree," David said. "I like to think that I'm here because I'm a talented journalist."

Baroli laughed. "A journalist," he mocked. If he'd been tasting the words, they'd have been long on sulfur and garlic. "You're so green you're still wet."

David waited for the rest. He was in fact new to his profession, but he was damn good at it. He met his deadlines and was ahead of the curve on developing sources. He sensed that the trouble he was in had nothing to do with his job skills.

"Grayson Cantrell was in my office about a half hour ago," Baroli said. Grayson owned the choice stories from the city beat. "He told me that when he contacted Malcolm Sanderson to get a quote on the DC City Council's decision to walk away from school vouchers, Councilman Sanderson told him that he'd already spoken to a reporter named Kirk. He was disinclined to repeat himself."

David gave the smug smile that he knew pissed

Baroli off. "I've known Mr. Sanderson my whole life," he said. "Peter Sanderson, his son, and I were best friends from elementary school through high school."

"How special for you," Baroli said. "But that was not your story. That story belonged to Grayson Cantrell."

"Grayson Cantrell is lazy." The words were out before David could stop them. He was like that sometimes when it came to stating the truth.

Baroli recoiled. "Grayson Cantrell was working sources before you were a viable sperm."

"Yet I didn't make my call to Councilman Sanderson until eight hours after the announcement," David said. "The story is up on my screen now, if you want to take a look at it."

"I want you to delete it," Baroli said. "I want you to concentrate on the job you were hired to do."

"I'm doing the Sanderson story on my time. If you don't want to print it, I can put it on my blog. Mr. Daniels told me that he reads my blog regularly. I'm just sayin' . . ." Preston Daniels owned the *Washington Enquirer*, having inherited it from three previous generations of Danielses.

Somewhere below the layers of facial flesh, a muscle twitched in Baroli's jaw. "You signed a noncompete," he said.

David shrugged. "My words for you are work for hire. My words for me are mine to do with as I please. If it makes you feel better, I don't pay myself very well."

But his advertisers did. *Kirk Nation*, David's blog, had just north of 172,000 subscribers now, and was viewed by well over a million people every day. He had influence peddlers lined up at the door to throw money at him in return for visibility on his masthead. David worked at the *Enquirer* for the 401(k) plan and the health insurance. And it didn't hurt to pad your résumé with time served on one of the most read and most influential newspapers on the planet. He was in the Big Leagues.

Baroli would have made a shitty poker player. His eyes grew hot and his jowls trembled. A poster child for the old generation of editors who no longer understood the realities of their own jobs, he clearly couldn't think of anything to say.

Baroli blurted, "Get out of my office."

CHAPTER THREE

About five miles into the drive, Jonathan began suspecting that he knew where they were headed. As they drove through Virginia's Piedmont, the relentless farmland was spotted with shacks and mansions, all of this in the vicinity of George Washington's birthplace on the banks of the Potomac River.

His suspicions were confirmed when Shrom directed Boxers to pilot the Batmobile through the open gate in the stone wall that defined Meadowlark Farms, a sprawling spread owned by a freelance spook named Griffin Horne, with whom Jonathan had worked a few times in the past.

Boxers shot his boss a knowing look in the rearview mirror, but he said nothing. If Irene Rivers was in fact here to meet them, she would not want her Fibbie minions to know that Jonathan and the Bureau used the same freelancers. That was especially true of the likes of Horne, whose allegiances had everything to do with good guys versus bad, and less than nothing to do with the alphabet soup that defined inside-the-Beltway rivalries. Jonathan had no doubt that Horne had worked for the FBI against the CIA or State, and then switched teams to work the other way around. Inside the government, where everyone claimed to be on the side of God and country, the border between good guys and bad guys was more of a blurry stripe than a fine line.

Boxers pulled to a stop just inside the gate. "Where to?" he asked. It was a bluff, of course. Horne conducted all of his business in the same place.

"To the barn," Shrom said. "They said it would be easy to find."

Easier for some than others, Jonathan didn't say.

Easily fifty feet wide and seventy-five feet long, Jonathan suspected the barn was visible from a low orbit. The last time Jonathan conducted business here, Horne had left the huge double doors open for them. This time, they not only were closed, but they were guarded by clones of Agent Kane.

"Well, shit," Boxers said, noting the guards. "Now I'm all scared and stuff."

"Stop the vehicle," Jonathan ordered when they were still fifty yards from the barn. "Time for all government employees to walk."

"What's going on?" Kane asked, indignant. Jonathan was beginning to think that indignant was the only trick Kane knew.

Jonathan explained. "You're getting out and walking ahead. You're going to tell the gentlemen with the squiggles in their ears to open the big doors and step aside. Tell them to keep their hands neutral, and assure them that if I see anything that looks remotely threatening, I won't hesitate to kill them."

Kane objected, "Who do—"

"Don't," Jonathan interrupted. "I've got eggs in my

refrigerator older than you. You want me, you play by my rules. None of this is negotiable." He paused a few seconds, waiting for them to read the subtext. "Including the part where you get out of my truck."

Shrom poked his protégé in the arm. "That's our cue to leave." He tried to open the door, but it was locked.

Jonathan saw Boxers' eyes looking for confirmation, and then the Big Guy released the locks from the front seat. The FBI agents slid out, pushed the doors shut, and started walking toward their doppelgängers at the barn door.

With the locks reset, Boxers drilled Jonathan with a glare in the rearview mirror. "Does any of this feel right to you?"

"Nope." And being at Horne's place didn't improve things. The fact that his loyalties shifted so easily with the source of the paycheck made it dangerous to be the last to arrive at the party.

"Worst case," Jonathan said, "we back out through the doors and run over a few people getting out of Dodge." The Batmobile was as heavily armored as any government limousine, capable of deflecting armor-piercing ammunition. Combined with run-flat tires and massively reinforced bumpers, there was no fear of getting caught in a kill zone.

As additional insurance, Jonathan lifted a patch of carpet at his feet and revealed a push-button keypad. He entered the code, lifted a hatch, and revealed a cache of weapons. He lifted two collapsed M4 assault rifles and four loaded thirty-round magazines of 5.56 millimeter ammunition. He loaded and chambered both, and then wended his way past the middle row of seats to place a rifle and mag on the passenger seat next to

Boxers. He then settled into the seat previously occupied by Agent Shrom and laid the second rifle across his lap.

They waited until Shrom and Kane finished palavering with the guards and the barn doors were wide open before Boxers started moving. "What do you think?" the Big Guy asked. "Slow or fast?"

"Split the difference, but with attitude."

Boxers brought the Batmobile up to about twenty-five miles an hour approaching the opening—fast enough to make the guards think twice about getting in the way, but not so fast as to overcommit to the unknown. It helped that they both knew what the barn looked like inside.

As soon as they crossed the threshold, Jonathan relaxed. The first face he saw belonged to Irene Rivers. She stood with two men who looked vaguely familiar, but whose faces he couldn't quite place. Irene's posture, with her weight shifted to one foot and her arms crossed, told him that she wasn't surprised by the drama of his entrance, and her smirk told him that they had nothing to fear from this meeting. "Okay," Jonathan said. "We're cool."

Boxers hit the brakes and they jerked to a stop. "Who are the suits?" Big Guy asked.

"Ask me in five minutes."

"Isn't the tall one a White House guy?"

Of the two men, one stood a head taller than the other. With slicked black hair, white shirt, and thin black tie, he looked like he stepped off the set of a lawyer TV show, and yes, his face did look like one that was frequently featured on the evening news.

"Holy shit," Jonathan said. "That's Doug Winters."

"White House chief of staff, right?"

Jonathan and Boxers exchanged grins. Yeah, this was going to be interesting.

"Leave the long guns in the truck?" Boxers asked.

Jonathan laughed. "Yeah, I think that's probably best."

They exited the vehicle together, and as they stepped down to the ground Irene started toward them. They met about halfway in the cavernous space. She extended her hand. "Leave it to Digger Grave to enter big," she said.

Jonathan grasped her hand and covered the handshake with his left. He'd always liked Irene, even beyond what was necessary for their business relationship. Tall for a woman—he pegged her at five-ten—she clearly worked hard to stay in shape, and her strawberry hair was somehow always perfectly coiffed. She had a kind of perpetual smirk that told the world that it would be useless to ply her with bullshit. She'd worked her way through the ranks of the FBI the hard way, and still occasionally crashed a door or two just to keep her skills sharp. What was there not to love?

"It's always a pleasure, Director Rivers." Because of the other personalities in the room, he kept it formal.

She smiled and offered her hand to the Big Guy. "How are you, Boxers?"

He grumbled something that probably meant "Fine." Ever conscious of his size, Boxers occasionally looked awkward when he shook hands with people—as if he were afraid he might hurt them accidentally. This was one of those times.

"Is that the White House chief of staff?" Jonathan asked quietly.

She winked. "Come on over. I'll introduce you."

The inside of Horne's barn looked more like a movie set for a barn than a working one. An old baling machine sat in the corner along with a John Deere tractor that might have been new in the sixties. Lots of sharp implements hung from the walls, but the rust on the blades made Jonathan wonder if they'd ever been used. Sixteen-by-sixteen-inch columns supported the network of eight-inch beams, which in turn held up the thirty-foot ceiling. Typical of every time Jonathan had visited the place, the sheer volume of space seemed to absorb all the available light, bathing everything and everyone in perpetual dusk.

Jonathan and Boxers followed as Irene led the way to the pair of men, who made no move to step forward to meet them. Jonathan wondered if maybe Irene had instructed them to hang back, so as not to spook the newcomers.

Irene gestured with an open palm to the man Jonathan recognized. "Douglas Winters, meet Jonathan Grave of Fisherman's Cove, Virginia." To Jonathan, she added, "And as you guessed, Mr. Winters is the president's chief of staff."

Winters flashed a politician's smile and extended his hand. "It's a pleasure," he said.

Jonathan hated politicians' smiles. They rang too many warning bells. But there was no reason not to shake hands. He said nothing, though.

The smile faltered. "I'm getting the feeling that maybe you didn't vote for my boss," Winters said.

"I don't remember who I voted for," Jonathan said, refusing to rise to the bait. "Far as I'm concerned, it doesn't matter. Been sent to war by both parties, been lied to by both." On the spectrum of species that Jonathan admired, politicians occupied a spot significantly south of the sand flea.

"And to think you were never a diplomat," Irene said. "This is Jonathan's business partner, Boxers."

Winters' eyes flashed. "Boxer? More like mastiff, if you ask me. You're a big fella."

This time, Boxers looked less concerned about hurting the hand he shook, and the corners of Winters' eyes twitched from the pressure. Boxers didn't like to be teased.

Irene next gestured toward the shortest of the suits, the one whose distended jacket spoke of a holstered pistol. "And this is Director Ramsey Miller," she said. "My counterpart at the United States Secret Service."

Miller nodded instead of shaking, and that was fine with Jonathan.

"Quite the high-level meeting," Jonathan said. "Secrecy, too. You've got my attention."

"Have you paid attention to the news this morning, Mr. Graves?" Miller asked.

"It's Grave," Jonathan corrected. "No *S*. Get to it."

Every clandestine meeting Jonathan had ever attended—and there'd been hundreds of them over the years—presented a kind of tarantella that required early posturing. Such meetings always involved strong personalities, and all of the players wanted to be in charge. Jonathan thought of it as dick-knocking, and in this case, since he was clearly the one with the skills that others wanted, he got to be the obnoxious one.

"The news reported a drive-by shooting last night," Irene said, hijacking the narrative. "Six Secret Service agents were killed."

Actually, that did ring a bell. "At a DC nightclub, right?"

"Exactly."

Jonathan gave another nod to Miller. "I'm sorry for your loss, sir." He meant it, too. Losing a member of your unit felt like losing a member of your family.

Miller said, "Thank you."

Jonathan said, "Not to get ahead, but the fact that we're here leads me to believe that maybe the media got a few details wrong?"

Miller deferred to Winters. "Well, they got it right insofar as they reported what we told them."

"Uh-oh," Boxers grumbled.

Winters continued. "The version of the story floated to the media has the agents dying on their own time during a random shooting. In reality, they were on duty, and protecting the First Lady."

Boxers rumbled out a chuckle. "I *knew* this was going to be good."

Jonathan said, "Was she stepping out again to someplace embarrassing?"

"She was kidnapped, Mr. Grave," Winters said.

Jonathan's jaw dropped. He didn't surprise easily, but this one nailed him. He waited for the rest.

"That's all we know," Winters said. "Her entire detail was killed, and she was taken away."

"By whom?" Jonathan asked.

"We don't know."

Jonathan looked to Irene. "How is that possible? She's the First-freakin'-Lady. How does she get out of anyone's sight?"

"The first step is to kill her security detail," Miller said.

Okay, this was getting circular. "What do you want from us?" Boxers asked. "You're the FBI."

"We want to keep this incident low profile," Winters said.

A laugh escaped from Jonathan's throat before he could stop it. Irene put a hand on his arm to silence him.

"These are difficult times," Winters said. "Our enemies feel more empowered than they have in years—"

And whose fault is that? Jonathan didn't ask.

"—financial markets are fragile. Americans' confidence in their government is at an all-time low. If this news leaked out, the results could be devastating."

"Shouldn't it be devastating?" Jonathan asked. "I mean, agents are dead and the First Lady is being held hostage. That's pretty damned hot stuff."

"Of course it is," Winters said. "We're willing to move heaven and earth to clear this up. That's why we're turning to you, Mr. Grave."

Boxers laughed. "You're shitting me, right? What, you got more important things to take care of? The president too consumed with raising campaign money to devote time to this little detail?"

Winters shot a forefinger at Boxers' nose. From the posture, he might have been pointing at a hole in the ceiling. "Watch yourself," he snapped.

Boxers growled.

"Let it go, both of you," Jonathan said. "Why us? You are, you know, the federal government. A few million folks in uniform and all that."

"It's a domestic matter," Miller said. "The military is banned by law."

"Jesus." Jonathan turned to Irene. "And last time I

checked, you have a few ambitious people working for you, too."

Irene held up her hands. "Don't think I haven't offered."

"We can't risk it," Winters said. "The news is just too big. To do what we have to do would require the involvement of courts and other law enforcement agencies. There's no way the secret wouldn't leak out."

"And the secret is more important than Mrs. Darmond's life?"

"Of course not," Winters scoffed.

"But kinda?" Jonathan prompted.

Winters set his jaw and took a loud, deep breath. "Are you willing to help us or not?"

Jonathan squinted and looked to Boxers for a hint to what he was missing. "You're not willing to trust the entire United States government, but you're willing to trust me? How does that work?"

Winters nodded toward Irene. "You come very highly recommended. Director Rivers assures me that you're very good at what you do, and that you know how to keep secrets. We'll give you all the access you need. And we'll pay your gate rate."

Jonathan started to say something, but Irene cut him off. "Do this for us, Dig," she said. "I swear to you that we'll give you all the resources you need."

"People?"

"Except people. We figure that we've got some time to work. Whoever took Mrs. Darmond hasn't yet contacted us with a ransom demand, and they haven't put her picture up on a website. That means they want this to stay quiet, too. Or, they're waiting for us to break the news."

"Or maybe they're in the process of killing her now," Boxers offered.

"In which case, we still have the benefit of time," Miller said. "If she is dead, then she will be no less dead in a week."

In a twisted way, Jonathan actually admired the honesty, despite the coldness of the delivery. "Does the president know about this?" he asked.

"Of course he does," Winters replied. "He's worried sick, but he also understands the gravity of the global concerns."

Boxers shook his head. "You're telling me that in the entirety of the US government, you can't cobble together a handful—" He stopped and turned his gaze to Jonathan.

They both got the Big Picture at the same instant. "You want us to break the law," Jonathan said.

"We want you to find the First Lady," Miller said, and he looked like the words might have upset his stomach.

Jonathan looked to Irene. She shrugged with her eyebrows. "If we follow the rules, we leave a paper trail. The paper trail will most certainly be leaked, and then it will be followed."

Just to be sure, Jonathan said, "No warrants, no due process?"

"I'm told this might not be the first time you've done that," Winters said. "In fact, rumor has it that you might have had something to do with thwarting an assassination attempt at one point."

"Not that they have any evidence to that effect," Irene said interjected quickly.

Jonathan's mind raced. If Irene hadn't been in the room, he'd have been out of there. But she had so much cred with him that he was nearly willing to ignore the warning bells in his head. At least temporarily.

"What about prosecuting the bad guys?" Boxers asked. Most of their conversations in the past had implied dire consequences for the Security Solutions team if they'd sullied evidence and therefore endangered the government's case.

"Not all that much of a concern to us," Miller said. "If you can find Mrs. Darmond, we don't care what happens to the people who took her."

Jonathan's eyes narrowed. "You're saying you want us to kill them."

"I'm saying that we don't care one way or the other."

Jonathan shifted his eyes to the White House chief of staff. "I want to hear you say that."

Winters didn't drop a beat. "We don't care one way or the other what happens to the kidnappers."

Boxers said, "Cool."

Jonathan held up a hand for silence and drilled his gaze through Winters. "Then we'll let them go," he said. "We're not assassins."

The words hung untouched. The unspoken truth was that each of them knew people who *were* assassins, but no one wanted it on even this small a record.

"Are you in or not?" Winters said, finally.

"What happens in three or four days if we can't make this thing happen?" Jonathan asked. "People are going to find out."

"And if they do, we'll handle it," Winters said. "We'd prefer that it not get to that. If it does, then we can take over the whole operation. You'll be off the hook and the world's economy and security will be destabilized."

Jonathan ears grew hot. It was a cheap shot to lay all of that at his feet. "I'll shoulder the responsibility that I sign on for, Mr. Winters. I don't do politics." He turned to Irene. "What resources do I get?"

"Whatever you need. In fact, I've got something for you both." She reached into the pocket of her suit jacket and produced two pocket-sized leather folders, which she handed to Jonathan. He recognized them as FBI credentials. "I believe you already have the appropriate badges. But you need new names."

The old aliases were now permanent fixtures on the Interpol list of fugitives. Jonathan thumbed open the first folder and saw Boxers' picture. "Here you go, Jason Kaufman," he said, passing it over. He noted that his own read Richard Horgan. "Are these real?" he asked.

"Real enough to get you through a background check, but not enough to get you a pension."

Jonathan craned his neck to get Boxers' vote.

"I'm in," Big Guy said.

This was a mistake. Enough of the circumstances didn't make sense, and the fingers of the kidnapping reached far too high into the world power structure for any good to come of this, but Irene had never once said no to him when he needed her.

"Fine," he said with a sigh. "Start at the beginning and tell me everything you know."

CHAPTER FOUR

David knew he was in trouble the instant he heard his cell phone ring. He'd gone home to his apartment at the Watergate after work and scarfed down the rest of last night's Stouffer's lasagna. After a pair of Yuenglings, he'd decided to lie on the sofa to watch the news.

And now it was 8:05.

Shit, shit, shit.

David snatched up the phone from the coffee table and swiped the virtual slide bar to answer it. "Deeshy," he said. "I'm sorry I'm late. I'm on my way."

"Jesus, David, this is scary shit, okay? I'm not kidding. How close are you?"

"I'm driving out of the garage now," David said, pushing his left foot into his black Ecco loafer.

"No shit? You're not like just waking up, right? Promise me?"

"No, dude, I'm like ten minutes away. I swear."

"David, this is important," DeShawn said. "You've got to hurry. I think I might've bit off way too much on this one. I'm in serious deep shit."

David snatched the key fob off the Kirkland dresser

he'd bought to fill the empty spot in the foyer. Its drawers were empty, but the long, wide, faux ebony–inlaid surface made a terrific key fob holder. "I'm turning out of the garage now. I'm surprised you can't hear the traffic noise."

"Just hurry, okay?" DeShawn sounded close to tears.

For the very first time since their conversation this morning, David wondered if the big black cop might actually be in trouble. *Real* trouble, not the imagined crap that he usually conjured up for himself. "What's wrong, Deeshy? I mean, truly. You're like really spun up. What's going on?"

"Not on the phone."

"Jesus, Deeshy."

"Get here, okay? Just get here and bring your whole fourth estate with you."

God pulled that string at the base of David's spine that launched a shiver through his body. "Dude, you're a cop—"

"Not for this, I'm not. This is *about* cops, okay? Feds. Secret Service. I'm gonna hang out in the Smithsonian Metro Station where there are people and it's a little warmer. Call me when you're close. For real close. Earn a ticket for this one, okay?" DeShawn hung up.

Deep in that cynical place where David preferred to live his life, he wanted to dismiss this as bullshit. DeShawn *so* wanted to break the big case, and the sensible part of David's brain told him that this was mostly a made-up emergency.

Then there was the other part that heard the impending tears in his friend's voice, the genuine fear. It turned out that fear begat fear, which pounded like a drum in David's temples as he fast-walked to the elevator. He'd have loved to believe that his fear was rooted in an empathetic, philanthropic concern for his friend, but who was he kidding? David was scared shitless of getting into the middle of anything that scared a gun-toting officer of the law in a city as corrupt as Washington, DC. Hell, ex-mayors got to smoke crack before they're reelected to the city council, and then don't have to pay speeding tickets or federal income tax after they beat their wives and watch kiddie porn. If a cop in that environment is this scared, what the hell business did a Radford journalism grad have getting involved?

The elevator took David to the parking garage, where his black Honda Civic sat waiting in the parking space that came with his rent. The car chirped as he pushed the unlock button, and David climbed inside. The door was barely closed when the engine roared to life. Two minutes later, he was clear of the garage and on his way to God only knew what.

Earn a ticket.

David Kirk knew the streets of Washington as well as anyone, and he made good time. By this time of night, the congressional staffers had all gone home, and the lobbyists were done feting their clients in the big-name restaurants along the K Street corridor, leaving the city looking like someone had dropped a neutron bomb on the place—all the structures were there, but no one was inside. Visiting businessmen might be cramming the lobby bars at the Mayflower or the Saint Regis, but in the wide swath of real estate known as the National Mall, homeless vagrants outnumbered everyone else three to one.

That meant there was plenty of parking.

David punched DeShawn's speed dial as he swung the turn onto Jefferson Street SW to tell him that he was only a quarter mile away. After five rings, the call went to voice mail and he hung up.

David nosed into a space twenty yards past the swollen phone booth of a building that marked the entrance to Ripley Center, more or less splitting the distance between the carousel and the Smithsonian Metro Station. If he hadn't already slept through the meeting time, he might have waited in the car with the motor running while Deeshy climbed the steps from the Metro platform, but as it was, he owed his friend the courtesy of meeting halfway. He pulled the brake and killed the engine.

The frigid air felt like a wall as he climbed out of the Honda. He raised the collar of his peacoat against it, wishing that he'd thought to bring a stocking cap. He hated to embrace the reality of his thinning hair, but there was no denying the fact that breezes were a hell of a lot colder than they used to be.

The Smithsonian Castle loomed red and huge to his right, and as he crossed the street he cast a glance to the dormant and unused carousel, whose galloping horses, draped in shadows, seemed frozen in space and time. What was it about circus icons—clowns chief among them—that felt so very creepy?

He was still in the middle of the street when he tried Deeshy's phone again. It didn't make sense to go all the way down the escalator to the station just to come back up again thirty seconds later. He brought the phone to his ear and listened as it rang.

As he listened with his left ear, his right brought the

sound of the reggae jingle that David recognized as Deeshy's ringtone. Rather than coming from the station below, it was from the direction of the carousel. He turned, expecting to see his buddy waving and walking toward him, but instead saw nothing but carousel, naked trees, and the deserted Mall.

He was still squinting into the wind when the ringing in the night stopped, and Deeshy's voice mail greeting kicked in. "If you don't know who you're calling, I'm not leaving a hint. Speak."

David clicked the phone off.

"Deesh?" he called at a whisper into the night. "Deeshy, you're creeping me out, dude."

The night returned only the sound of the wind, and honest to God, it felt as if the temperature dropped another ten degrees.

A little louder, he said, "Come on, Deeshy, I know I was an asshole to be late, but this isn't funny." Still nothing.

"Dude, I know you're there, so step out, or I'm driving away. I'm not playing this game." He feigned a move back toward his car, but he knew there was no way he could walk away. Deeshy could be over there and be hurt.

Because someone hurt him.

The smart move would be to call the cops, but according to Deeshy himself, the cops couldn't be trusted. If Deeshy was hurt, and the cops had hurt him, then who the hell *could* David call for help?

"Oh, this *so* sucks." His feet started taking him toward the source of the ringtone before he was aware that his brain had given them permission to do so.

During the spring and summer, full, leafy trees provided shade for the kids and the kids at heart, a respite from the blistering heat of the largely shadeless Mall. In the darkness of the night, the dim illumination from the streetlights transformed the shadows of leafless tree limbs into menacing shadows of bony fingers beckoning him closer. His heart slammed behind his breastbone with so much force that it surely left a bruise.

"Dammit, Deeshy, stop this shit!" There, he'd yelled it, announcing to the world that he was pissed.

Apparently, the world didn't care. Still, no sign.

He was on the carousel side of Jefferson Drive now, on the outer fringe of the malevolent shadows.

David tried the number again. Maybe he'd imagined the whole thing. That wasn't possible, of course, but maybe if you wanted hard enough for the thing to be true—

The reggae beat launched again, a bit of Bob Marley dancing from the shadows. If David hadn't known better, he'd have sworn that the noise had moved from last time. He blamed the wind. And his imagination, the curse of being a writer. Honest to God, if it turned out that Deeshy wasn't dead—or at least seriously hurt—David was going to kill him.

When the phone went to voice mail, David disconnected, waited a few seconds, and then dialed it again. He'd let the sound of the ringtone bring him closer—if not to DeShawn, then at least to his phone.

David was among the trees now, just twenty or thirty yards from the carousel, and when it rang this time, there was absolutely no doubt that it had moved. Whoever was playing this game with him was circling around behind him. The skin on his back felt alive as he spun to confront the threat that was finally visible to him. Actually, it was two threats, and they were both overdressed for the cold. They wore all black, and even though it was hard to see in the dark, David could see enough of their faces to know they looked angry.

"David Kirk," one of them said in an accent that sounded Eastern European. "We need to have a word with you." The one who remained silent held something in his hand that reflected the streetlight. Not for long—just a blink—but it was all David needed.

He spun on his heel to bolt away when he saw a third figure emerging from among the dormant horses of the carousel itself. For the space of a heartbeat, David hoped that it might be Deeshy, but from the size of the silhouette alone, he knew that it wasn't. And if he wasn't Deeshy, he was trouble.

A second heartbeat later, David sprinted into the wide open spaces of the Mall. The other option would have been to streak toward the Smithsonian Castle with its gardens and shadows, but he rejected that instinctively. What the Mall lacked in cover, it made up for in the ability to maneuver. At least the Mall would allow him to run his fastest, reliving the glory days of his high school years, which had vanished from his rearview mirror nearly seven years ago.

He pumped his arms and legs hard, as if by gripping the air with his fists he could pull himself faster, force his fashionable, slick-bottomed black loafers to dig more dirt with every stride.

They were right behind him. He knew without looking, and he didn't dare look for fear of freezing when he saw how close they were. Or, more reasonably, for fear of losing a half step of whatever lead he had on them.

The cold air tore at his face and dried out his eyes. His throat burned at the great gulps of breath. David had not run this fast in a long time—not since those days of high school stardom, if even then—yet it still felt like slow motion. He focused on the southwest corner of the Natural History Museum as his first landmark, and even though his muscles screamed and his throat ached, the goal never seemed to get closer.

The shortest distance between two points was a straight line. He remembered that from high school geometry, the last math class he ever took. But a person running in a straight line made the perfect target. He thought he remembered reading something about that.

Zigzag. Wherever he'd read about the danger of the straight line, he remembered that the solution was to run a zigzag course.

Screw it. If they hadn't taken their shot already, they weren't going to take it at all—not now, when he was this close to Constitution Avenue with all its official buildings and requisite guard staffs. He was sure of it.

Right.

He was still thirty yards from the sidewalk on the far side of the Mall when the calf muscle in his left leg seized, locking up like a flesh-covered rock and sprawling him face-first into the frozen dirt that pretended to be grass.

He went down hard. "Shit! Help me!"

At first, he thought he'd been shot. The pain was that intense. Clutching his calf with his right hand and pulling up on his toes with his left to ease the spasm, David rolled to his back to confront his attackers. He hadn't been in a fight since elementary school, but he wasn't going to die without one.

"Help me!"

Somewhere in the night there had to be a tourist or two. A couple sets of eyes might help to run off the men who would kill him.

Or maybe they'd kill the tourists, too.

Not his problem.

David was certain beyond doubt that the one man had been holding a knife. As he struggled to his knees to engage his enemies, he yelled again, a guttural, animal sound that gave voice to his terror.

But no attacker appeared. Beyond the thrumming of blood in his ears, the starless night revealed no sound but the wind and the grumble of distant traffic.

Where the hell were they? This was their perfect opportunity to take him out, slit his throat without a sound, and they'd blown it. Or maybe that wasn't—

"Hey, are you all right?"

The voice came from David's blind side and it startled the crap out of him. He spun to see a fortysomething guy in a beige trench coat with what looked like a suit and tie underneath. The soft jowls and prominent paunch set him far apart from the guys at the carousel. His face showed a look of concern.

With the threat of imminent attack gone, and with it the need for immediate assistance, David saw no upside in sharing details with a stranger. "I'm fine," he said through gritted teeth. "Got a cramp. Hurts like hell."

The Samaritan squinted into the darkness beyond

David. "Somebody trying to mug you or something? I saw you tearing across the grass like your hair was on fire. If you don't mind me saying, you're not exactly dressed for a jog."

Jogging? I was running with everything I had and this guy thinks I was jogging? He chose to say nothing.

The man in the trench coat pulled an iPhone knock-off out of his pocket. "Do you need me to call a cop?"

"No," David said, and the answer sounded a little too quick. "No, I'm fine. Just got a little spooked." He cast one more look back toward the carousel to make sure that those who spooked him were still nowhere to be seen.

Trench Coat planted his fists on his hips. He wasn't buying.

"Honest to God," David said. The spasm was easing as he massaged the muscle. "I'm a reporter for the *Enquirer*. I was doing a story and my imagination got away from me." As soon as the words about his employer escaped his lips, he wished he could take them back.

He rose to his haunches to give his calf a good stretch. In another few seconds, he'd be able to trust it enough to stand.

"You looked awfully scared when you were running," Trench Coat said.

David pointed back toward the carousel. "Nothing to be afraid of."

"But you were yelling for help."

"Just because there's nothing to be afraid of doesn't mean I'm not afraid of it." *Whatever happened to the coldhearted city dwellers who never wanted to get in-*

volved? He reached out his hand. "Do you mind helping me up?"

Trench Coat didn't hesitate to grasp David's hand in a power grip, one that involved more thumb than fingers. The hand was heavily calloused. A shiver—a warning shot—launched from his tailbone to his skull. You don't expect a guy in a thousand-dollar coat to have workingman's hands. On a night like tonight, anything out of the ordinary was a threat.

As David shot to his feet, he pulled his hand free and thrust a forefinger at the stranger's face, the tip coming within an inch of the man's face. In the same instant, he yelled—shrieked, really—"Stay away from me!"

Trench Coat jumped and took a step back. "What the hell—"

"Don't you even!" David shouted. "Just stay the hell away from me!"

"What's wrong with you? Jesus, I was just—"

David knew that he must sound like a lunatic, but what did he care? In the worst case, the stranger really was a Good Samaritan who'd gotten his feelings hurt. In the best case, he was a potential killer who'd been startled out of his mission.

David used the momentary confusion to take off again. With his leg still sore, he looked more like he was skipping than running, but he was putting additional space between himself and the people who would do him harm.

Behind him, Trench Coat yelled, "Ungrateful piece of shit!"

David hobbled on, stepping into the paltry traffic that straggled up Constitution Avenue. In the first bit of good luck for the evening, he found a taxi within hailing range. It pulled to the curb and David climbed into the backseat. "The Riverside," he said, pointing the cabbie to his apartment building. "Quickly."

Taking his orders a little too literally, the cabbie swung a U-turn in the middle of the street. David had to hold on to keep from getting thrown across the bench seat. "Whoa. Easy."

What the hell had he gotten himself into? *Goddamn you, Deeshy.* Whatever his buddy had found, it had gotten the attention of some very bad people. What had he said? Something about the Secret Service, right? And he couldn't talk to his own commanders about it.

They knew my name.

"Stop the car!" he commanded.

The cabbie pivoted in his seat to look through the security barrier, but he didn't slow down.

"I said, stop."

"Before, you said to hurry."

"Well, I want you to stop now."

This triggered a string of angry Urdu. But the driver stopped the cab.

David felt sick. If the attackers knew his name, then they would know where he lived. There was no way he could go home, not without knowing what was going on and making sure that it was safe. So, what was the alternative? All his stuff was in his home—everything. He didn't even have a computer, unless you counted his iPhone, and as smart as the phone was, it was nobody's computer.

"Oh, shit," he muttered aloud. His phone! He'd used it to call Deeshy. If they had his phone, they had his number, and if they had his number, they could trace him. Like physically trace him. Wasn't that how it worked?

"Hey," the cabbie said. "You want to go someplace or not?"

"Your meter's running," David snapped.

"Waiting is not driving, my friend. You want to think, think outside. I make money driving."

"Then drive," David said. "Just not to the Riverside."

"Where?"

"You want to wait for directions, wait. You want to drive, drive."

The cabbie's eyes flashed humor in the rearview mirror. David winked and the driver pulled the transmission into drive.

What the hell was he going to do? The first step, he supposed, was to turn off his phone, but would that be enough? Did turning it off make it invisible, or did he have to pull out that card, whatever the hell it was called. The SIM card, that was it. Did he have to pull that out to make it invisible? And how do you do that on an iPhone? The thing was one solid piece. As a first step, he turned the phone off.

And where was he going to stay? Having grown up in mansions, wilderness survival skills were nowhere near his wheelhouse. In David's family, camping meant staying at the Four Seasons instead of the Ritz-Carlton.

I am so screwed.

He recognized that he might be panicking, blowing this out of proportion, but his gut told him that things were desperately wrong. Deeshy was as paranoid as they came, and he saw conspiracy in the sunrise, but this time, he was *scared*. He'd almost cried on the phone. He was *very* scared. Of the Secret Service and the police.

"Think," he told himself. "Prioritize." Oh, God, it had to be bad if he was channeling his father.

David needed to get off the streets. He needed to hole up somewhere in a place that would give him a measure of safety and buy him enough time to think things through rationally. But where? His parents' place was out because that was too logical. How freaking sad was it that after a lifetime living in DC, he couldn't think of a single person to call to take him in?

There had to be someone. Then he got it.

David leaned in close to the taxi's security barrier as he pulled his wallet out of his back pocket and withdrew a bill. "Excuse me, driver."

The cabbie met his eyes in the mirror.

"Here's five bucks. Can I please use your cell phone?"

The cabbie reflexively moved the phone from the center console where it lay and placed it on his lap. "No," he said. "Use your own phone. I saw it in your hand."

"I can't. That probably sounds crazy, but it's really complicated. C'mon, five bucks for one phone call. Two, actually."

The cabbie was clearly uncomfortable with this. "I will take you to a pay phone."

"No, no, no. You've got that look in your eye. The second I step out of your cab, you'll drive away." David pulled another bill from the wallet. "Here, then. Twenty-five dollars. For two phone calls. I could call the moon and you'd still make a couple of bucks. All I need is directory assistance and then a local call. I swear. C'mon, please let me borrow your phone."

The cabbie studied what he saw in the rearview mirror, his eyes leaving David only to check his progress on the road. "Fifty," he said at last.

"Fifty! For a phone call?"

"Twenty-five for the call, twenty-five to use my phone."

This was outrageous. No wonder the world was at war with these guys. David went back to his wallet and retrieved the appropriate bills. As he handed them through the opening, he also handed the driver his iPhone. "Here," he said. "A little extra something for your effort."

CHAPTER FIVE

The universe that Jonathan Grave cared about resided on Virginia's Northern Neck of the Potomac River in a waterfront burg named Fisherman's Cove. He'd grown up there, and as a teenager he'd fled from there, only to return many years later to prove the old saw, "lo the memories be painful, there's no place like home." Or something like that.

Commercial fishing still thrived in the Cove, as did the dozens of businesses that supported fishermen and their families. Thanks in no small part to anonymous deep-pocketed finagling by Jonathan over the years, the big box stores that had consumed so much of tranquil America were still far enough away to give local small businesses an even shot. Tourists streamed to the Cove during the summer months, but those who were looking to stay in a major chain hotel had to shift their sights to local establishments, including a few bed-and-breakfasts that reset the definition of peace.

There was a nightlife if you knew where to look for it, so long as said nightlife didn't extend beyond 10:00 P.M. Monday through Thursday and midnight on Friday and Saturday. Fisherman's Cove was the wrong place to go looking for nightlife on Sunday.

The two most impressive structures in Fisherman's Cove were Resurrection House—a residential school anonymously endowed by Jonathan Grave for the children of incarcerated parents—and Saint Katherine's Catholic Church, Saint Kate's to the locals. The two buildings sat adjacent to each other on Church Street, on the long hill that led down to the waterfront. At the end of the block, facing Water Street, sat the three-story converted firehouse that served as Jonathan's home on the first two floors, and as headquarters for his company, Security Solutions, on the third.

To their major corporate clients, Security Solutions was a high-end private investigation company that specialized in getting information that few others could obtain. It was all done legally, but it was also done aggressively, using means that sometimes pressed and bent—but never broke—the letter of the law. When a billion-dollar merger was in play, a board of directors could never have enough information, and information was what Security Solutions specialized in.

Those were the very sorts of investigations that bored Jonathan Grave to the point of misery. His passion lay exclusively with the unspoken, covert part of the company's operations—the part about which even his most experienced investigators—employees who had been with him for years—knew nothing. Jonathan was reasonably sure they suspected, but they all knew to keep their mouths shut and to not ask questions.

Jonathan's 0300 missions—hostage rescue missions, in the parlance of the Unit, with which he'd served for many years—were run out of the Cave, the half of the third floor to which only a handful of people had access, and which was guarded 24/7 by retired military policemen whose longtime specialty was convincing people to stay out of places where they did not belong. Building security had been heightened enormously after an unfortunate incident several years ago when an intruder had been able to make his way inside and nearly killed Jonathan's most valued employee.

This evening, Jonathan sat with Boxers and Venice Alexander in the War Room, the Cave's high-tech teak conference room, talking through this business about the First Lady, trying to cobble together some semblance of a plan.

Jonathan had known Venice Alexander (it's pronounced Ven-EE-chay) since she was a little girl, the daughter of his family's lead housekeeper. Separated in age by an improper number of years when he was in his teens, he'd enjoyed the crush she'd had on him, and he'd been moved by the emotion she'd shown on the day he moved out.

While Jonathan was off saving the world in the United States Army, Venice had become something of a wizard—and, strictly speaking, a criminal—in things computer related. In the early days of Security Solutions, as soon as it became apparent that advanced computer skills were needed, Venice had been Jonathan's first choice. Now, she pretty much ran the place, stimulating ones and zeroes to accomplish amazing feats.

"I don't understand why there's been no ransom demand," Venice said. She looked like she wanted to be typing something on her terminal, but was frustrated that she didn't know what to type.

"And no announcement to the media," Boxers added.

"If this was a bunch of terrorists, it seems to me that they'd be all over the airwaves announcing their prize."

"I agree on both counts," Jonathan said. "And those two things together tell me that this isn't your standard kidnapping."

"Did the White House people give you any theories at all?"

Jonathan shook his head. "No. In fact, they seemed sort of intent on not going there."

Venice cocked her head.

Jonathan elaborated. "Call it intuition. They want us to do our own legwork. I don't know why."

"Didn't you say they promised to share all the intel they gathered?"

Boxers chuckled. "Promises from a politician. Now there's something to take to the bank."

"Ven, I know you must have done some research since our phone conversation," Jonathan said. "What have you come up with?"

She beamed. Finally, a chance to play with the computer. "Let's start with the troubling details," she said. "In the aftermath of nine-eleven, you can't scratch your ear or pick your nose in Washington without it being recorded by a camera. But guess what."

Jonathan was way ahead. "None of the cameras near the Wild Times Bar were working."

"Right. Now, that could be a coincidence—"

"But I don't believe in those," Jonathan finished for her.

"Exactly."

"I sense that you have a theory," Jonathan said.

Venice's smile grew larger. "Look at the big screen." Her fingers worked the keys. At the far end of the rectangular conference room, an enormous television screen came to life. There was no sound, but the images showed a list of news stories from various periodicals.

"Last night's outing to the Wild Times was far from Mrs. Darmond's first extracurricular nighttime adventure." She clicked through the headlines.

First Lady Startles Crowd at Georgetown Nightclub

Anna Darmond Steps Out

Is The First Lady Really the First Liability?

Arguments Rock White House Residence

Rumors of Darmond Divorce Cast Pall Over State Dinner

POTUS Said to Be Distracted By Marital Stress

First Step Supports Mom in Divorce Rumors

They went on and on.

"This is all background," Venice explained. "I don't know how relevant it is, but Anna Darmond is no Pat Nixon. Apparently, the public eye is not something she relishes."

"What's a 'First Step'?" Boxers asked.

"The stepson," Venice explained. "The son born before she was married. Remember when he made a point of telling the press that he voted for the other candidate?" It was big news at the time, capturing the imagination of every television comic on the planet.

"And these only scratch the surface. The Darmonds make the Clintons look like lifelong lovers."

"Among all the pundits, are there theories as to why there's so much discord?" Jonathan asked.

Venice gave him an annoying smirk. "You really are not dialed into pop culture at all, are you?"

Jonathan smirked back. "We've met, right?"

"She doesn't like his politics. She says he's wandered from the principles he held when he first ran for Congress. She's been very vocal. She's even done talk shows dissing her husband. How can you not know this?"

"I stopped watching television when the morning news shows stopped doing news and started hawking movie stars. Newspapers are only half a step better."

"I say the prez off'd her to shut her up," Boxers said.

Jonathan shot him a look. "Are you serious?"

Big Guy shrugged with one shoulder. "Half serious, anyway."

Venice made a puffing sound, her ultimate dismissal.

The theory actually rang as not outrageous with Jonathan. If there was one lesson he'd learned over all those years serving as Uncle Sam's muscle—and the additional years serving as an anonymous watchdog—it was that there was no limit to the degree to which power corrupts. If the president of the United States—particularly this president of the United States, whose own cabinet had already proven itself to be murderous—needed only to kill someone to gain reelection, Jonathan could imagine that being an easy decision.

"Let's table that theory for a while," Jonathan said. "Any others?"

"Maybe she just wanted to get away," Venice offered. "Having everybody assuming that she was kidnapped is way better than having the country hate her for walking away from her husband."

"You know that would make her a murderer, right?" Jonathan asked. "People were killed in that shoot-out. If it turns out to be some kind of tantrum-inspired ruse, that would spell really bad things for her."

"You asked for other theories," Venice said. "That was the first one that popped into my head."

Jonathan's gaze narrowed. "You've got some back-pocket research."

Venice smiled. "I confess that I accessed some files that Wolverine might not want to know I know about."

Time after time, Venice proved herself to be the mistress of electrons. As an analog guy trapped in a digital world, Jonathan had no idea how she worked the magic she did, but he'd come to think of her abilities as a force of nature.

"Anna Nazarov emigrated to the United States from Russia in 1986, the year before her future—and much older—second husband first ran for Congress. She had her only child, Nicholas, eighteen months later, courtesy of Pavel Mishin, an electrician whom she never married."

"How old was she when she arrived?" Jonathan asked.

"Sixteen, and not by much."

"Nothing wrong with her youthful libido," Boxers said.

"It's that clean American water," Jonathan said.

"Can we grow up, please?" Venice chided. "Those years marked the last desperate breaths of the Soviet

Union. Her baby was a natural-born citizen, and her ticket to stay in the US of A. There's not a lot else on the record until she met Tony Darmond on a blind date in 2002. Apparently, it was a whirlwind romance, and yada, yada, yada, she's FLOTUS."

Jonathan recognized the acronym for First Lady of the United States. Something in the way Venice said the yada, yada, yada rang a warning bell. "You've got a suspicion," he said.

"Not a suspicion, really. Okay, yes, a suspicion. It was hard to come to the United States back in the eighties. You had to be somebody over there, but when I search her family name, I don't really get much. She held menial jobs, but never really made an impact anywhere. Here's a woman who sleeps with the most powerful man in the world, and all we've got on a major chunk of her life is generalities. That makes me suspicious."

"Be less mysterious," Jonathan said. "Say what's on your mind."

"Really, that's it. I don't have a larger theory. It just seems incongruous to me that the First Lady would go so . . . unexamined."

"Well, her husband does belong to the news media's favorite political party," Boxers said. In the Big Guy's mind, being a member of the media put you very close to being an enemy of the state.

"But what about the bloggers?" Venice pressed. "And the networks of the opposition? Nobody's given this chick a hard look."

Jonathan grinned. "But I sense that someone's about to."

"I've tried," Venice said. "I mean, I've *really* tried. She sort of disappears." She drilled Jonathan with her eyes. "Remind you of anyone you know?"

Because of his covert work, Jonathan and Boxers had both disappeared off the grid a long time ago. Jonathan laughed. "What, you think she was an operator?"

"I don't know what I think. I really mean that. But everybody leaves a footprint. Emigrés leave a *big* footprint. Mrs. Darmond, not so much. Just seems odd to me. I don't know if she's a Special Forces operator or part of witness protection, but it seems very, very weird to me."

Jonathan thought about that. These were the days of the twenty-four-hour news cycle. CNN reported on zits that appeared on celebrities' noses. First Ladies should have complete pasts. "Are you telling me that she's invisible for those years between having her kid and marrying the future president?"

"Essentially, yes. I can't even find a driver's license application."

"How about tax returns?" Boxers asked.

"Yes. There's a tax return for every year. Not surprisingly, I suppose, they show a geometric growth in charitable contributions after she met Darmond."

"Feeding the poor through pure ambition," Boxers said. "A noble and long-standing American tradition."

Jonathan smiled. No one did cynicism better than Big Guy.

Venice continued, "I even looked for good works. Maybe she worked for a soup kitchen or a homeless shelter. There's nothing."

Jonathan weighed the meaning in his mind, forcing

himself to assume the worst, if only because years of experience had shown him that the worst was the norm. When people disappeared from view, it was either by their own choice, or by the choice of others. In Jonathan's case, he was a cipher in official records because of the good—and occasionally bad—works he'd performed in service to Uncle Sam. Others disappeared because of testimony they'd provided for the US attorney, and still others—think the Unabomber—disappeared because they wanted to be anonymous. Nobody—*nobody*—disappeared accidentally.

"Plus, there's one other big thing that bothers me. The first three digits of her Social Security number are one two eight. That's a New York series."

Jonathan leaned closer. "And?"

"There's no record of Mrs. Darmond ever living in New York. How would she get a Social from an area where she never lived?"

Jonathan smiled. "You know what?" He reached into his pocket. "This is worth a phone call." He pressed the speed-dial number for Wolverine.

She answered on the second ring. "Scorpion."

"We've been doing some research here," Jonathan said. "Is it possible that you've been holding out on us?"

"I need more than that."

It took all of thirty seconds to lay out his concerns. "Has Mrs. Darmond been disappeared for a reason?" he concluded.

Irene said, "This is not a conversation for the telephone."

Jonathan felt excitement stir in his gut. "Well, Wolfie, I have it on good authority that time is of the essence. It's your call."

Hesitation. "Is it fair to assume that Mother Hen has found a way to stymie the National Security Agency yet again?"

"I have no idea what you're talking about." Mother Hen had long been Venice's radio handle, but Jonathan wasn't about to confirm that.

"One day, you know we're all going to share a jail cell, right?"

"Not me," Jonathan said. "I have immunity. Don't tie my hands, Irene. You've asked me to find the First Lady. If you withdraw the request, I'll sleep fine. But if you want me to do my job, please don't get in the way."

Another hesitation. Much longer this time. "Bravo Four Three," she said. "In two."

Jonathan checked his watch. It was well past rush hour, but it would still be tight to get downtown to Saint Matthew's Cathedral in two hours. Then again, he was carrying a badge now—the absolute privilege to drive at killer speeds with impunity. "Okay," he said, but Irene had already hung up.

"Come on, Big Guy. We're going to church."

David forced himself to suppress a gasp when Becky Beckeman answered the door of her Alexandria Apartment. She wore skinny jeans and some kind of a gauzy peasant shirt that somehow emphasized her nipples in high relief. She'd clearly tied her longish dark blond hair up in a hurry, creating a flyaway disheveled look that he'd never seen before. Her normally painted face was free of makeup, and in a weird way, the plainness of it looked better than the mask she wore at work.

"David!" she exclaimed. "My goodness, are you okay?"

"Can I come in?"

She stepped aside, clearing a path. "Yes, yes, of course. Please, let me take your coat."

As he shrugged out of his North Face jacket, he took in the details of her apartment. Lots of yellow and lots of cat pictures. And daisies. Maybe they were sunflowers. Only the pictures, none of the living variety of either flora or fauna. Typical, he was sure, of twenty-somethings living in the residential purgatory that Eastern Towers was, her chief designer appeared to be the Salvation Army thrift store, accessorized by the occasional slipcover. In yellow, of course.

"You sounded so concerned on the phone," she said. "Is everything all right?"

Cue the pivotal moment. What was the appropriate amount to share when you suspected that representatives of the United States government, augmented by the Metropolitan Police Department, were conspiring to kill you?

"I don't think you're in any danger," he said. He'd meant the words to be reassuring, but when he heard them, he realized that they were terrifying. Becky's wide-eyed expression confirmed that for him. "I mean—"

"Oh my God, David. What have you done?"

The presumption of fault startled him. "Nothing. I haven't done anything. It's my friend Deeshy."

"Who?"

"DeShawn Lincoln. You met him once in the office."

"The African American police officer?"

David would have said the black cop. "Yes. Him."

"What did he do?"

"I think he got himself killed."

"Oh my God."

"Yeah. And I think the guys who killed him know that I know. And they know who I am. That's why I can't go home."

Realization fell across Becky's face like a shade draping a window.

David spoke quickly. "I didn't call you from my own phone," he said. "And I took a cab, and I had the cab drop me off at the Hilton on Seminary Road. I walked over here. It should be untraceable."

"It's entirely traceable," Becky argued. "The Hilton's a quarter mile from here. We're coworkers. If people know how to look for you, why wouldn't they look for you here? Certainly, they'd come by here to ask if I've seen you."

David sighed. "Can we sit down?"

The question seemed to startle her. "Oh. Of course. Yes, please, have a seat." She gestured toward the yellow love seat, while she headed toward the yellow chair that sat opposite. "Can I get you something to drink?"

"Any dark liquor."

Becky winced. "I don't keep alcohol in the apartment. I have iced tea. It's freshly brewed."

"No, thanks," he said. "I'm fine." He lowered himself into the puffy love seat and was surprised to find it comfortable. He inhaled deeply. "Maybe I shouldn't have put you in this position," he said. "I was in a panic, and I couldn't think of anyone else."

From her reaction, he wondered if the words offended her.

Becky eased herself into her chair. "So, you think that your friend was murdered."

"Yes."

"By whom?"

David shifted uncomfortably, and crossed his legs. "I don't know for sure," he said. He relayed the details of his last conversations with Deeshy, including the parts about the Secret Service and the police.

Becky's face formed a giant O. "He was killed by the Secret Service? Do you know how crazy that sounds?"

"I think that 'crazy' doesn't touch how it sounds," David confessed. "But it is what it is."

Becky looked to the floor, and silence consumed the room for a good two minutes as the gravity of it all sank in. At last, Becky said, "So, what's your next step?"

"I need cash," David said. "Not that I have anything in particular to buy, but once Uncle Sam gets his act together, he's going to start tracking every electronic transaction. My credit cards are going to be off-limits, and even ATM transactions are going to be like footprints in the snow. I need to pocket as much cash as I can before they lock down my accounts."

"And how are you going to do that?"

David felt his cheeks turn red. "I was hoping that you might drive me to Annapolis tonight. We could cruise some ATMs there. I don't know how much they'll let me take before the system locks down, but I'll grab as much as I can, and then we come back here. With luck, the cops will think that I'm moving north, and that'll give them even less reason to come sniffing around here." It was an unspeakably selfish plan.

Becky looked at him for a long time. He'd never noticed the intensity and intelligence of her brown eyes before. She stood. "Okay," she said. "It's after ten. We should get started."

CHAPTER SIX

Jonathan left the Batmobile in its garage and took the BMW M5 instead. It was a long haul from Fisherman's Cove to downtown Washington, and he decided to make the trip in style. Since Boxers lived in the District to begin with, he drove separately, thus saving Jonathan the needless bitching about the small size of the sports car. The Big Guy's vehicle of choice was a black on black on black Cadillac Escalade.

At this time of night, parking was not a problem. Jonathan pulled into a spot directly across the street from the cathedral's front entrance. Saint Matthew's looked like a black stain against the night, towering over its corner of Rhode Island Avenue like a monstrous architectural sentry. As Jonathan climbed the steps toward the massive wooden doors, he couldn't help but recall the iconic photographs of John F. Kennedy's flag-draped casket making this same journey on the shoulders of Honor Guards selected from every branch of the service.

Once at the top, he paused before entering to cast a suspicious glance to the two homeless men who flanked the doors. Paranoia was a survival skill in Jonathan's world, and he wondered why they would choose to hunker down outside on a night like this when they could be inside instead. Or even camped on a steam grate.

For that matter, why didn't the chronically homeless spend their summers hiking to Florida where it was perpetually warm, and they wouldn't have to worry about freezing at all? He'd never walked in their shoes, so he wasn't passing judgment, exactly, but he had to wonder.

The sanctuary looked even more enormous than usual in the dim nighttime lighting. Off to the right, the glimmer of candles attracted him to the Our Lady Chapel, where he knew he'd find Irene Rivers waiting, but was surprised to see that Boxers had beaten him here. Just outside the chapel's entrance, her two-man security detail stood with their backs to their boss, their arms folded across their chests. In their matching suits, Jonathan thought that they resembled living chess pieces.

Only a handful of people in the intelligence community—none of them with the CIA—knew that the Our Lady Chapel was one of the most acoustically dead spots on the planet. Designed to absorb sound without echo and swept multiple times a day for listening devices, the Chapel—designated Bravo Four Three for reasons Jonathan didn't know—was one of only a handful of spots in the United States, apart from secure government facilities, where anyone could speak in complete candor without the remotest chance of being overheard or recorded.

Jonathan approached from behind Irene and Boxers, who sat next to each other with a chair separating them. Boxers made the chairs look like they were sized for elementary school students.

"Have I missed anything important?" Jonathan asked as he approached.

Irene stood to greet him. What would normally have been a peck on the cheek turned out to be a hearty handshake in front of witnesses. "I wish I could say I was glad to meet you here," she said.

"Haven't missed a thing, Boss. She wouldn't talk without you here."

Jonathan sat sideways in his seat, with his left leg folded under his right, his left arm slung over the seat back. "This must be big," Jonathan said.

"It is," Irene said. "At least, I think it is. I couldn't mention it before, because of the company in the room. I don't know who knows what, and under the circumstances, I'm paranoid about what I say to anyone."

Jonathan waited, knowing that the silence would eventually fill itself.

"The public record on Mrs. Darmond is inaccurate," she said. "In fact, it's elaborate fiction that was created with the full cooperation of my predecessor at the Bureau."

Boxers' jaw went slack at the news.

"How elaborate a fiction are we talking about?" Jonathan asked.

"The most. All of it."

"How can that be?"

Irene scowled. "Of all people, how can you ask that question?"

"We were unit operators," Jonathan said, feeling oddly defensive. "We're black out of necessity. And we're not part of the president's family."

"If it makes you feel any better, neither was she when it happened."

"You're going to get to the story, right?" Boxers said. Mr. Patience.

"I want to start by emphasizing that this might have nothing to do with the current circumstances," Irene said.

Jonathan cocked his head. "Which I interpret as meaning that it probably has everything to do with it."

Irene acknowledged the sentiment with a smirk. "The lady we know as Anna Darmond was actually born Yelena Poltanov." She spelled it. "Her father was a big-time apparatchik during the last years of the Soviet Union. Yuri Poltanov. Along about the time the Poles started making trouble, Yuri read the handwriting on the walls, and found a way to send his daughter to the United States on a student visa."

"I thought she was Anna Nazarov."

"That's what she wants you to think," Irene said. "In fact, Uncle Sam himself wishes you think that. Thing is, young Yelena had drunk the Kool-Aid big-time. She didn't want to leave, and in fact thought that the United States was the embodiment of evil. All that stuff they taught her in school about the evils of capitalism really stuck. She got herself wrapped up in a ton of anti-American activities. That's how my predecessor got wind of her, and that's how we were able to develop an extensive file on her."

This wasn't clicking for Jonathan at all. "So, how

come we haven't heard about any of this? Seems to me that the tabloids would be all over this story."

Irene shook her head. "Because outside of our files at headquarters, none of this ever happened. This is the part I was getting to. Back then, there were throngs of Soviet expats here in the US, most of them on student visas, and many of them under the same circumstances as Yelena—committed to duty, honor, and the Motherland, yet exiled by their highly placed fathers. They wreaked all kinds of havoc. Some of what they did was just harassment of the local police, but there were some high-profile robberies and a lot of drug trafficking, too. The big-dollar stuff was all about funding anti-American activities."

"You mean terrorism?" Boxers asked.

"We didn't call it that back then," Irene said. "They set some fires and a couple of bombs. They spent a lot of money and resources spinning up racial tension wherever they could find it. It was a bad group of people."

"And Mrs. Darmond was among them?" Jonathan asked. He was beginning to feel the seed of a headache.

"As far as we can tell, she was an organizer."

Boxers said, "The First Lady." Clearly, the pieces weren't coming together for him, either.

Irene continued, "The bottom line of all this was, Yelena wasn't very good at being covert. Whereas her partners in crime stayed well below the radar, she actually left hints to friends that she was up to no good. For example, she told one of her suite mates in college to stay away from the Marine recruiting station on a certain day. That afternoon, a bomb blew out the front windows. A handful of people were injured by shrapnel and blast effects, but none seriously. Yelena didn't tell the girl specifically about the bomb, but that's a hard kind of coincidence to ignore."

"So, you arrested Yelena?" Jonathan said.

Irene shook her head. "Just to be clear here, I personally had nothing to do with any of this. But no, we did not arrest her. The US attorney didn't think we had enough to put her away." Irene's smirk returned. "We did, however, have plenty enough to scare her. A counterintelligence agent picked her up and told her that if she didn't turn on her friends, she would go to prison for the rest of her life."

"It was a bluff?"

"Absolutely. But as I said, she'd gulped the Kool-Aid by the gallon. At first, she proclaimed to know nothing of what the agent told her, and then she shifted into martyr mode and swore her allegiance to the Motherland.

"Well, as it turned out, at the same time the Bureau was gathering intelligence on the network of expats, our friends in Langley had their sights on Yuri Poltanov in Moscow. The Wall was softening quickly, and apparatchiks were scrambling to reserve spots on the lifeboats for themselves. He turned on the Kremlin. The Bureau liaison to the Puzzle Palace got wind of it, and we were able to work a little magic.

"We told Yelena what her father had done, and that we would turn him over to the KGB if she didn't cooperate with us. That did the trick. With her testimony, we were able to nail the entire leadership of the expat network."

"WitSec?" Jonathan asked. Irene would recognize the acronym for the Marshal Service's Witness Security program.

Irene flicked her forefinger at him. "Bingo."

"And what about Comrade Daddy?" Boxers asked. "Yuri."

Wolverine's face darkened. "Actually, that didn't go so well. The agency wouldn't break him free from his agreement to snitch on the Kremlin. Things were coming undone so quickly by then that the need for intel was insatiable. Plus, he knew about what was happening with his daughter, and was convinced that the KGB would figure it out and kill him."

Jonathan could tell from body language alone what was coming next. "Let me guess. That's what happened."

Another forefinger. "It didn't happen until after Yelena's testimony. They took him to Lubyanka, and he never came out. We presume they executed him, but Perestroika didn't extend to the release of those records. Now that the new regime has re-embraced the Cold War mentality, I expect we'll never know for sure."

Silence reigned as Jonathan and Boxers processed what they'd just heard. Jonathan had to say it aloud, just to make sure that he hadn't gone nuts: "So, the First Lady of the United States is a former terrorist who is part of the witness protection program."

"Yes."

"And every hotheaded Russian with a jones for the good old days has a motivation to kidnap and kill her."

Irene seemed less certain on that score. "It's been a long time," she said. "And we paid for some major plastic surgery to change her appearance."

Boxers laughed. "Holy shit. Only in America."

Irene seized on it. "You know what, Big Guy? You're absolutely right. Only in America. The land of second chances. And third."

Jonathan intervened. "I don't think he meant to impugn the honor and dignity of the nation he's risked his life for dozens of times." Subtext: This was the wrong table at which to play the guilt card. "I find it astonishing, though, that some intrepid reporter didn't dig this stuff up during the campaign."

Irene gave a coy smile and a shrug. "We're good at what we do."

"That's not what astonishes me," Boxers said. His ears were red, a sure sign that he was pissed. "How is it that the FBI can know that a terrorist is on her way to the White House and still sit on the information?"

The coy smile turned into something malignant. "What are you suggesting, Big Guy?"

"Suggesting my ass." He shot a look to the statue of the Blessed Mother. "Sorry. I think it's irresponsible that the American people didn't get to know about this."

Irene steeled herself with a deep breath. "Two points," she said. "One: Never once in the history of this nation has a single American cast a vote for a spouse. They vote for the candidates."

Jonathan wasn't buying. "So, there's no restraint by the media if a candidate's teenage kids step out to grab a drink at a bar, but having a wife who's a bomber gets a pass? Come on, Wolfie. That can't sit right with you."

"Which brings me to point two," Irene said. "We have no way of knowing that the president himself knows of her past."

"Bullshit," Boxers said. Then, to the Blessed Mother: "Sorry. Again. He's the president, for God's sake."

Irene tossed off another shrug. "As I say, we're very good at this sort of thing. Or, more to the point, the Marshals Service is very good at this sort of thing. If Yelena didn't reveal the secret to him, then no one else would."

Jonathan thought his head might explode. "What about you guys, Wolfie? We're talking national security here. Don't the people of the United States have a right to know that there's a terrorist in the White House?"

"Digger, you want things to be blacker and whiter than they ever are. I'll use the T-word if that's what you want, but the fact of the matter is that the same woman you characterize as a terrorist in fact did a wonderful and noble thing for her adopted country by sending a lot of very bad people to prison."

It was Jonathan's turn to laugh. "You accuse me of not dealing in shades of gray, and then you put out a purple argument. By your own words, there wasn't a lick of patriotism in what she did. That was all about saving her father's ass. How do you know that her very presence in the White House isn't part of some massive plan for revenge?"

"I know that because we don't live in a James Bond novel. There is no Dr. No, there's no THRUSH, and there's no KAOS. And there's no way to plot a course to 1600 Pennsylvania Avenue—especially not as a First Lady. I mean, think about it."

She had a point. In fact, Venice had told him that Anna and Frank Darmond had met before he had even run for the House of Representatives. It would have been foolish to roll the dice on becoming a mole at the highest level even before a first vote was cast. What seemed less outrageous, though, was the thought of a developing plan to squeeze the most out of an evolving opportunity.

"While under protection, what were her political activities?" Jonathan asked.

"Mostly quiet. Once you cut off ties with your revolutionary brethren, and send the bosses to prison, there's not a lot left."

"What about the friendships she developed afterward?" Boxers asked.

"No one particularly scary, I don't think. You're not going to find any Tea Partiers in her Rolodex, but I'm guessing there aren't many Communists in there, either."

"Can you get us a list of acquaintances?" Jonathan asked.

Irene nodded, but said nothing. It was her tell for unease.

"A complete list," Jonathan pressed. "Anything less than complete, and we're all wasting a lot of time."

"I'll see what I can do."

Warning bells pounded like a great gong in his head. "Why are you gaming me like this, Irene? That's not like you."

"It's complicated."

"Life's complicated." Jonathan leaned in closer. "Understand me, Madam Director. I am a micrometer away from pulling the plug on this whole thing. The stakes here are huge, and whenever that happens, the danger to me and my team gets huge, too. As this is fundamentally not my problem, I will not go forward without the trust that I have earned from you and the rest of Uncle Sam's legions."

Irene nodded some more. Jonathan could read in her eyes that he'd nearly convinced her, so he let the silence prevail. She signaled that the decision was made when she inhaled deeply through her nose and blew the breath out as a silent whistle. "I'll give you everything we have," she said. "I'll have a courier bring it to your office first thing in the morning. And I won't insult you by telling you how sensitive it is."

Jonathan turned more in his seat, and settled in for the next chapter of this conversation. "Did you know that while there were street surveillance cameras in place at the Wild Times Bar on the night Mrs. Darmond was kidnapped, none of them were in fact working?"

"Yes," Irene said. "I own those cameras, at least in a manner of speaking."

"That doesn't seem odd to you?" Boxers prodded.

"Oh, it seems *very* odd to me. Just as it seems odd to me that the attackers knew that the First Lady was on an OTR to begin with. It's odder still that by all accounts, the car that pulled up with the shooters was a big SUV. There's some disagreement whether it was a Suburban, an Escalade, or a Yukon, but everyone agrees that it was a big, dark-colored sports utility vehicle."

"Like the ones your guys drive?" Jonathan asked.

"Like the ones that all of official Washington drives. I've got a few agents working that angle, trying to track the whereabouts of all of them, but I don't expect much. Heck, if I were a bad guy pulling off something like this, maybe I'd just rent a look-alike vehicle to throw everyone off the scent."

Bingo! In a flash, one giant piece of the puzzle fell into place for Jonathan. As the realization dawned, a smile bloomed. He wagged a forefinger at Irene as the reality clarified. "You guys didn't hire us to protect the world from financial calamity. Well, maybe that was part of it, but you hired us because you don't know if you can trust your own people."

"I already stipulated to that," Irene said, but she looked away as she did.

"No, you didn't," Jonathan pressed. "You said you couldn't trust your people to keep it quiet—the financial Armageddon argument. In reality, you think that maybe your people are running this thing."

A longer silence this time as the director measured her words. "It's not just my people," she confessed at last. "Ramsey Miller can't write off the possibility that his people might have a hand in it, too."

"But why?"

Irene shook her head. "I have no idea. That's the part that makes no sense to me. And because it makes no sense, I don't give that possibility any more weight than, say, a thirty percent possibility."

"Thirty percent is a lot," Boxers said.

Jonathan finished the thought: "Certainly too high to take a chance."

Irene held up her hands as if to stop someone approaching her. "Tell you what, guys. Let me pursue that possibility on my own, okay? There are plenty enough people in the universe with motivation to do harm to Yelena Poltanov—excuse me, Anna Darmond. Why don't you focus on those? If nothing else, those are the kinds of leads that my shop can't follow without asking a lot of questions."

"And you'll start sharing for real?" Jonathan pressed.

Another hesitation. "Let's do this," Irene said. "I'll tell you if this turns out to be a problem within the federal law enforcement community, and I promise I'll tell you early. However, I will not gratuitously share dirty laundry with you."

Jonathan weighed the deal. Irene had dedicated well over half her life to the Bureau, and if it turned out that her tree was full of bad apples, she had every right to manage the problem from within.

Finally, Jonathan offered a handshake. "Deal," he said.

CHAPTER SEVEN

It was nearly one in the morning when Becky pulled her Volkswagen Jetta back into her parking space at Eastern Towers. They'd hit four ATMs in Annapolis for a total of $1,200. If people were indeed tracking him, there could be no clearer beacon than a cash withdrawal, and this one would lead his enemies in exactly the wrong direction. He worried, of course, that his pursuers might read the ruse for what it was and therefore concentrate their search for him in Virginia, but he recognized that that kind of double-reverse logic could drive a person insane.

There'd been no tolls to pay along the way, and Becky had made a point to call her mother while she drove, staging a casual conversation that would give her plausible deniability if she needed it one day. They'd no doubt passed through some traffic cameras, but David figured that if the police didn't know who they were looking for, the hazards posed by cameras were minimal.

"What are you going to do now?" Becky asked as she pulled the parking brake.

He looked at her, and for the first time, he began to realize just how hopeless a situation he'd created for himself. "I haven't a clue," he said. "I don't even know for sure that I'm not being ridiculously paranoid. I'm afraid to do anything, but I feel stupid doing nothing."

Becky slid the key from the ignition, triggering the interior light. She gave him a hard look. "You look like you're a mess," she said. "Well, you *are* a mess on the outside, but you look like you're a mess inside, too. You're welcome to stay with me, if you'd like."

He wasn't sure why, but the offer stunned him. "Really?"

"Sure. I just went to the store, so there's plenty of food in the apartment. I don't have much in the way of guest accessories, but what I've got is yours. For the time being, anyway. For tonight."

Without all the makeup, she really did look three years younger and ten degrees hotter. Her offer tugged at him, causing him to feel guilty about all the months of shittiness he'd thrown her way.

"Sure," he said. "Thank you. The minute there's any danger, I swear—"

"Okay, I'll be really honest with you," she interrupted. "I really do think that you're making a lot out of nothing. Or maybe I just hope you are. But I don't worry too much about the danger."

The dome light turned itself out, and it was time to climb out of the car. As they walked to the exterior door of the complex, David unconsciously kept his hand over the pocket where he'd stuffed the cash. He thought he saw Becky notice, and he thought she rolled her eyes, but in the darkness, he couldn't tell for sure.

As they rode up together in the elevator, David wondered what it would be like to have to live in this kind of squalor. David knew that he hadn't earned his wealth—unless you could compensate someone for the trauma of living with the poster child of a right-wing-nut-job father—but he was confident that one day he would make good on the debt, if only by virtue of his intellect.

For the people who lived here, though—for the people who actually depended on the next paycheck for their very existence—this might be the pinnacle for them, the moment for which they'd waited all their lives. He didn't understand how you could wake up every morning if every morning guaranteed a shit-smelling elevator ride.

The elevator dinged on the eleventh floor, and Becky led the way into the institutionalized dreariness. The hallway was a cavern of doors, and although more lights were functional than non-, the overall effect was a yellow pall that portended bad things.

"Are you all right?" Becky asked. "You look . . . funny."

He forced a smile. "It's been a long night."

Becky's apartment was the third from the end of the hallway, on the right. He noted that she had her key out well in advance of her arrival at the door, and David concluded from that that she was perpetually ready to fend off a hallway attacker with a Schlage in the eye.

She slipped the key into the lock, and a few seconds later, they were swallowed by the land of yellow. When the door was closed, she turned two dead bolts, and then used her key to turn a third. She left the key ring dangling from the slot.

"Want that iced tea?" Becky asked.

"Sure."

"Take off your coat and have a seat," Becky instructed, pointing toward the living room that was separated by an imaginary line from the dining room, which in turn was separated from the kitchen by a half wall.

David stripped off his coat, then realized he didn't know what to do with it.

"That's the closet there," Becky said, pointing with her forehead.

David opened it to reveal a level of order and neatness that was foreign to him. The closet couldn't have been more than thirty inches wide, yet it held four coats to cover the needs of each season, plus a vacuum cleaner, and somehow it didn't look crammed. She even had spare hangers.

With his coat hung, he walked to the same loveseat he'd occupied before.

Becky joined him in the living room with two glasses of tea. She handed him one and helped herself to her chair.

"So," Becky said, the word constituting a complete sentence. "What's your next move?"

"I don't know," David confessed. "For now, I'm trying to stay focused on staving off the panic. And please don't tell me again that you think I'm making this up."

"I didn't mean that as an insult. I just like to lean on the positive side of things until there's no other choice."

"So I should look at this mess as if my glass is one-eighth full, not seven-eighths empty?" He sold the comment with a smile and took a sip of tea. It was better than he'd expected.

"Are you hungry?"

He shook his head. "I should be, but I'm not. You feel free to eat if you want."

"I already did." Her posture changed in her seat. She sat back, crossed her legs, and smirked at him.

"What?"

"I don't get you," she said. "You've grown up here your whole life, your family has more money than God, yet you still don't have anyone to run to when you need help. How can that be?"

David chuckled as he shook his head. "Now those are some seriously barricaded mind-doors," he said. "Suffice to say that money truly does not buy happiness. Except maybe for the house staff."

"You had house staff?"

Her shocked tone made him laugh. "Well, we're not talking footmen and dressers, but yeah. Two full-time housekeepers and a driver."

Becky joined him in the laugh. "A chauffeur? In a uniform and everything?"

"Mostly he just wore a dark suit. His name was Tommy. Still is, actually. If it was some official Washington thing, or a movie premiere or something like that, he'd wear the hat."

"Boots?"

"No, no boots. We had a car, not a team of horses."

"A car or a limousine?"

David laughed again. "Can we compromise on a big car?"

"That is just so cool! I never knew anybody who had his own limousine."

David considered pointing out that the limo wasn't his, but rather his father's, but he was enjoying the lightness of the conversation, so he let it go.

"You know, it's not that much different than growing up in suburbia," he said. "You've got all the same problems. You get zits like everybody else, and you get bullied like everybody else."

The phone rang. "Oh, yeah, I'm sure," Becky said as she rose to answer it. "But you've got top dermatologists for the zits and lawyer daddies to handle the bullies."

"Don't forget the hit men," David added.

"Oh, of course." Becky picked up the cordless handset from its cradle on the wall where the dining room met the kitchen. "Hello?" Her face darkened instantly. "Oh, hi, Charlie." She covered the phone with her other hand and mouthed, *Baroli*.

"Um, no, I haven't seen him," she said. Her face flushed as she pointed at David. "Oh my God, are you sure? That doesn't sound like him at all."

David's gut twisted. There were many things that didn't sound like him—many of them nice, unfortunately—but he didn't imagine that many of those would prompt a call from the city desk editor at this hour.

"There must be some mistake, Charlie. DeShawn Lincoln was his friend. A really *good* friend, I think. Why would he kill him?"

Bang! At that sentence, David felt his window of hope slam shut. This was as bad as it could get. He'd been set up for the murder of a cop. Holy shit.

"Okay, Charlie. Yeah, I'll keep an eye out for him, but I can't imagine him coming here." She listened, and then chuckled dismissively. "Oh, I hardly think so. All right, I'll see you tomorrow."

She pushed the disconnect, and for a long stretch, they just stared at each other. Finally, Becky cleared her throat. "So, uh, I guess you caught the gist of that. Your friend is dead, and the police are looking for you as the prime suspect."

The room suddenly seemed short of oxygen. It was one thing to suspect that you were neck deep in a pile of shit, but something else entirely to learn beyond doubt that it was true. "I don't understand this," David said.

"Did your friend—did DeShawn—tell you anything about what specifically was going on?"

David closed his eyes tightly—winced, really—as he scoured his memory for anything that might be useful. "He was scared. He thought that it had something to do with the Secret Service, and it was too big to speak of over the phone. That means he suspected he was being watched." He opened his eyes. "And apparently, he *was* being watched."

"But why you? Why are you dragged into this?"

He shook his head. "I don't know. The best I can figure out is that they knew Deeshy was talking to me. I mean, they had his cell phone and I called a couple of times right before he was killed. Maybe I was just convenient."

A minute or two passed in silence. "Maybe you should just go to the police and turn yourself in."

"That's crazy. I didn't do anything."

Becky cocked her head to the side. "Well, David, no offense, but that's what every guilty person says. I mean, I believe you—if I didn't, you wouldn't be here—but once this story hits the news tomorrow morning, the act of remaining a fugitive just drives home the fact of your guilt to the police."

"Innocent until proven guilty," David said.

"Oh, come on, David. You're not that naïve. You're the rich son of a fabulously rich father, and you're a reporter wanted for murder. This has *Today* show written all over it. If it's not the featured story on the morning broadcasts tomorrow, then it certainly will be the next day. By the time they finish milking the angle that you didn't step forward to let justice take its course, you'll be ruined. Even if a court finds you not guilty, you'll be famous as the rich kid whose money let him skip a murder charge."

He felt light-headed. "Jesus, Becky. And you're the optimist?"

"I'm just saying—"

"I know what you're just saying. And I also know that you're right. But you forgot the part about what a crackpot I'll sound like when I start talking about some giant conspiracy."

"I don't suppose you recorded any of DeShawn's panicky phone calls."

"Of course not. But if this whole thing is being run by the Secret Service or even the DC Police, the last thing I'm going to do is just walk into a police station and let them determine my future."

"What's the alternative?"

"Not doing that. That's the first step. Steps two through three thousand are a little fuzzy. But I'm not going to do the one thing that will guarantee spending the rest of my life in prison. Even if everything you predict comes true, the result will be the same, so what's the sense in stepping forward now?"

Becky took some time to think about that. "Well, you've got a much better chance of survival if you walk in to be arrested than you do if you wait till some SWAT team crashes the doors to take you the hard way."

David faked a smile. "Yeah, but the SWAT scenario is way more interesting."

"That's not funny."

He let it go and guzzled the rest of his tea. He stood. He had to stand. If he didn't move, he'd go crazy.

There had to be a thread to pull. He refused to accept that there were no alternatives to a ruined life. He hadn't been the nicest guy over the years, but he deserved better than this.

He pressed his hands against the sides of his head to keep it from exploding.

"Here's the problem," he said. "I don't know how to untangle this without either being visible to the world or leaving an electronic trail a mile wide. Not that I know where to find answers, but even if I did, I couldn't go there to look."

"Don't you have a lot of police sources?"

"I do, but I can't call them. Not when the crime under investigation is a murder of one of their own."

"I'd think they'd want justice."

"Right now, they apparently think that hauling my ass in is the definition of justice. I can't risk it." His eyes narrowed as he focused in on Becky. "What about you? Are you willing to do some detective work?"

She blanched. "I do society pieces. I don't know anyone among the police. And if I called your sources, all your concerns would inure to me. That's not a solution. Can you think of anyone else?"

Hearing the question asked that directly made the answer seem ridiculously obvious. When he told her, she laughed.

"You're kidding, right?" she said.

David smiled and shrugged. "Can you think of a better solution?"

She stewed on it. "Not at the moment," she said at last. "I guess I'll call him in the morning."

David checked his watch. Technically speaking, it was morning already, but by any standard too early to call. He steadied himself with a deep breath. "All right, then. We have a plan. It's a sucky one, but it's a plan. So now we just have to wait for daylight." He eyed the sofa. "So, can I sleep there?"

Becky stood, too. She approached him with a smile that stirred something deep in him. "Well, here's the thing, David Kirk. Do you know why Charlie Baroli called here looking for you?"

His heart started to race. Whatever was coming was going to be very good or very bad.

She stepped up very close to him. "Apparently there's a rumor in the office that I have this big crush on you." She reached to his chest and unbuttoned the top button on his shirt. "But that's not true."

David didn't move. This was new territory for him. When it came to hitting on people, he'd always been the hitter.

"Does that surprise you?" Becky asked. "That I don't have a crush on you?" She undid another button.

"I don't know if it surprises me, but I confess it confuses me."

A third button revealed enough of his chest for her to slip her hands under the fabric. She caressed him, and he felt heat rising in his face. And something else rising elsewhere. "It's never been about a crush," she said. "It's about a strong, strong desire to see you naked."

CHAPTER EIGHT

When his landline rang at 0730, Jonathan knew that it was Venice. Only a handful of people knew the number, and of those, only she had the courage to wake him at this hour. He fingered the handset from its cradle and brought it to his ear without opening his eyes.

"I hate you," he said. Next to him on the bed, Joe-Dog stretched and farted. The seventy-pound black Labrador retriever had no official home—she was the town's dog with special dispensation from leash laws—but more times than not, when Jonathan was in town, his bed was her bed.

"And good morning to you, too." Yep, Venice. "A stern voiceless gentleman from the FBI delivered about two tons of paper. I believe they are the files you insisted on having. You know, because we're in a hurry. Charlie and Rick were kind enough to stack them in the War Room."

"Have you started sorting through them yet?" When he asked that, he made sure to project a smile that was louder than his words.

"And *you* hate *me*. Right. Please shower before you come up." The line went dead.

The instant Jonathan pulled away the covers and sat up, JoeDog was on her feet and ready to play. Or eat. Or, if all else failed, to go back to sleep again. Jonathan gave her enough of an ear rub to elicit a moan of ecstasy, and then stood. "Okay, Killer. Time to go to work."

Thirty-five minutes later, the three *S*'s were taken care of, and JoeDog and Jonathan were climbing the stairs together. At the top, Rick Hare tossed off a two-fingered salute. "Morning, Boss. Looks like you've got some research to do." A former military policeman, Rick carried a .40 caliber Glock on his hip with which he could write his name in a target at twenty-five yards. His job was to serve as the first line of defense—offense, really—if anyone tried to duplicate the attack that nearly killed Venice a while ago. The HK MP5 he wore slung across his chest would help in that effort as well.

"Hi, Rick. I understand that you got stuck with schlepping duty. Sorry about that."

"Well, that FBI troll wasn't going to do it, and I didn't see Ms. Alexander doing it all on her own. That wouldn't have been right. So me and Charlie pitched in."

Typical of many former military noncoms, Rick had a hard time addressing superiors by their first names. "I appreciate it," Jonathan said, suppressing the urge to chastise him for abandoning his post and cooperating in what could have been a trap. Given the bucolic nature of Fisherman's Cove, it would have sounded outrageously paranoid. Besides, Venice should have known better.

Jonathan pressed his thumb to the print reader and winked at the camera. When the lock buzzed, he pushed the door open and entered the hive of activity that was Security Solutions. As usual, it appeared that he was the last to arrive. You got to do that when you owned the place.

"Good morning everyone," he said to the room. A few people spoke a greeting in return, but it wasn't necessary. Jonathan turned left inside the door and approached Charlie Keeling, another member of the guard staff. The two guards on duty split their time between guarding the front door and guarding the entrance to the Cave.

"Listen, Mr. G," Charlie said, his voice barely above a whisper. "I owe you an apology for this morning. Rick and I never should have helped with those boxes, but I couldn't think of another way. Won't happen again."

Jonathan smiled. "I appreciate that, Charlie." All was forgiven.

"Hey, JoeDog," Charlie said. He patted his chest with both hands—a spot on his vest just above his slung MP5—and JoeDog planted her forepaws there, thus earning another ear rub.

Charlie buzzed the door and Jonathan and JoeDog both stepped into the Inner Sanctum. The beast made a beeline for her favorite leather chair near the fireplace in Jonathan's office while her nominal master peeled off and headed for the War Room.

The teak conference table was buried in stacks of what had to be fifty file boxes, each of them marked with a sticker from the FBI proclaiming them to be SE-CRET: EYES ONLY.

"Holy shit," Jonathan said.

"Welcome to my world." Venice sat on the far side of the stack, the top of her head barely visible. "How many times do I have to remind you to be careful what you ask for?"

Jonathan stepped to the table and peeled the lid off a box, revealing file folders. Lots and lots of file folders. "I guess I underestimated the number of her enemies."

"Oh, I think this is a more comprehensive file than just enemies," Venice said. "This is essentially every person Yelena Poltanov ever talked to while she was in the United States."

Jonathan gave a low whistle. "This will take days."

Venice didn't answer.

Jonathan pushed up the sleeves of his sweater and started paging through the box nearest him. From what he could tell, the files were organized by date. He started fingering through a box that seemed to span the month of March, 1985—part of the month, anyway. A counter-espionage agent codenamed Watchdog had been following Yelena's every move and taking annoyingly complete notes. As a random sample, Yelena had entered the chemistry lab at 09:54 and emerged in the company of two unknown students at 11:42. From there, she'd proceeded to the campus cafeteria, arriving at 11:57.

"Oh my God," Jonathan said. "Imagine the poor SOB who had to read through all this minutiae and analyze it."

"Your tax dollars at work," Venice said.

Jonathan pulled out one of the rolling chairs that surrounded the conference table and sat. "We need context," he said. "We don't have the time to read through this stuff cold and figure out the cast of characters."

"What do you suggest?"

"I've got nothing."

"Then keep reading."

"Have you called in Boxers for this?" Jonathan asked.

Venice laughed. "Right. This is definitely in his wheelhouse."

Jonathan wanted to argue, but what was the point? Boxers' attention span in fact did not lend itself to hours of document analysis. Still, it would be nice to have the extra set—

"Bingo!" Venice announced.

"What?"

She held aloft a compact disk. "An index. I've been looking for it. The feds always index boxes of files like this." She swung around to her computer terminal as she spoke, opened the cup holder, and inserted the disk. "I'll put it up on the wall," she said.

Her fingers tapped wildly, but for the longest time, all Jonathan saw on the screen were inconsequential numbers and figures. There were dozens of file names— maybe hundreds—but they weren't organized, and from what Jonathan could tell, the file names themselves were unreadable. Periodically, the cursor would move and Venice would make a satisfied noise, and then the screen would change all over again. Jonathan knew from years of experience not to interrupt her when she got into the zone like this. She was on the hunt, and she'd either find her prey or she would not, but it was always a bad idea to interrupt her concentration.

Meanwhile, Jonathan amused himself by lifting another file out of a box, this one from June 13, 1986.

"Don't get those out of order," Venice snapped without looking up from her keyboard. "Indexes don't do a thing if the papers aren't in order."

Jonathan rolled his eyes. "I promise to be careful." This time, there were pictures. A much, much younger version of the First Lady sat in a bar with friends, her mouth open wide in a big laugh, while the three men who were with her seemed equally amused. According to the caption, the men were Peter Crenshaw, Albert Banks, and Stephen Gutowski, and the bar was the Bombay Bicycle Club in Alexandria, Virginia. Watchdog had either shot the picture from very close range, or he had a terrific telescopic lens. Either way, this was a picture of four friends having a wonderful time. It was the kind of image that every college student everywhere could have had taken of themselves at one point or another.

Crenshaw, Banks, and Gutowski were described in the narrative as frequent acquaintances of Yelena's, but they were largely dismissed as inconsequential to the case that was being built against her. Jonathan tucked the photos back into their folder, and tucked the folder back into the spot from which he'd removed it.

Two additional random checks of files for June of 1986 showed equally boring activities, as did five random checks of July. When he reviewed the contents of the file from July 19, 1986, though, he sat a little straighter in his chair. In these photographs, Yelena was nose to nose in an intense conversation with a man who appeared to be slightly older than she. To Jonathan's eye, they both appeared to be angry, but of course there was no way to be sure. Apparently, the FBI wasn't using listening technology in their efforts to track Yelena's movements. Accompanying documentation showed that the picture had been shot in a place called the Hairy Lemon, and that the man in the photo was one Leonard Baxter, a.k.a. Leonid Brava. This was apparently their seventeenth documented meeting.

Jonathan flipped to the next photo in the file, which revealed another man and a woman, Peter and Marcia Carlson, husband and wife, whose names apparently were real. While the scenery from the first photo hadn't changed, the number of empty glasses on the table had multiplied. While the women preferred wine, the men drank clear liquor straight. None appeared to be having a very good time.

According to the narrative, *The conversation at the Hairy Lemon lasted three hours and fourteen mins. This was the seventeenth meeting of all subs. While unable to hear the words that were spoken, the conversation was animated throughout. For a short while, all subjects got angry, but then they settled down. I believe that when all the evidence is finally analyzed, it will show that an important decision was made. Photo 7.19.86–3 documents the final moments before parting. It is clearly celebratory.*

Jonathan turned the page again, and the referenced photo showed all the subjects in a four-way handshake, a clear indicator of an agreement made.

The narrative continued, *Addendum added 7/24/86: On 7/23/86, twenty-five pounds of Semtex was stolen from Allied Armaments, Inc. in Radford, Virginia. Three days later, Semtex was used in a bomb that killed*

Soviet Attaché Yuri Brensk in his home in Arlington, Virginia. The explosion was reported to the media as a gas leak.

"Huh," Jonathan said. He remembered that explosion, just as he remembered the media clamor to turn it into something other than a gas explosion. For a Soviet diplomat to die of a peaceful explosion—as opposed to one created by his enemies—at a time of such political flux—was a hard gap to bridge. If he remembered correctly, it took a statement from the head of ATF—the Bureau of Alcohol, Tobacco, Firearms and Explosives— to eventually calm the waters.

"Okay, I've got something," Venice said. "Take a look at the screen."

At the far end of the table, the projection screen blinked, and what had been a mishmash of files was now sorted into well-defined columns.

"It seems that our friend Watchdog was one organized fellow," Venice said. "And his worldview fell into a very convenient black-and-white division." She used her cursor as a pointer to highlight folders as she spoke. "When we last looked at this mess, it was organized by date, showing what could be found in every folder, date by date." She clicked and the screen changed. "Here, though, is the topical listing that takes an incident or a question and then cross-references it back to the dates where the events happened."

Jonathan gave a low whistle. "That's a lot of work."

"Yes, it is. I'm guessing they did it for the prosecutors in the case so that they could find what they were looking for." She clicked again. "But here's the Holy Grail for us." The screen filled with a heading that read *Cast of Characters*, below which there were two files, one labeled *Conspirators* and the other labeled *Acquaintances.*

Venice clicked on the Conspirators file, and after a second or two of electronic contemplation, the computer launched a screen full of pictures and names. There were more than a few—more than would fit on the screen—but Jonathan zeroed right in on Leonid Brava and the Carlsons.

"I clearly haven't had time to review all of this, but these appear to be the bad guys," Venice explained.

"Click on that Brensk guy for me," Jonathan said. This picture, like the one he'd seen in the file, showed a man who'd stepped out of KBG Central Casting. He had a round, pugilist's face with a jet-black hairline that nearly met his jet-black eyebrows.

When Venice clicked the file open, the screen filled with personal data—name, address, phone number, place of employment, relatives, that sort of thing. When she clicked again, the screen blinked to another list of files cross-referenced to dates.

"That's a lot of information," Venice said. "I'll grant that it's well organized, but it's still a lot."

"Well, yes and no," Jonathan countered. "We don't need to try the case here. We don't care about who they blew up or conspired to kill back in the eighties. We just need to track down the bad guys and find out where they took the First Lady."

"Shouldn't they all be in jail?" Venice asked.

"I think they *should* all be dead," Jonathan said. "If they are, then we need to start looking at their friends and families. How long should the first cut take?"

Venice backed out of the files and returned to the stacked pictures. She scrolled through them. "It looks like there are eighteen," she said. "Give me forty-five minutes."

David Kirk had always wanted to be on television, though not in the way that so many of his classmates in J-school wanted to be there. While the others strove for fame as on-camera reporters, David wanted to find fame the way Bob Woodward or Charles Krauthammer did— by being so respected as a print reporter and columnist that the serious news shows would seek him out as the intelligent guest who could explain the news of the day. Respect was the key, and he was willing to earn it from the bottom up.

He'd never dreamed that he'd end up reaching bottom on the very day that he first appeared on television. He'd awoken still tired—and, frankly, a little raw and achy in his southern parts, thanks to a series of carnal stunts that startled the hell out of him. It turned out that Becky had studied the *Kama Sutra*. Or yoga. Or maybe was a gymnast in her past life. Either way, it had been a hell of a night. It had apparently been good for Becky, too, because the deep rhythm of her breathing never changed as he reached over her to lift the remote from her nightstand. The clock read 6:59.

Still glowing, he tuned into the *Today* show to catch the top-of-the-hour news. He didn't learn much that he didn't already know. The economy was still slogging along on its anemic recovery, the Arabs still didn't like the Jews, and the American military was slumping back to the meals-on-wheels mission that had dominated it during his childhood years.

At the quarter-hour break, when the "news" show

switched to promoting upcoming movies and their stars, he rolled out of bed and padded to the bathroom for morning chores, as his mother used to call them. He'd just gotten the water temperature right for his shower when he heard Becky calling from the other room. Her voice had a touch of panic to it. "David! Come here! Quickly!"

He damn near killed himself dashing back into the bedroom, where he found Becky sitting upright and bare breasted, pointing at the television screen. And what fine breasts they were. He allowed his eyes to follow the line of her finger, and that's when his world ended. Again.

The television screen had transformed into a giant portrait of his face. Along the bottom, just under his chin, an electronic caption read, *Wanted in Cop's Murder*. What was it, he wondered, about seeing it on television made it more real than merely knowing it to be true? Just like that, the air in the room seemed to thin and he needed to sit on the edge of the bed, one foot curled under his butt, and the other dangling to the floor, as if to keep him in contact with the reality of the hardwood. Without looking, Becky laid a reassuring hand on his knee.

The newsreader from Washington's Channel Four said something about the "brutal murder" of DeShawn Lincoln around nine o'clock the previous evening, but David didn't pay attention to the actual words. He was too overwhelmed by their meaning. This wasn't just bad news anymore. This was an all-out call for the people closest to him to call the police. If his bank accounts hadn't been locked out before, they sure as hell were now. At his apartment, his computer and his records and probably his underwear and socks were all in an evidence locker now, being pored over by cops who would sell their souls for the honor of shooting a cop killer.

"We need to move quicker than I thought," Becky said, and then she was on her feet. "Let's shower together," she said. "It'll save time."

That had been two hours ago.

Now, he sat on a bench in Farragut Park with the collar of his new down coat standing high and a stocking cap pulled low against the bitter cold. If there was one ray of sunshine to be found in the black pall that his life had become in the last twelve hours, it was the fact that the frigid weather made it easier to be disguised.

He sat on the bench nearest the western side of Daniel Farragut's towering statue, keeping a close eye on the mouth of the Farragut West Metro Station. Becky had called the other party for this meeting under the auspices of introducing him to a news source. She and David had both been surprised that he'd agree so readily, and that fact alone added more stress to the day.

At a few minutes before nine-thirty, Grayson Cantrell emerged from the shadows of the subway station and stood at the corner of H Street and Connecticut Avenue, waiting for the light to turn, and for the red sign to turn white so that he could cross the street to the park. Seventy pounds overweight and bearing the ruddy complexion of a heavy drinker, Cantrell was to David part of the last of the old-school Washington journalists, for whom research meant a phone call to an old buddy, and source development meant buying a couple of rounds at lunch. At least thirty years younger, David didn't so much feel sorry for the old guy who'd been caught in a weird time warp as he did envy him for having lived the life of the reporter that he'd always dreamed of one day being.

Cantrell didn't seem the least bit anxious or even curious about what lay ahead as the light changed and he strolled across the street and entered the park. In the summer, this was a place of Frisbee games and impromptu concerts. This time of year, however, Farragut Park was merely a place of transit, a spot for commuters to hurry through, on their way to their offices in the morning, and to their homes at night. Of the precious few who occupied the park benches, the vast majority were homeless people who lay insulated in a dozen layers of fabric.

Grayson Cantrell walked right up to David and sat down. "How's life as a fugitive?" he asked.

David's insides melted at the question. "You knew?"

True to the overall image, Cantrell wore an old-style London Fog trench coat—with the wool lining installed—the collar of which he scrunched up around his throat as he helped himself to the seat next to the younger man. "Knew what?" he baited. "That you were you, or that you were wanted for murder?"

"Um, both."

"I've known since last night that you were suspected of killing that cop," Cantrell explained. As he spoke, he seemed more interested in the passing crowd than he did in David. "But I thought from the beginning that that was bullshit. You're a lot of things—most of them less than complimentary—but I don't see you as a murderer."

David found himself smiling. "Thank you."

"For what? I'm neither a jury nor a cop who'd mortgage his nut sack for a chance to shoot you. As for knowing that you were you, well, suffice to say that disguises are not your long suit."

David pulled his hat further down on his ears.

"Is it safe to assume that you put Becky up to calling me?" Cantrell asked.

David cleared his throat. "Well," he said. It was all he could come up with.

Cantrell chuckled. "Let me amend my last comment," he said. "Deception in general is not your long suit. Tell me what is going on."

David didn't know precisely how he thought this meeting was going to go, but he knew for a fact that this was not it. He'd been shitty with Cantrell for both of the two years that he'd been at the *Enquirer*, and as such, Cantrell had every right to be shitty back to him. This niceness routine made him uncomfortable. It took David the better part of ten minutes to catch Cantrell up on the essential elements of what had transpired in the last twenty-four hours.

Cantrell listened intently through the whole recitation, and when David was finally done, he let out a low whistle. "Jesus, David. You're in serious trouble."

"I knew that."

"No, I mean *serious* trouble." He pulled his hands from his pockets, cupped them, and blew into them before stuffing them back. "If what you and your friend are implying is true, then the Secret Service is framing you for murder. In my experience, if the feds want to hurt you, you're going to end up hurt."

David scowled and stretched his neck on his shoulders. This wasn't turning out to be as helpful or empowering as he'd hoped.

"So, why did you call me?" Cantrell asked.

"You know everybody," David replied. "You have forty years' worth of sources, and I'm going to guess that they'll be happy to talk with you about anything. I need to know what I'm really up against."

"And you can't approach these sources yourself."

"Exactly," David said. "After watching the news this morning, I was close to ratting *myself* out. Their case seems damn strong. Except, you know, for the part where they're completely wrong."

"Jails are filled with the innocent," Cantrell said. "Just ask them." As he spoke, he continued to seem more interested in the crowd than he was in David.

David craned his neck to check what he was checking. "What are you looking at?"

"For," Cantrell said. "I'm looking *for* anyone who might see through your brilliant disguise. Unlike you, at this precise moment in time, I still have a great deal to lose." It was classic Cantrell, simultaneously insulting and helpful.

"Why did you come if you knew I was going to be here?" David asked. At this point, life was literally too short to be subtle.

When Cantrell looked at him this time, David caught the first glimpse of real kindness in the grumpy old fart's eyes. Nestled under thick, droopy lids and surrounded by squint lines, the irises were a remarkable blue, nearly gray. "First of all, I didn't *know* you would be here. I merely suspected. But to your larger point—

why am I here alone instead of with a SWAT team in tow—I told you before that I thought from the very beginning that the news reports were wrong."

Grayson placed a hand on David's shoulder in a fatherly gesture that stirred emotion in David's throat.

"My boy, I am an old man. I'd been three times around the block before Woodstein got their first sniff of Watergate. My first big story was the DC riots of sixty-eight. Over that many years, you get a sense for people, a kind of sixth sense that is more compelling than any curriculum vitae. It's never let me down."

David scowled. "I don't—"

"Listen," Cantrell said, finishing the sentence in a way David had not intended. "You don't listen. And that's a terrible flaw in a reporter. It's also a trait common to every reporter your age. Hell, maybe it's common to every *person* your age." The statement ended in a glare that somehow froze David's vocal cords.

"In any event, while I find you to be arrogant, narcissistic, and in general way too full of yourself, you have never for a moment impressed me as a person capable of murder. Sitting here next to you, I've seen nothing to change my mind."

For a second, David wondered if the appropriate response was to thank him. On further consideration, though, finding no compliment, he decided not to. "Still," he said, "I appreciate you taking the chance and coming to see me. I wanted to ask you a favor."

Cantrell held up his hand for silence.

Yeah, and I'm the arrogant one, David didn't say.

"Your friend DeShawn Lincoln was not liked among his fellow cops. My sources have independently referred to him as twitchy, paranoid, obnoxious, and one who bristled at authority. The phrase common to all sources was 'pain in the ass.' And please know that I mean no offense to the dead, or to your friendship."

David scowled. "You've already started looking into the case?"

"I've been at my desk since six this morning. I'm always at my desk by six. All of this notwithstanding, those who knew him all agreed that he seemed genuinely unnerved yesterday. Two actually used the word 'frightened.' The law of the police locker room being what it is, though, no one ventured to ask him why."

"I assumed that he didn't want to talk to his fellow cops because he feared that they were in on whatever bad things were happening," David explained.

"Oh, how I love to depend on assumptions. They have served me so well over the years." Cantrell did sarcasm better than most. "Based on what your friend Becky told me on the phone, I did some research on the shooting at the Wild Times Bar the other night. Before I get into it, though, tell me again what your friend said about the Secret Service."

David shook his head. "He didn't really *say* much of anything. There was just a mention that whatever bad things were happening, the Secret Service might be involved. Beyond being the victims of the shooting, I mean."

"He suspected that the Secret Service might have shot their own?"

David checked himself before answering. "Admittedly another assumption," he said, "but that's what I got by reading between the lines."

Cantrell inhaled deeply, and ran the back of his hand between his neck and the collar of his coat. "Interesting indeed," he said. He scanned the park one more time, then poked David with his elbow. "Come on," he said. "Let's walk and talk."

They headed north, away from the White House, which lay only three blocks to the south. As they headed toward Connecticut Avenue, it occurred to David that every morning and evening, the Secret Service closed this road in a rolling roadblock as the vice president headed back to his residence in the Naval Observatory. David's legs felt stiff after having sat for so long.

"In such a short time, I haven't had a lot of time to speak with witnesses," Cantrell said. It was his habit to start with an apology before launching the game-changing revelation. "One of the bartenders, though, is friends with my nephew, and he told me that he thought for sure that Anna Darmond was there when the shooting started."

David felt his jaw slacken. "The First Lady?"

"Exactly she."

"The president's wife. In a sleazoid bar." David had a hard time wrapping his head around that one.

"She's famous for nighttime jaunts," Cantrell said. "And that would explain the Secret Service presence."

David cocked his head as he tried to connect the dots. "So, you're saying this was an attempted assassination?"

"I'm saying nothing of the sort, because no one can prove that Mrs. Darmond was even there. Andy Wahl, the ABC White House stringer for NBC, sort of floated the question during the morning news briefing, but the suit behind the lectern piffled the question away, as if to say such a thing was preposterous."

"Did he actually *say* it was preposterous?"

Cantrell gave him a disappointed look. "Does this administration ever actually *say* anything?"

David tried to make it work in his mind. "Why wouldn't it be all over the news? That's not exactly a little thing."

"It could mean the cover-up of cover-ups."

David stopped for the light at L Street. "You say this as if you think it sounds reasonable." He felt way too exposed out here in the commuting crowd, but between the cold-weather gear and the prevailing lack of eye contact among city dwellers, he might as well have been invisible.

Cantrell looked straight ahead as he said, "Not to patronize, but a few more years in this job will teach you not to make sense of a story as you're collecting information. Once you have the facts assembled, they will make sense out of themselves."

The light changed, and they stepped off the curb together. "You *are* patronizing," David said, "and in this case, not well. We're making assumptions based upon third-party rumors. That's not the same as chasing facts."

"Don't believe it then," Cantrell said. "I'm just passing along information. Out of the goodness of my heart, I hasten to add. And there's more if you'd like to hear it."

David waited for it, and then realized that Cantrell actually wanted an answer. "Of course."

Cantrell gave a satisfied smirk. "All of the witnesses to the shooting last night spoke of a third big SUV as the vehicle containing the shooters. According to my nephew's friend—the bartender—the guys in the shooting vehicle grabbed a homeless guy who looked to be dead and threw him in the back of their vehicle and then tore off with him."

David scoured his memory. "I don't remember a report of a dead homeless guy."

Cantrell shot him with a gloved finger-gun. "Bingo."

"What bingo? What are you trying to tell me?"

"That whoever these guys are, whatever they're doing, they're also covering up a murder."

"Did anyone else see this dead homeless guy?"

"I'm sure they did," Cantrell said. "I just need to find them. Problem is, from what I can tell, of the people the cops interviewed after it was over—the few that were left after they all ran the other way—none of them mentioned the homeless man."

"Maybe because he wasn't there?"

Cantrell smacked the back of David's head. "Get in the spirit of things, will you? You've got dead Secret Service agents, you've got a government-looking van, a vanished dead guy, and the likelihood that the First Lady was there. I don't scream 'conspiracy' very often, but I'm screaming it now. And then there's the not insignificant detail that the person who wanted to talk to a reporter about it ends up murdered, with the reporter he was going to talk to framed for his killing."

David had to stop. They stood just outside the Mayflower Hotel, amid the morning taxi-catching scrum. Hearing Grayson Cantrell sum it all up like that made things seem suddenly hopeless. David had never been much of a fighter—he talked a good game, but for the most part just rolled over when the going got too tough—and he had no idea how to take on the federal government, if that was what it was coming to.

"Maybe the homeless guy was the target of the hit,"

David said. It felt like a random comment under the circumstances.

"Maybe," Cantrell agreed. He lightly grasped David's arm at the elbow and urged him forward. "Let's keep moving. But if that were the case, it would mean that the rest was all coincidence—that the Secret Service just happened to be there, and that the corresponding likelihood of the First Lady being present was just one of those things."

David gave a wry chuckle. "If the alternative is some great national conspiracy, I think I prefer the co-incidence."

"As you wish."

They walked in silence for the half block that took them to the complicated intersection where Connecti-cut Avenue met M Street and Rhode Island Avenue. David didn't like where his head went without talking. "I really do thank you for this, Grayson."

"You're very welcome."

"And what's the quid pro quo?"

Cantrell recoiled, clearly feigning insult. "I'm shocked, young man. *Shocked* I tell you. Isn't it possible that I am merely feeling altruistic?"

"Never occurred to me."

Cantrell laughed. "See? You really do have reporter's instincts. But this time, contrary to character, I truly am acting merely out of the goodness of my heart."

David's gut tightened. "Um, why?"

Cantrell laughed harder at whatever he saw in David's face. "Good God. Is it really my reputation to be such a prick?"

"I'm actually not sure what you want the answer to be," David said.

"No answer is necessary. Perhaps when all of this settles out, you'll be able to set the record straight and tell all who will listen that Grayson Cantrell is willing to lend a helping hand to a needy colleague."

"So you'll help me with the story?"

"I thought that's what I'm doing now," Cantrell said. A veil of sadness edged out some of the twinkle in his eye.

"Well, you are," David said. "But now that everyone's looking for me, I thought that maybe—"

Cantrell shook his head slowly. "I can't do shoe-leather work for you," he said. "More precisely—more *honestly*—I *won't* do shoe-leather work for you."

David's stomach fell. It's precisely what he was going to ask, and while he recognized that it was an outrageous favor, the disappointment tasted bitter. "Okay," he said.

Cantrell sighed. "Look, David. I'm an old man. The job that I used to love bears little resemblance today to what it was like back when I loved it. In a year or two, when I retire, I want to be remembered for my decades of hard work as a journeyman reporter."

"But this—"

"Hear me out. I've lost my taste for the big kill. I don't want the big story anymore. I can't afford the risk."

David scowled.

"You're young. You can swing for the fences and take big chances. If you get the story wrong, you have years to recover. If I go for the big one and blow it, that's all I'll be remembered for. The rest of it—all those years—won't mean anything. It's as if I would never have existed. I can't live with that."

The emotion on Cantrell's face looked a lot like

shame. David didn't begin to understand the rationale behind the older man's words, but he recognized finality when he heard it.

"Well, thanks then," David said. "I think."

"You think I'm a coward," Cantrell said. "And that's okay. Perhaps I am."

"You don't have to explain anything to me."

"Now who's patronizing?"

David felt his ears turn red. "I'm sorry," he said. "You're right. That's not my place. I'm just feeling very alone right now."

"Reporters are about getting the story. We're not used to *being* the story. It's a lonely place to be."

Lonely and crushing and soul stealing. Panic inducing. David didn't know how he was going to breathe through the encroaching panic attack.

"Are you interested in a suggestion from a cowardly old man?" Cantrell asked.

"Right now, I'm just interested in conversation. Human contact." A beat. "I'd love to hear whatever you have to tell me.

"Your blog," Cantrell said. "I believe it's called *Kirk Nation*, right?"

"You mean you don't read it?"

"I don't partake of the medium that will soon kill the medium that pays my bills. But I understand that many people do read it."

"About a hundred twenty thousand hits a day," David said.

"That's nice. Barely ten percent of what our readership used to be."

"But nearly a quarter of what it is now," David countered.

"Indeed. I was thinking that you might do well to write a piece that posits exactly the scenario you outlined to me this morning."

"But I don't have the facts."

"It's the Internet, David. When did hard facts become a requisite for writing a story?"

"*Kirk Nation* is not like that." David hated it when these Stone Age paper guys took shots at the future that they feared to enter.

"Hear the rest," Cantrell said. "And I meant no harm. The point of writing the piece would not be to report the facts, per se, but rather to float out a bit of bait. Given that you are the focus of an international manhunt, what you posit by way of this incident will get a lot of attention."

"From the very people I'm trying to avoid."

"From *everyone*. If you put it out there, people will start asking questions. If your theory is right, it should trigger a panic somewhere. When people panic, they make mistakes."

"They also start shooting people."

Cantrell's eyes flashed. "Well, there's that, yes. But that's more of a constant in your personal equation than a variable, is it not? The important fact is that people will start pressing for more details. The universe can support only a finite number of lies. With enough people searching for the truth, the cover-up will collapse. At least it should."

David let the words bounce around his head for a while. "That's a pretty aggressive strategy," he said. "It's a little putting on a Speedo to go out and kick a hornet's nest."

"Imagery that I neither want nor need," Cantrell

said. "From where I sit—and remember, I'm the coward among us—a passive approach largely guarantees you a grave or a jail cell. If the hornets are going to sting you anyway, why not make a game of it?"

"Pretty damn high stakes," David thought aloud. Then, to Cantrell: "This is the First Lady we're talking about. This could have tentacles that reach to the White House. I'm just one guy. I don't have any White House sources. I don't have a single layer of protection."

Cantrell put a hand on David's shoulder. "It's your life, son. You've got to live it the way you want. Do you own a gun?"

"A *gun*! Who the hell am I going to shoot?"

"Yourself, I'd think," Cantrell said. "If it comes to that. Die or live. Run or live. Hide or live. Go to prison or live. Each is the opposite of living, as far as I'm concerned. It's just a matter of choosing your method."

Suddenly this entire meeting felt like a terrible mistake. David felt his world collapsing into a dark, dense void. Cantrell was right, of course. Not about the suicide—he'd never be able to do that—but about the need to be aggressive.

"Are you sure you don't want to come along for the ride?" David asked.

"I've never been surer of anything in my life. And I'm sorry it's that way." As he looked down at his feet, the slate-gray sky gave up a few flakes of snow. Not enough to accumulate, but more than enough to start snarling traffic in Washington.

"I guess that's it, then," David said. "Thank you, Grayson."

"Billy Zanger," Cantrell said.

"Excuse me?"

"Billy Zanger. He's a deputy assistant press secretary at the White House. Maybe a deputy deputy. He's junior, but he was appointed by President Darmond. You might even be older than he. He's a child. No offense."

David was well beyond being sensitive to insult. "What about him?"

"He's a source," Cantrell said. "He's an unnamed knowledgeable insider. If you need to sweat someone, he's the one."

David pulled up short. "Why would he help me? He doesn't know me from Adam."

Grayson shrugged. "It's what confidential sources do. They talk."

"Only when they trust you."

Grayson donned the condescending smile that suited him so well. "David, my boy, there are only three reasons why sources talk to reporters, and none of them are rooted in trust." He counted them off with his fingers, starting off with his thumb. "One: They leak information that their bosses want them to leak—the policy statement that comes with full deniability. Two: They realize that their careers aren't going the way they want them to, and they see opportunity in betrayal. The common denominator there is the advancement of their own careers. We journalists are merely their vectors."

David felt anger brewing in his gut. "Wow, you really are the cynic, aren't you?"

"I prefer the term 'realist.' And we listen to them for the same reason. Their betrayals give us the stories that make our careers. And as a class, I have to say that we reporters are not all that incentivized to determine whether the underlying facts behind the leaks are truth or fiction. The fact that an important person said it is itself newsworthy."

David shook his head, a rattling motion to make the loose pieces fall into place. "Why are we having this conversation?"

"Because you asked about motivation, and you made a speech about getting the facts right. You're wading into deep, deep waters, and I wanted you to know how much different the rules of the game are from what you think they are."

"Because I'm naïve."

"I was going to say idealistic, but naïve works, too. This is Washington, David. There are no legitimate high horses to mount, and all houses are made of glass. Never forget that. Leave the speech making and the lofty phrases to the politicians. They deliver them better, and no one believes them anyway."

"What does this have to do with this Zaney guy?"

"It's Zanger. William Henry Zanger of Concordia, Kansas, via Northwestern University. He lives in Lake Ridge, Virginia, with his public school teacher wife, Barbie, and baby daughter, Hope. Lake Ridge isn't quite the end of the world, but you can see it from there."

"This is important?"

"Damned straight it's important. Billy still owes eighty-seven thousand dollars to Northwestern for his English literature degree. On top of that, they've got a two hundred ten thousand dollar mortgage on their tiny little townhouse. That's almost three hundred thousand dollars in debt to be paid for from combined incomes of under a hundred-fifty-K a year. Do the math."

"How'd he qualify for that kind of mortgage in this kind of market?" Even as he asked the question, he realized that he'd locked on to the wrong detail.

Cantrell saw it, too, and laughed. "Lending institutions have done very well by currying favor with this administration. But this brings us to the third and most powerful motivation to talk to a reporter."

David saw it, but was horrified. "Money?"

"Money."

"You pay sources? That's unethical."

This time, Cantrell's laugh was pure derision. "Now you're definitely being naïve."

"The *Washington Enquirer*, the city's leading newspaper, allows you to buy information from sources?"

"Of course they don't allow it. But they also don't look all that carefully into the 'miscellaneous' category on expense reports." He used finger quotes.

"And Charlie Baroli knows you're doing it?"

A shrug. "I can't say that we've ever discussed it, but yeah, there've been winks along the way. It's how the system works."

"But if you're buying information, how can you ever trust what you get?"

"How can you not? If the information is good, the buyer keeps coming back. If it's not, then the game ends quickly. Simple supply and demand."

David felt sick.

"Come on, David. Don't look so devastated. Our relationship to politicians is equal parts symbiotic and parasitic. Neither can flourish without the other. Keeping the pump primed is good for business."

David wanted to move on. "So you have this symbiotic parasitic relationship with Billy Zanger. How does that help me?"

"That's the beautiful part, the part that gives us scribes the upper hand when all is said and done. One could argue that by buying information, we violate some universal ethical code. Clearly, that's what you think. But when they accept the money, they break the law. That fact—and the fact that we can expose them for what they are—gives us ownership rights."

David wasn't sure that he understood.

"I can trade him," Cantrell said.

David felt his jaw drop open.

Cantrell laughed again. David was getting tired of that sound. "It's the dirtiest of businesses, isn't it?" He clapped David on the shoulder. "Anyway, he's yours if you want him. Believe it or not, his address is in the book."

Cantrell offered his hand. "Good luck, David. I've got to get back to resting on my laurels."

David shook, and felt oddly ashamed for doing so.

CHAPTER NINE

"All of her enemies are accounted for," Venice said. It was just shy of 10:00 A.M. "Everyone in the database who is identified as a subject of the FBI investigation is still in prison, due largely to the testimony delivered by Yelena Poltanov. What's your next theory?"

Behind him, beyond the glass wall, the door to the Cave crashed open, announcing Boxers' arrival. "Have we decided who to shoot yet?" he quipped. It was his way of saying good morning.

Jonathan caught him up in a two-minute soliloquy. It doesn't take long to relay that there's nothing to tell.

"What about her friends?" Big Guy asked.

"What about them?" Venice replied.

"Well, if her enemies are all accounted for, what about her friends? Maybe they have something to do with this."

Jonathan scowled. "What are you suggesting?"

Boxers shrugged with one shoulder. "Wasn't it Sherlock Holmes who said that when the unlikely is all that is left, then it is probably the answer?"

"No," Venice said. "The quote is that when you eliminate the impossible, whatever remains, however improbable, must be the truth."

"Welcome to English class," Jonathan said. "Big Guy's larger point is worth looking at."

"Why would the First Lady's friends be trying to kill her?" Venice asked.

"Why would she be in a bar meeting with enemies?" Jonathan countered. "Maybe the kidnapping was secondary to a happy meeting with friends."

"Or maybe friends and relatives of the people she put in jail are looking for revenge," Venice said.

"Mine is quicker to research," Jonathan said. "The clock is ticking here."

"I didn't know we had a clock."

"There's always a clock, Ven. You know that. Mrs. Darmond has been missing for nearly thirty hours now, and still there's been no word. That's concerning at multiple levels, and we're still one hundred percent in the dark. Let's swing at the easy pitches first, shall we?"

Clearly annoyed that Jonathan had taken Boxers' side against her, Venice turned back to her keyboard and got lost in the keystrokes.

Boxers capitalized on the silence to ask, "Have you given any thought to the resources we might need if this thing goes hot?"

Jonathan sighed. It was always in the back of his mind, but until there were details to pin on the possibilities, weapons and equipment were hard to specify. "At this point, I think we prepare for the worst," he said. "The normal complement of small arms, a couple of claymores, some grenades, and GPCs."

Boxers nodded. He appeared to agree with Jonathan's assessment. "Okay, then. I'm gonna head down to the armory and start assembling the go bags. I need something to do anyway, and this has the feel of an op where the balloon's gonna go up fast."

Jonathan couldn't disagree.

The armory for the covert side of Security Solutions lay underground in a tunnel that ran the length of the yard and parking lot that separated the firehouse from the basement of Saint Kate's, and contained enough weaponry to sustain an invasion of Mexico. Jonathan considered it a sanctuary of sorts—a place to relax, enveloped in the aroma of gun oil while smithing weapons to improve their function or merely to erase the signatures of previous operations. For Boxers, the armory was less about the poetry than the practicality, but Jonathan envied his escape.

As Big Guy exited the War Room, Jonathan turned back to Venice, whose face at once showed annoyance and amusement. "What?"

"I hate it when Boxers is right," she said.

"What've you got?"

"One of the guys in the photos you looked at—Albert Banks—lives out in Warrenton, Virginia. I took a look at him because he's local, and guess where his cell phone was night before last?"

Jonathan felt a tingle of hope in his spine. "Southeast DC?"

Venice smiled. "I can dial it in even closer than that. He was within two hundred feet of the Wild Times Bar."

When Venice continued to grin, Jonathan knew there

was more. She loved savoring her Big Reveals. "You look like you have a gas pain," Jonathan said.

"Steve Gutowski was in the area, too."

Another name from the FBI's list of friendly contacts. "Interesting," Jonathan said.

"The question is why would her old friends be out to kidnap her?"

An idea bloomed in Jonathan's head, triggering a smile. "Maybe it was a reunion," he said. "And the shootings were an attempted three-fer."

"An attempted what?"

"Three-fer. One more than a two-fer. Revenge times three. If word got out to bad guys that the old friends were out reliving their past lives, what better time to take them all out?"

"That would mean a big leak in the Secret Service. If Boxers' theory is right, maybe they were there to help her get away from Washington."

"And the shooting?"

"Random coincidence?" Venice read the expression on her boss's face for what it was and quickly added, "They do happen, Dig. I know you don't like to admit that, but sometimes they do."

It had long been a central underpinning of Jonathan's life that when two or more unusual events occur simultaneously or in quick succession, they were directly related until proven otherwise. He'd seen too many people get hurt—hell, he'd seen too many wars start—when people ignore the proverbial elephant in the room.

"You said Albert Banks lives in Warrenton?"

Venice spouted off the address, as if Jonathan had

memorized every street in the Union. "I'll upload it to your GPS." She had already figured out that he was planning to pay a visit.

On his way out the door, he called over his shoulder, "I'll stay in touch."

"I'm sorry, sir, but Mr. Banks isn't in the office today." The voice coming through the speaker was young and far too chipper.

Jonathan didn't understand why everyone wanted to sound like a cheerleader these days when they answered the phone. "When do you expect him? I have a very important matter to discuss."

A pause as papers shuffled in the background. "I don't see any appointments on his calendar," Melinda replied. He thought that's what she'd said her name was. Or maybe Belinda. Just Linda?

"I didn't make an appointment," Jonathan said.

"Was he expecting you?"

We're done with this. "Let's get back to when you expect him."

"He won't be in at all today." The effervescence in her bubbly voice had dropped by half. "Who's calling?"

"This is Special Agent Horgan with the FBI."

Next to him, in the driver's seat, Boxers fanned the fingers of his right hand and waved from a limp wrist. *Hubba hubba.*

"Oh, my goodness. Is everything all right?"

Jonathan went Joe Friday on her. "I prefer to be the one asking the questions," he said.

"Oh, yes. Of course. I'm sorry. He called in sick today."

"Do you know if he's at home now?"

"I presume so. Is he in trouble?" All the bubbles were gone now.

"Ma'am, do you know what obstruction of justice is?"

"Excuse me?"

"Obstruction of justice. Ever heard of it?"

"It's a crime, right?"

"A serious crime," Jonathan clarified. "It comes complete with serious jail time."

"Oh my God, is that what Mr. Banks did?"

"No. It's what you will have done if I arrive at his home and find that he's not there anymore because you warned him."

"Oh, Mr. Horgan, I would never—"

"*Agent* Horgan," Jonathan corrected. Hey, if you're going to play a role, commit to it, right? "The very best thing you could do right now would be to pretend that this conversation never happened."

"Oh, I will, sir. I wouldn't dream of calling him or warning him. I won't even tell Mr. Grossman about the call."

As if he knew who the hell Mr. Grossman was. "Thank you for that."

"Are you going to need me to testify?"

Jonathan brought the fingers of his free hand to his forehead. "We'll see." He was already finished with the conversation. Now he just needed a way to shut it down. "Thank you so much for your help."

"Don't you need my contact information?"

He took it and ignored it. After three phone numbers and two e-mail addresses, he said, "I have to move on now," and he clicked off.

Boxers laughed. "That's one of your very best G-man impersonations ever."

Jonathan flipped him off. "We're going to his house now. Not his office."

"Works for me." They were maybe ten minutes out.

Warrenton, Virginia, lay in the near part of Fauquier County, about an hour and a half west of Fisherman's Cove. Twenty years ago, the sleepy little burg defined the leading edge of nowhere, but as people flooded to Washington, DC, and its suburbs in pursuit of government and computer jobs, there wasn't much about Warrenton that was country anymore. Travel a mile beyond it, though, and you'd feel naked if you weren't carrying a hunting rifle for food.

They'd taken the Batmobile. With Boxers at the wheel—Jonathan never drove when they were on an op together—the trip took fifteen minutes less than it should have. With a right foot made of lead, the Big Guy seemed empowered by the FBI creds in his pocket. If you drove like Boxers, the get-out-of-jail-free badge was a significant benefit of impersonating a cop.

"This guy's a *lawyer*, right?" Big Guy asked. He weighted the word to reflect his disdain.

"Civil engineer," Jonathan corrected. A much nobler profession, he thought, since engineers made their living building things that never were, while lawyers made theirs by sticking their hands into the pockets of others.

"How are we handling this?"

"Softly. We're going to talk and to learn."

"Suppose he doesn't want to cooperate?"

Good question. Banks might very well have a critical piece of information, or he may have nothing. Jonathan didn't mind twisting information out of someone he knew to be a bad guy, but he needed to be really sure before he resorted to physical persuasion.

"If it comes to that," Jonathan said, "we'll just have to wing it. For now, we'll proceed on the assumption that he has Mrs. Darmond's interests front and center in his heart."

"So you're telling me you don't have a clue."

"Pretty much."

Boxers' laugh made a low rumbling sound. "Just sidearms?"

"Yes." Jonathan made sure the answer sounded emphatic. The weapons and explosives locked in the compartment under the cargo bay weren't the kind of hardware you could carry out on the street. Jonathan would make do with the Colt 1911 .45 on his hip, and Boxers with his ever-present 9 millimeter Beretta.

"Our cover is just the FBI thing," Jonathan said. "We're there to ask him questions about why he was downtown last night."

"Suppose he denies it?"

"Then we'll know he's a liar." Effective planning was defined by baby steps.

Venice had loaded both the work and home addresses into Jonathan's GPS, so the shift in targets meant little. The residential neighborhood where Albert Banks lived might as well have been Levittown after a deep breath. The lots and houses were two or three times the size of those 1950s suburbs, but the sameness of the construction was nearly identical. Two stories instead of one, colonials instead of ramblers, but still the worst that suburbia had to offer. The yards were an equal shade of green, and even cut to a uniform length. Jonathan didn't begin to understand what compelled people to live in a place where every house had the same floor plan.

"That's his up there," Boxers said, pointing past the windshield. Banks's iteration of the ubiquitous colonial sat on a corner before a cul-de-sac. Red brick, green shutters. His lawn had bald spots, though, which no doubt made him a pariah of the community.

Boxers nosed the Batmobile into the driveway and parked it diagonally, blocking the whole thing in case Banks tried to make a run for it in the Subaru that sat parked outside the garage. A ridiculously heavy vehicle when it rolled off the factory floor, the Batmobile was so massively armored that the Subaru would shred itself if it tried to ram it. And it wouldn't even scratch the Hummer's paint.

They climbed out of the vehicle and closed the doors quietly. Boxers thumbed the button on the key fob and the locks seated without a honk of the horn.

Jonathan produced an earbud that looked remarkably like an invisible hearing aid and pressed it into his ear canal. It was a wireless transceiver mated to a radio on his belt. He pushed the transmit button on the radio and said, "Radio check."

Venice answered first. "Loud and clear."

Boxers gave a thumbs-up, and then said for Venice's benefit, "Me too." To his boss, Big Guy said, "I'll find the back door and give you a shout when I'm in place." Often as not, the back door man got a lot of action after the front door was knocked on.

Jonathan loitered on the lawn while Boxers disappeared around the back. The place had a startlingly unkempt look about it. Beyond the bald spots in the lawn, the shrubs along the front porch were untrimmed in the extreme, with one errant boxwood branch extending to within a foot or two of the porch roof gutter. Jonathan wondered if the scofflaw boxwood triggered apoplexy among the residents of Warrenton Woods.

Of greater concern to Jonathan were the drawn curtains on a sunny day. While the world was filled with people who preferred darkness to light, Jonathan's experience had taught him that people who chose to live behind closed curtains did so because they had secrets to hide.

"I'm in place in the rear," Boxers said in Jonathan's ear. "To my eye, it's shotgun construction."

Jonathan understood that to mean that you could fire a shotgun through the front door and the pellets would exit the back door. Translation: the front door and the back door were both located in the center of the building.

Jonathan thumbed his mike. "Roger that. Here we go." He paused ten seconds to scan the environment behind him to make sure that there were no curious children or intrusive dog walkers who could screw things up. He mounted the three steps up to the porch and then walked two strides to the cheaply constructed red door. He pounded heavily with his fist. "Albert Banks! FBI! Open the door!"

He waited five seconds and then said the same thing. No response.

"I'm kicking the door," Jonathan said into his radio. He drew his Colt.

"Me too," Boxers replied.

A big concern in kicking a light hollow-core door like this one was the threat of plowing all the way through and trapping your leg. Jonathan took careful aim at the strong part of the door, along the edge, and fired the sole of his boot into a spot just below the knob, where the tongue of the lock met the jamb. The door blasted open as if he'd used explosives.

He stepped into the foyer, half-crouched in an isosceles stance, weapon drawn and safety off, to find Boxers thirty feet away on the far side of the house, amid twice the amount of doorjamb shrapnel as that which surrounded Jonathan.

"Albert Banks!" Jonathan yelled. "Federal agents. Show yourself."

Movement upstairs. Boxers heard it, too. They moved as one, Jonathan leading the way, first up seven steps to the landing, where he paused to scan what he could see of the second floor, and then up the remaining six steps to the top. "Albert Banks! Step out and show your hands!"

The second floor presented four closed doors that Jonathan could see at a glance: One at the far end of the house on his left, and then two on the front side on the left of what appeared to be a louvered door linen closet, and then beyond that, a door in a longer wall that he assumed must be the master bedroom.

"I need orders, Boss," Boxers said from the landing, below and behind.

"Albert Banks, we are federal agents! Don't make us—"

Jonathan heard movement—sounded like the shuffling of papers—behind the door directly ahead, just to the left of the linen closet. "Cover the hall," he said to Boxers, and he darted forward. He covered the ten feet of distance in two long strides. He tried the knob on the door and was surprised to find it unlocked.

As the door swung inward, Jonathan brought his pistol to bear, again gripped with both hands, his finger poised just outside the trigger guard. The room was clearly intended to be a home office, but with all the trash and papers and assorted junk on the floor it had a ransacked look about it. At first glance, the closed closet doors concerned him, but when he realized how much crap was stacked in front of them, he all but eliminated the possibility of someone hiding inside. If they couldn't get the doors open, they couldn't pose much of a problem.

The more immediate concern was the terrified man on the far side of the desk. He was pounding frantically on his keyboard, his eyes never straying from the screen. Jonathan recognized the features he'd seen in the old photographs, but they hid behind folds of jowls. This was a man who needed to stay away from all-you-can-eat buffets for a while.

"Mr. Banks," Jonathan warned, "I'm a federal officer. Step back from the desk right now and show me a set of empty hands."

Boxers appeared in the doorway behind Jonathan, filling the frame. "Floor's clear."

Banks never looked up from his screen. If he thought he was pretending not to hear, he needed to work on his poker face.

"Banks!" Jonathan shouted it this time. "What could possibly be more important than getting shot?" He took a step forward.

"No," Banks said. "Please don't."

"We just need to talk to you, sir."

The speed of his typing seemed to pick up, as if that were even possible. "Please stay away," Banks said. He never made eye contact, and his hands remained concealed behind the stack of crap and his computer monitor.

"Mr. Banks, you need—"

"I said *please*!" Banks yelled. When he finally looked up, his hand held a big chrome-plated .357 magnum.

"No!" Jonathan shouted.

Banks brought the revolver to his own temple. His eyes burned wild, as if he'd been pushed past anything that resembled reality and reason.

"Mr. Banks, don't," Jonathan said.

"I won't let you do that to me," he said.

Jonathan's hands never moved from his weapon, and his eyes never left Banks. "Suicide doesn't solve anything," he said. "Just put—"

Banks's face hardened. He started to lower the weapon from his head, but Jonathan didn't buy it. He prepared for—

Banks jerked the gun up and pointed it at Jonathan. The .45 barked twice, as if by reflex, sending two bullets through the same hole into Banks's heart and dropping him in a heap into his chair. As the echo cleared, the man looked as if he might have fallen asleep at his desk.

"God*dammit*!" Jonathan spat. "Really?"

"That went well," Boxers said.

"He's a moron. He pointed a weapon at me."

Boxers' hand touched his shoulder. "You had no choice, Boss. Suicide by cop."

Jonathan kicked the front of the desk. "Shit."

"I don't think we should be dawdling here," Boxers said. "In case the neighbors heard or get curious."

Jonathan didn't disagree, but he wasn't going to let this be a total bust. He holstered his weapon and walked around to Banks's side of the desk. He rolled the chair and the body out of the way and examined the computer screen. It showed lists of files. Jonathan figured he must have been trying to erase them. If they were worthy of being erased, they were worthy of being read.

Jonathan pulled his Leatherman tool from the pouch on his belt and tossed it to Boxers. "Pull the drives out," he said, nodding to the CPU that sat among the detritus atop the desk. While the Big Guy took care of that, Jonathan scanned the assembled crap for anything that looked relevant. There wasn't enough time to scour thoroughly, but his attention was drawn to the stack of ancient five-and-a-quarter-inch floppy disks that seemed to have been staged at the edge of his desk. He hadn't seen any of those in years—since, say, the early nineties, just about the time when Banks would have been hanging out with his revolutionary buddies.

There were also a dozen or so thumb drives and a

couple of CDs. Jonathan pulled the plastic liner out of the trash can, dumped the garbage onto the floor, and loaded the bag with the disks.

A minute later, Boxers held two hard drives in his hand. He gave the Leatherman back to Jonathan, and then it was time to go.

CHAPTER TEN

"Please tell me you're calling from a secure line," Irene said.

"Encrypted satellite phone," Jonathan assured. He and Boxers were in the Batmobile, on their way back to the Cove.

"You *killed* him?"

"He pulled a weapon on me. I had no choice. I thought you should know."

"How thoughtful. I presume the body is still in the house?"

"Yes. He's not dead an hour yet. Can you, uh, take care of that for me? As far as I know, he lived alone." A small but very profitable slice of the covert world dealt with the surreptitious disposal of bodies. The contractors were good enough at their jobs that many of their projects remained listed as missing persons forever.

Wolverine's sigh came through the speakerphone loud and clear. "Good God, Scorpion. Yes, I'll take care of it. Did you kill Gutowski too?"

"Haven't yet had the chance," Jonathan said. "He's next on our list to visit."

"Don't bother," Irene said. "He's already dead."

Boxers and Jonathan exchanged looks. "When?"

"His body was found this morning in his house." Irene spoke as if she were describing a household event. "His fingers and toes were broken. A needle had been inserted in his right eye."

"Suicide?" Boxers asked with a chuckle. Ever the king of bad timing.

Jonathan silenced him with a raised hand. He wanted to think this through.

"Is anyone there?" Irene asked after the long silence.

"I'm thinking," Jonathan said. "People are tortured to deliver information, Wolfie. The more important the info, the more brutal the torture. Banks was out-of-his-head terrified. He said, 'I'm not going to let you do that.' Somehow, I think he knew about Gutowski's torture. That would certainly explain the suicide. Anything's better than death by torture."

"You're suggesting that they shared a secret?"

"I think so, yes. We pulled the hard drives out of his computer and made off with a bunch of data storage. We'll start plowing through that stuff and get back to you when we know something. Meanwhile, what's happening on your end? Any developments?"

"The White House press corps is beginning to sniff around Mrs. Darmond's absence, but that hasn't reached critical mass yet." Irene cleared her throat.

Jonathan had learned that that was a tell. "But there's more, right?"

"Well, yes, there is. I've been made aware of a disturbing blog post by a young man named David Kirk. Have you ever heard of *Kirk Nation*?"

"Um, no." A glance to Boxers confirmed that he hadn't heard of it, either.

"Well, it's fairly influential among some of the, shall we say, more paranoid sector of the commonweal. It's got thousands of followers, and Mr. Kirk posted this afternoon that a DC cop named DeShawn Lincoln was killed last night by the Secret Service in the middle of the Mall."

"Which mall?"

"The one in Washington. Across from the Smithsonian Castle. He said that Officer Lincoln was killed to keep him quiet about the details of the shooting at the Wild Times Bar."

"Uh-oh."

"You bet, uh-oh. But it gets even more interesting. David Kirk is in fact the District's primary suspect in the murder."

"So, they've got him in custody."

"Not yet. He seems to have disappeared."

"You're the FBI," Boxers growled. "You got phone records to work with, credit cards, God knows what else."

"Thank you for a lesson in my capabilities," Irene said. "We're searching for him. But between us, not necessarily for the same reason."

Jonathan got it. "You're thinking protective custody."

"Exactly. At least until we can sort out fact from fiction. Paranoia from truth."

"This is Washington," Boxers said. "Paranoia and truth are the same thing."

Irene continued, "According to *Kirk Nation*, Officer Lincoln called Kirk in a panic, saying that he had to meet with him ASAP to reveal something about the Secret Service's role in the shooting of other Secret Service agents at the Wild Times."

"Sounds to me like this Kirk kid is aching to get himself whacked," Boxers said.

"Apparently they already tried," Irene said. "His blog entry this morning read like he'd lost his mind. He talked about going to meet his friend—he referred to him as Deeshy—but when he wasn't at the appointed place and he wouldn't answer his cell phone, he went looking. Then he tells about two men emerging from behind the carousel—apparently the place where the officer's body was found—and they approached him to kill him."

"Can't say much for the talent they're using," Jonathan said. "How'd they miss?"

"I don't know. The blog entry said that the bad guys had a knife. Maybe he just outran them. In any case, Kirk took a cab from Constitution Avenue and dumped his cell phone with the cabbie."

A piece fell into place for Jonathan. "You said that he made calls to the decedent's phone just before all the crazy stuff happened?"

Irene paused. In Jonathan's mind, he could see it dawning on her face. "They didn't have to chase him," she said. "The fact of the phone call, combined with the kid's decision to run, gave them everything they needed to get a warrant."

"Who filed for the warrant?" Boxers asked.

"I'll find that out," Irene said. "Guys, I really want David Kirk put someplace safe."

"Finding him is an important first step," Jonathan said.

"I know where he is," Irene said. "At least I know where he was about twenty minutes ago."

Jonathan scowled and looked to Boxers. Got a shrug in return. "But you said—"

"I can't find him legally," Irene said. "It's against the law to troll private conversations looking for key words. That doesn't mean it can't be done by certain resourceful people who make their living violating the law."

Boxers chuckled. "I think she means us, Boss."

"Last time I played with the NSA on domestic matters they got really cranky," Jonathan said.

"Everybody at Fort Meade is cranky these days," Irene said. "It helps to be connected."

"You already have the address, don't you?"

"In fact I do. Are you ready to copy?"

Jonathan keyed the mike on his portable radio. "Mother Hen, Scorpion."

He had to wait an uncharacteristically long time for her to answer. "Scorpion, Mother Hen. Did you just call me?"

"Affirm. Everything okay?"

"It is, now that I'm out of the bathroom. Why are we on the radio all of a sudden? I had my phone with me."

"We're going hot," Jonathan said. He knew she'd understand that to mean they had a new op. "I need you to find out what the physical security of Eastern Towers Apartments is like in Alexandria, Virginia. You need me to spell it?"

"Unless there's something weird about the words 'eastern' or 'towers,' I would say no. Stand by."

As Venice took care of the research, Boxers navigated the Batmobile toward the sprawling apartment complex. Finding a spot for the enormous vehicle was always a challenge, and here it proved to be particularly difficult. The beast took up two spaces if you wanted to open the doors all the way, and at this hour, when just about everybody was home, they had to drive out to the back forty to find a suitable spot.

"Okay, I've got it," Venice said. "ProtecTall Security. This should be a cinch. I presume you want me to override their cameras?"

"Exactly," Jonathan said. ProtecTall was one of Northern Virginia's largest contractors for providing electronic security for offices, apartments, and individual residences. They were the people on the other side of the electrical impulses when someone opened a door they shouldn't have or when a wisp of smoke passed in front of a smoke detector. More to the point for Jonathan, they also supervised hundreds if not thousands of unmonitored security cameras. When you saw grainy images of missing persons or wanted fugitives on the evening news, chances were good that the recording came from ProtecTall.

Because they were so ubiquitous, Venice had long ago learned the codes to override their systems. Now, it was only a matter of knocking out the cameras for the next ten or fifteen minutes to make sure that there would be no electronic trail of images. If possible, she'd even go back a little on the recordings to erase the footage of Jonathan and Boxers arriving in the parking lot.

"We doin' the straight FBI thing again?" Boxers asked as they started the hike toward the main entrance.

"It's been working well so far, don't you think?"

"It's been an exciting day, I'll give you that," Boxers said. "I say he's not here. This feels too easy. Or if he is here, he's ready for a body bag."

Jonathan didn't respond. What could he say? Irene had talked someone at the NSA into breaking about a dozen laws to scan cell phone traffic in a radius of fifty miles from the center of DC looking for a short list of key words that would connect David Kirk to either the Wild Times Bar, the First Lady, or DeShawn Lincoln. There'd of course been thousands of hits—this was an ongoing criminal investigation, after all—but when they filtered them through the list of Kirk's known associates, they came up with two. One belonged to Charlie Baroli, Kirk's boss at the *Enquirer*, and Becky Beckeman, a coworker at the paper. The playback from Becky's featured a voice that was four-nines consistent with the voice of David Kirk.

Jonathan felt no guilt about stealing three-quarters of one second of taxpayers' computing time. Like Boxers, however, he worried that the solution was so obvious that that the bad guys would think of it, too.

The stroll to the front of the building took all of two minutes. Jonathan switched his radio to VOX, which meant that every word he spoke would be transmitted. That kept him from having to press a transmit button— a gesture that never failed to draw attention. "Are we ready to go yet, Mother Hen?"

A pause.

"Mother Hen?"

"I need another minute or two." Her voice sounded stressed. Maybe even angry. Jonathan knew better than to press her for information before she was ready to offer it.

An apartment complex of this size—there had to be a thousand units, distributed among several buildings—was like its own little city, teeming with people. The front doors never stayed closed for more than a few seconds as residents and visitors arrived and departed. Jonathan was struck by the fact that the mean age seemed ten years older than he would have expected. Back in the day, these roach mills were the domain of youngsters new to their careers. What he saw today were forty- and fiftysomethings. He wrote it off as another sign of the economic nightmare that would be the legacy of the Darmond administration.

"I don't like standing here like this," Boxers said. "People are beginning to notice me."

He spoke the truth. It came with the territory when you were six-foot-huge.

"I'm gonna wander," Big Guy said. "I'll be back when Mother says she's set."

Jonathan didn't object. It was probably just as well that they not be seen together. If things went really south, those were the kinds of details that people would remember.

Ten seconds later, Jonathan's earbud popped and Boxers' voice said, "Hey, Boss, look to your one o'clock. The guys climbing out of the black Chevy sedan. They look like feds to you?"

Dark gray overcoats, cut just a little bigger than they should, dark glasses and matching high-and-tight hairstyles. They were missing the curlicue from their ears, but even the Secret Service was getting away from those unless they wanted to be identified as who they were.

"Mother Hen?" Jonathan whispered.

The two men, trim but not especially muscled, walked with purpose toward the front doors where Jonathan was standing. As they passed within ten feet of him, the taller of the two—by only an inch or two—clearly made note of Jonathan through his dark glasses. The glasses and the scowl were well practiced to intimidate, so Jonathan made sure to smile and offer up a little finger-wave with his left hand. All of his fingers, not just the one.

"Big Guy, come back. Mother Hen, I need information now. What's our status?"

Venice's voice had a panicked edge. "Go," she said. "Stop them."

Jonathan spun and pulled open the doors to step inside.

"I thought I was coding things wrong," Venice explained. "I couldn't shut down the videos because it had already been done. I'm sorry, Scorpion." The bad guys had beaten them to the punch.

And none of that mattered now because none of it could be changed.

Somehow, the inside of the lobby looked less crowded than the outside. Must have been the choke point of the doors. The place was done in the simple style of the early 1960s, and apparently not much freshening up had been done since the original construction. A fifty-by-fifty-foot sea of white tile floors melded with blond paneling whose plainness was broken only by a waist-level strip of stainless steel that ran the entire interior perimeter, except for the six-foot section that was missing near the elevators.

The very elevators into which Mutt and Jeff disappeared before Jonathan had taken five steps inside the front door.

"Shit," Jonathan spat. "They're on their way up. Big Guy, I need you here now."

"Right behind you, Boss," Boxers said off the air. It was easy to forget how quickly Big Guy could move when he had to. So long as it wasn't for great distances.

"Stairs," Jonathan said, pointing to the sign next to the elevators.

"Not another elevator?"

"Suppose it's a local and stops at every floor?" Jonathan asked.

"Ah, damn," Boxers said. "My leg hates stairs." Years before, Boxers had had a significant hunk of his femur replaced with a titanium rod. Shoulda seen what the other guy looked like.

Jonathan went first. He always went first. He moved faster, but even more important, he couldn't shoot over Boxers' head. "Mother Hen, I need you to call this Beckeman chick's cell phone. Tell her what's happening and tell not to open the door for anyone but me."

"I might be able to stop the elevator," Venice said.

"But you might not. Call."

As Jonathan climbed the stairs two at a time, he heard Boxers' effort to keep up, but by the third floor, Big Guy was already half a flight behind.

* * *

David couldn't believe the numbers. "Holy shit, Becky. The story's not two hours old, and I'm already at three hundred thousand hits. This is amazing."

"It's *scary*," Becky said. She'd never been on board with this broadcast plan. "A few dozen of those three hundred thousand want you dead."

David pretended not to hear. "At this rate, I'll be at a million by midnight. God knows what it'll be by six a.m. tomorrow." He clicked away from *Kirk Nation* to the Google Diagnostics page. "Look at this. Twenty-seven countries. Christ, what time is it in Austria now? Two in the morning? And I've got over three hundred hits just from there. This is friggin' *huge*."

"David, look at me." Becky's tone was identical to one his mother used just before something really bad happened to him.

"Please don't speak to me that way."

Becky's jaw dropped. "Really? That's your comment to me? *Don't speak to me that way?* You let Grayson talk you into a bad idea."

David gaped. How could she be this far out of touch? This was the twenty-first-century Watergate, and he was Woodward and Bernstein combined. How could she not see the significance? "I'm reporting *fact*, Becky. When this all settles out, I'm going to be famous."

"Jack the Ripper is famous, David. Erik and Lyle Menendez are famous. Jeffrey Dahmer, Lee Harvey Oswald, and John Wilkes Booth are all famous."

He felt as if he'd been slapped. "What are you saying?"

Her face red, she leaned forward and planted her

hands on her hips, her shoulders out. The posture reminded David of a chicken. "I'm saying that fame for fame's sake is a fool's errand. You've invited millions of people who'd otherwise never have known about this stuff to join the rabble that's calling for your head."

David shook his head emphatically. "No," he said. "I'm the voice of reason here. I'm the one who's telling the truth here."

She looked stunned. "The *truth*?"

He waited for it.

"At what point in your life did the *truth* become the driving element of media coverage?"

David didn't know where she was going, so he didn't know what to say.

"Jesus, David. What we do isn't about discovering the truth. It's about telling compelling stories that happen to be true. Well, within the sleeve of being true. There is no absolute value to truth."

Something tugged in his gut. "What are you saying?"

"Nixon," Becky said. "He ended the war in Vietnam, he opened China to the West. What's he remembered for? Watergate. Clinton. He balanced the budget, he ended genocide in the Balkans. What's he remembered for? Boffing trailer park trash. Both sides are true, but only one side is the good story. You're dishing up conspiracies, and the government is dishing up simple cause and effect. Which one do you think is going to resonate more loudly with the average citizen?"

"I don't get it," David said. "Which side are you on?"

"I'm on—" Becky's cell phone rang. She pulled it

from the pocket of her jeans. "Does an 804 area code mean anything to you?"

"Richmond?" David offered. It was a guess.

Becky pressed the button to dump the call to voice mail.

At the seventh-floor turn, Jonathan felt the first sign of fatigue in his legs. This is the kind of shit he used to be able to do without limit, and the tingling in his thighs pissed him off. Big Guy had dropped three half-flights behind now.

"Scorpion, Mother Hen. They're not answering."

"Keep trying," Jonathan commanded. "It's all we've got."

"I disagree," David said. "Is it a risky strategy? Yeah, but it's the only one that—"

Someone knocked at the door.

He shot Becky a concerned look. "You expecting someone?"

"I never expect anyone who knocks at my door. Including the one who turned out to be on the run from police." When her little joke turned out to be not funny, she winced. "It's usually Jehovah's Witnesses, Girl Scouts, or—"

Her cell phone rang again.

"Jesus, when it rains it—"

Another knock. This one sounded more like a pound. "Federal officers. Open the door, Ms. Beckeman."

David felt the blood drain from his head. "How did they find me?" He spoke at a whisper.

"Dammit, David," Becky spat. "I told you this would happen." She checked the number on the ringing phone and dumped it again. "Same number." She plowed her fingers into her hair. "Oh, Christ, what am I going to do?"

"You're going to ignore them," David hissed. "You sure as hell can't open the door."

Another pounding. "Ms. Beckeman, this is your last chance. Open the door before we open it for you."

"I have to, David." Becky's face was a panicked mask. Her cheeks were red even though her lips had turned pale. Tears balanced on her lower eyelids. "I cannot go to jail for you. I don't mind helping, but I just can't." She started walking toward the door.

David launched himself from the sofa to get between her and the door. "Please don't. Please just give me a chance."

"To do what? You can't run from here, David. You know, we have laws for a reason. Maybe if you just—"

The phone chirped again.

"God *damn* it," she said. She pushed the connect button while she undid the bolt on the door. *"What?"*

"Don't open the door," a woman's voice said. "No matter what you do, don't—"

It was too late. The instant the knob turned, the door exploded open. It hit Becky hard in the face, sending her tumbling to the floor.

David recognized these men the instant he saw them. They were the men from the carousel last night.

Only now they carried guns.

CHAPTER ELEVEN

All semblance of fatigue evaporated when Jonathan's feet hit the eleventh-floor landing and it was time to do business. He never looked behind as he shouldered open the stairwell door and stepped into the minimally carpeted hallway. One stride in, he heard someone bellowing a command to open the door.

"Step it up, Big Guy. This thing's going down now."

Boxers didn't answer, and he didn't need to. An impending fight was the perfect Boxers bait.

Tactical options spun through Jonathan's mind as he quick-walked around the corner to the right, toward the source of the shouting and pounding. He wanted to avoid firearms because of the population density. An errant bullet fired in this cheap construction could travel through walls from the front of the building to the rear until it hit either a structural member or somebody's body. Plus guns made a lot of noise and raised a lot of attention.

Not wanting to shoot brought with it a necessity not to draw fire from the opposing force. If he rushed the bad guys, they likely would panic and start firing. If he just strolled in, he might arrive too late. In this business, a microsecond too late meant forever as a corpse.

He slowed his gait, settled himself with a breath, and straightened the front of his suit, making sure that the coat was unbuttoned, but his .45 still concealed. He walked with purpose to the turn in the hall. He was a step or two away from the turn when he heard the stairwell door open and close, and Boxers' heavy footsteps approaching from behind.

"I was gonna kick your ass if you started without me," Big Guy said.

"Hey, if you stroll when others are running, you miss the good stuff." Jonathan noted that for all the effort, Boxers wasn't even breathing heavily. "Our guys are right up here."

Scorpion and Big Guy turned the corner together, nearly in step. Jonathan saw the two guys in the suits braced against the wall on either side of a door six or seven apartments away. Both had pistols drawn—they looked like SIG Sauer P226s, but it was hard to tell from this distance—and they stood off to the side, as if preparing to dodge bullets fired through the door.

Boxers reached to his hip to draw his weapon, but Jonathan placed a hand on his forearm. *Not yet.*

The look he got in return was exactly the one he'd been expecting. *Are you nuts?*

It wasn't the first time the question had been asked of Jonathan. Whoever these guys were, they hadn't yet noticed their approach, and if they did and saw weapons—

The guys moved like lightning as they crashed the door open and slipped inside.

It was time to run.

* * *

They say everything happens in slow motion during moments of mortal terror, but for David Kirk, life became a freeze-frame, an impossibly distended moment in which the entire world reduced to the reality of the gun muzzle that seemed bigger than a railroad tunnel when it was pointed directly at his head.

He had some vague awareness that he was diving to the floor, but even as he fell, his eyes stayed focused on the big black circle that would launch the bullet that would kill him.

Becky had been in the midst of saying something about there being no escape, and the precise accuracy of the statement pissed him off. Maybe if she'd shown a little more positive—

More men charged the room, one of them a man like any other, though lean and powerful with piercing blue eyes that burned with anger. It was the other one, though, that triggered a new round of fear. The guy was huge. And he seemed to be enjoying himself.

In seconds, it was over.

Jonathan crossed the apartment's threshold at a full run, and never slowed as he lowered his head and drove his shoulder hard into the middle of a gunman's back. He heard something crack and worried for an instant that it might have been his own collarbone. As he saw the gunman's weapon leave his hand and cartwheel through the air, he knew that he had earned them all a second or two—all the time necessary to settle what needed to be settled.

As he and his prey lunged forward toward the floor,

Jonathan made an effort to drive the bad guy's face into the edge of the coffee table, but they fell short, so he drove the face into the parquet floor. Teeth broke, blood spattered.

Jonathan used his driving momentum to roll to his feet, from which position he drove a savage kick to the gunman's ear. The bad guy didn't move.

Through his peripheral vision, Jonathan saw Boxers' punch nearly rip the second would-be shooter's head from his shoulders. The way the guy dropped, he might have been dead. Either way, the imminent threats had been neutralized.

"I'm clear," Jonathan said, largely for Venice's benefit on the far end of the radio.

"Clear," Boxers echoed. Big Guy closed the apartment door.

Jonathan drew his .45 and pointed it at the chest of the man he assumed to be his Precious Cargo. "Are you David Kirk?" Behind him, Boxers drew down on the girl.

The kid threw his hands in the air. "Please don't shoot me."

"Please answer the question," Jonathan countered. "Are you David Kirk?"

The kid's face made snow look pink. "Y-yes. P-please don't shoot."

Without looking at the girl, Jonathan said, "And are you Becky Beckeman?"

She made a squeaking sound that sensible people would agree meant yes.

"Are either of you armed?" Jonathan asked.

"No," David said, with such speed and emphasis that it had to be true.

"Becky, I need an answer from you, too."

"No, of course not." As if having a weapon at a moment like this would be a bad thing.

Jonathan made a show of holstering his Colt. Boxers, by contrast, merely let his Beretta dangle at his side, muzzle to the floor.

"I'm here to take you to safety," Jonathan said.

"To *safety*?" David said. "Who the hell are you?"

"You ask that as if you had options," Boxers grumbled.

"You can call me Scorpion," Jonathan said. "This is Big Guy. It seems that some people at the highest level of government want you dead. Others at that level want you protected. I'm on the protection side. Are you really inclined to debate?"

The kid raised his hands even higher. "Dude, I just want something to start making sense."

"That makes you a member of a big club," Jonathan said. "You have to believe me that I'm a friend. If you choose not to, and you instead produce a gun or a knife or a really ugly face, I promise you that I won't hesitate to kill you. Big Guy *really* won't hesitate to kill you. It's extremely important that you understand this."

David looked even more frightened. As if that were possible. "Dude, I just want this shit to stop."

Jonathan laughed. "And the best way to do that was to poke a stick into the hornet's nest?"

"I *told* you," Becky said.

"Big Guy, get prints from the shooters. And a pulse if they have one." Jonathan locked David's and Becky's attention with a glare and an aimed forefinger. "I'm here to be your best friend, but you can turn me into your worst enemy. Behave yourselves."

"Scorpion, Mother Hen," Jonathan heard in his ear piece. "Is everything stable there?"

"We're stable," Jonathan said, drawing a look from the young folks who no doubt thought that he was talking to himself. "We'll be out of here in a few minutes. Get ready to receive fingerprints."

Both of the bad guys were alive, and both had strong pulses. Neither of them moved, however, as Boxers dipped their hands into their own blood and pressed their fingertips against a stray envelope he found on the coffee table. There were higher-tech electronic means to do this, but neither Jonathan nor Boxers had planned for the day to go the way it was going.

While the Big Guy busied himself with fingers, Jonathan used his iPhone to take pictures of the gunmen's faces—full face and profile—in order to do a more thorough database search. When the recordings were completed, Jonathan and Boxers handcuffed them to the old-fashioned radiators in what Jonathan called the elephant position, with their arms extended through their crotches, with the chain wrapped around the radiator's water pipe.

Jonathan turned his attention back to David and Becky. They literally had not moved. "Are you two okay?"

They nodded in unison.

"Are you up for a little more adventure?"

Another choreographed nod.

"I assume you know that you can't stay here," Jonathan said. "And with some very bad people hunting for your head, you're in desperate need of a friend."

David said, "You're that friend. Or so you keep telling me."

"Yes," Jonathan said. "And if that somehow doesn't resonate for you, I suggest you look at who's lying on the floor and who didn't just get shot."

"Where are you taking us?" Becky asked.

"Damned interesting question," Boxers said.

"To a secure place," Jonathan said.

Boxers scowled, waiting for the answer.

In his ear, Venice said, "Are you bringing them here? To the Cove?"

"Affirmative," Jonathan said.

Boxers' shoulders slumped. "Oh, shit. What about OpSec?" Operational security.

"It's a chance we have to take," Jonathan said. "I'm open to alternatives if you have them."

"Who are you talking to?" David asked.

"Voices in my head," Jonathan said. He was being deliberately provocative, and the look he got in return was more than worth the price of admission.

"We'll put them in the mansion's basement," Venice said. The basement she referred to was more opulent than most college dorm rooms. Back in the day, those rooms had served as the servants' quarters, the rooms in which Venice had spent her childhood.

"I'm switching off VOX," Jonathan announced, and he reached behind his back and flipped the appropriate switch by feel. He was no longer broadcasting every word he said.

"Here's the deal," he said to his new charges. "You're in a world of shit. David, you have stumbled into territory that is way beyond your abilities, and Becky, David has sucked you into his sucky world. We'll work out all the finer points as we go along, but for the time being, you need to know that your friends in the world can be counted on one hand. Big Guy and I take up two whole fingers. Are you with me so far?"

They both just stared. The two-plus-twos of their worlds no longer equaled four.

"Bottom line, you can come with us and live, or you can stay and die. Sorry to be so blunt, but it's hard to sugarcoat binary choices." He paused.

They stared.

He said, "Now would be a good time to say 'okay.'"

They spoke in unison: "Okay."

Something about the delivery, in the context of the facial expressions, made Jonathan laugh. "Guys, you're not walking the Last Mile here. Don't look so terrified."

"You just killed two men in my apartment," Becky said.

"They're both still alive," Jonathan said.

"But they're sleeping very soundly," Boxers added. "And when they wake up you'll be able to light New York from the energy of their headaches."

As so often was the case, Boxers' attempt at humor landed like a turd.

Jonathan focused on Becky. "Young lady, my orders are to take David with me. I have no business with you. Under the circumstances, though, you're welcome to come along. But you have to make your choice now."

"Where are we going?"

"I can't tell you that. And frankly, you don't want to know if you're not coming along."

"Suppose *I* don't want to come along?" David asked. Jonathan prayed that it was a rhetorical question.

"Trust me, kid," Boxers said. "You're coming along.

The only variable for you is whether you'll remember the trip."

Becky's head still hadn't joined the game. "You come in here and beat up a couple of guys and I'm—"

"We saved your life," Jonathan corrected. "At least get your facts straight."

She searched for the right words, for the right thing to do. "But I need time. I have obligations. I can't just leave."

Jonathan acknowledged her with a brief, percussive nod. "Fine. Big Guy, David, let's go."

"Wait!" Becky said. "These men—"

"I'd give them a wide berth when they wake up," Boxers said. "They're gonna be cranky."

"Becky, you can't stay," David said.

"Don't you say anything," she snapped. "You're the reason I'm in this."

"Pardon me for trying to—"

"No," Jonathan said. "That shit stops now, before it begins. We're not doing the boyfriend-girlfriend spat thing. Becky, make a decision."

Pundits talk about the twelve stages of grieving, but you never hear about the stages of accepting the inevitable. You go through the denial and the anger, and whatever the hell else you go through, but sometimes, there's only one correct decision. Jonathan saw it dawn on Becky's face.

"Okay," she said. "I'll come. But I need to gather a few things. I need, like, five minutes."

"You can have two," Jonathan said.

As Becky turned and headed toward the bedroom, Jonathan followed.

She stopped and turned. "Where are you going?"

"With you," he said. He didn't tell her about his concern that she might call 911, or that she might pull a weapon out of a nightstand drawer. Instead, he said, "Trust is a two-way street. I earned mine a few minutes ago. It's your turn."

Jonathan ended up granting Becky six minutes to gather her meds and makeup and a few pairs of shoes and other clothing, which she tossed into a small suitcase. Returning to the living room, Jonathan noted with some amusement that Boxers and David were standing farther apart than they were before. Being afraid of Big Guy was never a bad idea.

"Do you both know what a blood oath is?" Jonathan asked.

Their faces donned identical scowls, and they cocked their heads like curious puppies, David to the right and Becky to the left.

"I need a response."

"Like a pinky swear with attitude?" Becky offered.

Boxers rolled his eyes.

"With extreme attitude," Jonathan corrected. "It means a solemn promise for which the penalty for violation is death."

Boxers seemed to swell at the notion. The kids both shrunk a little.

"What are you suggesting?" David asked.

"I'm suggesting that from this point forward, you will see things and hear things that you have no right to see or hear. As reporters, you have a genetic desire to share this kind of stuff with other people. I need a blood oath from each of you that that will never happen. I want you to understand that if Big Guy or I ever see in writing anything that remotely resembles the truth, we will be very, very unhappy. That means you will be extraordinarily very unhappy." He gave it a couple of seconds to sink in. "I'm not being too cryptic, am I?"

"You're saying you'll kill us if we ever report what we're about to see," David said.

"I certainly reserve the right," Jonathan said. "Whether I exercise it or not should be a source of sleepless nights for the rest of your lives if you betray me."

"Who *are* you people?" Becky asked. "I don't believe for a moment that you're the police."

"If I were the police, your buddy David would be on his way to a life term in the hoosegow," Jonathan said. "Take comfort in the fact that we're good guys and let it go. I still need to hear you swear the oath."

It took a while, as it should.

Probably the better part of a minute as they searched their souls and consciences to decide what they could live with.

David went first. "Okay," he said. "I swear that I will never write about what I see."

That was a relief. It saved Jonathan the effort of blindfolding him for the trip out to Fisherman's Cove. People hated blindfolds.

"I don't think this is fair," Becky said. "I feel coerced. But if it's the only way for me to be safe, I guess I—"

Boxers held up his hand. "Be careful now, young lady," he said. His voice had taken on a tone that rumbled the parquet floors. "Don't say anything you don't mean. Once the words are out, they can't be with-drawn."

She hesitated, her mouth slightly agape. "Okay," she said. "I swear that I will never write about what lies ahead."

"Okay, then," Jonathan said quickly. He didn't want a morose pall to cloud a clear victory. "Let's get moving." He pointed toward the door. "You follow Big Guy here."

They both bristled. No one looked forward to alone time with Boxers.

"I'll be along in a minute," Jonathan assured. "I just need to make a phone call about our friends here." He tossed a glance toward the sleeping attackers. "Don't worry about Big Guy. He's just a big ol' puppy dog."

To emphasize the point, Boxers growled.

On the way out the door, Becky slapped David in the arm, apparently just for good measure.

When he was alone in the apartment, Jonathan dialed Wolverine's number from memory. She answered on the third ring.

"I have another cleanup job for you," he said.

CHAPTER TWELVE

After Jonathan separated from the army, he'd deeded his boyhood mansion to Saint Kate's Catholic Church to become Resurrection House, with only one restriction: that Venice and her family would have a home there for as long as they wanted. Venice's mother, known to the world simply as Mama Alexander, had been the family's lead housekeeper, and a surrogate mother to Jonathan after his real mom died when he was little. These days, Mama served as surrogate mother to the dozens of children who lived in the dorms at Rez House.

Venice and JoeDog were waiting for Jonathan and his team under the porte cochere in the rear of the mansion as they parked.

"Where is this place?" David Kirk asked as he climbed out of the Batmobile into the night.

"A place where you have a low likelihood of being murdered tonight," Jonathan answered. The kid had talked so incessantly during the ride in that Jonathan felt confident that David wouldn't be able to retrace his steps. Becky was another matter, however. He wouldn't be surprised if she'd found a way to count wheel rotations.

Jonathan led them through the center hall from the back door to the stairs that led to the basement. The rooms down here were spacious yet imposing. They would have been perfectly acceptable as English-basement apartments.

"I'm sort of claustrophobic," David said. "You're not going to lock us in, are you?"

"Separately," Jonathan said. "One to a room. Note that you've got a window and a bathroom. And somewhere around seven hundred square feet. We're not talking Rikers Island. Make do."

The four of them—David, Becky, Boxers, and Jonathan—stood in a clump in the hallway. Jonathan made a sweeping motion with his arm, ushering David into his assigned space. The kid looked terrified, but he followed directions. When he crossed the threshold, Jonathan closed the door behind him and threw the lock with a twist of an old-fashioned key in an old-fashioned keyhole.

Becky was next. Jonathan walked her three doors down the hall and indicated a door with an open hand. She started to walk through, but Jonathan put a hand on her shoulder to stop her.

"One more time," Jonathan said. "You are here voluntarily. If you want to walk away, you're welcome to do so. But there may well come a point where that window of opportunity closes. Think seriously about your options."

When Becky cocked her head, he saw real beauty that hadn't been present before. Her luminescent brown eyes seemed especially sharp, and there was something about her one-sided smile that intrigued him. She exuded a level of intelligence that worried him.

"I don't have any options," she said. Her tone bordered on incredulity. "My options evaporated the second I let David into my apartment. I guess I'm your prisoner."

She tried to enter the room again, and Jonathan stopped her again. "No," he said. "You are not a prisoner. If you even suspect that you are, you need to leave."

"But if I leave, I'll be a target."

"Different thing," Jonathan said. "Being your preferred option for safety is a world apart from being your jailer. I need to hear you acknowledge that."

She scowled and cocked her head. "Are you serious?"

"As a heart attack. I don't think you understand the reality of your situation," Jonathan pressed. "Forces are in play that can kill all of us. My colleagues and I have carved a respectable career out of defending good guys against bad guys, but that differentiation—bad versus good—requires a black-and-white split. Do you understand what I'm telling you?"

"I really don't," she said.

Jonathan inhaled deeply through his nose. "None of what has happened to David—and, by extension, to you—makes total sense to anyone yet. All the indications, though, point to a high-level conspiracy that makes all of us nervous."

"Are you saying—"

"Hush," Jonathan said. "I'm speaking. You're listening. You need to choose your camp right now. I represent the good guys, and the men chained up in your apartment represent the bad guys. If you stay here, that whole blood oath thing kicks in. If you betray me, you will suffer. I promise you that at a holy, religious level. You will suffer."

Color drained from Becky's cheeks.

"Be frightened," Jonathan said. "If my life is at stake—and it is—so should yours be at stake. Those are the rules. If you can live with them, you're welcome to stay. If you can't, then you're welcome to leave."

"How will you trust me if I leave? How do I know that you won't just shoot me in the back?"

Boxers took that one with his characteristic rumbling laugh. "Honey, if either one of us wanted you dead, it'd be done already and you'd've been the last to know."

Jonathan found the delivery a little harsh, but he didn't correct him. "I don't think you want to spend every night for the rest of your life wondering if one of us is coming through your window."

Tears balanced on Becky's eyelids. "I *am* frightened," she said. "I'm freaking scared shitless. I didn't want any of this in my life." She paused, as if expecting a different reaction than the one she got the last time she said the same thing. In the end, she said nothing more. She stepped across the threshold and made a point of gazing out the window, her back turned, as Jonathan closed the door.

"You know she's a problem, right?" Boxers said under his breath.

Jonathan shrugged. "Let's cut her some slack. It's

been a tough couple of days, and we came on pretty strong."

Boxers chuckled.

"What?"

"It's the big brown eyes, isn't it?" the Big Guy poked. "You've always had a soft spot for big brown eyes."

By the time they walked back down to David's room, Venice had appeared in the hallway. She stood with her hands on her hips, taking in the surroundings. "I don't come down here very much," she said. "It's like traveling back in time." Back in the day, hers had been the second room off this hallway, though not for long. By the time of her early teens, she and Mama Alexander had been moved to the mansion's third floor, from there better to serve the needs of the Gravenow family.

"Thanks for joining us," Jonathan said. "I wanted us all to hear this story at the same time. Feel free to ask questions as they pop into your head. Use handles only, no real names. And Big Guy?"

Boxers' forehead wrinkled. He waited for it.

"Try not to scare the kid to death, okay?"

"I'll spread nothing but love and happiness," Big Guy said. "Just like always."

Jonathan slipped the key into the door and turned the lock.

The toothpaste-blue room was set up in the style of a college dorm, with a desk and a chair, and a sofa that folded out to become a bed. Jonathan had no idea how old the decorations or the furnishings were, but they looked dated to him. Neither comfortable nor especially uncomfortable, the sofa felt understuffed, and the desk chair creaked whenever David moved to cross or uncross his legs. They'd moved the young man's chair to the center of the room so that he could address his questioners all at once. Boxers sat awkwardly on the edge of the desk while Venice occupied the cushion next to Jonathan on the sofa.

David Kirk told his story quickly and emphatically, relaying details of his conversations with DeShawn Lincoln and of his initial encounter with the men that Jonathan and Boxers had so recently dispatched.

Jonathan worked hard to poke holes in David's story, but it held together well. It didn't make any more sense than it had when Jonathan knew fewer details, but after twenty-five minutes, he was confident that the kid wasn't lying.

As they chatted, David's shoulders relaxed and his overall posture became less rigid. He was becoming comfortable. If not comfortable, then perhaps less suspicious that Jonathan intended to hurt him.

"I've got a question for *you*," David said after some of the edge had worn off. "You said something about a big-time conspiracy," David said. "Do you think the Secret Service killed Deeshy? And is this like some kind of rogue action?"

Jonathan paused before answering. As a rule, he made it a point to keep his opinions on such things to himself—certainly, he kept them away from relative strangers. During the silence, in fact, Boxers caught his eye and gave him a surreptitious shake of his head.

Thing was, this kid had lived a part of whatever was

going on, and by sharing theories with him, maybe there was a chance that something important might shake loose. He decided that it was worth the risk.

"I have no idea if the Secret Service killed your friend," Jonathan said, finally. "I suspect that they're involved in this somehow—that seems self-evident, given the events of the shoot-out at the Wild Times. But there's a subtle difference between suspicion and paranoia. Both are reasonable under the circumstances, but for now, I don't know how to tell one from the other."

"Well, I don't think there's any doubt," David said. He seemed to think people were arguing with him. "Deeshy sure as hell was convinced. And why is Becky being held separately?"

The suddenness of that question startled Jonathan. "About her," he said. "How stable is she?"

"Scorpion!" Venice's tone was that of a scolding mother.

Jonathan ignored her and waited for his answer.

"I don't know what to say," David said. "How *stable*? What does that mean?"

Boxers simplified the question: "Is she going to be part of the solution or an extension of the problem?"

David still didn't get it.

"Can you trust her?" Jonathan said.

"Of course I can trust her. She took me in."

"She's awfully angry," Jonathan said. "Disproportionately angry, I would say."

"How can you say that?" Venice said. "Think about everything that has happened to her in the past twenty-four hours. How could she not be furious?"

David smiled at her, a look of genuine relief.

"I mean really," Venice went on. "She's lost everything. And she lost it by helping a friend. Yet you ask if *she* is the one who is trustworthy. Imagine the questions that are streaming through her head right now."

She looked to Boxers. "Did he give her the blood oath speech?"

The Big Guy nodded.

"Oh, for heaven's sake." She stood and held out her hand. "Key."

Jonathan knew better than to argue. He handed over the entire ring. JoeDog curled herself into the vacated cushion the instant Venice left the room. A minute later, when the two women appeared in the doorway, the beast slunk back to the floor. She looked ashamed of herself. It was a look that made her invulnerable to scolding.

"Here you go, sweetie," Venice said, pointing to the sofa. "Have a seat next to the boss."

Becky hesitated.

Jonathan stood. "It seems I owe you an apology," he said. "Soft talk has never been my strong suit. Your anger bothered me. Abundant caution has always served me well."

"Fine." Becky sat. "Whatever. What I want to know is what's next. Clearly, neither of us can go home, and while staying here is a fine option in the short term, what happens tomorrow or the next day?"

This was the sticky part. Jonathan resumed his seat. "I think that in two or three days, this whole thing is going to be set in concrete. The evidence that needs to be covered up will be, and David, your future will be permanently bleak."

David blanched. "What do you mean by bleak?"

"Just exactly what you think I do. You will stand trial and be convicted of murder. Or, at best, you'll have an outstanding warrant that will keep you on the run for the rest of your life."

"But I didn't do anything. Somebody has to believe that because they hired you. In court—"

"Your day in court won't matter," Jonathan said.

"I'm *innocent*."

"So what?" Boxers said. "Jails are full of innocent people."

"That's because all the guilty people say they're innocent," Becky said. "That's cynical. David's actually—"

"No, Becky," Jonathan interrupted. "While everyone in prison was convicted of a crime, a good many of the people rotting in cells didn't do what the jury believes they did. Courts aren't about finding truth. They're about lawyers winning and losing, based on their ability to sell a jury on their version of the facts."

Becky made a huffing sound. "That's paranoid bullshit."

Boxers huffed back at her. "God, I love young people."

"Look at what happened in your apartment today," Jonathan said. "Men with Secret Service badges—men with the authority to step into your home—tried to kill you. If they turn out to be who I think they are, Big Guy and I are guilty of assaulting federal officers. We met all the elements of the law. If they had died, we would have committed murder upon a federal officer. Is that what you saw?"

"That's such a specific case," Becky said.

"All assaults are specific cases," Jonathan pressed. "A white security guard kills a black teenager in a late-night struggle. The police decide that it was self-defense. But then the press gets ahold of it, and suddenly it's a chargeable offense. The guy is convicted by the world before he ever stands trial. Jurors know that if they find the guy not guilty, the city will likely burn with riots. Is that a fair trial?"

"Is this really the time for a civics lesson?" Venice asked.

Jonathan paused to let some of the wind out of his sails. "Okay. My point ultimately is that whoever is behind whatever is going on is actively building whatever fiction is necessary to pull off his plan. Somehow, David, you're a pawn, and Becky, you're an accomplice."

"What does that make you?" David asked.

Jonathan smiled. "I'm the problem solver."

"Speaking of which," Venice said. "I need to speak to you in the hallway. Big Guy too."

They both stood. He addressed his new guests. "Okay, guys, I'll make a deal with you. I'll keep the doors unlocked if you promise me that you won't leave the basement."

"I don't understand why we need to be treated like prisoners," Becky said. "You tell us that we need to be here of our own free will, but then you restrict our every movement."

Ever the optimist, Jonathan took one more shot at explaining. "It's about keeping your location a secret," he said. "This building is more than a home. It's also an office, with people moving about on the floor above. Children wander in and out at times, making the presence of a stranger even more notable. Never forget that you, David, are wanted for a very serious crime. People are actively looking for you."

"Becky, too, unfortunately," Venice said. Then with a sheepish smile, she added, "Late breaking news. They've named you as an accomplice."

Becky's jaw dropped.

"Powerful people move with remarkable speed," Jonathan said.

A lightbulb went on over Becky's head. Her eyes grew wide. "There was a shooting here a few years ago," she said. "And a kidnapping, too, right?"

Venice's quick glance to Jonathan eliminated any chance of Jonathan bluffing his way out. "Let's not go there," he said. "The point is that there's too much opportunity for you to be seen and recognized. If that happens, a lot of bad stuff follows."

"So we just hang here?" David asked.

"Pretty much, yes," Jonathan said. "And just to sweeten the pot, Doug Kramer, the local chief of police, is a good friend of mine, and it's not out of the question that he might wander in upstairs, too." He saw those words hit home.

Venice said, "My mother—you can call her Mama— will be sure that you get enough food to gain five pounds every day. Honestly, it won't be that bad."

Jonathan left before they could ask any more questions. He pulled the door to on his way out, but he didn't latch it.

Back in the hallway, he asked, "What've you got?"

"I looked at the files you took from Albert Banks. I think I know what they're up to."

CHAPTER THIRTEEN

Lover of drama that she was, Venice kept them in suspense until they wandered back to the third floor of the firehouse and gathered around the conference table.

"Good thing we're not in a hurry," Boxers grumped as he pulled a seat out for himself.

"I'll do the easy stuff first," Venice said, her fingers already pounding the keys. "Eyes on the screen, gents."

At the far end of the room, the massive screen switched from dark to blue, and then two faces appeared. They looked vaguely familiar, but before Jonathan could process them, Venice said, "Those men in the apartment were not Secret Service agents. I found both of their fingerprints in the Interpol computers. Here are their names."

The screen displayed Vasily Alistratov and Pyotr Zabolotny. "I'll let you figure out how to pronounce the last names. Vasily served six years at hard labor about fifteen years ago for assaulting a police officer. He was elevated to Interpol's list in 2002 when he disappeared from view. Nine-eleven paranoia was running at its fevered height back then, if you recall, and it was easy to move from petty criminal to public enemy without a lot of justification.

"Pyotr, on the other hand, didn't serve any jail time that I can see, but does have some spotty history of petty crimes. Nothing serious and nothing violent."

"So why is he listed on Interpol?" Jonathan asked.

"I have no idea. He is, however, listed as a potential terrorist."

"Now *that's* interesting," Boxers said. "How did that happen?"

"Again, no idea. But both are listed as known to be in the company of the other, and both are on all the no-fly lists."

"Yet here they are," Jonathan said.

Venice chuckled. "You've got to love it. The TSA pokes every nook and crevice of Granny's wheelchair, but suspected terrorists somehow get in."

"Granny needs better handlers," Jonathan said. "You know, people who can give her a fake identity to sneak her in and out."

"I bet a First Lady could figure out how to pull those strings," Boxers said. "I'm not the only one who caught the Iron Curtain connection, am I?"

"It was subtle," Venice said, her voice dripping with irony, "but yes, I managed to catch it."

"This is really helpful, Ven," Jonathan said. "I'm sure Irene has our friends in custody by now. She'll certainly have all of this. I wonder what else she'll come up with."

Venice shifted in her chair and gave a coy smile. "I have something else," she said. "On the files from Banks's computers."

Jonathan's jaw dropped. "You couldn't possibly

have read through all the files already. You only had them for a little over an hour."

"It helps to be brilliant," she said.

Her boastfulness was way out of character, prompting an exchange of glances between Jonathan and Boxers.

A subtle smile bloomed as she added, "It also helps to be really lucky. Look at the screen."

At the far end of the room, the 106-inch screen filled with lists of files.

"After I transferred all the data from all the files on all the disks you brought in onto a single drive, I decided that the best bet to find what we're looking for was to search the files that were accessed most recently, and then to work backwards." She glanced over at Jonathan. "I'm extrapolating from 'manual methods first.' "

Jonathan recognized the reference to one of his most inviolable philosophies: that the simplest, most elegant explanations were most often the correct ones.

Venice continued, moving the cursor on the screen to highlight her points as she spoke. "There are tons of correspondence and assorted other details that I haven't had a chance to look at yet, but my attention was first drawn to these files here." The arrow-point cursor stroked a list of ten or twelve files that all ended in a similar suffix.

"Note the dates," she said. "These were all opened yesterday, and they all came from one of the thumb drives."

She said this stuff as if people could read her mind and understand the implications. Jonathan feigned patience and waited, confident that a sensible explanation was on the way.

"But if you look here," she continued, clicking to a different screen that to Jonathan's eye showed more files that looked essentially the same as the others, "you'll see that the same files were erased from the computer's hard drive just today."

Jonathan raised his hand, as if in a classroom. "If they've been erased, how can we be looking at them?"

Venice gave him a look of pure disappointment. "Come on, Dig. You're not new at this. You know that no file is truly erased. Not if they don't use a magnet or a shredder. If you know what to look for, you can search for recently erased files. You might not be able to pull up the files themselves without some extra work, but the file names will still be there."

"Let me guess," Boxers said. "You did the extra work."

She beamed. "You said that you thought Banks was in the process of erasing files when you crashed his place. Building on that, I went to the erased files and entered today's date, and I got this."

She switched back to the first screen. "I searched on the file names. You see that they're kind of weird? That 'dot pic' suffix? Well I copied and pasted, this is what I came up with. The backup file from the thumb drive."

Jonathan felt a tingle in the small of his back. He sensed that something big was on the way. "Albert Banks hadn't gotten to the backup yet to erase it."

Venice nodded. "That, or he didn't know that a backup had been made. You're welcome, by the way, for forcing you to buy all that memory and storage space. It helps to be able to load all these files simultaneously."

"Have I ever denied you anything?" Jonathan asked. One of the advantages of owning limitless funds was the ability to have it all. He never said no to a technology request from Venice. Most of the time, he didn't even know what he was saying yes to.

"I'd be even more impressed if the files were open and we knew what they were," Boxers said.

"I was thinking the same thing," Venice said, oblivious to Big Guy's sarcasm. "And let me tell you, I had to search for a while to figure out a way to open them. It turns out that the files were done in a partially encrypted program that I'd read about a couple of years ago. It's used for the transmission of large documents, often architectural drawings."

She clicked again, and the screen filled with a detailed drawing of what appeared to be a bridge. It was a skeletal view, revealing structural members in both plan and elevation views. Venice clicked again, and the screen revealed what looked to be a small part of the larger drawing shown in cross-section.

"Engineering sketches?" Jonathan wondered aloud.

"That would be my guess," Venice said. "There are dozens of drawings like this within the file. Maybe hundreds."

"What am I missing?" Boxers asked. "Banks was an engineer. Shouldn't he have lots of this kind of stuff in his computer?"

"Ah, you weren't paying attention," Venice said. She clicked back to the first image. "What are we looking at?"

Jonathan held up his hand. "Ven, please. I know you groove on this, but is there a way to cut to the chase?"

"*Look*, Digger," Venice insisted. "Look at the lower right-hand corner. Look at the name of the bridge."

Then he saw it. "The Brooklyn Bridge? The original? Wow, I thought the drawing looked old. But why is that significant?"

"Because it was built over a hundred years ago. You said it yourself, it's an old bridge. Engineers design new things, not old things." Her eyes narrowed. "On the other hand, what group of people can you think of that would want to see detailed drawings of existing structures?"

Jonathan felt a chill. "Terrorists?"

She smiled.

"Whoa, whoa, whoa," Boxers said. "At what point did I become the voice of reason? You can't conclude something like that from the presence of a drawing. Maybe he just likes old bridges."

"You saw how feverishly he was trying to erase the files when we got to his house," Jonathan said. He looked to Venice for confirmation. "That's the timing, right?"

"I checked my record of your phone call after the shooting at Banks's place. Just about a perfect match."

Jonathan could tell that Boxers was close to being convinced, but didn't want to be.

"But there's more," Venice said. She had the most stunning smile when she thought she'd come up with something big. She started clicking more files, and more drawings popped up on the screen. "This is the file on the Chesapeake Bay Bridge," she said. "And here is the Holland Tunnel. The Sumner Tunnel in Boston. New York's Penn Station." She stopped there. "There are more, but from what I can tell, they're all major commuter routes. Can you think of a better terrorist target than a place that is guaranteed to have thousands of people at risk for the initial blast, and then millions more inconvenienced for years to come? Think of the economic consequences."

Jonathan sat back in his seat, rubbing his face vigorously with his hands. He knew that she'd found the pulse of the plot they'd been looking for, but the ramifications made him feel a little dizzy. He held out his hands as if to stop the onslaught of ideas.

"Okay, let's hang on a second. Let's take a step back. We're about three steps away from proclaiming that FLOTUS is a terrorist. Is that where we're going here?"

Even Boxers looked shocked. "I believe that's exactly where we're going."

Venice said, "It's perfectly consistent with her past. Maybe this has been her plan all along."

Jonathan scoffed, "Okay, that's a step too far. Not even the president knew he wanted to be president until after they'd married."

"She didn't have to be First Lady to pull off an attack," Venice said.

Jonathan liked that. "And maybe the reason why she didn't pull the trigger before was because of her trajectory toward the White House. Whether she was biding her time for the perfect moment or delaying so that she wouldn't screw things up for her husband, either way would explain the long leash on her plan."

"Might explain why the Secret Service was shooting

at each other," Boxers offered. "Word got out that she was trying to pull the trigger and they decided to take her out."

Therein lay the glitch in the theory that Jonathan just couldn't embrace. "Come on, folks. Even my cynicism has limits. If that hit last night was truly executed by the Secret Service, that means killing each other. Box, could you have opened up on a unit operator?"

"If I thought he'd turned to the other side? You betchum, Red Rider. Without flinching."

Jonathan let it go, but it sounded like more talk than truth. Soldiers and cops and firefighters developed a brotherhood of shared fear and sacrifice that made them a family. Fratricide would be no easier among them than it would be among brothers born of the same mother.

Still, some crimes were so egregious that all the old rules needed to be disposed of. Could this be one of those?

"Sometimes, I really hate my job," he said.

"I've got a question for you," Boxers said. "If FLOTUS is planning the destruction of mankind as we know it, where does that put POTUS? More to the point, if we've really stumbled upon the truth here, where does that put us? We know a bunch of shit that they're not going to want us to know."

"We've made a living knowing shit that Uncle didn't want us to know," Jonathan said.

"Not at this level," Boxers said. "A president willing to kill his own wife is a guy prone to scorching the earth."

"You're assuming he's an accomplice," Venice said. "That might not be the case."

"I'm assuming nothing of the kind," Jonathan said. "Stipulating that all of this impossible shit is true in the first place, I think that we could call President Darmond an ally. We all want to stop her."

"It's a little different, Dig," Boxers said with an eye roll. "He killed innocents at the Wild Times. We're not talking about a stable man."

"We're talking about a panicking man," Venice said. "There's a difference between killing in a panic and being a murderer."

Jonathan smiled. "Tell that to the mourning families," he said. Venice had campaigned damned hard to get Darmond elected. She would be the last constituent to abandon him.

After a brief silence, Boxers said, "Holy shit, Boss. What have we gotten into?"

Jonathan shook his head. "Scary, huh? Even scarier when you think that Mr. Chief of Staff Winters invited us to the party. I've got lots of alarm bells sounding right now. Think of the damage we've done to this administration," Jonathan said. "We kicked his SecDef in the balls and we stirred the Agency pretty good."

Venice's jaw dropped. "You don't think they know about Trevor Munro, do you?"

Jonathan wished he'd never told her about the way he'd settled that score. "The absence of handcuffs would say no," he said.

"Maybe that's because you saved Darmond's sorry-ass life," Boxers said.

"He shouldn't know about that, either," Jonathan

said. "But facts are facts. From this point on, we double down on OpSec. We need to assume that we're under siege."

Boxers cocked his head. "Don't we still have a PC to find?"

Jonathan shrugged. "I'm beginning to look at that cargo as less and less precious."

"But we made a deal, Dig. The official version is that FLOTUS is in danger, and we have to snatch her away from it. If I were you, I wouldn't want to have to call the White House and tell them that you're walking away."

Another bell rang in Jonathan's head. It was a church bell, actually. A gong. "Back up," he said. "Why did they bring us in?"

The question stopped conversation. Drew stares from both of them.

"Don't look at me that way. Think about the order of events. There's a shoot-out at the Wild Times bar and a bunch of people are killed, mostly Secret Service. We hear rumors of a cleanup operation, where a homeless guy only one guy saw is carted off. No official record of that. There's a lot right there to make me uncomfortable. Can we agree on that?"

"I don't remember the last time I was comfortable," Venice said.

Boxers made an undefinable noise that Jonathan interpreted as agreement.

"If this was a hit on the First Lady to shut down her terror operations, why would Douglas Winters contact Irene Rivers to have us brought into the case? Why wouldn't they just let it run its course?"

As soon as the question had left his lips, he saw the answer. "Oh my God," he said. "We're pawns. We're being used. They don't want us to find her and bring her back. They want us to find her so they can finish the job of killing her."

Boxers saw it too. "They turned to us because legitimate law enforcement would leave a paper trail," Boxers said.

"And what happens when we do find her?" Venice asked.

Jonathan let the question hang in the air. He hoped that the answer was obvious.

"They're going to kill her?" Venice gasped. Realization hit her hard.

"I don't know," Jonathan said. "Hell, we don't *know* anything. We're just trying to feel our way through this mess. But a commitment to kill is a commitment to kill, isn't it?"

"Sweet system," Boxers said. "We hand over the victim and then we all get popped. I seriously cannot wait until I see Doug Winters again. I'll pull his brain through his nose."

"We're missing something," Jonathan said. "The stuff that makes sense only makes sense till it doesn't. That always means we're missing something."

"But the basics are solid," Boxers said. "Can we agree that FLOTUS was up to no good?"

Jonathan's cell phone rang, displaying the name J. Edgar, his little joke to himself. It was Irene Rivers's phone number. He pressed the connect button. "This is Scorpion."

He was startled to hear a male voice say, "Arc Flash is ready."

Jonathan recognized the voice as that of Paul Boer-sky, Irene's longtime confidant and body man. Her Clyde Tolson, but without the sexual overtones.

"Good to know," Jonathan said. "Why are you telling me this?"

"Because we thought you'd want to ask some questions."

"You mean because you don't want to be the one asking them," Jonathan corrected, but the line went dead.

He looked to Boxers. "We've got to go."

CHAPTER FOURTEEN

It had been a long time since Griffin Horne had been enough of an insider to warrant a code name, but as soon as Jonathan heard the phrase "Arc Flash," he knew exactly who it referred to. He also knew the origin of the name, and took no pleasure from the memories. Horne's corner of the covert world involved the extraction of information from people who were intent on remaining silent. All too often, his tactics involved the application of electricity to the most sensitive parts of his subjects' bodies.

Jonathan abhorred torture. On the occasions when he'd employed it, he'd had great success inflicting pain just once or twice at the beginning of the session, and then developing the source through the mere threat of additional unpleasantness. Hurting people was never a legitimate goal for a professional, but he'd known far too many operators and spooks who found genuine pleasure in hurting people.

Griffin Horne was one such man, and Jonathan always felt as if he needed a shower after being in a room with the man. That said, there was no denying that Horne's methods were effective. Jonathan knew of at least two post-9/11 terrorist plots that died in their planning stages thanks to information that was extracted by Arc Flash.

The drive to Horne's farm took about forty minutes. "I hate this son of a bitch," Boxers said as they closed in on the place. "Every time I see him, I want to pop his head like a zit."

Jonathan agreed. "Thing that scares me is, I imagine he has equipment at his fingertips that could do exactly that."

The call from Paul Boersky—not Irene, yet from Irene's number—told Jonathan that the Secret Service agents from Becky's apartment—or whoever they were who pretended to be Secret Service agents—had been prepped for questioning. He didn't know what that meant, exactly, but he was confident that the next hour or two were going to be unpleasant for everyone.

"Pull to the side," Jonathan said when they were still half a mile from the farm.

Boxers followed instructions and waited till they were stopped before he asked why.

Jonathan pointed to the barely recognizable silhouette of a dilapidated old house that looked like it hadn't seen an occupant in decades. "Pull up behind there," he said. "We'll walk into Horne's place."

As Boxers piloted the Batmobile up the remains of the rutted driveway, Jonathan explained. "What I said back in the Cave about increased security. Given what we know about Horne and his less-than-stable loyalties, I don't want to provide more of a target that we have to. I want to make a tactical approach."

Jonathan more sensed than saw the surprised glance from Big Guy. "You're really spooked by this shit, aren't you?"

"Damn skippy I'm spooked. The president has a lot of toys at his disposal. We're good, but our abilities have limits."

Boxers stared for a long time. After a few seconds of silence, Big Guy smiled and said, "Pussy." Then he opened his door.

It took them all of five minutes to kit up. When they were done, they each wore a sidearm, a rifle, and a personal defense weapon, plus a ballistic vest whose pockets were stuffed with ten thirty-round magazines—5.56 millimeter for Jonathan's M27 and 7.62 millimeter for Boxers' HK417—plus one flashbang grenade and three frags each. Jonathan shifted his Colt to a thigh rig on his right side, and balanced it on the left with a folded MP7 in a holster on his thigh. Other pouches in his vest carried five spare mags for the .45 and three spares for the MP7. All told, including the existing loads in their weapons, each of them carried over four hundred rounds of ammunition. With decent marksmanship—both of them were far better than decent—it was enough armament to sack a well-fortified castle.

"Lids or no lids?" Boxers asked. It was his way of asking if they would be wearing Kevlar helmets.

"Sure," Jonathan said. "In for a dime, right?"

When they were done, they looked like they were ready for battle. In fact, they *were* ready for battle.

Jonathan rocked his NVGs—night vision goggles—into place and instantly, the night became day, only tinted green. A glance to his left showed him that Boxers had already put his on. They'd only recently upgraded their night vision to a four-tube array, transforming their view from tunnel vision with the old two-tube models to nearly panoramic.

"Okay," Jonathan said. "Let's do this."

Boxers rumbled out a laugh. "We're going to scare the shit out of Horne."

As they approached the farmhouse from the left side—the green side, as Jonathan thought of it—they moved as stealthily as they could. With winter in full swing, the forest floor was covered with dry, noisy leaves. They placed their feet carefully, but noisy was noisy.

"Good lord," Boxers whispered. "I feel like we might as well be blasting music."

"We're still half a click away," Jonathan said. "They won't hear a thing." He tried to sound assuring, but he didn't think he pulled it off.

Sometimes, this business was easier when you knew for a fact that the guys on the other end of the mission were trying to kill you. In those cases, anybody you saw was a target, and the disposition options were obvious. Here, everything was a variable.

If he saw someone, was he friend or foe? If the person had a weapon, was the weapon for personal protection or for killing approaching good guys?

The only absolute was when the guy with the gun pointed said gun at Jonathan or Boxers. That was a capital offense, and the penalty was bestowed immediately.

That was a lot of thinking to do when the bad guy's bullet could come at you at two thousand feet per second.

The route to the big barn took them over two fences, one built of stone, thanks, no doubt, to the labor of slaves two hundred years ago, and the other made of chain link and barbed wire. Boxers took out the wire with a pair of cutters.

The approach to the barn on Horne's property took all of thirty minutes. Jonathan found the absence of threats to be unnerving. He wanted to see sentries and snipers. The fact that he didn't see them merely made him wonder where the shooters were hiding.

Finally, they arrived at the green side of the barn itself. Solidly constructed of heavy timbers, almost no light escaped the structure.

They approached shoulder to shoulder, each of them cheating out ninety degrees to keep watch for threats that may materialize from any compass point. When they reached the near wall, they both spun to press their backs against the heavy timber.

With their backs against the wall, they sidestepped toward the corner where the green side met the white side, the front. With his M27 pressed to his shoulder, Jonathan led with the muzzle as he peered down the front wall. The image flared as his goggles amplified the light that spilled from under the enormous front doors.

He looked away from the flash of light, and scanned

the night beyond the barn and to his left. "I don't see any threats," he said.

"I'm clear," Big Guy agreed.

Still using the wall as cover, they glided through the night to a spot on the near side of the door.

"How do you want to handle it?" Boxers asked.

Jonathan lifted his NVGs out of the way. "Diplomatically," he whispered. Then he bellowed, "Arc Flash! This is Scorpion. If you are inside the barn, speak up loudly and speak up now!"

"Diplomatic *and* subtle," Boxers observed.

Jonathan heard movement beyond the walls, but nothing that he could make out as voices.

"Arc Flash! You do not want to cross me. I have Big Guy with me, and we are both heavily armed, and we are coming in. If you have a weapon, put it down, or I will shoot you when I see you! Acknowledge, please!"

He heard more movement from inside. Nothing sounded panicked, and he didn't hear any of the characteristic sounds of rifle bolts being cycled. If anything, the noises from inside sounded routine, though even Jonathan couldn't quite put his finger on what that meant. Sometimes you get a bad feeling about an entry, and sometimes you get a good feeling. This one fell in the middle.

Jonathan checked the latch on the big double doors. The thumb lever moved, and when he pulled the wooden panel, it swung open. He looked to Boxers. "You go high-right."

"Rog."

This was the moment that Jonathan simultaneously

hated and loved, these few seconds before throwing open a door to the unknown, with heart, mind, and soul fully committed to dealing with whatever lay beyond.

He pulled open the left-hand door panel, weapon at the ready, and used his left heel to push it out of the way. Without a word between them, Jonathan and Boxers squirted inside. The room hadn't changed much in the eighteen hours since they'd last been here, except there were no people.

Boxers said, "Who was making the noise?"

As if on cue, Jonathan heard it again. Closer this time, it sounded like furniture being moved. "Where is that coming from?" he wondered aloud.

They moved together, deeper into the vastness of the barn. They kept their rifles at their shoulders, scanning the shadows for threats. They scanned left-right, up-down, over and over again, fingers poised just outside their trigger guards.

When they'd made it to the halfway point—about to the spot where they had met with Irene and the White House people—Jonathan dared to let his weapon fall against its sling. He kept his gloved hand on the grip, just in case.

The noise happened again. Definitely the sound of something being dragged across wood.

What the hell?

Then Jonathan noticed something. "Hey, Big Guy. Does this room seem smaller on the inside than it does when you look at it from the outside?

Boxers took a few seconds to look around. "Come to think of it, yes."

More dragging.

"It's coming from behind there." Jonathan pointed to the array of farm implements that hung from mounting brackets on the wall.

"How do you suppose you get in? I didn't see any doors—"

A workbench moved just five feet to Boxers' right, causing them both to snatch their rifles back to their shoulders, poised to shoot.

The movement stuttered, and then started again. Only it was more than just the bench. It was the entire section of wall that contained the bench. It was a door, and because it was opening toward them, they wouldn't be able to see who was behind it until he'd stepped into the clear.

Jonathan tugged on Boxers' sleeve, then mimed with a patting motion in the air for them drop down to one knee.

The door opened all the way.

And the silhouette of a man emerged into the expanding wedge of light on the floor. The silhouette held a pistol in its hand.

"Is somebody out here?" the shadow called. "Show yourself or get shot." It was Horne.

Boxers gave Jonathan a curious look. *What do you want to do?*

"It's Scorpion," Jonathan said in a conversational tone. He didn't want to sound overly threatening.

The silhouette jumped and raised its weapon.

"Arc Flash, if I eyeball you and you still have that pistol in your hand, I'll kill you."

"Unless I do it first," Boxers added.

As often happened, the deep rumble of that second

voice sealed the deal. "I'm putting it on the ground," Horne said. And the shadow did exactly that.

"Is that the only weapon?" Jonathan asked.

"The only one on me," Horne answered. His voice had always had a tinny, boyish quality to it, but the quaver in it tonight made it sound particularly young.

"Is there anyone else back there with you?"

"Only the ones that were sent to me. For crying out loud, Scorpion, why are we—"

"Because I don't trust anyone tonight," Jonathan said. "After what's been going on, everyone is a threat until they've earned otherwise."

"Even after all these years? I'm hurt." The silhouette stretched its arms out to the sides and splayed its fingers. "What's next?"

"Step into the open where I can see you," Jonathan instructed. "And keep your hands exposed."

Griffin Horne emerged slowly and tentatively from behind the door. Maybe five-eight and thick through the middle, Horne looked like he'd been born into a long tradition of bureaucrats. The pastiness of his skin told of far more hours indoors than out. If you saw the guy on the street, you might mistake him for a lawyer or an association executive. You'd never in a million lifetimes guess him to possess the special skills for which he was so famous in the covert community.

"Big Guy, check the inside of that room while I check out Arc Flash."

Boxers made a point of growling as he brushed past Horne and disappeared into the back room.

"I'm getting an ungrateful vibe from you, Jonny," Horne said as Jonathan patted him down for weapons.

"Code names, Torture Boy."

"After all the good times you've had here at my place, I'd think a little deference would be in order."

It was cold enough to see your breath in here, yet somehow Horne had managed to work up a sweat. "It's nothing personal," Jonathan said. With the thorough frisking completed, he picked up the revolver Horne had dropped, unloaded it by dumping the cartridges on the floor, then slipped it into the patch pocket on his thigh. "You get this back when I leave."

"May I put my arms down now?"

Jonathan answered with a nod. "So, what's going on in there?"

Horne gestured to the open door with his palm. "Look for yourself. I've been setting up for you."

"You first," Jonathan said.

Horne smiled. "You really are spooked, aren't you?"

"I'm not one to toy with tonight. Read the body language. If not mine, then the Big Guy's."

Arc Flash made a point of smiling even more broadly before stepping through the open doorway into a brightly lit room. Five steps in, the temperature had climbed twenty degrees

Boxers turned to meet their approach, his fists planted on his hips. "Wait till you get a load of this," he said.

The hidden room turned out to be only about twelve by twelve feet—leading Jonathan to conclude that there must be several more such rooms lining the back side of the barn. To the left, on the far end, Vasily and Pyotr sat naked in high, straight-backed chairs, bathed in bright white light that emphasized their facial bruises in a kind of three-dimensional relief. Horne had positioned them so that they were facing each other, and he'd spared no expense in dispensing the duct tape. Loops of the stuff bound every joint to the structural elements of the chairs—forehead, chin, biceps, waist, thighs, knees, and ankles. Every tender part of their bodies was fully exposed, and they would be powerless to protect themselves.

Jonathan found himself recalling his last encounter with Arc Flash in a stinky, steamy basement in Yemen. The prep there had been nearly identical.

"What's the plan?" Jonathan asked.

"We're going to learn things that we didn't know before," Horne replied. "I've been tendering them up with a little electricity, but I thought you'd want to ask the questions."

It wasn't until Horne mentioned the electricity that Jonathan noted the cables that disappeared from view into the men's respective crotches. He knew without looking that the cables led to heavy alligator clips on the prisoners' genitals. On the other end, the cables led to a hand-cranked generator.

Jonathan looked away. The pain of the clamps alone would be unbearable. The thought of high-voltage electricity turned his stomach.

"Take those off," Jonathan said.

"But they haven't told us anything useful."

"I said take them off." Jonathan drilled the man with a glare. "My interrogation, my rules."

Arc Flash glared right back. "Don't kid yourself, Scorpion. My property, my rules. And *you* are not my client. I'm letting you ask the questions as a courtesy."

Jonathan said nothing.

After maybe ten seconds, Horne broke. "Fine," he said. "If you want to play the good cop, I suppose I can go along. For a while."

As Horne removed the clamps, Jonathan found what could have been a milking stool and carried it to a spot roughly between the two prisoners.

Boxers stood at the back of the room, blocking access to the closed door. He kept his hand on the grip of his rifle, poised to hurt anyone who posed a threat.

Jonathan shrugged out of his rucksack and laid it on the floor. He worked his shoulders a couple of times to ease away the phantom strap marks and sat on the stool.

"Hello, Vasily," Jonathan said. Under the bruising, the man had broad Slavic features, complete with the orbital ridge and the pugilist's nose. Something flashed behind his eyes—it was there and gone in a second, but long enough to show Jonathan that he'd struck the truth.

"You, too, Peter," he said to the other one. Jonathan wasn't going to take a shot at the pronunciation of Pyotr. He figured he was close enough. "Welcome to America. I apologize for my friend's attraction to male genitalia. Are you both reasonably comfortable now?"

Neither prisoner spoke. Instead, they stared at each other.

Jonathan pulled his iPhone out of his trousers pocket, thumbed it to life, and navigated to the dossiers Venice had downloaded to him. He recapped the intel that they'd discussed in the War Room.

"So, let's get past all the covers and bullshit Secret Service identities," he concluded. "You know how this works. You answer my questions through a haze of agony, or you answer them because you know it's the better solution. Which will it be? Peter, I'll ask you first. Are you going to cooperate, or are we going to hurt you?"

Pyotr started to answer, but Vasily cut him off. "We are here legally," he said. David had made no mention of so thick a Russian accent. Jonathan figured that under stress, he'd forgotten to fake his words. "I don't know what you want to know."

Jonathan laughed. "Really? Is that the best you can come up with? I guess you don't remember that we're the ones who kicked your asses when you were trying to kill an innocent couple."

The prisoners continued to look exclusively at each other.

"Okay," Jonathan said. "Let's start with the obvious. Why were you intent on killing David Kirk?"

"Who?" Vasily said.

Jonathan sighed. "Oh, dear. This is going to be such a long night." He shifted his gaze to the other prisoner. "How about you, Peter? Are you going to be this difficult?"

Pyotr shifted his eyes to the floor. "I don't know what you're talking about," he said.

"Very well, then," Jonathan said. "Let's come at it this way. Why were you at the Eastern Towers Apartments this afternoon?"

"You don't have to answer him, Pyotr," Vasily said.

"He's not the boss anymore, Peter," Jonathan said. "Never again will be. You should feel free to answer if you want."

"Say nothing, Pyotr."

Jonathan kept his gaze locked on Pyotr. Vasily didn't matter; that was the context. *Just a chat between you and me, Pete.*

"Peter, it will be so, so much easier in the long run," Jonathan said. His tone had never sounded so reasonable. So kind. "I don't like to see people get hurt. I am not like my little friend. While he may be a monster, I assure you that I am not."

Pyotr cheated with his eyes, leaving their lock on Vasily's face and shifting to evaluate Jonathan.

"Pyotr, don't!"

Jonathan pointed to his own eyes. "Look here, Peter. Not at him. Right here. Right at my eyes. I'm telling you the truth. This doesn't have to be difficult."

Pyotr's eyes shifted back over to Vasily. And they grew huge.

From his black side, Jonathan more sensed than heard Boxers shifting his weight. "Threat left!" he yelled.

Jonathan reacted as reflex, rolling from the stool to the floor. A half-second later, he was back up on his knee, his .45 drawn and gripped in both hands, ready to neutralize the threat he still hadn't seen. Boxers hadn't yet fired a shot, and that fact alone kept Jonathan's finger off the trigger.

If he'd turned a few milliseconds later, Jonathan would not have seen Arc Flash deliver the full overhead swing of a sledgehammer onto Vasily's left shoulder. The crushing blow landed squarely on the sweet spot where the clavicle, scapula, and the proximal condyle of the humerus met to form the shoulder joint. The bones splintered with a sickening crunch, and Vasily's entire left side sagged from the impact. Somehow, the sound of shattering bone reverberated more loudly than Vasily's guttural shriek.

"Aw, fuck!" Boxers yelled.

Jonathan's stomach nearly emptied itself. "Arc Flash!" he yelled. "Jesus!"

Horne beamed with delight as he spun the sledge in his hand the way a drum major might flourish a baton.

"Like that," Horne said. The effort left him short of breath. He pointed the sledge at Pyotr, an extension of his arm. "Aren't a few answers worth not having that happen to you?" He emphasized the point by tapping the white flash of bone that protruded from the ruined shoulder, triggering another scream.

Pyotr vomited into his own lap.

Jonathan hadn't yet broken his aim. "Put that down, Arc Flash. For Christ's sake."

Horne grabbed the back of Vasily's chair and jostled it. Vasily howled like a wounded animal.

"Stop!" Boxers boomed.

Horne turned to face the Big Guy full on. He stepped out in front of Vasily, his arms held wide, cruciform. In the bright light, blood shimmered on the sledge's head.

"What are you going to do, Big Guy? Shoot me?" he pivoted a quarter-turn to his left to address Jonathan. "How about you Scorpion? I'm all the way over here and you're all the way over there. Are you going to separate my soul from my body just because I break a few *bones*?" He emphasized the last word with a golf swing that brought the face of the sledge through the face of Vasily's right kneecap. An erection showed through Horne's trousers.

He turned back to face Boxers. "All right, Mr. Snake Eating Delta Operator. What are you going to do? Decision time. Either shoot that thing or holster it."

"Big Guy, don't," Jonathan said.

Boxers had a long history of treating rhetorical challenges as real. Jonathan didn't want to deal with the Horne's corpse. Not tonight. "Disengage," he commanded.

When he didn't hear sounds of appropriate movement, he looked back to see Boxers thoroughly committed to a shooter's stance. Eight feet away, Horne's entire being screamed, *Shoot me.*

"Hey, Big Guy," Jonathan coaxed. "He's a shit, but he's on our side."

Boxers hesitated for maybe a second, and then let go of his 417, letting it fall against its sling. "This isn't right, Scorpion," he said. "We don't do this shit."

You knew you'd crossed a moment in the space-time continuum when Boxers was the conscience of the group. What was done was done. Arc Flash's tactics were disgusting, but they were already in play. This wasn't the time to put righteous indignation in the way of collecting valuable information.

Jonathan slipped his Colt back into its holster and resumed his seat on the stool.

Everything about Pyotr had changed. He was three shades paler, he was drenched in his own nastiness, and though it was physically impossible, he looked ten years younger and ten pounds lighter. By any measure, that meant he was ready to talk.

Jonathan cleared his throat. "So, what'll it be, Peter? The easy way or the hard way?"

CHAPTER FIFTEEN

"**T**his is bullshit," David said. He and Becky sat together in his room. For the past couple of hours, they'd been biding time by doing nothing. So far, this Scorpion guy had been true to his word, up to and including the nice old black lady who'd seen to their every need.

"There's been a lot of that today," Becky said. "Which part are you finding particularly bullshitty?"

"It's stupid to trust my future—my life—to people I've never met before," he said.

Becky stewed on that for a few seconds. "I can't disagree entirely," she said. "But give credit for the fact that we're alive because of them."

"I thought you were against all of this," David said.

"I don't have a clue what I'm for or against anymore, David. Everything I've ever known, everything I've ever been—all of my accomplishments, such as they are—don't mean anything anymore. Maybe I'm just grasping at straws. Pretending that I still have choices."

"Here's the thing," David explained. "When I met

with Grayson, he gave me the name and address of a
guy in Lake Ridge—it's in Prince William County—
who he said should be able to give us some information."

"A guy. Which guy?"

"His name is Billy Zanger. He's on the president's
staff."

"President of the United States?"

"That would be the one."

"You want to meet with a staffer of the president of
the United States?"

Hearing the question asked with such incredulity
gave him pause. "He's been bought and paid for by
Grayson. Or so Grayson says." The bought-and-paid-
for line didn't even raise an eyebrow.

"Why is Grayson sharing his sources with you?"

David gave her the thirty-second précis of his chat.

When he was finished, Becky cocked her head.
"What, exactly, would you ask him?"

David started to answer, then stopped. "I have no
idea. But sitting here does nothing but make me nervous. This is my life we're talking about. And it's all
collapsing around me."

"You can't, David. Your face is all over the news.
Suppose someone notices you?"

"People don't look for faces," David said. "Nobody
pays attention to those pictures unless they're watching
America's Most Wanted."

"But if they do?"

"Then they do and I go to jail. That's not a whole
hell of a lot different than where I am right now."

"Except for the locks on the doors, and the absence
of anal rape," Becky said.

David scowled. "Where did the ironic sense of humor come from? You've never had an ironic sense of humor."

She folded her arms, emphasizing her breasts. "You have no idea what I've had or haven't had. I was invisible to you until last night." The way she delivered the line, it sounded less like a shot than it probably was.

David let it go. "I'm going to visit and talk with him," he said. "It feels like the right thing to do. Do you believe in karma?"

Becky laughed. "Oh, please," she said. "Tell me that the cynical David Kirk is not going all woo-woo when the chips are down."

"Things happen for a reason," he insisted. "If Grayson went to the trouble of telling me about this guy, there has to be a reason for me to speak with him."

Becky stared at him.

"What?"

"Nothing," she said. "You just continue to surprise me."

David sighed. "So, are you coming with me?"

Her smile collapsed into a look of total shock. "You mean you're really going? How are you going to get there? You don't have a car."

He shrugged. "They've got to have taxis, don't they? Every place has taxis. And I have a pocket full of fresh money."

"I have the drawings, Peter," Jonathan said. "I know what your targets are. What I don't have are the details of the how or the when." Behind him, Vasily had fallen unconscious. The wetness of his breathing sounds told Jonathan that Arc Flash's blows had caused one of the many broken bones to puncture the man's lung. He sounded like he was drowning. Jonathan avoided looking at him.

Pyotr, on the other hand, kept staring, and as he did, he became increasingly unnerved. He said something in Russian that might have been a prayer.

"English," Jonathan said.

Pyotr took his time answering, dividing the silence between Jonathan and Vasily. "You don't understand," he said, finally. "You don't understand because you don't want to understand."

"Enlighten me," Jonathan said.

"Americans are always focused on the wrong thing," Pyotr said. His accent had grown thick enough that Jonathan had a hard time understanding what he was saying. "You determine that there is a single threat to your country, and then you focus all of your resources on that one thing. Even as the threat is weakened and ultimately destroyed, you refuse to look any further."

"I'm not sure I understand what we're talking about," Jonathan said.

"We are talking about the downfall of the United States," Pyotr said. "It is the thing upon which so much of the world is focused." He allowed himself a smile. "You pretend that your enemies are religious enemies, and you fear only Muslims. You believe this even though those enemies die by the dozens under the rain of your bombs and the bullets of your secret killers."

Vasily made a desperate choking sound that drew Jonathan's attention. The man's lips had turned a dull blue, and while his head bobbed as if asleep, his eyes remained open. Vasily was dying.

"I'm sorry about your friend," Jonathan said. "It's a

terrible way to die. But a brutal death is part of the deal we all make when we go into this line of work." Jonathan cringed at his own words. Hearing a man die as the result of torture meted out in his presence had stolen something from his soul.

"Look at me, Peter," Jonathan said. "Try to ignore Vasily. It's clear that he'll be dead soon."

Hesitantly, Pyotr retuned his gaze.

"You say that we don't understand what are the greatest threats against us, but then you don't tell me what the real threats are."

"But you already know" Pyotr said. "We are right here."

Boxers said, "I don't know if you've noticed that you're tied naked to a chair. I'm not feeling all that threatened."

Sometimes, Jonathan wished that Boxers would keep his mouth shut.

"Ask any one of the passengers on that airplane in Chicago," Pyotr said. "Americans are bullies. It's not about your religion or about your so-called freedom. The world hates you for making war against peaceful people."

Jonathan suppressed a sigh. With zealots, lectures all too often came as part of the package. Islamists were the worst of the lot, but former Communists came in a close second. He'd learned, though, that if you waited long enough, they'd abandon the bullshit and get around to the point.

"For Christ's sake, Scorpion," Arc Flash said, hefting his sledge.

Jonathan held out his hand to stop him, though he sensed that Horne was bluffing.

"Everybody benefits if you speed this along, Peter," Jonathan said.

Horne said, "Screw this," and he crashed the sledge down onto Vasily's other shoulder, caving in that side, too. The blow elicited another shriek from the otherwise unconscious man.

"Screw *you*," Boxers growled. He closed the distance to Arc Flash in three long, quick strides.

The little man tried to back up, but he couldn't move fast enough.

Boxers ripped the sledge away with one hand, and drove Arc Flash into the back wall with the other. A shelf broke, raining torture tools onto the floor. When there was no place left to go, he pressed the sledge's head under Horne's jaw, at the spot where it met his neck, effectively cutting off his ability to breathe.

"No more," the Big Guy said. His voice had turned raspy, a tell that Jonathan had come to recognize as the last station before Homicideville.

Jonathan considered intervening, but then decided that he didn't care.

"Once more," Boxers continued, "and I'll gut shoot you and watch you bleed to death."

Delivered by a different guy, those words might have sounded empty. Coming from Boxers, they sounded like a promise. As Horne's face reddened, his eyes showed real terror.

His point made, Boxers pulled the sledge away and let the man breathe again.

Horne's hands shot to his neck and he slid to the floor, gasping for air.

"Sit," Boxers said. "Stay." To Jonathan: "Sorry, Boss. He got on my last nerve."

Big Guy recovered as quickly as he'd erupted, and Jonathan reminded himself for the millionth time how much better it was to have Boxers as a friend than an enemy.

Jonathan returned his attention to Pyotr. "They never did get along," he said. "The good news is, for now Big Guy is on your side. He gets that you lost a friend—or will as soon as he dies of his injuries, but the fact remains that you are trying to blow up my country. In the process, you tried to kill the president's wife. That's bad juju, Pete."

Pyotr scowled. "Jew?"

Jonathan laughed. "Juju," he said. "Like voodoo." The Russian still didn't get it. "Never mind. The plan, Pete. What's the plan?"

"Is already in play," he said. He'd never sounded more Russian. "You cannot stop it."

"Humor me."

Pyotr looked down to his feet, a gesture of resolve to shut up. He'd said enough.

Jonathan inhaled noisily. "Please don't make it go this way," he said.

Pyotr continued to look at the floor.

"Hey Big Guy," Jonathan said without shifting his gaze. "Do you still have the sledge?"

"Yup."

"Would you shatter Pete's left knee, please?"

"Love to."

Jonathan more sensed than felt the Big Guy's approach from behind.

Pyotr's eyes grew huge. "No, no, no," he said. "I tell you."

Jonathan dared a look over his shoulder and saw the

Big Guy with the sledge raised over his shoulder, poised for a home run swing. He'd never know if he was bluffing because he'd never ask.

"One chance, Pete," Jonathan said. "I abhor torture, but I'll watch you scream for mercy for hours before I let another tourist die on an airliner. Do you get where I'm coming from?"

Pyotr nodded like a bobble head. "Yes, yes. I understand. Please don't hurt knee."

Boxers' shadow retreated.

"I won't hurt knee if you tell truth," Jonathan said. His Russian accent sucked.

"We have sleeping cells in your country," Pyotr said. "They wait for orders to do violence."

"What kind of violence?"

"Big violence. Big as East-West Airlines and even bigger."

"Was that you?" Jonathan asked. "Did your sleeper cell shoot down the airliner?"

Pyotr smiled as he nodded. "Was perfect operation, no? You still do not know who was person who shot down."

Jonathan shrugged. "We will," he said. "We Americans aren't good at everything, but we're really good at ferreting out our enemies." He didn't add that Pyotr would be the very man to give them the intel they'd need to close that loop. "What does any of this have to do with Mrs. Darmond? Why did you attack her?"

Pyotr smiled. "Did you know she used to be one of us?"

Jonathan said nothing. In an interrogation, it was of utmost importance that information flow in only one direction. He asked the questions and the prisoner provided the answers. "Is it revenge?" he asked.

Pyotr scowled as if he didn't fully understand the question. "Revenge is same as payback, yes?"

"I suppose."

"Payback for how she betray her friends?"

"You tell me, Peter."

"No. We are not interested in revenge. She knows secrets."

"Of the targets you're planning to hit," Jonathan presumed.

"I don't know what the secrets are," Pyotr said. "I only know that she needed to be silenced."

A piece of the puzzle fell into place. "So, the hit on the Wild Times Bar was an assassination attempt?"

Pyotr looked away.

"I need an answer, Pete."

He nodded.

"And what about the police officer on the Mall?" Jonathan asked. "DeShawn Lincoln."

"He saw too much and talked too much," Pyotr said.

"What did he see and say?"

Pyotr shook his head. "I do not know. It doesn't matter that I know. I do not design the machine. I am merely a mechanic."

Across from Pyotr, Vasily managed one more giant breath, and then he died. The death rattle seemed to give Pyotr a moment of peace. Jonathan wondered whether it was because his friend was finally out of pain, or if it was because his boss could never rat him out for telling.

"By mechanic you mean killer," Boxers clarified.

Pyotr did his best to pivot his head to see the Big Guy. "By mechanic I mean I fix things and make them right. I am a soldier."

"Don't honor yourself, asshole," Boxers said. "You're no soldier."

Jonathan knew that the current path couldn't lead to anywhere good, so he changed the subject. "And what about David Kirk and Becky Beckeman? What did they do that you had to fix?"

"The girl meant nothing to us," Pyotr said. "She was—what is your word? Collateral damage. She was with Kirk."

"And what had Kirk done?"

"Is that not obvious?"

"I need to hear it from you."

"He also knew too much. He was Officer Lincoln's last phone call."

And so it was with cover-ups. Jonathan had seen the pattern a hundred times. Once a secret is blown, the only way to get the genie back into the bottle is to engage in a scorched-earth strategy of cleanups.

"The group that is doing this," Jonathan said. The group you're a part of. Does it have a name? Is it organized?"

"We don't need a name," Pyotr said. "We have memories and we have a mission."

"Who's the leader?"

Pyotr shook his head. "I do not know."

"Then who is your boss? Who do you take orders from?"

He said a phrase in Russian that Jonathan didn't understand. When pressed, he said, "I do not know the English. Perhaps drop dead?"

Boxers bristled. "Easy there, pal."

"I think he meant dead drop," Jonathan said, a term of art in the espionage trade that meant a pre-established location to leave and retrieve messages. It remained one of the most reliable means by which clandestine people communicated with each other. "Explain to me how it worked."

Pyotr hesitated, but Jonathan sensed that it was mainly for show. The thing about breaking somebody was once the information started to trickle, a flow was generally close behind. As much as Scorpion hated to admit it, watching Vasily be tortured to death had loosened Pyotr's tongue. People in pain may or may not give reliable information; but people in fear of pain would give up anyone and anything.

"My phone would ring at a precise hour. If it rang, then I would go to the drop dead. Dead drop. The instructions would be there."

"Who called you?"

"I do not know."

"Well, who was on the other end of the line when you answered?"

"I did not answer it," Pyotr said. "The phone would ring at only one of two times per day if it was going to ring at all. At four fifty-seven exactly. Same time, morning or afternoon. Not a minute sooner or later. If it rang, I would go."

"He's lying," Arc Flash said. He hadn't yet dared to stand from where Boxers had planted him.

"Shut up," Big Guy said.

Jonathan said, "You mean to tell me that you were never curious?"

"Of course I was curious. But I have orders, and the orders were not to answer when phone rang at four fifty-seven."

Soldiers the world over suppressed all manner of emotions and foibles when their orders told them to. The story made sense to Jonathan.

"What sorts of things would you be instructed to do?"

"Mostly, I would be deliveryman. Pick up a package at one place and drop it at another. And before you ask, I never saw the people on either end of the delivery. I would pick up at a place and drop off at a place."

"Always the same pick-up location?" Jonathan asked.

"No. Always same dead drop. It would then give location for pick-up. At pick-up, I get instruction for drop-off."

It was a good way to control the flow of information, Jonathan thought. You never wanted human assets to know more than they needed to. Even now, under the heat of a coerced confession of sorts, Pyotr's betrayal of his superiors could only go so far.

"Where is the dead drop?"

"In a restroom in Fairfax, Virginia. In hotel."

"Which hotel?"

"Hilton Garden Inn on Route Fifty. Instructions would be taped behind toilet in men's room off of the lobby. No one could see it if they were not looking for it."

"And these packages. What would be in them?"

"Always orders not to look."

"How often did you and Vasily work together?"

"Never before now. Never before this mission."

"This mission to kill," Jonathan clarified.

"*Da*. This mission to kill. But I do not know why. The dead drop told me to go to the park outside of the Foggy Bottom Metro Station wearing New England Patriots knit cap with blue Levis and white tennis shoes. I would meet a man wearing brown shoes, tan pants, and a blue ski parka. I would say to him, 'sure is cold,' and he would say, 'I am ready for vacation in Saint Kitts.' That person was Vasily."

"This isn't the first time you've seen him," Jonathan said.

"Was first time in years. Since we arrive in America. He had orders for killing. I only assisted."

"Who did his orders come from?"

"Should have asked him," Pyotr said. It was his first jab back at his captors.

Jonathan shot a look to Horne. "Would have been nice to have a chance to. In fact—"

His earpiece popped to life. "Scorpion, Mother Hen."

He pressed the transmit button on his vest. "Go ahead."

"Two bits of news. First: Our recent houseguests have left. I have no idea where they went."

"Idiots," Boxers said to Jonathan. He was plugged into the same net and heard everything.

"I just received a message from Wolverine. She needs to see you ASAP. No details. And she said it has to be here."

"Where's here?"

"In the Cave." While they spoke on encrypted radio channels, Jonathan was keenly aware that there was nothing that couldn't be listened to or jammed by someone who knew what they were doing. The Cave meant the office. And it was an extraordinarily odd place to meet.

"That's crossing the worlds a little too closely, don't you think?" Boxers asked on the air.

"No argument from me," Venice said. "I'm just reporting the request."

"What's her ETA?" Jonathan asked.

"You are to notify me when you're an hour out, and then I will notify her."

Jonathan looked to Boxers, gave his signature shrug. "I don't like it," Big Guy said off the air.

Jonathan pressed the transmit button. "Make the call. We'll be there in thirty."

"Stand up, Arc Flash," Jonathan commanded.

The little man did as he was told. He might have been beaten, but he hadn't been cowed. "More problems afoot?" he asked.

Jonathan took a step forward, and Horne responded with a concomitant step backward. "Listen to me, Torture Boy," he said, leveling a finger at the man. "What's done here is done, and by that I mean that you leave both of these men alone. I'll get some of Wolverine's people out here to take care of them. You just lock the door. Are we clear on this?"

Horne recovered his lost ground with a step forward. "I hear you, Scorpion, but never forget who I am, and where you are. I do my job, and you do yours, and if we both do them right, the world becomes a safer place. But don't think for a moment that you scare me."

"How about me?" Boxers said, stepping forward. "I figure I've got to make you at least a little nervous."

He stood close enough that Horne had to crane his neck to see Big Guy's face. He showed wisdom in not replying.

"Just don't hurt them any more than you already have," Jonathan said.

CHAPTER SIXTEEN

It was as if Billy Zanger had investigative reporters in mind when he selected his home. Out here in Prince William County, Virginia, the primary industries were support services for the midgrade military officers who comprised the main demographic. Neighbors might be impressed with Zanger's title of deputy press secretary, but they wouldn't obsess over it. Awareness of national politics decreased exponentially with every mile outside the Beltway. In Prince William County, the chances of being seen and reported by a curious blogger were pretty slim.

Becky and David had been sitting in their rental car in the parking lot of the little townhouse cluster for over an hour, awaiting Zanger's return from his late shift at the news desk in the West Wing.

"He should be getting home anytime now," David said. "He was supposed to get off at midnight. Even if he stays to work late, he should be here soon."

"How sure are you that he's going to cooperate?" Becky asked from the driver's seat. "What's his incentive?"

"I told you. He either speaks with us, or we out him."

"Would you really do that?"

David forced a laugh. "You bet I'd really do that. Journalistic integrity is important to me, but I'm more concerned about my ass."

He felt the chill radiating from Becky, and as much as he wanted to ignore it, he couldn't. "Look," he said. "I'm sorry about all of this. You have every right to be pissed at me, and I have no business asking you to participate as deeply as you are. You did a good deed letting me into your place, and now, true to the saying, you're not going unpunished."

"That was a double negative," she said without dropping a beat. "You're better than that."

She seemed to enjoy his confusion.

"I'm not pissed at you," she said. "I'm not pissed at anybody." She reached across the center console and gripped David's arm. "What I am is scared. Shitlessly."

"I get that," David said. "And as adverbs go, 'shitlessly' is a pretty good one."

"But really, David. This thing has the White House involved. That's huge."

"We don't know that the White House is *involved*," David said. "Correlation and causation are different things."

"Oh, good," Becky mocked with a smile. "Freshman logic. That's what we need. Where I grew up, if it walked like a duck and quacked like a duck, we drew conclusions and lived with the margin of error."

David watched her as she spoke. In the deflected silver light of the street lamp, he saw cheekbones that stayed hidden most of the time. When she smiled, her teeth actually flashed.

Becky pointed through the windshield. "That's him," she said. "Drives a Fusion, right?"

David followed where she was pointing. They knew he drove a black Ford Fusion, and in the darkness, the one they saw parking in front of Billy Zanger's townhouse could just as easily have been brown or navy blue.

"Okay," David said. "Let's try not to get killed."

They opened their doors in unison and stepped out into the frigid night. David noted that the dome light didn't come on as the door opened, and he realized that Becky had already thought of that. Damned impressive.

When the door on the Fusion opened up ahead, that dome light did work, and its glare revealed exactly the person they were hoping to see. Billy Zanger was far too absorbed in whatever was playing through his head to notice the two approaching strangers.

Zanger climbed out of his car, slung his European man-bag over his shoulder, and pressed the button on his key fob to make the Fusion chirp as its locks set. He was in no hurry as he dragged himself across the sidewalk and up the three concrete steps that led to his front door.

The whole time, David and Becky closed the distance that separated them. The timing worked out perfectly, with them arriving at the steps the moment that Zanger turned the lock and opened the door.

"Hi, Billy," David said, causing the other man to yelp and spin around.

"Who are you?"

"I'm a friend of Grayson Cantrell. Ring any bells?"

Zanger said, "Shit."

"Clearly, you know him," Becky said.

"What are you doing here?" Zanger said.

"Invite us in, Billy," David said.

Zanger looked past David and craned his neck to scan the street in both directions. "You can't do this," he said. "You can't come here. Not to my *house*. Suppose someone sees?"

"If they saw us, they'd think nothing. If they saw you looking like you've just been caught in a drug bust, they might start e-mailing each other." David gave him a second to make sense of his words. "Now, let us in, please."

His cheeks red, Zanger stepped through the door and then stepped aside to make room for his unwanted houseguests. "My family is sleeping," he said.

"We'll be quiet," David said. The Zanger townhouse looked like every other suburban Virginia townhouse of its era. A narrow center hallway stretched from the front door to a sliding glass door in the rear. A stairway with a wrought-iron railing rose parallel to the hallway on the right, and on the left, a small living area led to a small dining area, which dead-ended at the linoleum-tiled kitchen that appeared to span the entire width of the house in the rear. While not especially cramped, you could see nearly every inch of the main floor in a single glance.

"I don't like you being here," Zanger said. "This is twenty levels of inappropriate."

"I have no idea what that means," David said. He walked past his host and helped himself to a red-patterned sofa in the living room, where none of the furniture matched. "We'll only be here for as long as it takes."

"As it takes to do what?" Despite the suit—David pegged it as off-the-rack from Jos. A. Bank—Zanger looked more like a college student than a White House adviser.

"Please sit down, Billy."

Zanger sat on the edge of the coffee table, of all places, ignoring the inviting brown La-Z-Boy that David wished he had chosen for himself. Becky took it instead.

"Who did you say you're a friend of?" Zanger asked.

David smiled. "Promise me that you'll never play poker," he said. "Grayson Cantrell. And before you deny knowing him, may I remind you that you just let two strangers into your house on the power of his name?"

Zanger's eyes flashed surrender. "Ask your question and get out." He didn't pull off tough guy very well, either.

"Okay, I'll get right to it," David said. "What did you think of *Kirk Nation* today?"

Zanger looked way too confused by the question. "Kirk what?"

David smiled. "*Kirk Nation.* The blog. What did you think of it today?"

Zanger stood. "I really have no idea what you're talking about. You need to leave."

David looked to Becky, who winked. "I'm not going anywhere, Billy. Not until we have this conversation."

"You really think that you can just barge into my home and speak to me—"

"Billy, it's your schedule," David said. "I have all night. I have all the nights and days I need." He made a show of checking his watch. "I believe that you, on the other hand, must be awfully tired."

Zanger tried blustering again. "Who do you think you—"

"Oh, for Christ's sake, Billy. Be righteously indignant if you must, but you're wasting time. I'm not buying it. *Kirk Nation*. What are your thoughts?"

Zanger's eyes narrowed as he connected some important dots. "I know you," he said.

David arched his eyebrows. He knew where they were going, but they hadn't gotten there yet. "Not personally, you don't," he said.

You could almost see the Rolodex cards spinning in Zanger's head. "You're him," he said. "You're David Kirk."

David smiled with only his mouth, making a conscious effort to keep any inkling of humor out of his eyes.

"You wrote that shit about the First Lady. You had no proof about any of that."

David smiled.

"What's the grin for?" Billy still had not sat back down.

"What you said," David explained. "You just confirmed a lot of my story."

"I did no such thing." He seemed to grow taller. He most definitely grew redder.

"There's no podium here, Billy. No microphones. Because it's just you and me talking, there's not even a record to stay off of. Yet, you just told me that I leveled accusations that I couldn't prove."

"That's exactly right."

"Yet you didn't say that they were false."

"Oh, for God's sake. Don't parse words with me."

"Oh, for God's sake, Billy, that's what we both do for a living. Answer me this: Did you have anything to do with getting my site taken down?"

Zanger put both hands on the top of his head, his fingers disappearing in the tangled mop of brown hair. He started to speak, but then his filters kicked in, silencing him.

"If you've got something to say, say it," David said.

Another aborted attempt. "Who's she?" he nodded toward Becky.

"She's my last remaining friend," David said. "She's my witness."

"Are you armed?" Zanger asked.

It was a weird question, and David recoiled from it. "Maybe," he said. "But if you're thinking of starting some kind of fight, forget about it. I haven't been in a fight since eighth grade, but I guaran-damn-tee that I could kick your ass."

Zanger seemed to do the math in his head, and the results ended with a nervous smirk. "Okay," he said. "You want the truth?"

"It's as good a place to start as any," David said.

Zanger took a few seconds to screw up his courage. "You're a murderer, Kirk. You killed a cop last night. Now you're concocting some kind of bullshit conspiracy. It's nuts."

"Then why did you deny knowing about my blog when I first asked you?"

The question hit Zanger like a slap. He clearly was trying to formulate an answer, but it wouldn't come.

"Come on, Billy. You're busted and you know it. There's something huge going down on Pennsylvania Avenue, isn't there? Something bad is going down, and you're a part of it." David watched Zanger's face as his words hit home. "I'm not a murderer, Billy. And looking at you—looking at the absence of panic when you realized who I was—I'm guessing you already knew that. I'm guessing that you want to put a stop to whatever shit is going down. God knows I want to. So what do you say?"

Zanger went to a place in his mind that brought tears to his eyelids. "It's not supposed to be like this," he said. When he looked to Becky, they spilled in single tracks down both cheeks.

"I could go to jail for this," he said.

"You're too young for that," Becky said. "You look like a clean-cut nice guy. Whatever this secret is, you shouldn't have to pay the price for it."

Zanger swiped at the tears with the heels of his hands. "I got into this for all the right reasons," he said. "Nobody gets into government to kill people."

David's heart jumped, but he worked hard not to show it. "I know," he said. "Nobody goes into anything to do harm." He had no idea if that was true, but it sounded like the words he should say.

Zanger looked at David for a long time without saying anything. His smooth jaw—he was one of those twentysomethings who looked as if he hadn't yet shaved for the first time—flexed the whole time. David didn't know if the stories on the Internet about prison rapes were true, but it occurred to him that Zanger had a femininity about him that would make incarceration particularly difficult.

"It started out seeming like the right thing to do," Zanger said. "You know, it started out as protecting people. This first time you think it might be spinning out of control, you sort of look the other way and figure that you just have to tweak a few things, you know what I mean?"

"I think so," David said. Clearly, Zanger thought that David had more concrete knowledge than he really did, but David didn't want to interrupt the confession. Oftentimes, if you just kept listening, the lost details would line themselves up into a logical order. If they didn't, you could always catch up when the monologue was over.

"Then you realize that the fixes you tried to do caused more problems. And then you try to fix those problems and five more things break." He looked directly at Becky when he said, "I never in a million years thought that people would die. Would be killed."

"Who was killed, Billy?" Becky asked. She leaned forward in her lounge chair and reached for his hand. "Tell me."

"Surely you know," he said.

"Tell me," Becky repeated.

"Those poor people at the Wild Times Bar the other night," he said. "I read the brief on that—I wasn't supposed to, but I did, you know, because it was lying there on a desk."

Becky continued to nod, devoting all of her energy and attention to Zanger, except for the flash from her eyes that told David to shut up when he took a breath to interrupt.

Zanger continued, "Nobody was supposed to die. In retrospect, I guess that the shooting was inevitable, but you don't think that way during the planning stages, you know? Not when your boss is telling you that everything is going to be fine."

"So the president is involved with this?" Becky asked. She tried to remain cool when she asked the question, but the fact was she should probably stay away from the poker tables, too.

Zanger showed confusion for a few seconds. "Oh, I get it," he said. "It's the job title. Deputy White House press secretary. Okay. Well, they don't let me touch any of the high-profile stuff. I work for Doug Winters, the chief of staff. I'm sort of, nominally, his spokesperson." He looked away. "Only really, I'm more of his personal assistant. He and my family go way, way back. He trusts me."

"Ah," Becky said. "So the guy telling you that everything's going to be fine is just the president's chief of staff."

"Right."

"It's not the president himself."

"Exactly."

David found himself not blinking as he listened, his mind screaming to him that this was going to make Watergate look like a minor distraction.

Zanger continued, "You can't use any of this on the record."

"It's all deep background," Becky assured. While she might well have been playing a bluff, her promise concerned David. If they did, indeed, come out the other end of this ordeal whole and free, they would have to tell the FBI and others about what they'd just heard. How could they do that and still accept the Pulitzer that would be coming their way?

Zanger seemed satisfied, though no less disturbed. "But I never in a million years thought that tonight would ever happen."

Becky cocked her head. "Tonight?" she asked. "What part about tonight?"

Zanger cocked his head, too, albeit in the opposite direction. He seemed equal parts confused and concerned. "Isn't that why you're here? Isn't that why the two of you came to my door?"

Becky waited for it, and David was glad. Some issues be allowed to play themselves out.

Zanger looked shocked. "Really?" he asked. "The kidnapping. I thought for sure that you were here about the kidnapping."

CHAPTER SEVENTEEN

Nicholas Mishin loved the sound of his sleeping house. Most nights, the one-story rancher in the Colorado hill country was too damn quiet. Ever since Marcie left with Josef—he was Joey now, he mustn't forget—the house seemed to have lost its heartbeat. She'd taken the dog, too, so for too many nights and days, the otherwise comfortable house had been anything but a home.

For this week and next, though, that would all be different. Marcie had jetted off to some far-flung place with her rich new husband, leaving him alone with his son for the first time in ten months.

It was amazing how much children could change in a year. You expect it when they're little, when every day brings a new skill and new adventures, but Nicholas had not been prepared for the metamorphosis that had consumed his boy between his thirteenth and fourteenth birthdays. He'd grown tall and lean—Nicholas estimated him to be five-nine—and despite the adolescent hair that would go from clean to oily in half a day, and the zits on his nose and cheeks and chin that were the focus of so much of his vanity, he fit every person's definition of handsome. The California sun that was so much a part of his life while living with his mother had even managed to lighten his dark brown hair.

When Nicholas first saw Josef stepping out of the people mover into the arrival lounge in Denver International Airport, his gut seized at the magnitude of the change. He worried that in the months since they'd seen each other, the boy would have become a man so quickly that they would now have to get to know each other again as strangers.

Then Joey fired up that smile, and all the fears dissolved away. Without hesitation or embarrassment, he gave his old man a big hug, and from that second on, the missing slice of time stopped mattering.

It had been a great week, including three day-trips to the slopes—Vail, Copper, and Breckenridge—and an afternoon at the movies. Tonight, during dinner in front of the television in the family room, they'd agreed that tomorrow would be a lazy, do-nothing day, giving Joey a chance to catch up on his gaming and his e-mails, while allowing Nicholas to reestablish contact with the clients and colleagues he'd been pretending did not exist.

The evening had ended with a mind-numbing tutorial on World of Warcraft, a dizzying role-playing game that to Nicholas just felt like random violence, but he had to admit that the graphics were stunning.

That had taken them to the beginning of a new day, and much to Nicholas's surprise, Joey had been the one to call it quits.

Now, an hour later, Nicholas still lay awake, listening to the peaceful sounds of the sleeping house.

He missed the old days when they were a complete

family, but family dynamics were complicated things. While Marcie had been the first to wander from fidelity, he understood that he'd played a role in that. The obsession with work—he was an environmental engineer, which in fact was a far more interesting line of work than it sounded to people on the outside—combined with his even less healthy obsession with his mother's current husband, had made him a pain in the ass to be around.

And it didn't help that the media was so desperately anxious to throw fuel on his fires. They baited him and he swallowed the hook every time. All that negative energy and negative attention was too much for Marcie. He could have told them to mind their own business.

But he didn't. And now the house had its heartbeat for only a few weeks out of the year. Yet more evidence of life's most vivid lesson: Actions have consequences.

So, here he was, awash in consequences, and left with the struggle to fulfill another of life's challenges: He could accept things as they were and enjoy his time alone with Joey, or he could burn with bitterness and be miserable. He could provide a happy environment for Joey or he could push his son away.

You only get one shot at any given moment in your life, and the wise man doesn't squander a single one.

Nicholas sensed that he'd been lying awake since first getting into bed, but in a dark room, it was always hard to tell. You slip in and out.

Right now, though, he felt his heart hammering in his chest, and he didn't know why. A bad dream, perhaps? A bout of sleep apnea, for which he refused to wear that ridiculous fighter-pilot's mask?

He heard something.

He couldn't quite place it, but it was different from the normal sounds of the house.

Had to take the dog, didn't you, Marcie? It was more fuzz ball than watchdog, but that puffy little mutt had ears as sharp as any hound's.

He lay on his back, watching the ceiling, which showed itself only as a darker shade of black in an otherwise black room.

He heard it again. The pop of a floorboard outside the master bedroom door, the one you had to step on to gain access to the room. He'd often called it his ninja burglar alarm.

Nicholas sat up in bed and squinted to see the closed door. "Josef?" he said. "Is that you?" Who else could it be?

Joey's scream split the night like a hot ax, equal parts pain and fear. "Let go of me! Dad! Ow!"

Nicholas tore the covers away and threw his feet to the floor. "Josef! What is it?"

He'd taken only two steps when the door exploded open, and then they were on him.

There was something unnerving about seeing the third-floor offices lit up in the middle of the night. Jonathan noticed it as Boxers pulled the Batmobile into the garage at the rear of the firehouse.

As he stepped out, he waited for the sound that so often came next. The pounding of paws rumbled in the night as JoeDog, completely invisible in the dark, galloped from wherever she'd been to greet him with a running body-block.

He stooped and braced for it, and took it without

falling. "Hello, Beast," he said, rubbing her ears. He allowed his face to be licked a couple of times, and then the reunion ritual was complete. If he'd been coming in through the front door, she'd have had to run a couple of victory laps up and down the sidewalk. Who knew why?

"You treat her better than you treat people," Boxers said.

"I like her better than I like people."

Jonathan led the way through the back door into the mudroom that led to his living room, swatting wall switches to illuminate his sprawling man-cave. Fearless, protective creature that she was, JoeDog was careful to keep Jonathan between herself and Boxers.

Once inside, all semblance of firehouse disappeared, giving way to ornate oriental carpets and elegant yet cushy furniture. Jonathan had a thing for leather, and the upholstery in the place showed it. Dom D'Angelo, his best friend and local parish priest, once told him that his decorating aesthetic ran toward early hotel lobby.

JoeDog headed for her favorite club chair and settled in for the night.

An open stairway midway down the right-hand wall was the only architectural detail that remained of the old fire station—along with the brass pole that extended from the second-floor landing to the ground floor. Having spent so many hours polishing it as a boy, Jonathan couldn't bring himself to take it out when he remodeled the place.

The door at the top of the stairs led to a vestibule that to the right opened to the second floor, the sleeping floor, and to the left through a reinforced steel door that joined the stairway that led from the street to the office spaces on the third floor.

Jonathan opened the stairway door and let Boxers go first onto the landing. The night guard—a youngish former Air Force PJ named Sam Franco, who'd left a leg behind in Afghanistan—stood at the third floor landing.

"What's up, Sam?" Jonathan asked.

"We've got a special surprise for you inside," Franco said. "But Ms. Alexander made me promise not to tell you."

"You know I don't like surprises, right, Sam?"

"Yes, sir, I do. But the worst you can do is fire me. Ms. Alexander can make my life hell forever."

"Kid's got a point," Boxers said. "He's already earned his combat badge."

Jonathan scanned his thumbprint, punched the code into the cipher lock, and entered what he figured was going to be an entertaining night.

If Jonathan's living room was the hotel lobby, then his office was the lounge. Huge by any reasonable standard for offices, the themes of oriental carpeting and comfy leather continued, but in here, the addition of carved walnut paneling gave the space a feeling of warmth that Jonathan loved. His tastes were the polar opposite of Venice's chrome-and-glass aesthetic.

His visitors sat in the expansive and expensive conversation group in front of the fireplace that dominated the right-hand wall. Jonathan's heart skipped a beat when he saw the source of the mystery.

First Lady of the United States Anna Darmond, née Yelena Poltanov, sat with perfect posture in the Hitchcock armchair on the far side of the hearth. In the frenetic light of the well-stoked fireplace, she somehow looked regal in stretch pants and a bulky sweater that would have made a perfect fashion statement in Telluride.

"Mrs. Darmond," Jonathan said. "How nice to see that you're not dead."

Irene shifted in her seat. "Jesus, Scorpion."

Jonathan's preferred seat in this section of his office was a wooden rocking chair marked with his name and the Seal of the College of William and Mary. After too many back injuries to count over the years, it was the only chair that reliably gave him the support he needed. No one else ever sat in his rocker.

"Okay, Yelena, let's have it," he said, settling in and crossing his legs. "How come your Secret Service detail is dead and you're not?" He used her old name in a deliberate effort to get a rise, but no one in the room flinched. If anything, the First Lady merely looked bored.

Behind him, he heard the rattle of glasses from the bar as Boxers helped himself.

"I know what you think of me, Mr. Grave," Yelena said. "Director Rivers has told me everything. I understand your anger, but I assure you that it is misplaced. I am not a murderer, and I am not plotting any terrorist schemes."

"Yet here you are hiding, when you could be lounging in the middle of the most secure cocoon in the universe."

The squeak of a cork told him that Boxers was going for the good stuff, and then the faintest aroma of peat confirmed that he'd selected scotch.

"Security cuts both ways, Mr. Grave," Yelena said.

"Digger."

"As you wish. But great fortresses make great prisons."

Jonathan rolled his eyes. "Promise me you're not going to whine about the loneliness of the bubble."

A glass bearing two fingers of Lagavulin arrived from over his right shoulder. In Boxers' hands, the tulip glass looked more like a shot.

"You need to hear her out, Dig," Irene said and the Big Guy helped himself to the remaining club chair. "Open that big mind of yours."

Jonathan recognized her words as a rebuke and he dialed it back. "Okay, Yelena, the floor is yours."

"I prefer to be called Mrs. Darmond."

"And I prefer to be in bed at this hour." Jonathan took a sip of scotch. Liquid contentment. He knew he was being a shit, but it was calculated shittiness. He wanted her to be off balance. Enough people sucked up to her every whim. She needed to know that he was not among them.

Yelena looked to Irene. "Is it important that I be humiliated?"

"My office, my rules," Jonathan said.

Irene narrowed one eye, clearly annoyed. "If you think Digger's annoying, wait till you get to know Big Guy."

Boxers threw Irene a kiss and took a sip from his glass.

Yelena drew a deep breath, settled herself. "I am not planning terrorism," she said. "However, my husband is."

Jonathan recoiled. "You mean the president of the United States?"

"He is the only husband I have."

"Now, anyway," Boxers said. He responded to the angry glare with a shrug. "Hey, I'm just keeping it honest."

"And honesty is important, Mrs. Darmond," Jonathan said. "Irene wouldn't have brought you here if you didn't need my help. I'm not putting my life on the line for anyone who doesn't tell me the complete truth. I don't care who they are, or what their husbands do for a living."

"I'm not asking you to risk anything," Yelena objected.

"Uh-huh," Jonathan said. "Now, who is President Darmond planning to terrorize?"

"I understand that you've already seen the drawings."

Jesus, was there anything Irene hadn't told her?

"I've seen a lot of drawings," Jonathan acknowledged. "Bridges, tunnels, a building here and there."

"The airliner that was shot down at O'Hare," Yelena said. "That was him."

"Bullshit," Jonathan said. The word was out before he could stop it. He conceded that Darmond was a disaster as a president, but come on. "Why would he do that?"

Her answer came with a shrug that indicated it was the most obvious answer in the world. "Because his numbers are down." The sibilant *s* got special emphasis with her accent.

"You mean poll numbers?" Venice asked, clearly aghast.

"Yes, poll numbers," Yelena said. "His popularity. We are coming up on an election year, no?"

"Interesting strategy," Boxers said with a laugh. "Vote for me or I'll bomb your neighborhood. Has that ever worked? Outside of Chicago, I mean?"

Yelena continued. "Every president profits from crisis. Every president wishes he could have been in office for Pearl Harbor or 9/11, to be the subject of such unity and patriotism. Every president wants a *Grand Moment*." She leaned on those last words.

Jonathan had occasionally thought that presidents thought such things, but hearing them verbalized by a president's wife took him to a dark place. "Ma'am, attacking your own countrymen is hardly—"

"It is not about the attack," Yelena interrupted. "It is about the response. It is about victory over an enemy."

That was exactly the rationale he would have expected. And given the president's track record for scandal, maybe it made some degree of sense, but good God. Jonathan decided on a different tack. "How do you know this?" he asked. "How does he plan to make it work?"

"I don't know the workings," she said. "But I know he is desperate about his poll numbers. America has stopped liking him."

"All respect, you're not helping much," Boxers said.

"I stopped liking him years ago. Everybody knows that. We hardly make it a secret. But I am not responsible for the bad economy or the big debt or the scandals in the administration. Tony—the president—is responsible for all that, and the people are angry."

Jonathan understood that anger all too well. In fact he'd been up close and personal with more of the scandals than he cared to think about.

"With a big national emergency, people will stop thinking about those things. They will start thinking about the emergency."

Jonathan asked, "So, what makes you think he's planning an attack on his own country?"

Yelena's response came quickly: "You thought I was going to do that—attack my own country. Why is it so difficult to think that the president might do the same thing?"

Boxers answered without dropping a beat. "Because he's the president of the United States and you're a dissident imposter who's been living a lie for decades."

Jonathan shot him an angry glare.

"What, like you're not thinking the same thing?"

Yelena's features reddened.

Irene said, "Come on, guys. A little civility here."

Jonathan got it. "Sorry, Mrs. Darmond, but we've dedicated a lot of energy to the proposition that you're the bad guy. That's only after we were told by Douglas Winters and Ramsey Miller that you had been kidnapped. Now you're telling us that the president is planning a terrorist attack. That's a lot of whiplash."

He gave her a few seconds to let it sink in.

"You mentioned Douglas Winters," Yelena said. "It was through him that I found out about Tony's plot."

"The White House chief of staff," Jonathan said. He just needed to be sure.

"Gettin' better and better," Boxers said.

"I overheard him talking with a man about the lack of security around bridges and tunnels and other infrastructure around the country. At first, I thought it might be some kind of security briefing, but the tone was wrong. There was excitement in his voice. Enthusiasm. It struck me as odd so I listened more, and it continued the same way."

"Was he on the phone or in person?" Jonathan asked.

"In person. Someone in a meeting."

"Who?" Irene asked.

"I don't know. The door was closed, but not all the way." As those words left her mouth, her eyes shifted, ringing a warning bell for Jonathan.

"*Where* did this happen?" he asked.

Hesitation. "That does not matter."

"Yeah, actually it does," Jonathan said. "Let the record show that my job was to find you, and here you are. You're free to leave and let me go to bed right now if you'd like. But if there's more, mine are the only rules that count. Either come off all the details or go home. I don't care which."

Yelena looked to Irene for help.

"Officially, I'm not even here," Irene said. "None of us are. If we go official, I need to arrest you for the murder of a lot of people at the Wild Times."

"But I didn't do those things."

Irene shrugged a gesture of helplessness. "I don't make the rules, I merely enforce them. You say you're innocent, and I happen to believe you. We're here in the first place *because* I happen to believe you. But that doesn't matter."

"So, you would put me in jail?"

"I'd have to, because I'm paid to believe in the system. If you're innocent, then either the prosecutors would not be able to prove their case, or your defense team would be able to uncover the truth."

Yelena looked pained, deep creases appearing over her eyes. "But if the government is involved . . ." She let the words trail away.

"This isn't your first trip to the dance," Irene said. The deference had suddenly disappeared from her tone. "Scorpion and his team are the best at what they do, and what they do is all done under the radar. If you want help from me, you have to sit in jail. You want help from him, you stay free. The choice is yours."

Yelena shifted her gaze to Jonathan. "That is not much choice," she said.

He smiled. "The details, Yelena. All of them."

"Please stop calling me by that name."

The room waited for her answer.

The First Lady folded her hands on her lap and rocked ever so slightly back and forth in her chair. Finally, she blurted, "We were at a hotel."

Boxers reflexively coughed out something like a laugh. "Uh-oh."

That pretty much said it all.

"You and Winters?" Jonathan asked, just to be sure. "Together?"

Yelena started to answer, then shrugged. "What can I say? The rumors are true."

Jonathan looked to Venice. "There were rumors?"

She nodded.

"Why didn't we talk about this?"

"There are a lot of rumors about Mrs. Darmond that we didn't talk about," Venice said. "Actually, the rumors say that you and Douglas Winters have been having an affair off and on for many years."

"But no one could find enough evidence to make the accusations stick," Yelena said. "We have long been friends. That does not mean that we have long been lovers."

"But have you?"

She sat straighter in the chair. "We were that night, yes."

"I don't understand," Irene said. Clearly, she was hearing details for the first time as well. "How can you be in the same hotel room and not know who Winters was talking to?"

"It was a big room," Yelena said. "Several rooms, actually. A suite at the Apex. And because of, well, propriety, we arrived at different times. I showed up earlier than expected, and they were in one of the bedrooms. I listened from the living room. When it sounded like the meeting was breaking up, I ran to the other bedroom and closed the door."

"Why?" Jonathan asked. "Why wouldn't you want to confront a credible suspicion of terrorism? You're the First Lady of the United States."

"I was concerned for my safety."

"Bullshit," Boxers said. "You travel with an army of bodyguards."

Yelena shook her head. "Not that day. I had shaken them all off. I've gotten pretty good at that."

Jonathan wanted something to make sense. "So, this guy you're having an affair with. You thought he was going to kill you?"

"I didn't know what to think. The subject matter was so startling. It was the last thing I expected to hear. At a moment like that, everything changes. Suddenly, you begin to question if what you'd always assumed to be black was in fact white. I didn't know what to think. So, yes, in that moment, I was frightened. If not of Douglas, then of whoever he was talking with."

"After you darted back to the other room," Irene said, "did you peek out of the door to see who was leaving?"

"Ultimately, yes. But not at first. Not until I was certain that they would not see me at the door. By the time I looked, the man was nearly at the door. All I saw was the back of his head. He had gray hair, that's all I can tell you. Same height as Douglas and maybe a little heavier, but not much."

"He didn't look familiar at all?"

"It was the back of his head. Backs of heads are backs of heads."

"So then what?" Jonathan asked. "How do you go from hiding to stepping out to greet Douglas?"

"I took a shower," she said. "When I came out of the shower, I told him that I had arrived early and that when I heard he was in the middle of a meeting, I decided to leave him alone."

"How did he handle that?"

Yelena thought before answering. "He seemed . . .

nervous. He didn't ask me outright if I had overheard his conversation, but he went all around it. When I asked him who he was talking to, he said it was a work matter. Those were his words. A work matter."

"How long ago was this?" Jonathan asked.

She pondered. "About six weeks. When I asked him who he was meeting with, he told me that it would be inappropriate to say. He implied that it was a national security matter. But that was bullshit, of course." It came out *bool sheet*, causing Jonathan to smile. "We were meeting for a tryst. Who would invite official business for that?"

"Who would invite a terrorist?" Jonathan countered.

"He didn't expect me for a half hour. This was a good off-the-record place to meet. In official offices, records are kept of who comes and who goes. Records are kept of phone calls. In hotels, especially in hotels like the Apex, people make a point of not noticing who comes and goes."

"But how do you do that?" Venice asked. "Your face has been on every magazine cover in the world."

Finally, a smile from the First Lady. "Thanks to the Marshals Service, I have become very accomplished with disguises over the years. You'd be surprised what a wig and different eyebrows will do. Throw in a pair of glasses and maybe some prosthetic teeth, and you can be a whole different person in less than fifteen minutes."

"Let's get back to the original track," Jonathan said. "Let's go back to the night before last at the Wild Times Bar. What was that about?"

"I have to go back even further," Yelena said. "That

night when I heard the conversation, I tried a couple more times to get Douglas to expand on what he was talking about, but the harder I pushed, the more uncomfortable he became. To the point of being angry. So I stopped pushing. But in what I heard, it sounded to me like Douglas was pointing to something, as if he had documents or even diagrams. Referring to something as he spoke. The next morning, I woke up early and I sneaked over to that other room."

She looked up at Boxers. "Yes, we slept in the same bed, not in separate rooms."

Big Guy showed no emotion at all.

"I looked all around, but I didn't see anything. I tried to be quiet, but you have to make some noise just to sift through things. I found his briefcase, but it was locked. I was trying to get into it when I heard Douglas moving around. I quickly put everything down and went back out to the living room. I was back out there before Douglas came out of the room, but I think he suspected I was up to something. He asked me what I was doing and I told him that I was just restless.

" 'Why are you acting so strangely?' he asked me. I told him that I don't know what he is talking about. I made some excuse why I needed to be back at the White House, and then we get dressed and leave.

"Nothing was the same after that. We would meet, but he would always be nervous. In between time, I called old friends, Albert Banks and Steven Gutowski. We met for lunch at the White House and when I told them what I thought was going on, they said I should call the FBI." She glanced at Irene.

"Did you?" Irene asked with a defensive edge to her voice.

"What would I say? Already, I am considered a liability to my husband. The press and the White House staff all think I am crazy. If I make an accusation like this, the best thing that would happen is that no one would listen. Worst thing . . . well, I don't know. My friends tell me that I should tell my protection detail, but it's the same problem there. No one would listen. I need proof."

"Are you getting to the computer files soon?" Jonathan asked.

"Yes, exactly," Yelena said. "Three nights ago, Douglas and I meet again. Different hotel, but we spend the night. I begin to think that maybe I am crazy. But that afternoon, as I walked into the hotel—remember I am in disguise—I saw a man I have not seen in many years. Dmitri Boykin was walking across the lobby from the elevator to the front door."

"Let me guess," Jonathan said. "Gray hair, same height as Douglas Winters and maybe a little heavier."

"Yes. Exactly."

"I sense that we all should have gasped when you said that name," Jonathan said. "But I don't get it. Who is he?"

"Russian mafia," Irene said. "Former GRU, bosom buddies to the old Soviet network. Deeply committed to anything that hurts the US. Great friend to Iran, great friend to Syria, and we suspect strong ties to Venezuela. Cuba goes without saying."

Jonathan felt a chill. "You're suggesting that this was the man Winters was meeting with?"

"Exactly," Yelena said.

"It'd be a hell of a coincidence otherwise, wouldn't it?" Boxers said.

Jonathan sat back in his chair. The potential enormity was just beginning to dawn on him.

Yelena continued, "So when I got up to the room that afternoon, something was very wrong with Douglas. He was pale. He looked shaken. I thought maybe he was having a heart attack. No, he said, he just had to think some things through. But his hands were shaking. I asked what I could do and he said nothing. He said that he was going to take a shower before dinner."

Yelena stopped her narrative and looked to the ceiling, as if for support. "That's when I went through his pockets and found the flash drive. I didn't know if it was anything, but it was all I could find. It was in an inside, inside pocket of his suit coat, and I took it and put it in my purse. When he came out of the shower, I talked him into doing room service and eating in the hotel's bathrobes. Just as a way to keep him from finding out what I'd done.

"The next morning, I left before he was awake. Back at the residence in the White House, I tried opening files, but I couldn't. I just knew, though, that the evidence I needed was there. So I called Steve Gutowski and we agreed that we would meet at the Wild Times that night, where I would give the flash drive to him. He is a computer genius. He brought Albert Banks with him. And, of course, because of everything that was happening, I brought my Secret Service detail with me. But it was a very small detail.

"I gave the flash drive to Steve, who had brought a laptop with him, so he made a copy for Albert. Between the two of them, we were sure we would find out what was on the drives. When that was done, we partied for a while longer, and then my Secret Service detail insisted that it was time to leave."

"What happened when the shooting started?" Jonathan asked.

Her eyes glazed with tears. "That was terrible. Those poor people. The shooting started when I was nearly to the car. It started with an explosion, and then I was pushed and shoved and I don't know what all happened. I found myself back inside the bar, and then Steve had his arm around me, and we were on our way out the back door. We sneaked away in all the confusion."

The room remained silent for the better part of a minute when someone knocked lightly on the door.

Boxers opened it to reveal Sam Franco standing on the other side.

"I'm sorry to interrupt," he said. "But two people downstairs say they have to see you right now."

Jonathan cocked his head.

"Their names are David and Becky."

CHAPTER EIGHTEEN

"Dad! There's—" Josef's words were cut short by what sounded like a slap.

In the fog of the assault, Nicholas couldn't react fast enough. He raised his hands to fight his attackers, but a kick to his testicles followed by a blow to his belly made his knees sag.

The men said nothing, but when they spoke, it was in Russian. Just a few words at a time. They worked with what seemed to be a practiced efficiency. They slipped a hood over his head, and cinched it in place. Even as that was happening, they planted a foot in his back and stretched his arms painfully behind him. He knew from the sound and the feel that the bindings on his wrists were handcuffs, but then it felt as if they'd wrapped another length of rope around his elbows.

In less than fifteen seconds, he'd been completely immobilized.

"Where is Josef?" Nicholas grunted. They kicked him again in the balls, but they wouldn't let him fall. "Please don't hurt my boy," he said. "He's only thirteen. He's done nothing." Nicholas had done nothing wrong, either, but he'd confess to the crucifixion of Jesus if would spare his boy this kind of treatment.

They'd *hit* Josef, for God's sake. Men beating on a little boy. How could anyone—

Still without a word exchanged between them, the attackers pulled on the rope at his neck, leading him out of his bedroom and into the hallway.

"Josef!" Nicholas cried. "Joey! Are you—"

This time the punch landed in his right kidney, hard enough to make him think that something had maybe ruptured. It was a command to be silent.

"Joey!"

The next punch had to have broken a rib. The pain from the kidney shot lit up his entire torso, from his hip to his shoulder.

"Dad!" It came more as a shriek than a word, and it sounded muffled. The boy yelped in pain after that and fell silent.

But at least he was alive.

And Nicholas was powerless to protect him.

He fought the urge to beg for mercy. Not only would it be useless, but it would give even more of an upper hand to these brutes who already held all the cards. Whatever was going on, Nicholas would be even less a protector—no, he'd become a burden—if he were crippled by these people.

They led him from the front, pulling on the rope as if he were a recalcitrant dog on a leash. Because he'd walked this path countless times over the years, he knew to expect the stairs, but they still arrived before he was ready. A captor in the rear grabbed the triangle formed by his bound arms to keep him falling face-first, but the pace never slowed.

He reflexively counted the thirteen steps to the tile foyer. It all felt so cold on his bare chest and bare feet. He wondered if they'd left the door open.

Then he was outside, surrounded by cold. Combined with the fear, it triggered convulsive shivers. He wanted to ask where they were taking him, and whether they were taking Josef to the same place, but he realized the futility.

Nicholas told himself that there was no reason to kill Josef. Whatever this was about, it had to be Nicholas that they were angry with. Josef was merely—what? In the way, perhaps.

He hadn't realized that it had snowed until they marched him through it. It didn't feel more than ankle deep, but after only a few frigid steps, his feet started to cramp from the cold.

Good God, was Josef enduring this same treatment? This same fear and this same pain? He knew they had struck him, but how hard? Was he still conscious?

Was he still—

No. Don't go there.

It made no sense to consider the worst outcome until he had some idea of what was going on.

Among the thousands of thoughts that raced through his head as his body tried to adjust to the cold and the pain, the one that registered more clearly than any other was how angry Marcie was going to be when she found out what had happened during Josef's visit to his father.

The thought brought sadness, and the sadness displaced much of his fear. If Nicholas had been a better father, they would still be a family. And if they were still a family, then none of this would have happened. If he were a stronger man, he would be fighting back and his son would be safe.

His kidnappers pulled him to a stop, and then he was airborne, lying faceup in the air with hands firmly around his torso and his legs. They were lifting him.

Seconds later, air barked out of his lungs as they dropped him roughly onto a hard surface. He landed on his side, and as his handcuffs hit the floor, he heard a metallic clank. Metal on metal. And the surface felt corrugated. It felt as if he were on the floor of a van. Or a workingman's truck.

Panic seized his gut as he thought through the possibilities. They could take him anywhere. Or they could push the vehicle over a cliff, or they could set it on fire with him inside.

Whatever it was, he would be powerless—

He felt something sharp hit his thigh, and then he felt the spreading coldness that could only come from an injection.

Then he felt nothing at all.

Yelena looked confused. "Who are David and Becky?"

Jonathan explained. "According to the man who tried to kill them, they were collateral damage." He gave a brief recap of his interview with the two assassins, leaving out the gory details.

"Do I want to know how you got them to give all of that up?" Irene asked when he was done.

"You know where your people took them, right?" Jonathan asked.

Irene looked at the floor.

"Then you know how we got them to talk. If it makes a difference, I had nothing to do with the methods chosen."

He shifted his attention back to the First Lady. "So, Mrs. Darmond. Where have you been and what have you been doing since the time of the shooting at the Wild Times?"

"I've been trying to get my bearings," she said. "Trying to make sense of the world. In the confusion after the shootings, Steve and Albert rushed me out a back door. I gave them each a copy of the files I couldn't decode, and they dropped me off out in the suburbs, in a Hampton Inn."

This time it was Venice. "Oh, come on. You mean you checked into a hotel and no one recognized you?"

"I already told you," Yelena said. "I'm very good at disguises." She paused and took a deep breath. "Then, the next morning, when I was watching the news, I heard that DeShawn Lincoln had been killed and I started to panic."

Jonathan kept his poker face. "Who's DeShawn Lincoln?" he baited.

"He's a DC cop," she said. "Was. Such a shame. He was friends with Steve, who probably told him more than he should have. We were just so desperate to find out what our options were. Steve told him what we suspected was going on, and he, DeShawn, promised to keep an eye out. Then, what happened happened, and DeShawn ended up killed.

"I tried calling Steve when I heard the news, and when I couldn't get through, I knew something terrible had happened to him, too. I called Albert Banks, and he had already heard about Steve and he was in a panic. The White House knew what we were trying to do, and they'd put the Secret Service up to cleaning us all out. I was terrified."

Irene said, "We're all here, right now, because I got a call from General Grand, chief of staff of the Army. He told me that he had heard from Mrs. Darmond that there was trouble. In fact, he called it a dire threat to the nation."

"So why are you in Fisherman's Cove instead of in some situation room somewhere?" Jonathan asked. "Why haven't you activated some counterterrorism task force to expose the plot and bring the bad guys to justice?"

Irene said, "Accusations are not evidence. If we were to come forward with what we have, the administration would merely deny everything, cancel whatever they had in motion, and make us a laughingstock. And as a flag officer in the United States Army, General Grand would be guilty of high treason."

Whatever burden Jonathan was feeling before quadrupled. "So, again. Why are you here?"

A long pause.

Irene broke the silence. "You're a patriot's patriot," she said. "We knew you could provide a safe haven."

"And then what?" Venice asked.

"That's where it starts to get sketchy," Irene said with a smile that was clearly designed to disarm.

A double-tap knock on the door prompted Boxers to rise and open it.

David and Becky stood on the other side, and they both looked like hammered shit.

"Welcome back," Jonathan said. "Did you have a nice escape?"

David led the way into the library. "Oh, man," he said. "You wouldn't believe—" He caught his first glimpse of the First Lady and stopped so abruptly that Becky collided into him.

"Oh. My. God," he said.

It took only a few more seconds for the color to drain from Becky's face. "Mrs. Darmond?" she said.

Yelena flashed the smile that the tabloids knew so well. "The one and only." She extended her hand.

Becky took it in both of hers. "It's an honor to meet you," she said. "But I'm so sorry about your family."

Yelena's face turned to stone as everyone in the room froze. "What about my family?"

"Oh, shit," David said. "You don't know."

Yelena stood. For the first time, Jonathan saw real emotion in her eyes. And the emotion was fear. "What about my family?"

David seemed shocked to be delivering the news. "Your son," he said. "Nicholas. He's been kidnapped."

CHAPTER NINETEEN

"**W**ho?" Yelena asked. Her tone was just this side of panic. "Who kidnapped him?"

"A Russian," David said. "That's all I know."

"And how do you know that?" Irene asked.

For the first time, David took in the faces he saw in the room. His shoulders and jaw both sagged in unison. "Holy God," he said. "Are you Director Rivers? Of the FBI?"

"I was this morning." She shot a look to Jonathan. *Can I trust him?*

Jonathan shrugged. *We'll find out together.*

"I believe you have the advantage," Irene said as she shook hands.

"Huh? Oh. My name is David. David Kirk. I work for the *Washington Enquirer*."

"Oh, shit." That came out before Irene could stop it.

Jonathan tried to defuse the moment. "And this is Becky Beckeman," he said. "Also with the *Enquirer*. For what it's worth, they have both pledged not to report anything of what they see."

Yelena connected the dots in her head. "You're the

boy Mr. Grave was telling me about. You knew Officer Lincoln."

David brightened. "You knew Deeshy?"

She demurred. "In a manner of speaking. Please tell me about my family."

Davis fished a reporter's notebook out of his back pocket. "I'm really sorry to have been so blunt," he said as he fished through for the right page. "We're talking about Nicholas Mishin, right?"

Yelena paled and sat heavily in her chair.

"Okay," David said. "Well, my source told me—"

"Stop there," Jonathan commanded.

David's head snapped up.

"Names," Jonathan said. "At this stage, we need names. Who is your source?"

David looked to Becky, who looked at a spot on the ceiling. It took the better part of a half-minute for him to search his conscience. Jonathan got that he was conflicted, but he also got that there were too many secrets on the table now to start holding back selectively.

"It's a guy in the White House press office," he said, finally. "His name is Billy."

"Billy Zanger?" Yelena said. She seemed startled.

"Yes, ma'am," David said. "He told me that they'd just gotten word. Apparently, you were—" He stopped himself.

"Candor, Mr. Kirk," Irene said. "That's really all we've got at this point."

He nodded. "Okay. Apparently, you were supposed to be killed last night," he said to the First Lady. "That, or you were supposed to be brought back to the White House. That was Douglas Winters's preference, so you know. Being brought back, I mean."

"How does this Bobby what's-his-name know this?" Jonathan asked.

"Billy Zanger," David said. "And I don't know how he knows. I forgot to ask him."

"But he's telling the truth," Becky added. "I could tell. He was like totally relieved to get this off his chest. I think he's really scared."

"Billy Zanger is Douglas's press liaison," Yelena explained. "They work very closely with each other. The two of them thought each other's thoughts."

"All well and good," Jonathan said. "But what does this kidnapping have to do with anything?"

Becky said, "It was some kind of quid pro quo. Billy said he didn't understand the details, but apparently the kidnapping was in retaliation for something Mrs. Darmond had done. Billy didn't know what that was."

But Jonathan did. Except for the latecomers, the entire population of the room knew. The kidnapping had been triggered by the First Lady's decision to spirit the flash drive out of the White House.

Jonathan looked to Wolverine. "This sounds like a job for your shop," he said.

"Do you have any idea where they took them?" Irene asked.

David shook his head. "No. But Billy seemed to think that it would be out of the country."

"Shit," Jonathan said. "Any idea where? Even which country?"

David looked down at his feet. "No," he said. "I'm sorry I don't."

Yelena scanned the group with her gaze. "We have to get him back," she said. "He has my grandson with him this week."

"Oh, damn," Boxers said. He wasn't all that fond of small children, but he had a special hatred for those who abused them.

"How old is he?" Jonathan asked.

"Josef is thirteen," Yelena said. "And a half."

Jonathan nodded as he considered the ramifications. At that age, kids were far from rational, but they were able to respond to commands and participate in their own rescue. That was a good thing.

"Where were they kidnapped from?" Jonathan asked David.

Yelena answered, "Vail. In Colorado. David has a home out there." She took a deep, shaky breath. "They must be terrified. We have to get them back."

Easier said than done, Jonathan didn't say. "First, we have to figure out where they are." He looked to Wolverine. "Is this your op or is it mine?"

"So far, I don't have a vector into the case," Irene said. "If this goes international, it all gets very complicated."

"We should call the police," Yelena said. "They should be out looking for them."

"Did this Billy guy give any indication of how long ago the snatch went down?" Jonathan asked David.

"We were waiting for him when he got back to his house at about one this morning," David said. "And by then, it was already a done deal."

"And why didn't *they* call the police?" Venice asked.

David cleared his throat. "From what I could tell, the police are the last people that any of them want to talk to."

Jonathan faced the First Lady. "Mrs. Darmond, think. Does any of this make sense to you? Do you have any idea who would want to put you in this kind of jeopardy?"

Yelena closed her eyes and inhaled deeply. With her eyes still closed, she said, "You seem to know about my past, Mr. Grave. If that is the case, then you know there are a great many people who would want to hurt me through my family."

"Does any one of them float to the top?"

She waited long enough to answer that Jonathan thought she was formulating a lie. "Dmitri Boykin would be one," she said.

And just like that, it all came home. "I'm hearing that name a lot," Jonathan said. "Do you want to tell us the rest of the story?"

She closed her eyes again and seemed to transport herself to a different place. As she spoke, her cheek muscles tightened, creating a countenance of pain. "Back then," she said. "Back before, when we were all dissidents, Dmitri was among the worst of the worst. While I wanted to bring down institutions, he wanted to kill people. He believed, I think, that the Soviet Union could be avenged through violence in America. I think he never grew past that."

"I'm sorry, ma'am," Irene interrupted, "but that's too easy. I don't recall a mention of this Dmitri Boykin in any of your testimony."

Yelena's eyes opened. "I might not have mentioned him," she said.

"Might?"

"I did not mention him."

"But your deal with the government—"

"I know what my deal was, Director Rivers. I signed it, remember? I gave you everyone else. *Everyone* else.

But Dmitri was different. He was a crazy man. Capable of anything. And by then, I was a mother and I had greater concerns. I always worried that he would—"

The words caught in her throat, and she dislodged them with a cough. "Come after my family." She finished the sentence at barely a whisper.

Irene leaned in closer to Yelena. "Mrs. Darmond, this is the time to be one hundred percent forthcoming. We cannot help you if you don't give us all of the details."

"I don't have details," Yelena said. "It's been too long. Your predecessors wanted me to turn on the co-conspirators I worked with, and I did that. Except for Dmitri. He was just too connected and too unpredictable. Even if he was in prison, he would have found a way to get even."

"Was this a negotiated arrangement?" Jonathan asked. "Did you make a deal with him that if you withheld his name he would give you a pass?"

"I wish it had been that direct," Yelena said. "I was young and stupid and scared. I thought that if I just didn't mention him he wouldn't come looking for me."

Venice asked, "Have you been in touch with him at all since then?"

Yelena shook her head. "No. Of course, as the campaign kicked in, and I got more and more exposure on the news, I knew that he would see it and that there might be repercussions, but there was never a confrontation."

"Didn't that surprise you?" Jonathan asked.

She considered the question. "No, not really." She paused to reconsider. "Well, yes and no. I knew that he would be aware of the fact that he had a pressure point against me and by extension against my husband, but I also thought he would see that as his free pass for the rest of his life. Which it could have been."

"You let a murderer go," Boxers summarized, "so that you could feel safe."

Yelena seemed ready to do battle for just an instant, and then she calmed herself. "Do you have children, Mr. . . ." she clearly had forgotten his name.

"None that I know of," Boxers replied. "But if I did, I'd be sure to set a good example."

"What you'd do is protect them," Yelena said. "And you'd do it at any cost."

Her answer could not have been a more perfect way to disarm the Big Guy.

Yelena went to a place in her head that did not include anyone in the room. In the accompanying silence, Jonathan felt his anger swell.

"Yelena," he said, deliberately reverting to the name she didn't like, "you've been deceitful tonight, and I don't appreciate it."

She looked offended.

Jonathan leaned in close to the First Lady. It was a gesture designed to make her pull back. She responded just as she was supposed to. "You just finished walking us through this song and dance," Jonathan said, "about a gray-haired man who met with Douglas Winters and happened to turn out to be Dmitri Boykin. And through that entire story, you knew that this guy had a vendetta against you and your family. If David and Becky here had not come forward with the fact of their kidnapping, you would have kept that to yourself."

Yelena's eyes had a hard time finding a spot to settle

on as she worked through the accusation. "It's not like that," she said. "You don't understand—"

"I understand that you're a woman of many secrets, ma'am, and that when you live with secret upon secret, life becomes extraordinarily complicated. But that's never an excuse to lie to the people who may very well be the only allies you have left in the world."

Yelena made a waving motion with both hands. "I didn't think—"

Jonathan turned to Irene. "Okay, Wolverine, what are our options?"

Irene took a deep breath and looked to the newcomers. "David, is it?"

"Yes, ma'am."

"Did this Billy person say anything to you about a ransom, or conditions for release?"

David cleared his throat. "I actually asked that," he said. "Or essentially that. Billy didn't know."

That made perfect sense to Jonathan. "Their demand is to be left alone," he said. "And the First Lady's family is the leverage to make that happen. That means that this Dmitri guy doesn't know that you're not in the White House, ma'am."

Yelena scowled.

"If he thought you were on the run, as you are, he wouldn't assume that the president's chief of staff would have any sway in this. Winters couldn't talk to someone who wasn't there."

Jonathan asked Irene, "Can't you put HRT on this?" The FBI's Hostage Rescue Team.

"Where would I put them?" she asked. "We can check out the family's residence in Vail. I guess we should do that anyway, but there's really not much doubt what we're going to find."

"And there's the fact of the law enforcement connection," Paul Boersky said, his first statement of the evening. "The whole reason we brought Scorpion into this in the first place was the fear that we couldn't trust our own to keep things secret."

"I think that horse has left the barn, hasn't it?" Venice asked.

"Not necessarily," Jonathan said. "It's your call, Wolfie—my job is already done—but if the control of information is the endgame here, I'm thinking it might be a mistake to involve the real authorities too soon. They leak. You and I both know that."

"The whole world knows that," Boxers said. "Our enemies all count on it."

Irene rubbed her eyes, then looked at Yelena. "Ma'am, how much of this do you imagine that the president knows?"

Yelena shook her head slowly. "Tony and I have literally not spoken in two months. Not even hello in the morning. I have no idea what he knows."

"Is he close to your son?" Venice asked.

"Oh, good heavens, no. They hate each other." After the words were out, Yelena retreated. "By that, though, I don't mean to imply that he would consider hurting them."

"Good heavens no," Boxers mocked.

"You know," Irene said, "I think it speaks volumes that my cell phone has not been going crazy with reports of the kidnapping. Especially given that the White House knows."

"What are you suggesting?" Jonathan asked.

"I'm suggesting nothing," Irene said. "I'm merely observing. And at this point, my observations are leading me to believe that Scorpion is correct. It may well be too early to involve official Washington in any of this."

Yelena's face became a mask of disbelief. "But what about my family?"

"We'll get them back for you," Jonathan said.

"There's the words I've been dreading," Boxers grumbled.

"How?" Yelena and others asked in unison.

Jonathan smiled as he looked at Venice. "Let me get back to you on the specifics," he said. "After we do a little research."

Venice groaned. When Jonathan said *we* he actually meant *she*.

Venice held up a finger, as if to point to the lightbulb that had appeared over her head. She looked to Irene. "Do you remember that Yelena's group had a sleeper cell in Canada?" she asked.

Irene scowled, scanning her memory. Then she saw the same lightbulb. "Toronto?"

"Ottawa. Yelena? Mrs. Darmond? Does this ring any bells?"

The First Lady's eyes grew large, as if she were considering a new detail for the first time. "Yes," she said. "Back then, it was easy to be anti-American if you were from Canada."

"Is that where this Dmitri guy comes from?" Jonathan asked.

"No," Yelena said. "But it would not be unreasonable for him to know about it. Personally, I have no idea if that cell even exists anymore."

"Which means that you have no idea that it went away, either," Boxers observed.

Yelena conceded the point with a combined shrug and nod.

Venice stood abruptly, startling Jonathan. "You all stay here," she said. "It shouldn't take more than an hour to decide if we have a reliable lead or if we're dead in the water."

"What does that mean?" Jonathan asked.

Venice's eyes flashed. "It means that I'm going to go do what I do best."

They all watched as Venice left the room. When she was gone, Jonathan said to the group, "More times than not, it's worth waiting around for the answer."

CHAPTER TWENTY

It actually took Venice less than thirty minutes, but in that time, Jonathan had managed to fall asleep. The Lagavulin had a part in that, but so did the absence of sleep in the past thirty-six hours.

"I've got it!" Venice announced, blasting into the office without warning. "Leonard Shaw," she said. "Does that name mean anything to you?" She didn't address the question to anyone in particular, but Jonathan assumed it was for Yelena.

No one said anything.

"Alexei Petrov," Venice said, and Yelena's face lit up.

"You know him," Jonathan said, observing the obvious.

"Alexei," she said. "Yes, he was a sweet boy. What does that have to do with Leonard . . . who?"

"Shaw," Venice said. "Leonard Shaw. He prefers to go by Len. That's Petrov's new name. He's a Canadian now."

More recognition on Yelena's features. "He was a Canadian then." She chuckled at something that passed through her mind. "A socialist to his soul, he never fully understood what to do with his feelings. He has changed his name?"

"So it seems," Venice said. "Quite some time ago."

Jonathan raised his hand, partly to poke fun, but mostly to give Venice a chance to shine. "Dare we ask how you determined this?" he asked. Not everyone understood how thoroughly she terrorized electrons with her computer skills, and he thought a showcase was important for her credibility.

Venice explained. "After I scanned through the various drawings we pulled off the data retrieved from Banks, I briefly scanned what you sent me from Vasily and Pyotr. I remembered a reference to Ottawa, which didn't mean anything to me until David mentioned an international connection. I just worked backward until I found an e-mail about a visit to go see Len Shaw."

As she paused for a breath, Jonathan said, "This is the part that I always like. Wait till you see how she connected the dots." He said this in full confidence, having no idea how she in fact connected the dots.

Venice continued, "I matched Len Shaw with Ottawa, and of course that didn't mean anything to me. So then I threw in the list of names from Mrs. Darmond's participation with the FBI way back when, and I found a record that showed that Alexei Petrov had changed his name to Len Shaw."

She stopped, clearly assuming that she'd explained everything. Recognizing the blank stares for what they were, she said, "Come on, how could that be a coincidence? I looked him up, and I found that he's become quite the real estate investor."

"Investor?" Irene prompted.

"Investor," Venice confirmed. "He's assembled quite a few properties over the years, all of them in the greater Ottawa area."

"Relevance?" Jonathan said.

"International," Venice said. "I don't know why, but I guess I assume that if they're going to take high-profile hostages, they're going to stay contiguous to the United States. I didn't find any Mexican references."

Thank God for that, Jonathan didn't say. He'd spent enough time south of the border, thank you very much.

"How about it, Yelena?" Jonathan asked. "Is this the connection we're looking for?"

Yelena looked to Irene. "Is Alexei with Dmitri now? I could see that happening."

"Don't look at me," Irene said. "This is Venice's show. I have no idea where she's going."

"Why could you see it happening?" Jonathan asked. He suspected that Venice had already divined all the answers, but sometimes it's best to absorb other stake-holders into a problem to embrace the obvious on their own.

"You need to remember when we were together," Yelena said. "We all thought that for the Soviet Union to thrive, the United States had to die. I don't know to this day if that was true. As it turns out, the Soviet Union is gone and the United States is still here."

"Congregation say halleluiah and amen," Boxers said.

Yelena continued as if she hadn't heard. "Alexei, as I recall, believed that everything the USA did was wrong. Everything. His family had Vietnam deserters living in their home. It was that kind of a house. Right around the time I was arrested, he fled back to Canada, knowing that no one would prosecute him there. I had no idea that he changed his name, though."

Jonathan asked, "Do you think he is capable of kidnapping?"

"Maybe," she said. "He was all about loyalty back then. Loyalty and action. If he felt that I betrayed him, maybe he could be moved to kidnap."

"I don't want to put too fine a point on this," Boxers said, "but didn't you in fact betray him? Didn't you betray all of your friends when you turned government witness?" He winked at Irene. "Not that there's anything wrong with that."

Irene acknowledged his wink with a smirk. For Boxers, there was no greater crime than turning your back on a friend.

Venice brought the conversation back on track. "If it's even remotely possible that he would participate in such a thing," she said, "I think that he's where you all need to focus your attention."

They all waited for her to answer her own riddle.

When the answer didn't come in a few seconds, Jonathan primed the pump. "Why is that?" he asked.

"Because one of the properties he owns is an abandoned prison," she said. A smile bloomed on her face as she took in the shocked looks.

"Yes, a prison," she clarified. "Saint Stephen's Reformatory. On Saint Stephen's Island in the middle of the Ottawa River. It used to be Canada's own little Alcatraz. According to the zoning applications, he's planning to turn it into a hotel."

"What a romantic getaway," Boxers said.

Venice ignored him. Again. "But I can't find any records that he's followed through on the plan."

"I don't get it," Irene said. "Are you suggesting that he bought that property with the idea of kidnapping Mrs. Darmond's children?"

"No," Venice said. "I'm suggesting that he bought the property to fund whatever he's interested in funding. The fact that it's still a prison merely plays into his hand. Think about it. It's in the middle of a river, accessible from a single bridge. If I were going to run a summer camp for would-be terrorists, I could think of worse places. A great place to make a last stand, if it came to that."

Jonathan felt a chill at the realization that they might be dealing with a fortress. The room fell quiet as everyone thought through what they'd been told.

"It makes too much sense to dismiss it," Jonathan said, breaking the silence. "But how do we confirm it?" His eyes drilled Irene. "Do you have influence over the satellite taskers?"

"Not without making all of this official," she said. "But my guys have Peter in custody now. We can try leaning on him a little harder. He was pretty talkative for you."

Irene pulled out her cell phone and pressed buttons.

Jonathan pivoted to face David and Becky. He made a V with his first two fingers and pointed at both of them simultaneously. "Honest to God, you two. You're seeing shit that you have no right to see. If even a hint of this appears in some newspaper—"

"I get it," David said. His tone was harsh, his words percussive. "You've made that point already."

Becky held up her hands in surrender. "Ditto. I understand."

Jonathan held his glare, gauging their sincerity. He liked what he saw: equal parts fear and indignation.

Jonathan turned to Venice. "Have you already talked with our friend down south?"

She nodded, knowing that he was referring to Lee Burns, a former unit colleague who owned the Skys-Eye satellite network, for which Jonathan paid an astronomical fee every year to have access to a view from above that nearly rivaled the imagery that Uncle Sam could produce through the NSA and the air force.

Venice said, "I've actually pulled up some interesting imagery in the War Room. If you—"

"I need to speak to you both outside," Boxers said. "Now."

From the tone alone, Jonathan knew what he wanted to talk about, and it was probably a conversation worth having.

"Excuse us," Jonathan said. He followed Boxers and Venice out into the area—he supposed you could call it a lobby—that separated their offices and the War Room.

The door to Jonathan's office had barely closed when Boxers said, "What are we about to do?"

"Launch a rescue mission," Jonathan said. "We're going to do what we're good at."

"At what cost?" Boxers said. Even at a whisper, his voice was louder than it should have been. He leaned down when he spoke, an effort to get close to their faces. "And I don't mean dollars. Do you see how many people we're about to bring into the circle? Reporters, for God's sake. Are you crazy?"

Eighty percent of Jonathan's professional life these days was lived outside the law. Not the *wrong* side, but the outside. Whenever the covert element of Security Solutions kicked into gear, the laws of any land became irrelevant. This meant that he and Boxers routinely broke laws, and that Venice was an accomplice every time they did it. OpSec was a critical concern.

"Look," Jonathan said, "Wolverine already knows what we do. She's been involved in half of the ops anyway."

"I'm not worried about her," Boxers said. "She's got skin in the game. If we testify, she's toast. That makes her trustworthy. But these others . . ." He let his voice trail away.

"I agree with Boxers," Venice said, words that rarely escaped her lips. "And that very fact should tell you something."

"It's a hint that life as we know it is about to end," Jonathan quipped, but it fell flat. "Okay, Big Guy, tell me what our alternative is."

He shrugged. "We just walk away. A day ago, Yelena Anna Poltanov friggin' Darmond was our precious cargo. She's the one we signed on to rescue. Okay, she's safe. We're done. Declare victory and walk away."

"And her son and grandkid?" Jonathan addressed that question to Venice, who looked away.

"You see?" Boxers griped. "That's your weapon. You use it all the time. You try to make it about the *people* and not about the *operation*. I hate that."

"But the operation *is* the people," Jonathan said.

Boxers' eye grew hot, no doubt because Jonathan was being deliberately obtuse. He knew exactly where

Big Guy was coming from. Back in the day when they did what they did under the auspices of Uncle Sam, the operation meant everything—trumping all of humanity except that of the team members. You did what you did to accomplish the mission, and if that meant trading your life for that of the PC, that was fine. The difference—the wild card—back then was that someone else chose the mission for you. These days, the risks were all hand selected, and when you started stacking them on top of each other, it could get daunting.

Jonathan looked to Venice. "You?"

He could almost see her brain racing for options behind her eyes, but nothing formed.

"If it helps," Jonathan said, "I'm not thrilled by the cast of characters, either. The First Lady is . . . well she's whatever the hell she is, but this is for her kids, so I don't worry too much about her."

"Which brings me back to my original point," Big Guy said. "The reporters. There's no such thing as a trustworthy journalist. And that's a lesson all three of us have learned the hard way."

"We've never been screwed by anyone whose life we've saved," Jonathan said. Something about the words amused him—the fact that the world could be divided into slices that actually included such a category.

He sensed Boxers' frustration. Apparently, Venice could, too, because she moved to lighten the mood. "There's another way to think of this," she said. "Dig, you already gave your fear-of-God speech, and they already know where we are and what we're doing. You saved their lives."

"They're *reporters*," Boxers growled. How could he make his point any clearer?

"And as long as they're here," Venice said, "they're controllable."

"You know they're going to want to come along, right?" Boxers said. "They're going to try some embed bullshit, and you're going to buy it."

"The bright side," Jonathan said. "Maybe they'll get shot."

"Not a bad idea."

"You're always free to say no," Jonathan said. As soon as the words were out, he knew he'd made a mistake.

Boxers swelled to his full height, and somehow more than his full girth. His face turned red as his jaw set. Boxers had never once refused to follow Jonathan into any Golf Foxtrot—goat fuck—and as often as not, Big Guy had been the reason why Jonathan had gotten to come home to do it again.

"I'm sorry," Jonathan said quickly. "That was cheap and it was wrong. I'm really, really sorry." He had no business throwing a passive-aggressive guilt trip on him. It wasn't even Jonathan's nature to do such a thing. "Chalk it up to being really tired."

Boxers held his anger long enough to make his point, and then he deflated. A little. "Just what we freaking need," he said. "Here we are about to invade Canada, and you're too tired to think straight."

CHAPTER TWENTY-ONE

Joey was cold. So very, very cold. And scared. Shivers consumed him, convulsing him from his feet to his shoulders.

He took a deep breath and held it, trying to get control. It didn't work. Well, maybe a little. He tried again.

His head hurt. Not in the way that it hurt when you had the flu, but the way it hurt after someone hit you really hard and made sparks fly behind your eyes. The stars were still there, if he looked for them, little colored spots that swam through the darkness in the space between his eyes and his brain.

When he first awoke, he thought maybe he was blind—it was that dark—and then he remembered them slipping the hood over his head. It was heavy and thick, and now that he thought about it, it made breathing more difficult, and that launched another bout of panic until he realized that breathing was breathing, and he was doing it.

Who were these people?

Somehow, he knew that this was about his father,

because the language the men were speaking in the room sounded like Russian. Joey didn't understand Russian, but he recognized the hard vowels and the gurgling throat sounds as the ones he heard when his dad spoke with his babushka—the lady who was married to the president of the United States, whom he wasn't supposed to talk about.

The floor moved and made him bounce. In that moment, Joey realized that he was in a car of some sort, and that it was moving. He wondered if he was in the trunk, and that thought triggered another flash of fear over running out of air. When you'd been kidnapped and beaten, it was really amazing how many things there were to be afraid of.

Why are they doing this to me?

That was the question of questions. He'd spent the entire evening gaming—and yes, exploring porn—but that was no reason to yank him out of bed and throw a sack over his head.

And why did they have to hurt him like that? They punched him in the balls and in the stomach and yanked his arms behind him, doing that stretchy thing that Simon Parker did in gym class that made your shoulders feel like they were going to pop right out of their sockets. And then they punched him in the head. Twice. At least twice.

Maybe it was because he was fighting back so well. He liked the thought of that. He liked the thought of being tough.

Unless that toughness pissed them off and made them decide to bury him alive in the trunk of a car with a sack over his head.

The shivering returned.

"Stop it," he said aloud. The sound of his own voice startled him.

"Josef?" a voice said. "Joey?"

"Dad?"

"Are you hurt, son?"

Joey nodded, and the nodding hurt his head. "Yes," he said. And right away, he knew it was the wrong thing. When you're being brave, you're supposed to say that everything is all right. "I'm okay," he added quickly.

"We're going to be fine," Dad said.

"What's happening? Why are they doing this? I'm scared."

"I'm scared, too, son. I don't know why this is happening. But we're going to be okay. I won't let anything happen to you."

For just the flash of an instant—the space of a heartbeat—Joey considered asking if his father's hands were also tied behind his back, and if so, how was he going to keep anything from happening to anybody. He didn't ask, though, because he knew that Dad was trying to be brave, too.

"Are we in a car?" Joey asked.

"I think it's a van," Dad said. "I think we're being taken someplace."

Joey felt his heart race. "Why? What did we do?"

A long silence followed.

What did we do? How do you answer a question like that when it's coming from a thirteen-year-old? Do you go for the harsh truth, or do you try to shield him?

When you're blindfolded and tied, the harshest truth was hard to shield.

"I don't think we did anything, son. Don't think that way. You did nothing wrong."

"Then why—"

"I don't know." Only a couple dozen words into this, and he'd already told his first lie. He had a good idea that this had something to do with his mother's past, but how could he say that when Josef didn't even know about that past?

"They were speaking Russian," Joey said. "Wasn't that Russian? Isn't that the language you and Babushka talk to each other in?"

"Yes."

"What were they saying?"

"You said you were hurt. Where are you hurt?" It was a deliberate change of subject, but a topic far more important than the lethal threats of Russian Mafia thugs.

"A little bit everywhere. My head and my cheek where they hit me, but that will be okay. Mostly it's my shoulders and wrists now."

"From being tied," Nicholas said.

"Why do they have to do it so tight?"

Because they're ruthless asshole bullies, Nicholas didn't say. "Maybe they'll loosen them soon."

Silence followed for the next minute or two, filled only with the hum of tires on the roadway, and the sound of his own breathing, amplified and warmed by the hood. If he were a better father—maybe a full-time father—he would know what to say to calm his son. He would tell a story or sing a soothing song. He'd do something other than tell a lie or just be silent.

"Are they going to kill us?" Joey asked. For the first time in months, he sounded like a little boy again.

"I won't let that happen," Nicholas said again. Another lie, because he believed that the truth was one hundred eighty degrees separated from the answer he'd just given. No guilt for that one, though. Some things didn't need to be said aloud.

It took a crazy kind of courage to kidnap the president's stepson—the kind of courage that he couldn't imagine would have a good outcome for the victims.

Enter, yet again, the face of bad parenting: Nicholas had been offered yet had turned down Secret Service protection for himself and his family. He wanted nothing to do with Tony Darmond or his policies or his lies, and he certainly hadn't wanted anything to do with his henchmen.

How's that one working out for you now, Nicky? He could almost hear Tony's mocking tone in his head, almost see the self-righteous smirk.

You didn't see much of that smirk during the last few years when Nicholas was leading the protests against the son of a bitch.

Come to think of it, after all of that, maybe Nicholas had earned some portion of the smirk he saw in his head.

So, now Nicholas's stubbornness was going to cost the life of his son. For all he knew, Marcie might have been swept up in this, too.

No, that didn't make sense. Whatever was happening, it had everything to do with Nicholas being related, however distantly, to the president of the United States.

"Will my hands have to be cut off because I can't feel them anymore?" Joey asked.

"Wiggle your fingers," Nicholas said. "Can you wiggle your fingers?"

"I think so, but they feel funny."

"Feeling is feeling. That's a good sign. Try moving your shoulders, too." He tried to tell himself that this discomfort had to end soon, but reality came knocking yet again. He'd heard stories of Russian mobsters who'd learned at the feet of the KGB, who'd learned at the feet of Stalin's torturers. The notion of taking mercy on children was an entirely Western notion. In the rest of the world, a boy was merely a future enemy, to be treated with the same brutality.

"How are we going to get away?" Josef asked.

Nicholas took a deep breath that turned out to be far noisier than he had expected. "If we find our chance, we have to take it," he said. "But you have to leave that to me, okay? Will you promise that you'll leave that to me?"

"I don't know what you mean."

"I mean that I want you to trust me on the timing of things. If I say let's run, we run. But if I don't, I don't want you running on your own. Okay?" Joey had always been impulsive, and he'd always been suspicious of authority. In his mind, Nicholas could see the boy bolting the instant that his hands were free, regardless of the likelihood of getting shot in the process. However this worked out, they would live together or they would die together. And if only one of them had to die, it would be Nicholas.

"I'll try," Josef said. "I promise that I'll try."

Nicholas heard the hedge loud and clear, and he admired it. Josef was far from a perfect kid—he got into too many fights, and he was incapable of keeping his mouth shut if someone pushed him too hard—but he was as scrupulously honest as a thirteen-year-old could be, and that was a great source of pride.

The van decelerated quickly, causing Nicholas to slide a few inches along the floor, and then it turned abruptly to the right, causing him to slide the other way.

"Whoa," Josef said. "What the fuck—" He abruptly cut off his words.

Nicholas ignored the transgression. They were being kidnapped. Profanity was allowed.

After the turn was completed, the roadway became rougher. The bumps caused Nicholas to bounce on the floor, and the landings ignited jabs of pain through his body.

"Just hang on, Joey," he said. "I think we're going off-road." He said that as if it were a good thing—or a neutral thing—when in fact, he couldn't think of a single positive outcome from being delivered to an off-road location.

The Russians had a long history of bad things happening in the woods. Just ask the Romanov family.

As the bumps got more severe, the vehicle seemed to slow, then finally stopped.

"What's happening?" Josef asked.

"Just try to stay calm," Nicholas said. "I don't know yet. Whatever it is, we can get through it."

Just a blink later, he heard the sound of the back doors opening, and the accompanying blast of cold air.

"You two still alive?" someone said. The accent was comically thick.

"No thanks to you," Nicholas said. The tough talk was for the benefit of his son. No boy wanted to hear his father snivel.

"Sorry about the rough ride," the voice said. "The rest should be easier."

"Where are you taking us?"

The question triggered laughter among whomever stood outside the vehicle.

"To La-La Land," the captor said. "And I'm sorry to both of you for the bruise."

Pain erupted in Nicholas's thigh. By the time he realized they'd stuck him with a needle, he wasn't there anymore.

It was nearly 3:00 A.M. when they all gathered in the War Room to look at the reconnaissance photos. "This comes from SkysEye," Venice said. While not the very latest in imaging technology, it was every bit the equal of what Jonathan had used back in the day. With a little manipulation of the computer's mouse, they could see the texture of the mortar between the bricks.

David was clearly impressed by what he saw. "Is this the kind of detailed view military commanders get when they launch a mission?"

"Depends on where the mission is," Jonathan said. "Not all areas of the world are as well-viewed as the others."

They all sat around the teak conference table in various postures of engagement and exhaustion, all of their chairs cheated toward the big screen at the end of the room.

Boxers said, "I'd give you an 'ooh' and an 'ah' too, if I didn't know I had to get in and out of there."

Saint Stephen's Reformatory had clearly been modified and added to over the years. The twelve-foot exterior wall covered a rectangular footprint of about four acres. Those walls contained the prison complex itself, which consisted of four three-story buildings that themselves formed a square, with what Jonathan imagined to be an exercise yard in the middle. Another larger building extended perpendicularly from the middle of the northernmost annex of the complex.

Jonathan pointed to that larger building. "What is this?"

"Used to be the main cell block," Venice said. "Held a couple hundred inmates. The roof there is made of stained glass. All the better to inspire the residents to lead better lives.

"The jail closed its doors as a jail in 1978. Until 1952, none of the side windows in the cell blocks had glass. In Canada. Lots of prisoners died of hypothermia in the early days, but then they started stacking people eight to ten in a cell, and the hypothermia deaths plummeted. Of course, then there was the disease problem."

Irene looked confused. "How do you know this?"

"The Internet and I are very good friends," Venice said.

Jonathan asked, "Did you contract for thermal imaging?"

"We did," she said, and she started tapping the computer.

The image on the screen turned to various shades of black, gray, orange, and red. Jonathan used a laser pointer to trace the northern annex, where the thermal footprint was hottest. "This seems to be the most occupied building," he said. "They've clearly got the heat on, and if you look carefully, you can see an occasional human form."

The other buildings showed cold, except for a faint pink glow from the easternmost corner of the southernmost annex. "What's that?" Irene asked, pointing.

"With the walls and floors as thick as they are, it's hard to tell. My guess is that they're firing up the furnace."

"Which means they're expecting guests," Boxers said.

Irene nodded. "That's consistent with what I got from the police in Vail. I had our Denver field office ask around, and they found someone who saw Nicholas Mishin and a boy—I'm assuming that's his son—in the grocery store around six o'clock this evening. They then verified that the house had been broken into and that neither Nicholas nor Josef were there."

Yelena had moved to the very front of her chair. "What else did they find?"

"I told them to stop looking," Irene said. "I told them to seal the place up. Treating it as a crime scene right now will just grab attention we don't want. I think we're all comfortable that we're on the right track. If we're wrong, we'll know soon enough, and then we'll pull out all the stops for the investigation."

"How the hell are we going to get in there, Dig?" Boxers wanted to know.

"One step at a time. What else do we know about this prison place?"

"I found some pictures of the inside," Venice said. Fifteen seconds later, the screen blinked, and then displayed a terrible, tiny claustrophobic jail cell with stone walls and heavy plank flooring. A small arched window looked like a droopy eye, equal parts heavy bars and air.

"Oh my God," Yelena breathed. "My poor baby."

Jonathan felt a flash of pity, but then dismissed it. They were fast entering the phase where emotion posed nothing but liability.

"Wooden floors," Jonathan observed aloud.

"Is that good?" Yelena asked.

"Neither good nor bad," Jonathan said. "It just is."

Venice clicked again, and they were looking at what appeared to be an interior hallway that ran the length of a cell block. The doors were all open in this photo, but they looked to be made of heavy timber, with only a single, round observation window that was maybe two inches in diameter.

"This is all great," Boxers said. "But unless we know where within this complex the Mishins are being kept, it's not going to do us much good."

"I might have something for you there," Irene said, glancing at her buzzing cell phone. She pressed a button and said, "This is Director Rivers, and you're on speakerphone."

"With who?" a male voice asked.

"Not your concern," Irene said. A glance around the room told everyone else to remain silent.

"Okay," the voice said. "Do I need to introduce myself?"

"I'd prefer you didn't," Irene said. Jonathan got that that was her nod to give the agent on the other end of the phone plausible deniability if this whole thing came unzipped.

"Okay," the agent said, "I just finished a one-hour interview with . . . the Russian. Director Rivers, I don't know what's going on here, but I saw some of the marks on that man's body. I don't think—"

"Please report what you know," Irene interrupted. "What you *think* in these circumstances is less important to me."

"Yes, ma'am. Well, he tried to hedge on answering questions, but when I confronted him directly with Saint Stephen's, he seemed too tired and exhausted to resist. The prison is, in fact, a garrison of sorts, but they are not armed."

Jonathan's first instinct was to be buoyed by the words, but his bullshit bell rang just a few seconds later. A terrorist without weapons was like a doctor without a stethoscope. They just didn't occur in nature.

"Are you saying that there are no weapons at the prison?"

"No, ma'am. The weapons are there, but the occupants don't go around armed all day. They stockpile the weapons."

"What kind of weapons are we talking about?"

"Firearms and explosives, to be sure," the agent said. "But he wasn't able to give us numbers. He said that he hadn't been up there in a while."

"How many people?" Irene asked.

It was killing Jonathan not to be asking the questions.

"Under fifty."

"There are a lot of numbers between zero and fifty," Irene said.

"Yes ma'am, but that's all we've been able to get out of him so far. The guy is a mess."

Jonathan pointed to the northern annex, where all the heat was coming from.

"Did you show the Russian the photo of the prison?"

"Yes, ma'am."

"And what did he tell you about where things happen?"

"Well. Do you have a photo there with you?" the agent asked.

"I do."

"Okay, well, the weapons are stored in the part of the complex that used to be a chapel. If you look at the big part that used to be the main cell block, the chapel is connected to it on the western wall of the compound. Just north of the main entrance."

Jonathan's gut turned. The chapel occupied a big footprint. If it was anywhere close to being filled with weapons, that could be a lot of firepower. When he met Boxers' gaze the Big Guy was grinning. Clearly, he saw the opportunity to make a crater.

The agent continued, "Those four buildings in the middle of the compound that form the giant square are additional cell blocks. The northernmost building of that square—the one that runs east-west—is where the garrison sleeps."

That would be the garrison that numbers somewhere between one and forty-nine people.

"What do they do there during the day?" Jonathan asked. He didn't do silent well, and he'd reached his limit. Irene's glare actually gave him a chill.

"Who is that?" the agent asked.

"He's authorized," Irene said. "His identity doesn't matter."

"I don't understand the question."

Jonathan sensed that he was stalling for time, but he cut him some slack. "This unarmed, unnumbered garrison," Jonathan said. "What do they do when they're not garrisoning?"

A pause. "I don't know."

"Some of them have been busy shooting down airliners," Boxers said.

"Um, Director Rivers, how many people are there in the room where I'm speaking?"

Irene's ears had gone hot. "There's a good handful of us," she said. "But that should not concern you." She glared at Jonathan and drew an invisible zipper across her mouth. It was exactly the same gesture that Mama Alexander used with the kids at Resurrection House. The absurdity of it made him laugh.

"Here's the thing," Irene said, daring anyone in the room to speak. "If, hypothetically, someone were to try to gain entrance to Saint Stephen's Reformatory, how many people would they be likely to encounter at, say, midnight as opposed to noon?"

Silence on the other end of the phone.

"Are you still there?" Irene asked.

"Jesus, is that what you're planning to do?"

"Focus, young man," Irene said. "Answers are far more welcome than questions."

"I-I don't have an answer for that, ma'am."

"You mean you don't have an answer, ma'am, *yet*, right?"

In all these years, Jonathan had never seen Irene in badass boss mode. He was impressed.

"Right," the agent said. "That's exactly what I meant."

"And you'll get back to me as soon as you have answers?"

"Yes, ma'am."

"One more thing," Irene said. "I don't want to mention any names or locations, but are you still at the facility to which you were dispatched?" Jonathan knew she meant Arc Flash's farm.

"Yes, ma'am. But we're almost packed up to leave."

"Don't do that just yet," Irene said. "The owner of that facility—a little man who goes by the name of Arc Flash. Is he still there?"

"He's the reason why we're in a hurry to leave. I can't tell you how offensive—"

"There you go with opinions again," Irene said. "What did we say about those?"

"Yes, ma'am."

Irene closed her eyes as she spoke the rest, as if too ashamed to make eye contact. "Here's what I need you to do," she said. "I want you to return the Russian to the custody of Mr. Arc Flash. Then I want you to go and sit in whatever vehicle you brought while he asks the questions. It shouldn't take long. When he's done, call me with the details."

Another long silence.

"Hello?" Irene prompted.

"Ma'am, do you know that you're asking me to break the law? You know that nothing we get will be usable in court."

Irene stewed for a while before answering.

"Ma'am?"

"I'm going to tell you an interesting story," she said. "You might know that J. Edgar Hoover's body wasn't all that cold when I first joined the Bureau. Certainly, his fingerprints were still on everything we did, from the firearms we carried to the way we comported ourselves in public. My first supervisor was a devotee of Director Hoover. Are you familiar with Director Hoover?"

"I believe I've heard the name."

Ah, petulance, Jonathan thought. *Bad move.*

Irene continued, "He told me that Director Hoover valued loyalty over everything—that if you went crosswise with J. Edgar, you either needed to quit, or prepare yourself for a long career at an Indian reservation."

Pause. "I'm not sure I understand your meaning."

"I'm quite certain you do," Irene said. "How's your Chippewa, young man?"

"You're threatening me."

"Absolutely not. I'm promising. You need to decide if you trust me enough to believe that what I'm asking is in the critical interest of the United States, or if you want to file a protest that, one way or another, will have you living your working years along the shores of Lake Superior."

Jonathan almost felt sorry for the guy. Fibbies tended to be purists at heart—unless their careers were at stake, in which case Grandma *and* her wheelchair were both eligible to be slung under the bus.

Jonathan could hear the wheels turning in this poor guy's head. "I'll get back to you as soon as I can," he said.

When the line went dead, Irene winced to the rest of the room. "Well, that was ugly," she said. "I feel like I need a shower."

CHAPTER TWENTY-TWO

The Torture Report—that's what Boxers called it, ever one to make people feel at ease—revealed only one additional bit of data, and it was a doozey. Sometime in the next two days—Pyotr thought it would be tomorrow night—the stores of explosives in the chapel would be transferred to trucks and transported to the United States.

"Okay, now I'm interested," Boxers said.

Jonathan stopped him with a raised hand. "That's not our mission,' he said.

"It is now," Boxers countered.

"The rescue comes first," Jonathan said. "Not that we can't kill two birds with one detonator."

Boxers smiled. "Nice line. But unless and until we know where the family is being kept," Boxers said, "or where they will be kept if they haven't yet arrived, any planning we do is just conjecture."

"What's our worst case, then?" Jonathan asked. "Assuming that they're in the most remote part of the facility, how do we get in and out?"

"I actually have some construction details," Venice said.

All heads turned.

"Hey, if you're going to zone for public use, you have to tell people how the hotel rooms are constructed."

"Do you want to join the FBI?" Irene asked. She phrased the question as a joke, but Jonathan knew there was a serious offer in there.

"You can't afford her," he said. And he believed that to be true. In fact, he was willing to bet that what he paid Venice trumped what Irene made as director of the FBI. With change. A lot of change.

"The jail actually started life in 1792 as a single row of stone cells," Venice said. She highlighted the western wall of the compound—the part that looked on the photo to be part of the outer wall and contained the chapel with the explosives. The southern end of the section became the northern edge of the archway that served as the main entrance. "Back then, not only was there no glass in the windows, the doors themselves—then made only of iron bars—opened directly to the outside. Can you imagine what manner of wildlife must have crawled in there?"

The question was meant to be provocative, but Jonathan wasn't in the mood. Apparently, no one in the room was in the mood.

"Okay," Venice said. She clicked, and the picture of the cell returned to the screen. "Those floors are constructed of six-by-six oak timbers. It was an attempt at insulation, but after all these years, they must be dense as concrete."

"But nowhere as brittle," Boxers observed. Many in the room didn't realize it, but that was a vote against explosives. Whereas stone and old concrete will shatter with a relatively small hit of HE—high explosives—heavy timbers will absorb a lot of the shock. It was a crapshoot whether they'd break or merely heave up and bend.

"What about the roof?" Jonathan asked.

"Originally, it was timber, too," Venice said, "but sometime in the 1920s, it was covered with slate. It's not entirely clear from the info I've been able to read whether the slate was ultimately replaced with something else."

Jonathan calculated whether the roof would make a good entry point, and decided that it posed too many challenges. "What are our ground options?" Jonathan asked.

"I've got a better question," Big Guy said. "Who's our team?"

"I'm going," the First Lady said.

"Oh, no you're not," Jonathan said. "You're the rescuee, remember? And you're already safe. There aren't a lot of rules in my business, but one of them is that once a PC is safe, you don't throw them back into danger."

"PC means 'precious cargo,' " Venice explained to David and Becky.

Yelena smirked and cocked her head. "How sweet. You think I'm precious?"

Jonathan let it go.

"That's my son and grandson, Mr. Grave. You can't expect me to just—"

"I can expect you to let me do my job, which means you staying out of my way."

"Would you rather I take a commercial flight to Ottawa and then just drive to the front door?"

Jonathan stared. She was serious.

Yelena continued, "It's not as if I would be completely useless. You know, I have—" She checked herself and threw an uncomfortable glance at the director of the FBI. "Admitting to nothing, it's entirely possible that I have some experience setting explosives."

"Holy shit!" Boxers proclaimed with a giant laugh.

"Then I'm going for sure," David said.

"The hell you are." That came as a unanimous chorus from everyone else in the room, and the words seemed to press him back in his chair.

"Think of me as an embed."

"You're not writing about this, remember?"

David held up his forefinger. "Not true," he said. "I promised not to reveal details. No real names. I never said anything about the story itself." He looked directly at Jonathan. "A deal's a deal. You can't change the terms now."

"Watch me," Boxers growled.

Jonathan felt the weight of the others' anticipation as he considered his option. In his world, on an operation this small, an embed was another word for liability. This kid wasn't a war correspondent. To bring him along could actually endanger others.

On the other hand, he had already endured a lot, and seemed to be handling it well. "If you come, you're not coming to observe and write," he said. "You're coming to engage. Have you ever fired a weapon?"

David smiled. "Glock nineteen and twenty-three, Remington eleven hundred, Bushmaster M4 and 308, and, in one day of overkill, a Browning A-bolt composite stalker in three hundred Win Mag." He seemed to have been waiting for the question.

And his answer sucked all of the air out of the room.

"What kind of scope did you use on the Win Mag?" Boxers asked.

Without dropping a beat: "A Leupold Vari-X three."

"Did you hit what you were shooting at?"

"Dead center," David said. "At six hundred yards."

The room gaped in unison.

"My dad belongs to a gun club out in Loudoun County," he explained. "I went there a lot as a kid."

"Targets?" Boxers asked.

David rolled his eyes. "Generally, they don't let you shoot at people."

"So the targets never shot back at you." Boxers stated that as his point.

"In a perfect world, he can hit what he's shooting at," Jonathan said, summing it up. It also served as his decision that the kid could come. They needed the manpower.

When Becky sensed that it was her turn, she cleared her throat and gave a shy smile. "I took a gun safety course in Girl Scout camp," she said. "But I'm willing to go if I can be of any help. At the very least, I can carry stuff while my partner, Rambo, shoots up the place with his three hundred win-thing."

"There's a sentence every warrior wants to hear," Boxers said.

"Stop," Jonathan said. "We'll stipulate that everyone wants to or is willing to go. Now we need a plan."

"First we need to know where the PCs are going to be held," Boxers said.

"That's a level-three concern," Jonathan said. "First, we have to get in country with the appropriate tools." He knew it was stupid, but he resisted talking about weapons and explosives in front of the others. As if they didn't know what "appropriate tools" meant. "Next we have to figure out how to get into Canada and then onto the island. The actual extraction and evacuation don't happen unless we can get past those two points. Irene, I don't suppose you have any contacts in CBP, do you?" Customs and Border Protection.

"No one high enough on the food chain," she said.

"It'd take too long to get false passports for everyone," Jonathan thought aloud, "so driving is out."

"What's the hurry?" Becky asked. Then, to Yelena, "Sorry, but an extra few hours to get it right might be worth the delay."

Jonathan shook his head. "No. We know where the PCs are headed now. We don't know where they might be moved later. If they get whisked off again, we'll be out of business. The clock is definitely ticking."

"Not all roads are monitored," Boxers said.

"Yeah, they are," Jonathan corrected. "There might not be checkpoints, but there are ground sensors and drones in the air." He smiled at Irene, who seemed surprised that he knew about the drones. "It's not worth the risk to drive. Plus, that's a twelve-hour commute from here."

"We can always charter a jet," Boxers said, "but there's still the problem of customs."

Jonathan never quite understood why it was so much harder to get in and out of Canada that it was to traverse the Mexican border, but he figured it had something to the relative strengths of the two nations' respective lobbyists. Fact was, the border was carefully watched, and the penalties for illegal crossings were huge. At a minimum, it included impounding the vehicle that carried you, and in Jonathan's case, given all the weaponry that his vehicle would be transporting, that would be especially problematic.

Given the time constraints, they needed a way to literally pass under the radar between the two nations, but that would mean treetop flying, and that attracted a lot of attention. Unless, of course, they could start and end in relatively unpopulated areas.

In a perfect world, they'd use a helicopter. Working the logic, then, they needed a helpful contact in New England, close enough to make the flight out and back on a single tank of gas.

Vermont, maybe.

That's it!

When he looked to Boxers, the Big Guy was already grinning.

They said it together: "Striker."

Len Shaw, a.k.a. Alexei Petrov, arrived in his office to find Dmitri Boykin already seated in Len's chair, with his feet on the desk, paging through paperwork that he had no right seeing. "Excuse me," Len said.

Dmitri looked bored and slightly amused. He started to speak in Russian.

"No," Len said. "Not here. English. French if you must, but I do not allow Russian in my compound."

Dmitri's eyebrows raised halfway up his forehead. "You do not *allow*? Comrade Petrov, tell me you are not ashamed of your heritage."

"Those days are gone, Dmitri. Comrade this and comrade that, you sound like an old movie. You must embrace change. And the first change is to get out of my chair."

Dmitri didn't move. He was a bully in the most basic definition of the word. Built like a fire hydrant, he had a face that had survived too many fights, and the personality of a man who longed for more. While he intimidated most of the men with whom he interacted, Len was not among them.

"Are you going to make me?" he asked.

It was a level of discourse to which Len would not stoop. If it came to that, so be it. The odds in the ensuing fight would be even at best—and in Dmitri's favor, at worst—but there'd be a lot of blood on the walls, and no one would want that.

Dmitri held his posture for a few seconds—long enough to impress Len with his faux fearlessness—and then lowered his feet to the floor and stood. "You are getting bold in your old age, Alexei."

Len waited until he had clear passage—avoiding the temptation of the schoolyard shoulder-knock and the unspoken challenge it brought—before walking behind his desk and sitting down. "The name is Len. Len Shaw. And I am a real estate developer. That is the life I lead, mission notwithstanding. The men who live here are construction workers. The public is not welcome because a construction site is a dangerous place. That is our cover, and our cover is working."

"You seem to have taken deep ownership of a property I bought."

"It's a property that *I* bought," Len snapped. "Check the land records."

"What is it that the Americans like to say?" Dmitri asked. "Ah, yes. Follow the money."

Len sighed. "Must we engage in this—what else is it that the Americans say? Ah, yes. Must we engage in this dick-knocking? We are on the same side, Dmitri. We have known each other too long for this. We are too close to our mission's end. Nineteen eighty-eight was a long time ago." He was referring, of course, to the fall of the Soviet Union.

"The Mishins are on their way," Dmitri said, getting right to the point. "They should be here in the next few hours."

Len had taken special care to shower, shave, and fully dress before responding to Dmitri's summons at this ridiculous hour. He wore creased blue jeans and a crisply ironed white shirt. On his right hip he carried a Glock 23, a .40 with which he could hammer nails at twenty-five yards. He was not pleased to find out that he would be harboring high-profile hostages. As any senior leader of Al Qaeda could tell you—if you could raise them from the dead—few terrorists (and that's exactly what the Americans would consider Dmitri to be) died of old age.

"I've made my opinion known on the risk of this," Len said.

"Yes, you have."

"It is madness to risk all of the progress we have made on something so personal. To involve the president's family—"

"It is the bitch's family, not his."

"That's not how the American people will see it. They will see an attack on the first family, and they will react with violence. Everything you've worked for will be jeopardized."

"Everything I have worked for will be guaranteed," Dmitri said. He'd settled himself into the cane-backed guest chair in front of Len's desk. "I have told that fool Winters that if word ever leaks out, I will simply kill the hostages and move on. Just as I told him that I would take them in the first place if our operation became jeopardized."

Len understood that actions had to have consequences, that once a promise was made, it had to be fulfilled. He didn't argue with any of that. His difficulty with the current arrangement was the danger that came from mixing the missions. Saint Stephen's was first and foremost a weapons repository. In that light alone, it was a huge target, in recognition of which they'd gone so far as to prohibit incoming and outgoing phone calls. No one was to know what transpired within the twelve-foot walls of the compound. Shipments arrived at night, mostly by boat. Only a select few among the cadre knew the nature of the materials stored in the chapel, and none of them knew more than was necessary for them to do their jobs.

Now, in addition to those responsibilities, they would also become jailers. With the added duties came added risk. The Americans would move heaven and the stars to find the spawn of Yelena. To find them was to find everything. If their search brought them to Saint Stephen's the whole mission would be finished.

"Are you aware that we have not heard anything from Vasily or Pyotr?" Len asked.

"I'm sure they're fine," Dmitri said.

"Why would you be sure of that?" As he spoke, Len opened the top left-hand drawer of his desk and withdrew a Cohiba Espléndidos cigar and a cutter. "I've been monitoring the US news outlets, and there has been no word of a reporter being killed."

Dmitri pulled a silver cigarette case from the inside pocket of his suit coat. Dmitri always wore a suit. Always dark, always at least ten years out of date. As if in competition with Len, when the spring-loaded case opened, it revealed two complete rows of black Sobranies. "They no longer allow smoking in America," he said. "It's a law that makes for very long days."

"But much healthier fat Americans," Len said with a smile. He allowed the light moment to glow for a few seconds, and then returned the discussion to that which could kill them all. "They should have called in by now. One of them or both of them. The fact that we've heard from neither is of great concern. Nor have we heard that their targets were killed. I think they may have been compromised."

Dmitri's features darkened. "How compromised might they be?"

"Vasily and Pyotr know most of everything. They know this facility. They know what we keep here."

"Did they know about the plan to take the Mishin boys?"

Hearing a midthirties man referred to as a "boy" was startling. To hear the use of the plural in "boys" was troubling. "Did you know that the grandson would be visiting?" Len asked.

"I try to know as much as I can," Dmitri said.

"So you knew all along that the boy would be a part of this?" In Len's world—in the world of sanity and proportion—there was a sanctity to childhood that should never be breached.

"I did not choose the timing of the bitch's betrayal. She alone chose that." For years, Dmitri had refused to speak the name of Yelena Poltanov.

Len's mind reeled. This was the problem with zealots. They got so wrapped up in emotion and principle that they forgot about the practical ramifications of what they did. Americans would tolerate the taking of an adult as a hostage to a larger cause—they would profess dismay and make threatening gestures—Daniel Pearl, anyone?—but they would ultimately shrug it away and tolerate it. To take a child, though, was to invoke the wrath of the self-righteous.

"This is a mistake, Dmitri. We have the San Francisco operation ready to launch in just days. And after that, the Los Angeles operation and the Washington operation." Each focused on largely unprotected mass-transit systems. "Per your orders, I moved the explosives shipment from tomorrow to the next day. These little changes incur huge risks. Ours is a balancing act."

Dmitri had never been one to take bad news well. His features hardened. "We cannot project weakness," he said. "If we do that, then we lose all of the influence we have at the White House. They have to know that we say what we mean, and we mean what we say."

Len raised his hands, a gesture of surrender. With the argument lost, it became all about coping with the reality.

"If it helps," Dmitri said, "the Mishins will be here for only a few hours. Forty-eight at the most."

"Where do they go after that?"

"Do you really want to know?"

Len intentionally answered before he had much time to think about his words. "No," he said. "As long as I don't have to worry about them and about the fallout, I don't want to know." He heaved a deep breath and turned a page in his mind. "We are forty-five strong now. At any given moment, we will have fifteen men on guard detail, and fifteen on operational detail, doing whatever needs to be done. That leaves fifteen to be sleeping. I am confident that we can provide coverage for the Mishins when they arrive."

"I want everyone well-armed," Dmitri said. "Rifles and pistols for every on-duty guard, pistols for everyone, all the time."

"It is difficult showering with a pistol," Len joked, but it landed dead on arrival. When he saw the deep concern in Dmitri's face, he changed his approach. "Do you have information that I should know about?" he asked. "Information that I should share with my people?"

Dmirti took a long pull on his black cigarette, and then waved the smoke away after he'd exhaled. "You ask for *trust*, Len, yet you do not offer it in return. We have turned the corner in our struggle to hurt America, and those in power will soon wake up to the threat. It is the moment we have been waiting for, and the moment we have been training for. If we give our men the tools of strength, they will show strength. I want them to feel very, very strong."

Len found himself nodding as he listened. He'd seen it before: Good soldiers became great soldiers when they were entrusted with live ammunition. When all was said and done, potential became reality when the choice was to live or to kill.

But in all of Len's experience, these truisms only worked when the enemy was clearly identifiable, and the mission was clear. In this case, neither factor applied, and that worried him.

"I will make them feel as strong as I know how," Len said. As for the rest, the clock would tick as it ticked, and he would learn what history wanted him to know.

CHAPTER TWENTY-THREE

Striker—real name Carl Oppenheimer—had spent a career as a pilot for the 160th Special Operations Air Regiment—the Night Stalkers—flying Special Forces operators into and out of some of the hottest LZs on the planet. He'd been shot down once that Jonathan knew of, and ultimately was forced to retire with a bum leg, thanks to a lucky 7.62 round that came through the floor of his Blackhawk while he was flaring to land in a place that he couldn't even tell Jonathan about. The bullet took out three toes and just a tiny trace of his sanity.

In the intervening years, he'd either spent a lot of money or made a lot of money—Jonathan couldn't figure out which, but it had to be one or the other—buying discarded hulks of helicopters and restoring them to their former glory. According to the buzz mill within the Community, he made good coin renting out his equipment to people who needed to fly fast and hard and didn't want to leave a paper trail.

"You know this changes everything, right?" Boxers asked in a low whisper. He and Jonathan were huddled at Jonathan's desk while the others talked among themselves around the fireplace.

Jonathan looked up from the satellite photos he'd been studying. "What are we talking about?"

"Our business," Big Guy replied. "OpSec used to be king. We flew under the radar, no one knew who we were, and no one knew what we did. Now we're just lifting the kimono and showing all the goods to anyone who wants to see."

Over all the years that they'd worked together, Jonathan and Boxers had engaged in maybe a dozen serious conversations, and this was clearly one of them.

"Given the cast of characters, I think we have a fair amount of cover."

"I'd have agreed if Wolverine had decided to come along." He looked directly at Irene, who was hovering close. "It bugs me that you want to stay behind."

Irene crossed her arms and shifted her weight to one foot. The comment made her uncomfortable. "If I could be there, I would," she said. "I think our history proves that. And if this were going down in Des Moines or Bangor, I might well be all over it. But this is foreign soil, and I'm the director of the FBI. What you're planning—what *we're* planning—is an illegal act. If it goes bad and I'm there, it becomes an act of war. I swore my oath to the Constitution, not to you guys. I'm sorry."

"Forgive me, Wolverine," Boxers pressed, "but it feels like cowardice to me. Feels like a setup."

Jonathan jumped in, even as he felt a swell of anger. "No," he said. "Wolverine is too good a friend."

"No one is a friend in official Washington."

"Except those who have proven themselves," Jonathan

said. He shot an apologetic glance to Irene and she received it in kind. No one was more cynical than he, but there was no denying the number of times that Jonathan had saved Irene's ass, just as she had saved his. She'd earned not only his respect, but the benefit of his doubt. "Does it make you more comfortable to think of the damage we could do if we were ever called to testify?" It was of a magnitude that would topple this government and others.

"What about the reporters?"

"We've had this discussion."

"But I didn't get the answer I wanted," Boxers said. "On the one hand, they're reporter scum, and on the other, they've never engaged an enemy before."

"You know I can hear you, right?" David called from the sofa in front of the fire.

"Then quit listening!" Boxers yelled. When Boxers yelled, he caused seismic activity.

"Way to go, Big Guy," Jonathan said with a smile. "Pretty much guarantees that everyone listens to everything."

Becky stood from the spot next to David. "What do you want from us?" she asked. "We've promised to do everything you've asked, with the clear understanding that if we don't, you two will hunt us down and kill us, even if it takes the rest of your lives."

David reached for her arm, but she pulled away.

"I'm tired of being treated as if I did something wrong. I'm going on this *mission* because I care, and because I have nothing else to do. I can't go home, and without home, I have nowhere else."

Jonathan looked to Boxers. He'd made this bed, after all.

"You weren't supposed to hear what I was talking about," he said.

"Well, that genie's out of the bottle, isn't it?" Becky said. Shouted, actually, and she had a hell of a shout. "This is our lives, too, you know."

David Kirk chimed in with "Has it occurred to you that we want to do the right thing? That we want to help rescue people who should never have been taken hostage?"

Jonathan's first instinct was to roll his eyes. Overt statements of altruism were so rarely real that he wanted to dismiss this as ridiculous. Then he saw the look in the kid's eyes. Boxers might have seen it, too, because he became uncharacteristically quiet.

"One of my best friends was killed by these assholes," David said. "Then they tried to kill me and my girlfriend."

Jonathan caught the hiccup that came with the *g* word, and he wondered if it was the first time it had been uttered aloud.

"Throw in the fact that the United States—the country that even us reviled journalists are proud to call our home—is threatened, and maybe we've decided that there might just be a cause worth dying for."

The words hung in the air. Truth be told, the altruism angle had never occurred to Jonathan. In his mind, that gene had never been bestowed upon a reporter.

"Thank you," Yelena said.

All eyes focused on her.

"I don't know how to describe what this means," she said. "That you would risk your lives for my family . . ." The words trailed off.

Jonathan resisted the urge to tell her that public servants risked their lives for strangers every day, but it would have been rude. The glare he shot to Boxers said, *Let it go.*

Big Guy clearly didn't want to, but he did.

"Here's where we are," Jonathan said, turning his body to face the entire room. "I can't predict the future, but each of you needs to know that we'll be on an airplane soon, and on the far end of the flight is a helicopter ride that is going to insert all of you—all of us—into a spot from which there is no return. According to Wolverine's numbers, there are forty-five people at the facility we're about to assault, and they will not be pleased with what we are planning to do. For the plan to work, every one of you needs to perform at one hundred percent. If any one of you drops the ball, we all will likely die."

"So why are *you* doing this?" Yelena asked. "Of all of us, you two are the ones who could walk away without consequence."

It was the most obvious question in the world, yet it took Jonathan completely by surprise. "It's my job," he said. "It's *our* job."

"Too easy," Yelena said. "As I understand it from your own mouth, your *job* was to rescue *me*. That job was completed, and I confess that I have not been as grateful as I should have been. But now you are pressing to do more. Why would you do that?"

It felt odd having his own questions turned back on him. Jonathan looked to Boxers for the right words.

"Hey, you're the boss," he said. "I just go where you tell me."

That was a lie, of course, but it was a harmless one.

"Duty, honor, country," Jonathan said.

It landed like a punch line among the others, earning a group groan.

"Don't do that," Jonathan said. He put a sharpness in his tone that was designed to startle, and it worked. "You asked for an answer, and I gave it to you. Don't you dare dismiss it. When I say 'duty, honor, country' that's exactly what I mean. It's what I have always meant. That's what *we* have always meant."

A soapbox speech was blooming in Jonathan's gut.

"Next time your husband talks about soldiers or sailors or airmen as pawns in some geopolitical game—or the next time you"—he pointed at David—"start thinking of them as numbers on a budgetary spreadsheet, ask yourself why they do what they do. Even back in the day, there were a hell of a lot easier ways for me to earn fifty-five thousand dollars a year. And that was after seventeen years working for Uncle. We do what we do because there is, in fact, an absolute value to right and wrong."

He felt his ears growing hot, and, completely out of character, he felt tears pressing behind his eyes. "It's *wrong* to snatch innocent people out of their beds and take them hostage. I don't care who the players are or what the motivations are. That's wrong. And when the motivation behind it is to harm the government of the country I love, that makes it a cause worth dying for."

"You *are* getting paid, I assume," Becky said. "Pretty well, I imagine."

"I'm already rich. My fee is a rounding error, a test of commitment for my clients."

"And your life?" Yelena asked.

"What about it?"

"You're willing to risk that for people you've never met?"

Now his blood was boiling. "Yeah, Yelena, I am. Your family is my mission, I'm willing to die for them. And kill for them."

He leaned in closer as he delivered the rest. "Just as your Secret Service detail was willing to do for you."

He felt Boxers' hand on his arm, a signal that he was a few degrees too hot.

"Tell me what you're implying," Yelena said.

"I'm implying that a lot of good, dedicated people died in service to your security," Jonathan said. "Their wives and children will never see them again. I refuse to let that sacrifice be in vain."

A long silence followed—every bit of sixty seconds and more—as no one made eye contact with anyone, except for Jonathan, whose eyes demanded a response from the First Lady.

"I don't know what you want me to say," she said. "That I am sorry?"

"No," Jonathan said. "No one gives a shit whether you're sorry. The dead will remain dead, even if you drop to your knees and offer up a novena. What I want from you is acknowledgment that a lot of people have paid the ultimate price to protect you, and that now a bunch more are willing to pay that price for your family."

Tears welled in Yelena's eyes. "Why are you doing this? Did you think I didn't feel guilty enough?"

"I don't care," Jonathan said. "That's the key. Listen to it again: This isn't about your feelings. It isn't about publicity, and it isn't about anything that resembles politicking or selling papers. We're going into battle tomorrow. People are likely to die, but if we get home alive, then the killing will have been worth it. That's what mission focus is all about."

Ordinarily, Boxers would have driven the plane, but Austin Mannix announced that he needed his plane back later in the day. Thus, they had to accept a ride from two pilots who seemed very contented to know nothing about their passengers. It was a short flight, too. Just a little over an hour.

Venice had arranged for a Cadillac Escalade to meet the Lear on the tarmac at BTV—Burlington International Airport—where Jonathan and his team could transfer the tools of their trade directly from the plane without triggering about a thousand security traps that frowned upon the kinds of hardware they were transporting. To the casual observer, the Escalade was being filled with heavy duffel bags.

And Yelena Poltanov had transformed herself into a cross between June Cleaver and Granny Clampett. Her hair had gone from its natural brown to strawberry blond, and she'd cashed her après ski outfit in for an unremarkable brown dress that drooped to below her knees, where brown stockings took over and led to brown hiking boots.

Yelena caught Jonathan's amused look. "It's a lesson I learned from the Marshals Service," she said. "If people are noticing the outfit, they're not noticing the face."

But even her face had transformed to be unrecognizable. She'd broadened the bridge of her nose and donned a pair of clear-lens glasses. A prosthetic appliance on her upper teeth added puffiness to her cheeks which, combined with pale pink lipstick, erased the glamor that had made her such a hot property for ladies' magazines.

"I'm impressed," Jonathan said. "When this is all over, I'd like a lesson in disguises."

"Particularly that lipstick, Boss," Boxers said as he passed with the last of the duffels and laid them on the flat bed of the Escalade. "I'm tired of that red shit you usually wear."

Jonathan flipped him off.

"I can see you wearing that," Yelena quipped.

He flipped her off too. But added, "Ma'am."

Following the directions downloaded by Venice to Jonathan's GPS, Boxers piloted the enormous SUV through ever-narrowing roads in the general direction of Lake Champlain. The farther they got from the major thoroughfares, the more snow-covered the roads became. As they closed to within the last two miles, Big Guy had to throw the switch for four-wheel low. Though clearly built more for sports than utility, the Cadillac performed better as a truck than Jonathan had expected.

At just after 9:00 A.M., Jonathan held up his hand and said, "Okay, slow it down."

"I'm doing seven miles an hour. Slower would mean reverse."

Jonathan kept his eyes on his GPS. "According to this, we're coming up on the road that leads to the road to Striker's property. It'll be up here on the left."

Every occupant leaned forward and to the left to

help with the scanning. Encrusted in white, the woods looked stunning in a way that you can only see in New England. It must have snowed the night before because the coating on the branches was still powdery enough to whisper away from the breeze created by the monstrous vehicle.

"Is that it?" Becky asked from the second rank of rear seats. "See those red reflectors on the trees?"

Jonathan saw them just as she said the words—two round, red reflectors of the type you might see on a bicycle, mounted at about ten feet to two massive hardwoods that rose like columns from the ground to the sky. If he used his imagination, Jonathan could see a snow-covered path—it would be a vast overstatement to call it a roadway—that led deeper into the woods.

"I think that's it," Jonathan said. "The GPS shows that we're right on it."

"Well, let's be sure," Boxers said. "Because once we start up there, we won't be turning around for a while."

Yelena leaned forward until her head was even with theirs. "Are you sure you can fit it there at all?"

Boxers turned the wheel and gunned the engine to get traction. "The important parts will." He fishtailed just a little as he threaded the needle through the trees, shearing the right-hand sideview mirror from its mount. He laughed. "I've always said that nothing performs like a rental car."

Jonathan made a mental note to have Venice scare up the name of a local body shop.

Over the course of the next half mile or so, the pathway opened up a little, but not much. If another vehicle were coming the opposite direction, there would have been an interesting standoff.

"Here we go," Jonathan said at last. He pointed toward another gap in the trees. "That's the entrance to Striker's property." From the looks of the ground, no one had driven this way in several snowstorms. The coating of white was pristine, undisturbed.

Boxers made the hard left, this time clearing the tree sentries with room to spare.

"This Striker guy," David said. "He doesn't like people very much, does he?"

Jonathan chuckled at the understatement. "No, he doesn't. Never did, actually." While Oppenheimer had delivered Jonathan in and out of more than a few hotspots, the SOAR guys didn't interact all that much with the Unit guys outside training and missions—Fort Campbell was a long way from Fort Bragg—so all Jonathan knew of the guy was that he seemed intense, intelligent, and, frankly, scary. He took wild chances and had the medals to prove it, but Striker's heroism came with a suicidal edge that made Jonathan nervous.

Jonathan had seen Striker only once since the man had retired on disability, and on that occasion—a training seminar on infiltration strategies—Striker seemed . . . spent. To Jonathan, it seemed that when that bullet took away his ability to fly for Uncle Sam, it took away the pilot's sense of self. He didn't like people enough to return to headquarters as an instructor, and, from what Jonathan picked up through scuttlebutt, he'd just sort of disappeared to the old family homestead in Vermont and surrounded himself with the mechanical creatures he loved.

The Cadillac struggled some with the depth of the snow on the ground, but Boxers plowed on, never letting up on the throttle, and somehow finding traction despite bottoming out more than once.

The Oppenheimer spread was an impressive one, easily thirty acres, an equal mix of woods and fields. Being this remote, and knowing Striker's personality, Jonathan imagined that Oppenheimer was a survivalist at heart, living off the vegetables he could grow in the short summers and the meat he could shoot from his kitchen window.

"This is beautiful," Yelena said.

"A real slice of New England," Becky agreed. "The way Norman Rockwell pictured it."

Even the clapboard farmhouse looked like something from a postcard, with its gables and a wraparound porch that appeared to surround the entire structure. The house sat atop the long, gradual slope that rose from the opening in the fence, and as they came closer, what had initially looked like three large barns became more obvious as hangars for Striker's pet helicopters. Protected from the direct wind and snow by heavy timber walls, the double doors on one of the structures was gapped just enough to make out the unmistakable nose of a Vietnam-era UH-1 Huey. It was officially called an Iroquois, but Jonathan couldn't remember a single time that he had heard anyone refer to it that way.

"Park next to the Suburban," Jonathan said, pointing to the forest green SUV that sat either in the yard or in the driveway. It was impossible to tell which.

As they pulled to a stop, Boxers asked, "How do you want to play it? He's always been a little twitchy."

"We're just old friends who are paying a visit," Jonathan said. "I briefed him on the phone, and Mother

Hen was supposed to call him and remind him we were on the way."

"Doesn't mean he's not still twitchy," Boxers said.

He made a valid point. "Y'all stay in the truck till we get everything settled," Jonathan said to the others.

Jonathan didn't own any winter camouflage gear, so he and Boxers had opted for their standard black 5.11 Tactical kit, minus the ballistic vests and heavy rucks, which they left in the vehicle. Jonathan made sure that his Colt was visible and accessible. He didn't expect to use it, but twitchy people tended to get twitchier if they thought you were trying to conceal a weapon from them. If the weapon was in plain sight, they didn't feel duped.

Up close, where the paint was peeling, and the sag in the porch steps was obvious, the house lost a lot of its charm.

Jonathan climbed the four steps to the porch and stomped his feet, ostensibly to remove the snow from his boots, but also to make as much approaching noise as he could.

He'd just raised his hand to knock when the door pulled open.

Striker beamed a delighted smile. "Jonny-boy," he said, pushing open the fraying screen door. He'd lost a lot of weight and grown a lot of beard since Jonathan had last seen him, and his bald pate—now ringed with gray rather than black—gleamed white as bone. His pallor, combined with his Santa beard, painted a picture of ill health. The cane didn't help to improve the image.

Jonathan extended his hand. "Hello, Striker," he said.

"I don't answer to that name anymore, Jonny. Call me Carl."

"Only if you call me Digger. I've *never* responded to Jonny."

"It's a deal." As they shook, Carl's hand felt cold.

"You remember Boxers," Jonathan said, gesturing to Big Guy.

Another big smile. "The man who always caused me to rework my fuel charts."

Boxers didn't much like being teased about his size, but he managed a smile anyway as he shook Carl's hand.

"Come on in, boys," Carl said. "Let's get caught up."

"I have some other people to introduce you to," Jonathan said. He waved for the others in the car to join him. "One of them is going to startle you a little."

Becky led the way up the stairs, followed by David, and then Yelena. Jonathan introduced them one at a time, and then, when it came to Yelena, he paused for a moment for the recognition to materialize. The First Lady still wore her frumpy clothes, but she had removed all the feature-altering prosthetics.

Carl scowled. "Why are we all looking at each other like this?"

"I just wanted to give you a moment to recognize her."

Carl added pursed lips to his scowl. "Do we know each other? Please don't tell me I fathered one of your children."

Jonathan suppressed a laugh, but of course Boxers didn't, and Yelena just looked appalled.

"This is Anna Darmond," Jonathan said, and Yelena presented a demure hand.

"Hi, Anna." Carl shook her hand—her fingers, really, the way you're supposed to shake a lady's hand if you're of a certain age. "Why do I sense that I should have just heard a deep organ chord when I did that?"

Boxers crossed his arms and smiled even more broadly. "Yeah, Boss, why is that?"

Jonathan felt himself blushing.

Becky took a shot at it. "Anna Darmond," she said. "*The* Anna Darmond."

"Are there a lot of them to choose from?" Carl wasn't getting it.

"She's the First Lady of the United States," Becky said. She seemed to take pride in uttering the syllables.

"Huh," Carl said. "Well, welcome to Vermont. I gotta tell you, though, you needn't campaign here. Tony's got my vote for sure."

"I bet he doesn't tomorrow," Boxers said.

Jonathan shot him a glare.

"Come on in, have a seat and get warm."

The inside of Carl's house hadn't seen a dust cloth in a very long time. The low-angled morning light made the sun itself look dirty as it shined through the cloud of motes. The fifteen-by-fifteen-foot room was packed with mismatched furniture, making it look smaller than it actually was. Lots of old-style guns-and-cannons early American upholstery on sagging, overstuffed cushions. Jonathan noticed as many kerosene hurricane lamps as modern ones, calling into question the reliability of the electrical service. The heat from the woodstove made Jonathan wish he'd worn shorts and a T-shirt.

One chair in particular—the one that sat closest to

the front window—was surrounded by well-read and bookmarked magazines. At a glance, Jonathan saw copes of *Flying*, *Helicopter*, and *Aviation Week*. Given the collection of pornography that adorned the walls, everything from the merely risqué to truly offensive, he wasn't the least bit surprised to see copies of *Woman Pilot* in the mix as well.

"Sit, sit, sit," Carl said. He made a beeline for his chair, and let the rest fend for themselves. After he sat, he lifted a mason jar half-filled with clear liquid. "Can I offer anyone some vodka?" he asked. Then he looked to Jonathan. "Oh, that's right, you're a scotch fan. I can put some shoe polish in it for you."

The others were appalled, but Jonathan got it as the joke it was. He was also halfway surprised that Boxers didn't take him up on the offer.

"So," Carl said, clapping his hands together. "I understand that we're going to invade Canada."

CHAPTER TWENTY-FOUR

The first thing Nicholas noted as consciousness returned was that he had free access to his hands. Clearly time had passed—it was nowhere near as dark as it had been before—but as far as his brain was concerned, he'd been in the back of the van just a second ago, talking to—

"Josef!" he said. His vocal cords sounded crusty, and his voice came as a hoarse whisper. His eyes snapped open. "Joey, are you here?"

It took effort to sit up. His body felt beaten—bruised and stiff. As he rose, a heavy wool blanket fell away, and he felt enveloped by a shroud of cold.

"Joey?"

He heard a snore from behind him, and he turned to see his son on the floor, likewise wrapped in a heavy blanket identical to his, a sort of red-and-blue tartan plaid. Josef's eyes were closed and his face looked peaceful, his color good. Nicholas moved to wake him, then decided not to. What would be the point? Let the boy sleep through all the worry.

Awareness came in fragments. Nicholas sat in a tiny

unfurnished room whose floor was made of heavy wood and whose walls were stone. Up high, near the ten-foot ceiling, cold air rolled in through a half-moon window that was blocked with bars.

Could this be a prison?

Stupid question. It could be anything at all, just as this could be any day at all. Given the temperature of the place, it could even be Russia. And that would be the place they would be taken, wouldn't it? Why else would Russian-speaking kidnappers snatch them away in the middle of the night?

Could this be Tony Darmond's way of getting rid of the familial thorns in his side?

He pushed it away. That was the dullness of his brain talking. Even if weren't preposterous, it would make more sense just to kill them. To keep them around was just a liability. No, this was about something, but that wasn't it.

As he twisted in place to stretch his back, he noticed that someone had dressed him in a thick sweat suit. They'd even put heavy socks on his feet. Was it ridiculous to feel gratitude toward your kidnapper? Was that what the famed Stockholm syndrome was all about?

He brought his legs under him to stand, and he realized that his bladder was full to bursting. In the same moment, he saw the old style chamber pot throne in the corner, with a roll of toilet paper on the floor next to it.

"Oh, wait till Josef sees this," he mumbled aloud.

Gathered with the rest around the steel-and-Formica dining room table, Carl Oppenheimer seemed pretty much disinterested in knowing *why* they were invading Canada, but completely absorbed in the how of it all.

Jonathan shared the latest satellite imagery of Saint Stephen's Reformatory, now just over an hour old. What he saw concerned him.

"Last night, there were no guards outside this facility at all," he observed. "Now they've got them at the main gate, and then outside the entrances to the interior buildings. He zoomed in with the SkysEye imagery and saw men that were dressed in various styles of heavy clothing, each of them holding a rifle that was either at a loose port arms or slung over their shoulder.

"No uniforms," Boxers said. "That's encouraging."

"Why?" David asked.

"Because it implies a lower level of organization and training."

"Implies?" Yelena asked.

"Nothing's certain in this business, ma'am," Jonathan said.

"I saw *Black Hawk Down*," Becky said. "Untrained people can do a lot of damage."

Jonathan didn't reply. He'd lost some friends in that battle, and didn't want to open the door to all that.

Carl remained silent as he studied the photos, and then turned his attention to the topographical maps along with some flight charts he'd pulled out of a file cabinet next to the woodstove.

"If you're thinking of fast-roping into there, I can't help you," Carl said. "We'd get shot out of the sky and I've got no suppressing fire." His expression turned apologetic. "I bought a pair of seventies-era miniguns on the Internet a few weeks ago, but I won't be able to get them in shape in time."

"Jesus," Boxers said.

Jonathan kept a straight face. "Just as well. I wasn't thinking about a three-thousand-rounds-per-minute spray and slay anyway."

"Spray and slay?" Becky said. "Really? This is funny poetry to you?"

"I didn't know that I was trying to be funny," Jonathan said.

Boxers added, "And it's a damn fine tactic when a bunch of people are trying to make you dead."

Becky opened her mouth to say something, but Jonathan silenced her with a raised hand. "Nope," he said. "Both points have been made. The topic is closed."

Jonathan had no compunction against using overwhelming force to send bad guys to their maker, but in this case, where every round from the minigun that did not hit its target would travel on for miles until it found a different one, the weapon posed too high a risk for the population of Ottawa.

"I was thinking we'd come in from the water," Jonathan said. "There's a place on the outskirts of Ottawa, a warehouse on Ridge Road, where there's going to be a car and a boat waiting for us. It's mostly in the middle of nowhere, a hundred twelve miles from here as the crow flies. I figure Boxers will fly us to that spot, and we'll offload."

"Big Guy isn't flying anything," Carl said. "I'm the only one who flies my birds." The reversion back to code names was not lost on Jonathan. He wasn't sure what it meant, but it felt significant.

"Striker, I can't do that to you," Jonathan said.

"I won't let anyone else risk their lives for me," Yelena said.

"How'd I get on the short friggin' list of honor?" Boxers growled. To Carl, he said, "I'll fight you for the pilot's seat if you'd like." That came with just enough of a smile for it not to be offensive.

"No need to fight," Carl said. "You've got no bargaining power. My birds, my fuel, my rules."

"We'll pay you," Jonathan said. "No one expects you to foot the bill for this."

"You going to go to jail for me if you crash my chopper on Canadian soil?"

"You'd rather be the one to crash it?" Jonathan said.

Striker's pallor reddened up. "I've never crashed anything. Even after my foot was blown off, I kept that aircraft in the air." He pointed a finger at Boxers. "Can you say that you've never crashed anything?"

Big Guy recoiled from the question, then smiled. "I could say it," he said. Boxers was as good a pilot as Jonathan had ever seen, but thanks to circumstances that were mostly beyond his control, he'd endured a few hard landings along the way.

"Um," Jonathan said. That was it. Just "um." He needed to word his next question carefully. "The stakes are really high here, Carl. Be honest with me. And with yourself. I can't help but notice the cane. Are you really up for this anymore?"

Carl bristled, and then recovered, all over the course of maybe a second. He looked like he wanted to make a speech, but smiled instead. Jonathan was beginning to dislike the smile. Carl nodded once and said, "Yes."

Jonathan recognized the challenge to mix it up more, but he let it go. He sensed that Striker somehow needed this mission. He was reckless back when he did this every day. Jonathan had no desire to die on an op because some cowboy pilot couldn't do his job.

For right now, though, Carl had one undeniably good point: Jonathan had no leverage. He supposed he could create it if he needed it—hell, he could steal the chopper from him if it came to that—but the ripple effect of that as word spread through the Community would be devastating to Jonathan's business. Worse, it would undo a reputation for integrity that he'd spent a lifetime building.

Rule one in Jonathan's unofficial code: You never betray a friend.

They had time yet.

"How much equipment do you have to transport?" Striker asked. Just like that, it was back to business.

"All of us," Jonathan said, "plus about four hundred pounds of weapons and equipment."

"How much of that do you expect to expend?"

Jonathan shifted in his seat. It was bad form to discuss the practical details of a raid in front of people who found the phrase "spray and slay" offensive.

"Hopefully, none of it," Jonathan said. "In a perfect world, we'll knock on the door and they'll hand over the PCs without argument." He looked at Becky as he spoke, and she looked away.

"As a practical matter, probably a lot," he said to Carl.

"Are any of your weapons traceable?" Striker's entire demeanor had changed. The aging hippie vibe had been replaced with the soldier he used to be.

"No," Jonathan said.

"What have you—"

"Let's just leave it at no," Jonathan interrupted. "Nothing's traceable." The reality was that Jonathan retooled the barrels and receivers of all of his weapons after they'd been used on an op, and during all that work, his bare skin never touched the weapons. It was a bit of overkill, considering that his fingerprints didn't exist in any known file, but the little things could add up over time.

No one else in the room needed to know any of that.

Boxers said, "If you're choosing which aircraft to use, don't forget we're going to be two people heavier on the way out."

"But lighter in equipment." As Carl leaned over the table, his hair dangled in the middle of his performance charts and he pushed it away. "Do you really need all these people?"

"No," Jonathan said. "I need two for an exfil team. Actually, I could do with one, but since they're not pros, nobody should work alone."

"And the third one?" Striker asked.

"I promised them they could all come along."

"You know we're right here, right?" David asked.

The others ignored him. "When did an op become an amusement park ride?" Carl asked.

"Yeah, Boss, when did it become an amusement park ride?" Boxers said.

"We don't have the benefit of a trained army," Jonathan said. "The two of us can do a lot—we *do* do a lot—but sometimes, we can't do everything. We've had fair success getting more out of civilians than civilians thought they had to give."

"Yeah, okay," Carl said. "I get that. But why more people than you need?"

"Because they've all got a stake in this," Jonathan said. "If I were them, I'd want to be here, too."

Striker turned directly to the others. "You know you can get killed, right? Worse, you know you can get shot through the spine and be a quad for the rest of your life. Or through the gut and have to eat and shit through tubes. *That's* the kind of risk we're talking about. No video games, no do-overs, just real no-shit shoot-or-be-killed firefights. Is that really what you want to get into?"

"Jesus," Boxers said. "Now *I* don't want to go."

The speech had its desired effect. Yelena, David, and Becky all looked suddenly a little sheepish.

"I thought you said we'd be in support roles," Becky said. "Why would we have to do any shooting?"

Jonathan explained. "Carl von Clausewitz said it best two hundred years ago: no battle plan survives first contact with the enemy. We're developing a plan that should work, and should result in the fewest number of people on either side getting hurt. But for the plan to work, the enemy has to do what we want him to. Enemies don't like to do what *their* enemies want them to do. In fact, they're going to try to get us to do stuff to help them hurt us. It's as dynamic an environment as you can get."

Boxers added, "And why it's so friggin' unfair when you newsie types try to be lounge chair quarterbacks after the fact and tell the soldiers who were in the shit what they should have done when people were shooting at them."

"Easy, Big Guy," Jonathan said. "Same side, remember?" To David and Becky: "You have to excuse him. This is our first time with embeds."

"Are you crazy?" Carl said. "They're *reporters*?"

"We've had this discussion, Striker. Among us, I mean. Let it go." He let silence defuse the moment. "So, now you know the risks even better."

"You forgot to mention getting arrested by one of two governments—or maybe both—for the whole invasion thing," Yelena said. "He's my son. Everything you said is worth it."

"It's what they tried to do to me anyway," David said. "What the hell?"

Becky said nothing for a long moment. Finally, she asked, "Is somebody going to teach me how to work a gun?"

Len Shaw stood at his office window, looking past the front wall of the prison across the water to the western edge of the city's skyline. This place truly would make an outstanding hotel, he thought. Ottawa was an underappreciated jewel of a city. It had so much to offer both in summer and in winter. Skating on the Rideau Canal alone was reason enough to brave the frigid temperatures.

There was something poetic, he thought, in transforming a prison—a place of such misery—into a property that could bring happiness to so many. Likewise, it was tragic that in the interim it would be headquarters for such violence.

This was it for Len. He'd made that decision following his discussion last night with Dmitri. It took a lot of hatred and anger to drive the kind of zealotry that made the Movement what it was. Intellectually, at an academic level, he understood that if American power were not toppled, then the rest of the world would soon possess no power at all. In the United States, the wealthy became wealthier as the people became willing puppets to go to war to demand the resources of yet more powerless puppet regimes.

Even more than that, Len still mourned the loss of so many colleagues who were either killed or imprisoned when that Poltanov bitch betrayed them all. Should she pay? Yes. Was he ashamed that she'd been able to rise to such elevated levels of power with none of them even noticing for so many years? Yes.

And were it not for Jillian Lang, a zealot of another sort who targeted American secrets as her greatest conquest, they might never have discovered the truth about Anna Darmond. The transformation had really been something. Of course, that was when Jillian sold her secrets one at a time to the highest bidder, before she sensed that the FBI was on her tail and she just dumped them all for the world to read together.

As long as it was important for Washington to keep the First Lady's secret quiet, her identity was a point of leverage. And leverage gave them resources. The chapel on the north end of the Saint Stephen's compound was filled nearly to overflowing with weapons thanks to the largesse of the White House. A leaked transport route here, a lock combination there. Most of it procured without firing a shot.

For Len, this had all become a chess game, outwitting the other side to obtain that which they should never have had. But he'd lost the hatred, and with it had disappeared his desire to kill. He was just tired.

But soon it would end.

Blasting the airliner out of the sky at O'Hare last

week had merely been a test of the deployability of the Stinger missiles they'd procured. Day after tomorrow, between 8:00 and 11:00 A.M. local time, international flights would be shot down on takeoff in New York, Washington, San Francisco, Denver, Los Angeles, and Phoenix. Daily, for the next week, bombs would detonate in restaurants, office buildings, and shopping malls throughout Middle America, in cities like Fort Worth, Muncie, and Sheboygan—the cities that consider themselves off the radar for terrorist threats.

When America found itself at war on its own land, they would shift their focus away from their wars with other countries. And when they found out who their First Lady really was, and they realized the depth and scope of the lies they'd been told, they would react with anger. Trust in their government would evaporate overnight.

Around the world, leaders of other nations would express their deep concern and condolences even as they privately celebrated the plucking of the great American eagle's feathers.

Soon after that, the world would realize what a mistake it had been these past decades to ignore Russia as a cunning world power. They would see how the *Rodina* had been quietly pulling itself together after the glasnost nonsense. Mother Russia will have finally toppled the United States of America.

If, through some miracle, Len was able to survive the next few months, and if his participation was somehow never revealed, he would welcome the opportunity to try his hand at capitalism. He would love to become an innkeeper at this very spot.

It was a goal that seemed very, very far away.

"Are you dreaming in the day, Comrade?"

The voice startled him, but he didn't turn. "It's Len, Dmitri. And when did you stop knocking before entering?"

"I'm practicing my stealth."

Len turned to face the other man, who wore the same suit as yesterday, but with a fresh shirt.

"I see your new houseguests have arrived," Dmitri said. "It was good of you to give them clothes and blankets."

"I don't want them freezing to death," Len said. He pulled out his chair and sat, pretending to be distracted by the papers on his desk. "When do they leave?"

Dmitri took the wooden guest chair. "I'm not sure that's important for you to know." He reached for one of his black cigarettes.

"On the contrary," Len argued, handing him a lighter. "I need to provide for security. What it is not important for me to know is where you plan to take them next."

"Even I do not know that. Moscow has not shared their plans with me."

Len assumed Dmitri was lying because Dmitri didn't know how to tell the truth. "Then tell me what time the trucks arrive tonight to clear the chapel."

"After dark, that's all I know."

Len sighed. "Dmitri, I am not a spy. We have been colleagues long enough to dislike each other, but that is of no operational relevance. You have already doubled the guard here, and now you're bringing in even more. All of these people need to be fed. There are logistical concerns."

Dmitri waited a long time before answering. "They will arrive around midnight."

"And will they have guards to protect the shipments?"

"Impractical," Dmitri said. He waved away his cloud of smoke. "These will be unremarkable vehicles. Neither new nor old, big enough to carry a few launchers and warheads apiece, but not so large as to draw attention. Thus, no guards, no convoys."

"How do you get these to America?"

"Missiles are not so much larger than drugs."

Len took that to mean that they would use the same border crossings.

Dmitri laughed. "Americans are so predictable. If a smuggler is white with a nice haircut and a cross dangling from his rearview mirror, he can move anything across the border. You'll notice there's no talk of a fence across the Canadian border."

"That's because Canadians are happy to be in Canada." They chuckled together.

"About the new guards who showed up this morning," Len said, shifting back to business. "Where do they come from and how much do they know? They don't speak much to me or the rest of my normal staff."

"That is because I told them not to," Dmitri explained.

"I've heard them speak among themselves, and they don't sound Russian."

"They are not Russian," Dmitri said. "They are not Canadian, they are not American, and they are not Kenyan, although I believe that some were born in each of those countries. Their loyalty is to the man who is paying them today."

"Mercenaries."

Dmitri shrugged. "If you wish."

Len didn't wish. In his experience, mercenaries were merely well-paid thugs and murderers, fine for taking down a rival warlord, but useless for strategic thought.

"I can read your mind, Comrade. You do not respect such men."

"No one respects such men," Len said. "They don't even want respect as far as I can tell. They're all about fear."

"Fear and respect are very close cousins."

"But who are we trying to intimidate?" Len let the question hang in the air, and then he saw his own answer. "You no longer trust me, Dmitri?"

The other man exhaled a cloud and tapped the cigarette on the edge of the ash tray. "If I didn't trust you, you would be dead now," he said. "But I worry about how much you have changed. I worry that as we close in on victory, you seem to be pulling away."

"I will be loyal," Len insisted.

"I'm sure you will. But what was it that Comrade Gorbachev's best friend told the world? Trust but verify. Think of my little army as a form of insurance. Now, didn't you say something about food?"

CHAPTER TWENTY-FIVE

Boxers clearly was pissed to be consigned to firearms instruction while Jonathan checked out the aircraft, but even he knew that it was the best choice. Despite the fact the Big Guy didn't particularly like people—or perhaps because of it—he was a terrific instructor when it came to shooting. In the few hours that he would spend with David and Becky and the First Lady, they would know how to operate a Colt M4 and a Beretta M9 pistol with their eyes closed. That wouldn't necessarily make them good marksmen—that was a skill that took years to develop—but they would know enough to keep up a steady stream of fire without shooting each other.

Or, even better, they would know to keep the safety engaged until there was no choice but to shoot.

Carl led Jonathan through the snow across the expansive lawn toward the barn-hangars.

"How many aircraft do you have?" Jonathan asked.

"In total?" Striker looked toward the sky as he considered the question. "Right now, as we speak, I've got six on hand, but not all of them are in as good working order as the others." His cane seemed to be particularly important to him in the knee-deep snow.

"Where do you get them?" As he asked the question, Jonathan tried to modulate his tone to be conversational, when in fact the line about not all being in as good a shape as others had spooked him.

"All kinds of places," he said. "You just need to know where to look."

"Such as?"

"Company secret, Dig. A good businessman never shares company secrets."

Their trajectory was taking them directly toward the UH-1 Jonathan had seen poking through the door on the way in. "We're not taking a Huey, are we?" Jonathan asked.

"One of the best choppers ever made," Carl said.

"With all the stealth of a brass band," Jonathan countered.

Carl chuckled. "That sound scared the shit out of the Viet Cong back in the day."

In fact, the Viet Cong called that distinctive *wop-wop* sound "muttering death." Even battle-hardened NVA were known to dump their weapons in a ditch when they heard the sound, unaware of the swarm of copper-jacketed bees that were on their way.

"Well, you know, this mission of yours is a tough nut," Striker said. "You want to fly a heavy load, yet you want to be stealthy, and you have a lot of people." They arrived at the front door and Carl pulled on the left-hand door.

"Need me to pull the other one?" Jonathan offered.

"Nope, just need enough space to get through." He led the way inside.

Jonathan followed. The difference between the snow glare and the darkness of the hangar's interior left him momentarily blind. Reflexively, he moved his hand closer to his .45. Blindness was never an advantage.

"Easy there, cowboy," Carl said. "Weapons down. How long you been out of the unit?"

"A while," Jonathan said.

"You guys always were quick to draw down." Carl chuckled. "I remember flying some of you guys into some Golf Foxtrot and as we touched down, one of your Unit brothers pickled a round past my ear and out through the windscreen to kill a skinny who was running right at us. Scared the shit outta me and saved my life all at twenty-three hundred feet per second."

Jonathan knew exactly who that unit guy was. He stared back at him from the mirror every morning. "You're welcome."

Now that Jonathan's eyes were adjusting, he could see Carl just well enough to note the smile. "No shit, that was you?"

"It was," Jonathan said. He reminded him of the exact location on the world map.

"Well, then hell yeah. Thanks. Anyway, we've got this logistical problem of invading a friendly nation, snatching some good guys, and getting out without getting tagged."

Jonathan could make out the developing silhouettes of the various aircraft.

"For quiet, you can't beat the Little Bird," Striker said, patting the skin of the MH-6 that lurked just behind the Huey. "But you're talking a two-fifty round-trip with a heavy load. If she's got it in her, it isn't by much, know what I mean?"

"You don't want to break your record of zero crashes."

"Exactly. And even the Huey you're worried about. While it can handle the mileage and the load with change on both ends, look at the size of the son of a bitch. You need half a football field just to set her down. Plus, she's got some serious gray in her hair."

Anything that made Striker nervous scared the living shit out of Jonathan.

Carl wandered to the front wall and flipped a switch, igniting some intense floodlighting. "Given all of the variables, I think this bird is our best bet."

The two-handed reveal pose Carl struck reminded Jonathan of a television model from *The Price is Right*. The chopper he presented looked like a Little Bird that had taken a deep, deep breath. It still had the pregnant-mosquito look, but this one took up twice the footprint.

"European Helicopter?" Jonathan guessed, naming one of the world's most respected chopper-makers.

"The EC135," Carl said.

Jonathan planted his fists on his hips. "That's a new aircraft, isn't it?"

"This one is looking forward to her eighth birthday."

"That must be a million-dollar aircraft," Jonathan said. What he didn't say was, *where did you steal this from?*

"Actually, she's more like four million new," Striker said. "But I got a real deal on her."

Warning bell. "How?"

"Do you really want to know?"

Jonathan steeled himself with a breath. "Given the stakes," he said, "I think I do."

"Let's just say that this one landed kind of hard," Carl said.

Shit.

"But don't worry," Striker went on, "I've done all the repairs myself. She's like new."

The chopper looked like it just rolled off the factory floor, except for the rust-brown primer coat where there should have been paint.

"Note the shrouded tail rotor," Carl said. "That takes out a lot of the engine noise. You're still going to get some whopping from the main rotor disk, but against the night sky, we'll look like a medevac chopper. A lot of jurisdictions use these as medevacs. She's fast, and I sprung for SOTA FLIR."

Jonathan recognized SOTA as state-of-the-art, and FLIR as forward-looking infrared, which meant that the bird could fly full-throttle at treetop level.

"What do you know about US-Canada air defense?" Jonathan asked.

"Not a thing."

He appreciated the honesty, even if it didn't help him. Jonathan said, "I'm betting that the Canadians are less worried about people invading their air space from the US than America is worried about invasions from the north."

"If you feel good believing that, I'll feel good believing it, too."

In the distance, a ripple of gunfire rattled the otherwise still morning air. Boxers' students had taken their first shot.

"So, is this really what you do, Dig?" Carl asked. "I've heard rumors through the Community, but you know how reliable they are."

"Exactly," Jonathan said, being deliberately obtuse. "Company secrets."

Striker seemed to understand the gentle rebuke. "Well, for what it's worth, I heard that you did some very cool, very noble work on behalf of Boomer Nasbe. I won't ask you to verify, but if it's true, and I assume it is, I bow at your friggin' feet. If that's the shit you're doing to pay your bills, I want you to know that I'm part of your team any time you make the phone call."

Jonathan kept a poker face. He had, in fact, helped the Nasbe family out of a jam a while ago, but it made no sense to confirm the rumor.

"I've made you uncomfortable," Striker said. "I'm sorry. That's the polar opposite of what I wanted to do. You're still working for the Community, and I don't think there's a greater calling than that."

"Tell me that this bird is airworthy," Jonathan said.

"And then some," Striker said. "And like I said, she's quiet." He pointed again like a proud father to the shrouded tail rotor.

Unlike most helicopters, in which the tail rotor was open to the atmosphere and therefore noisy, the shrouded tail rotor provided the most basic of QTR—quiet tail rotor—technology, knocking the noise signature down by fifteen decibels, three times the sound pressure, as registered from the ground. That might just give them the edge they needed to get across the border and back without being reported by someone who was pissed because their rerun of *Seinfeld* was interrupted by aircraft noise.

Jonathan pulled open the side door. It should have revealed seats and restraints, but in fact revealed only open floor space. He cast a glance to Striker.

"Okay," Striker said. "It's not the most perfect, safest arrangement of floor space. But the beast will carry you and your equipment there, and you and your precious cargo back." Carl stood taller. "Is that, or is that not, the point of this exercise?"

Sometimes, you had to choose between the best of bad options. In this case, it was the promise of a sound airframe, despite the lack of seats or seatbelts.

"I promise not to crash," Carl said, as if reading Jonathan's thoughts.

"Oh," Jonathan said. "Well, in that case, you have a deal." They shook on it.

It was the kind of cold that radiated all the way through David's waterproof boots and into the bones of his feet. Boxers—Big Guy now because code names were important, though he never said why—had led them on a hike to the edge of the clearing that contained the house and barns. They faced the thick woods. Even with the leaves gone from the trees, you couldn't see more than thirty feet in.

David, like Mrs. Darmond and Becky, wore a heavy vest—a *ballistic* vest, not a bulletproof vest, and no, he would never make that mistake again—that looked like the ones he saw on the news coming from war zones. Its surface was covered with all kinds of patches and pockets into which Big Guy had jammed maybe a dozen ammunition magazines—oh, good God, not *clips* because *clips* are a specific kind of magazine designed for the M-1 rifle—each of which had been loaded with a single bullet.

They'd already learned that they were shooting Colt

M4 carbines, the same rifle that was standard issue to active-duty soldiers. They'd been introduced to the safety and to the switch that allowed them to change from single shot to automatic, which would turn the weapon into a submachine gun. That was the DFWI switch, according to the Big Guy—the don't fuck with it switch. Automatic mode was bad. It wasted ammunition.

The whole session was a waste as far as David was concerned. He'd fired his own M4 on the range countless times. Granted, it was a semiautomatic version, but Big Guy was telling them not to use full-auto anyway.

"I don't give a shit if you can hit your targets tonight," Big Guy said. "If it comes to that, so much shit will be broken that your marksmanship probably won't make a difference. Just don't shoot each other, and for God's sake, don't shoot me. And if you do shoot me, go for a head shot because if you shoot me and I live, you will die with a rifle up your ass. Are we communicating?"

Personable guy. David nodded while Becky said, "Yes, sir."

"The easiest shot you'll ever get at an enemy is when he's reloading. The best rifle in the world is just a glorified club when it's empty, and the guy who brings a club to a gunfight always loses."

From there David learned more than he ever thought he'd need to know about the technical aspects of reloading.

"You only have one round in your magazines because we don't need to practice pulling the trigger. The way these weapons are designed, when you fire the last round in a mag, the bolt locks open. You don't have to keep count of how many rounds you've fired. When that puppy locks open, you'll feel it. And if you don't feel it, you're going to know because the next time you pull the trigger, the weapon's going to say click instead of bang. Bang is good. Click is bad. Anybody need to take a note on that?"

By the time David realized that the Big Guy was trying to be funny, the moment had passed.

Big Guy brought his own weapon to his shoulder. His gun looked similar yet different from theirs, as if born of the same mother but with different fathers. He fired a shot at the woods, and then turned to face the class, his muzzle pointed toward the sky. The bolt was clearly locked open.

"Here's what I want you to do." He demonstrated that the mag release button was just above the trigger on either side of the weapon. "Let the mag drop to the ground. In the shit, don't worry about it after you drop it. Here in training, take care of it, because it's one of the ones you'll be using later if we're in the shit."

He fingered the release, and the empty mag dropped away.

"Take a new one from a pouch—" He demonstrated in live slow motion. "Put your forefinger along the nose of the bullets just to make sure they're in alignment, and insert it till it clicks." He did those steps. "Now what's wrong with the weapon?"

David raised his hand, happy to have something to contribute. "It won't fire. The bolt's still open."

"Jimmy Olsen gets a point," Big Guy said.

"He was a photographer," David said.

Big Guy fired off a glare that would have been funny

if it wasn't so friggin' scary. "Don't cross me, son," he said. Then he winked.

Big Guy demonstrated the bolt release button on the left-hand side of the breech. "If this isn't closed, the weapon won't fire." With the bolt closed, he turned and fired another round into the woods.

"So, that's the exercise," Big Guy said. "One round, drop the mag, insert a new one, seat the bolt, fire a round and drop the mag and seat a new one. We're going to do this until you're really tired of doing this."

Truer words had never been spoken.

By the time the exercise was done, David's "dead time"—the interval between the last shot fired from one mag and the first shot fired from the next—was down to three seconds. Big Guy pronounced that to be *survivable*.

Who would not feel confident with such gushing words of encouragement?

"Dad, I'm scared," Josef said.

"I know," Nicholas said. The boy had only been awake for maybe fifteen minutes. Thankfully (tragically?), the drugs they'd used to knock them out were far more effective on a child than on an adult. "Try not to be."

What a stupid thing to say. Try not to feel what every sane person in the universe would feel under the same circumstances.

"Why are they doing this?"

"Because they're bad people," Nicholas said. Was that an acceptable response from a father who cares?

"They're going to hurt us, aren't they?"

Nicholas looked at his son. Josef had chosen to place his face in the single shaft of light—single shaft of warmth—that invaded their shell. With his dark eyes and dark hair and bruised cheek and filth-streaked face, he looked like a picture from a movie poster. Gavroche from *Les Misérables*, perhaps, or the Artful Dodger from *Oliver!*

"They're going to *try* to hurt us," Nicholas said. "Just as they already hurt us. But we need to be brave and not let them do that."

The boy stared back at him, his face a giant question mark.

"Have you ever been in a fight, Joey?" It ripped at his heart to ask such a question. He was the boy's father, for heaven's sake. He should know every momentous event in his life. He had no doubt that Marcie did.

"Not many," Josef said. He looked down when he spoke, exuding shame.

"Look at me, Joey," Nicholas said.

The boy resisted.

"Please. Look at me."

Those huge Bambi eyes, with the eyelashes to match, rocked up to meet his. Nicholas had never seen him look more like his mother.

"I don't know what they have in store for us," Nicholas said, "but if they're left to their own means, I don't think it can be good."

The eyes reddened. "Do you think they're going to kill us?"

Nicholas shook his head and moved closer to his son on the floor. He offered his arm for a hug, but the boy refused. "No, I honestly don't think they're going to kill us. What I think they're going to do is take us to Russia."

Josef recoiled. "Why?"

"Because that's where your babushka is from. I think this is about her."

"Because she is the president's wife?"

"I think so. I think they are using us to get something from the Americans."

"But *we're* Americans."

Nicholas nodded. "Yes, we are." Once you start hearing the words spoken aloud, they become so complicated. "But these people who took us. I do not think they are."

Josef's eyes folded into a scowl. "But the police will rescue us," he said. "Babushka is the First Lady. She's the president's wife. They have to rescue us."

"I certainly hope they will try," Nicholas said. Josef knew nothing of his father's refusal to accept protection, but he'd felt the animosity from Tony Darmond. "But if that doesn't happen," Nicholas continued, "it will be up to you and me to determine our fate."

"What do you mean?"

"It means that we may have to fight."

"But they're bigger than us," the boy said. "And stronger."

"They seemed stronger than they really are because we were surprised at the house. We were asleep. If we had been awake—"

"The people who grabbed me were very strong," Josef said. "I tried to dig my fingers into his arm, but his skin felt like stone. He was very strong."

Nicholas lowered his voice. "But they have balls," he said.

Josef gasped. It was not the kind of thing he heard from his father every day.

"Testicles," Nicholas clarified, as if it were necessary. "And they have eyes and they have noses and knees. These are all very sensitive areas. If they come to take us away, I think we need to fight."

Those beautiful Bambi eyes clouded with fear, but Nicholas pressed on.

"If they drug us again, or take us onto another airplane, I don't think we'll ever see home again. We might not even see each other again. I don't want that to happen."

"I don't want that to happen, either."

This was the opening Nicholas had been hoping for. "Then we'll have to fight," he said.

"But they're big."

"They're not that big. And I don't think they're very smart. In fact, I think that we're smarter than they are."

The fear in the boy's eyes deepened.

"Didn't you hear the way they were talking?" Nicholas donned a comically heavy Russian accent. "You must come with us or we will hurt you. You must help me scratch my butt because I cannot find it."

The word "butt" was always a sure thing. Always elicited a giggle.

"I mean, think about it," Nicholas went on. "They were so scared of you that they had to pump you full of drugs so that you couldn't fight them back."

A smile bloomed.

"Look," Nicholas said, "Maybe it will never come to this. Maybe I'm wrong and this will turn into some kind of vacation—"

"A vacation in a prison?"

"Okay, a really shitty vacation."

Another laugh.

"But if it turns out that they want to take us away, or if they come at us with drugs again, I want you to know that I'm going to fight them."

"But they might kill you."

"They might. But if it comes to that, I'm going to die fighting. If we allow ourselves to be knocked unconscious, or if we allow ourselves to be put on an airplane, our lives as we know them will stop. Do you understand that?"

Josef started to cry, but Nicholas didn't think he was aware. "I really don't know how to fight grown-ups."

"Balls," Nicholas said. He pointed to his own. "Every man has them, and it doesn't matter how strong they are. A kick in the balls stops everyone."

"And the eyes?" Josef asked. "You said something about the eyes."

"A strong man who has a finger in his eye is not very strong anymore," Nicholas said.

"But they'll hurt me."

Nicholas took a deep breath. He'd been rehearsing this speech in his head for a while. "Maybe," he said. "I hope not, but they might hurt you. You've been hurt before, right?"

"Not like—"

"Hurt is hurt, Joey. When you broke your arm doing the trick on the skateboard, was it worth it?"

"That hurt *a lot*. I had to get surgery."

Five screws and a plate, Nicholas didn't say. He could still see the X-ray in the viewer, still feel the sense of helpless hopelessness in his gut. "Of course it hurt. You broke your arm. If broken arms didn't hurt, people would break them every day."

He got the smile he was trolling for.

"But it didn't stop you from skateboarding, did it?"

Joey shook his head.

"In fact, weren't you back out there skateboarding *with* a cast on your arm?"

A giggle. "Yeah."

"Well, that's the Joey I'm talking to right now," Nicholas pressed. "The one who's tough enough to face his fears."

"But they could kill us."

"They could kill us anyway. We could get hit by lighting." He reached out and pulled Josef's hand out from under the blanket. He held it, and then covered it with his other hand. At whisper, he said, "You need to know that if they come for us, I'm going to fight. In fact, I'm going to fight all the way. What you do is up to you, and I know this is a crappy kind of choice to have to make at your age, but I want you to know that I'll be able to use all the help I can get."

Josef nodded. "Okay," he said. "When do you think they'll come?"

Nicholas turned to look out the window. Purple hues had begun to infuse the perfect blue of the sky. "I would guess after dark," he said. "But I don't know."

"Suppose I fall asleep again?"

Nicholas waved away the concern as it were a pesky fly. "If you need to sleep, sleep. Who knows, but maybe you will need the rest. I'll stay awake."

As the boy settle back into his covers and closed his eyes, Nicholas thought about taking back the entire conversation. For sure, going along was the quickest way to stay alive in the short term, but in the long term, captivity meant only misery.

In less than a minute, Josef's breathing became rhythmic, and then there was the slightest trace of a snore.

As he watched his son sleep, he tried to come to grips with how desperately he hated Tony Darmond.

CHAPTER TWENTY-SIX

David felt as if he were living someone else's life. The events of the past couple of days were so far beyond the bounds that typically defined his existence that for a moment out there on the range in the glare and the cold and the sun, he felt a little dizzy. Was it possible to have so vivid a dream?

The answer, of course, was no, but that didn't make the surrealism of the moment any more . . . real.

Now they were gathered back in crazy Striker's little house, boots off and warming near the fire, while the entire team snarfed down pizza and hotdogs. Apparently, that was all Striker had in his fridge. It wasn't till he smelled the food that he realized how hungry he was.

He found out the hard way that Big Guy was hungry, too. Damn near lost his arm reaching for the same pizza slice as he.

Together, they ate like locusts, consuming every morsel within ten minutes.

When the table was cleared of dishes, Scorpion pulled a heavy-duty laptop out of his enormous backpack—he called it a rucksack—and positioned it so everyone could see the screen.

After a few taps on the keys, a daytime picture of Saint Stephen's Island appeared in high definition.

"This is the latest satellite imagery we have," Scorpion said. "The good news and bad news is the addition of more guards. Here, here, and here."

David couldn't see what he was pointing at.

"Look for the shadows," Scorpion explained. "They're easier to make out than the tops of heads."

Of course. Once he saw that, the human forms were obvious.

"These images refresh every four minutes," Scorpion went on. "Mother Hen will be monitoring them back at the War Room and will let us know if anything changes significantly."

Yelena raised her hand. "I don't understand how more guards can be anything but bad news."

"It means that there's something there on the property that's worth a closer guard than yesterday. In my mind, that means that your family has arrived."

He clicked another button, and the imagery changed to something that resembled a photographic negative. "This is thermal imaging," he said. "Remember yesterday, when we looked, only this area at the top appeared warm? Well look now at the southern wing. It's warm now, too. According to the drawings we found on the Internet, and augmented by records Mother Hen dug up, that entire building is stacked cell blocks. Three floors of them, except for the wing where we expect the PCs to be, which is four floors."

"How are we going to know which level they're on?" Becky asked.

Scorpion held up both hands, as if to ward off an attacker. "No. There is no *we* inside the compound, unless you're talking about Big Guy and me. You three will be outside the compound. More on that in a minute."

David felt an emotion that was hard to describe. Could it be disappointment that he wasn't going to be shot at? Maybe it was just disappointment that he wasn't trusted enough to be on the real team.

"I want to be there," Yelena said.

"I know you do," Scorpion said. "But this isn't about what's best for you, it's about what's best for your son and grandson. Big Guy and I have been doing this for a long time. The fact that we're here talking to you is perfect evidence that we're good at what we do."

"But—"

"Hear me out. In the very best case, if everything breaks our way, we'll already be dealing with two people who may or may not know up from down. To add a third—and with all respect, consider the possibility that you might get shot or be injured—now we'll have more victims than operators. It's not a sustainable model."

David watched as the words rolled over the First Lady—they pierced her, really—he saw her try to construct an argument, and then abandon the effort when the inherent sense of it all settled into her brain.

"Big Guy and I will move heaven and earth to reunite you with your family."

Becky tentatively raised a hand. It hadn't been going well for her thus far, and she seemed hesitant to step in something again. "Suppose you and Big Guy, you know, don't . . ." She couldn't complete the sentence.

"Make it?" Scorpion prompted. "Suppose we get killed? It won't happen."

"You can't know that."

"I have to know that. I have to know that beyond any shadow of doubt, because if I consider failure to be an option, then failure becomes the only possible outcome."

"That's hubris," Yelena said. "That's arrogance."

Scorpion seemed taken aback for just a few seconds, and then he shrugged. "Okay," he said. "But it won't happen."

David didn't understand the point of the question in the first place. If the rescuers died, then everyone died. What was the point of even discussing that?

Scorpion clicked another key. The thermal image became a map. "We leave from here," he said, pointing to a spot on a service road that ran parallel to the Ottawa River Parkway, roughly south-southwest of the southernmost point of Saint Stephen's Island. "David, you and Becky will just leave the boat trailer there, and Big Guy and I will paddle around to the northern tip of the island, and that's where we'll moor the boat."

In essence what he was describing was an inverted J, a route that seemed needlessly complicated and very long.

"Why not just go straight north to the southern tip of the island?" David asked. "It'd be a lot quicker."

Scorpion's jaw set and he drew in a quick breath. Apparently, Scorpion didn't appreciate being second-guessed. "Remember that getting in is the easy part. Everybody's dumb and happy because even though they've geared up with additional guards, none of those guards actually expects anything to happen. After things go boom and the shooting starts, it'll start getting hairy. It's the getting-out part that's difficult."

"More to my point," David pressed. "Since the shortest distance between two points is a straight line, I don't understand—"

Jonathan cut him off with a raised hand. "You will, okay? Let me finish, and when I'm done, we'll get to whatever questions you still have. Deal?"

David set his own jaw. Scorpion wasn't interested in input. David supposed he understood, but his life was on the line, too, you know?

"We're going to kick this thing off with a big-ass explosion," Scorpion said. The map on the screen moved, and they were looking at a satellite photo again. "The chapel is now designated Building Alpha. In fact let's get the rest of the labels out of the way."

The chapel—Building Alpha—sat nestled in the western wall. Across a tiny yard area, four wings comprised a near-perfect square. The northernmost east-west wing was designated Bravo. Then, moving counterclockwise around the remainder of the square, the wings were designated Charlie, Delta, and Echo. The north-south-oriented service buildings on the western wall of the compound were designated Foxtrot and Golf. The big building that was the main cell block—the northernmost building in the compound—was Hotel.

"The first seconds are key," Scorpion explained. "We're going to set charges in the chapel—Building Alpha—then move to the main gate between Foxtrot and Golf to set them off. That's going to get their attention. When they're running around trying to figure out where Armageddon just came from, we're going to get into the cell block inside Delta, snatch the good guys, and then run like bunny rabbits." He tossed a nod toward Big Guy. "Okay, three bunny rabbits and a big honkin' tortoise."

Big Guy flipped him off as David stifled a laugh.

"Won't people be shooting at you?" Becky asked. A stupider question had never been asked, and she seemed to realize it as she shrank away.

"We'll have contingencies in place to protect the Mishins," Scorpion assured. The way he said it reinforced David's feeling that Scorpion was deliberately holding back operational details. "But do I think it's going to be a hot extraction?" Scorpion continued. "Oh, yeah. And this is where you three come in."

David was aware of sitting taller in his chair.

"Once the noise starts, it's going to be pure bedlam. That's the intent. But since that River Street Bridge is the only way on or off the island, every cop and fire-fighter in Canada is going to be streaming in from there. We're talking roadblocks and God knows what else. Can you see that in your imagination?"

David thought it was interesting that he actually waited for an answer to what he'd assumed was a rhetorical question. They all said yes.

"So before we blow the first charge, I need for you to be on the other side of the river in Quebec at this spot right here." He pointed to a tiny inlet at the base of what appeared to be commercial buildings near the river shore on the Quebec side of the river. "This is our exfil spot, right here. If we do our jobs right, we'll be en route back to the chopper by the time anybody even knows what the hell has happened. If you're not there, everything else will have been for nothing. Do. Not. Screw. This. Up."

David felt a chill. Where Big Guy radiated pure menace all the time, Scorpion seemed like a nice enough guy. Polished, even. Someone you might want to meet for a drink after work. But in that last statement, his eyes flashed a homicidal intensity that took David's breath away.

Who was this man?

When the briefing was done, Jonathan and Boxers separated themselves from the others and wandered back to the barns. Striker had already moved the Huey out of the way so that he could hook a tractor to the EC135 and pull it out into the open.

"I don't like other people in the cockpit," Boxers said. "It's his bird, but it's our op. We have a way of doing things, and it's worked real good for us for a long time. Why are you giving in so easily?"

As happened every winter at this time, Jonathan was more than ready for spring. He was tired of schlepping through snow. "Why are you wrapped so tight about this?" he asked. "He's not a crop duster. He flew for the 160th, for God's sake."

"A long time ago."

"We left the unit a long time ago," Jonathan countered.

"But it ain't like we stopped practicing the craft, is it? He doesn't even have two feet."

"And you don't have two legs."

"Bullshit. One of 'em's just mostly titanium." Boxers was the only person Jonathan ever knew who'd learned to walk again after taking a hit with a fifty-cal.

Granted, it was a glancing blow, but still. "Why are you being so . . . flexible? You're never flexible on this stuff."

Jonathan didn't want to answer, because he knew how the answer would sound, and he wasn't in the mood to take Big Guy's shit.

"Okay, don't tell me," Boxers said. "What the hell, it's only my friggin' life. Not to mention the president's wife, and her spawn. Oh, yeah, and two reporters, but I plan to push them out of the chopper, anyway, as soon as we're airborne. I have no need to know."

"I think he needs it," Jonathan blurted. There, it was out.

Boxers pulled to a halt. "Oh, God. Tell me you didn't just say that. He *needs* it? I don't even know what that friggin' means."

But the level of his agitation told Jonathan that he knew exactly what it meant.

"He wants to feel relevant again," Jonathan said. "They're his birds, he's a goddamned war hero, and he wants to feel relevant again. I don't see anything wrong with giving him a shot."

Boxers gathered himself with a deep breath. "Good God, you've been sneaking off and watching PBS, haven't you? Oprah, maybe? When did we become the friggin' USO? I don't give a shit what he needs to *feel*. Christ, I don't give a shit what *you* need to feel and you're as close to a friend as I've ever had. This is all about the mission, Dig."

Jonathan planted his fists on his hips. "No shit, really? This is about a mission? Why hadn't I thought about that?"

"I don't mean to insult—"

"Then quit insulting. Quit insulting me and quit insulting Striker. That bullet took away more than his foot, don't you see that? Do you remember what an artist he was in the air?"

"I remember he was a cowboy."

"A cowboy who saved a shitload of good guys who would have been dead otherwise."

"But *look* at him, Boss. He looks like he stepped out of Woodstock."

"That's just hair and attitude," Jonathan said. "We're cutting him a break. If we need to punt him at the end, we'll punt him. You can take over midflight if it comes to that."

"No, I can't," Boxers said. "That's the thing. You haven't looked inside the cockpit of that bird, have you?"

"I thought I did."

"Well, next time, look again. There's no second seat up front. The left seat is a passenger seat. He could have a heart attack or just go suicidal and there'd be nothing I could do about it."

Jonathan had in fact not seen that. And it was outside his normal operating parameters to trust any outsiders with mission-critical responsibilities. But this felt like the right thing to do. "Striker flies the aircraft," he said. He started walking again.

Boxers followed. Jonathan could feel his displeasure, but he also knew that Big Guy was a soldier's soldier. Once a decision was made, he would respect it, even if he didn't like it.

But if things went to shit, Jonathan knew to expect an earful.

CHAPTER TWENTY-SEVEN

They cruised in total blackness at 180 miles per hour, the chopper's skids never more than ten feet above the leafless treetops. For a while, Jonathan watched through his NVGs, but ultimately switched them off and lifted them out of the way. He had no control over what kind of landing they were going to have, so what was the sense of stressing over it? Per Boxers' insistence, Big Guy sat in the left seat, where he could keep an eye on the pilot.

"We're one mile from the Canadian border," Striker announced. He flew with night vision in place, and with the aircraft completely blacked out. Before flipping off his NVGs, Jonathan did take note of how interesting the pilot's ponytail looked falling from the bottom of his flight helmet.

Jonathan pressed the transmit button in the center of his ballistic vest. "Mother Hen, Scorpion, how do you read?"

Venice replied without pause, "Loud and clear, and your GPS signal is strong. I'm monitoring emergency frequencies, and so far, you're not upsetting anyone."

"Roger," he said. *Give it a minute or two*, he didn't say.

Across from him, Yelena, David, and Becky sat on the floor. They said nothing. Instead, they stared into the darkness of the cabin, seemingly lost in whatever place their imaginations had taken them to. If they weren't scared, they were out of their minds. Each of them wore the requisite vest and helmet with ten spare mags of ammunition. While they had comm gear, Jonathan made sure to set theirs at a different channel than his. Too many people liked to hear themselves speak on the radio, and he didn't want to deal with any of that once this op went hot.

"We just crossed into hostile territory," Striker announced. "Assuming, that is, that the Canucks are hostiles. Kind of an odd thought, actually."

Fifteen minutes later, Jonathan felt the aircraft slow. He rose from his spot on the deck and duckwalked forward, where he could peer between shoulders to see out the front windscreen. With his NVGs back in place, the terrain looked identical to that which he had studied so intently in the satellite images.

"Here to check me out, too?" Striker asked.

"Just here to look," Jonathan said.

Striker pointed to a spot on the ground about five hundred yards away. "Can we agree that that's our LZ?"

"Looks good to me. I even see a boat and a truck," Jonathan noted.

"I'd love to know how you got those planted here," Striker said.

"Company secrets," Jonathan replied with a smile. It wasn't all that difficult, really. Venice had searched the

Internet for listings of boats for sale in Ottawa. The requirement was that the boat be inconspicuous and that it have its own trailer. A similar search through the for-sale listings found a crew cab pickup for sale. She negotiated the prices for both on the condition that they be delivered to this address, which was chosen in part because it was an abandoned property. She paid in real cash through a wire transfer from one of Jonathan's cutout companies. There was always a risk of getting ripped off, but when you pay twice the asking price, people generally respond. That was true in North America and Europe, anyway. On other continents, it paid to have face-to-face contact in any business deal.

Jonathan said, "Do a couple of passes before we touch down. I want to see if we have any lurkers." The downside to doing business over the phone and through wire transfers is that they stunk of criminal activity. Jonathan wanted to make sure that no one had called in the Mounties to stake out the place.

"Looks clean to me, Boss," Boxers said.

Jonathan agreed. The infrared showed only a lot of cold. "Set her down on the black side," said. He knew that Striker would recognize the side farthest away from the road.

A single structure resided on the property they'd chosen as their landing zone. It measured one hundred fifty feet by forty-five feet, and had most recently been used as a commercial woodworking shop. The owner had died, leaving debts that required foreclosure on the property. Now, the bank was trying desperately to unload the land and the building, but no one was interested. There was no end to the information Venice could squeeze out of a computer.

They landed in a cloud of blowing snow. As Striker went about the business of shutting things down, Jonathan addressed the others. "Okay," he said, "we are now officially in violation of about a million laws. From this moment on, our planning is just advanced dreaming. I hope everything goes the way we want, but if it does, this will be the first time.

"This is also your last chance to opt out before we break another *two* million laws. It's all for a good cause, but if we get caught or arrested, the cause won't matter to the prosecutor."

"Having Mrs. Darmond with us might help a little," David said.

"Or, it might make it worse," Yelena said.

"That's not going to happen if everyone does their jobs," Jonathan insisted. "Big Guy and I are golden. We'll get done what needs to be done. You just hold up your end and we'll be fine. Now let's load this gear into the truck and get started."

It wasn't until Becky stepped out of the helicopter and felt the assault of the frigid air that she realized she couldn't go through with this. Early on, maybe it was a pride thing, or maybe it was an adventure thing, but now that she stood in the blowing snow on Canadian soil, in the company of men who made their living by killing other men, she realized that it was just wrong.

There had to be another way. There *always* was a nonviolent solution to every problem.

But that horse had fled the barn a long time ago.

They were on a terminal course toward committing capital murder. This was just wrong, and she found herself frozen in place, unable to move or to speak. She wanted to cry, but she wouldn't allow it. She was afraid that the tears would freeze to her face. That her eyes would freeze shut.

David had already carried two duffel bags over to the truck, and as he returned, he said, "No, that's okay, Becky. We don't need any help."

She grabbed his arm and pulled him away from the open door of the chopper, into the darkness where they could speak in a place where the wind wouldn't carry her words to the others.

"What are you doing?" David protested. He yanked his arm away.

"We can't do this," she said.

His eyes flashed in the darkness. "What?"

"I said we can't do this. It's wrong. It's against the law. People are going to get killed."

David threw a look over at the others, and grabbed her shoulders in both his hands. His voice was barely a whisper when he said, "Becky, you can't back out now. People are counting on you."

"No, they're not. Scorpion doesn't even want me here. He made that very clear."

"So, what, this is like hurt feelings or something?" He looked back at the others and modulated his voice again. "People are counting on you. *I'm* counting on you."

"I can't start something when I know people will die because of what I'm doing. I don't believe that you can just rationalize this away."

"Where the hell was this discussion when we were still in Virginia? You didn't have to come."

"Neither did you."

"Yes, I did. These assholes tried to kill me. If we can put a stop to all of this shit, they won't want to do that anymore."

"Yo!" Scorpion called. "Is there a problem over there?"

"No," David said quickly.

"Yes," Becky said. "I'm not going. I can't. These things you're planning to do are—"

"Fine," Scorpion said. "Stay with Striker. Everybody else load up. We've got work to do."

Inexplicably—maybe even unreasonably—Scorpion's words stung her. She looked to David, but he'd already broken eye contact and was on his way back to the others.

She'd never felt more alone.

Boxers looked happy as hell to be back in the driver's seat. He drove the eight-year-old nondescript Chevy crew cab at posted speeds and obeyed every traffic sign. The nightmare scenarios lay in unanticipated turns of fate. In this case, the worst of the worst would be some kind of routine traffic stop where they were found to be carrying an arsenal of weapons and explosives.

The mood inside the vehicle was dark with anticipation, but Jonathan sensed something more.

"Don't think badly about her, David," he said. "She got spooked. No shame in that. Better to find out now than when we're in the thick of things." He turned in his shotgun seat to address David and the First Lady face-to-face in the back. "But she's the one, understand? We had one extra set of hands, which means that only one person had the luxury of backing out. She took that off the table for both of you."

"You give a lot of lectures to people," Yelena said. "Did you know that?"

Jonathan smiled. "Ma'am, I've seen shit go wrong in a thousand different ways, and I've never seen them go wrong the same way twice. When that happens, there's only two ways to go. You can panic and die, or you can improvise intelligently. The lectures are meant to scare you into being decisive if the time comes."

"Decisive about what?" David asked.

"About taking action. About trusting your gut and never acting out of fear. If you have to run away, run away, but don't turn your back on the guy who wants to shoot you. And for God's sake, if it comes to that, be the one who pulls the trigger first."

Jonathan thought it notable that Yelena's eyes showed no emotion. They were the eyes of a hardened warrior, so focused on the mission that risks didn't matter. David, on the other hand, looked like a kid in a classroom trying to memorize every word for an upcoming exam.

"Remember," Jonathan said, "Nine times out of ten, if you need to shoot, all you need to do is throw a lot of lead downrange. If our really spotty intel is correct, there will be exactly four good guys on the island, and that'll be the PCs, Big Guy, and me. Try really hard not to shoot us."

"I'm going to try really hard not to shoot anybody," David said. He cringed after he said it, probably be-

cause of the way the words echoed those of his girlfriend. Or whatever the hell she was to him.

"Not shooting at anybody is even better," Jonathan
said. "After we launch the boat, your job is to get the
hell out of Ottawa and into Quebec. Do not speed, do
not allow your firearms to show, and in general try to
be invisible."

"How long do we wait?" Yelena asked.

Jonathan didn't understand the question.

"On the other side," she expanded. "How will we
know if we've waited too long?"

"Jesus, lady," Boxers said. "They're your blood. You
tell me."

"I don't think she's talking about running away,"
Jonathan said. "I think she's wondering how long to
wait before she takes the fight directly to the bad guys."

She nodded.

"I don't have an answer for you," Jonathan said.

"If it comes to that, we're going to be very far out of
position," Yelena said. "We couldn't possibly help you
from the other side of the river."

Jonathan's gut flipped. He didn't like people messing with his plans. "Mrs. Darmond, with all respect, if
Big Guy and I can't handle this rescue, there's not
much that you'll be able to add."

"I can add firepower."

"You can stick to the damn plan," Jonathan said. He
felt anger rising. "When we come out of there, and the
world is on fire, we're going to be outnumbered by a lot
to one. Our only advantage is confusion and speed.
We're going to get in that boat, and we're going to
scream across six hundred yards of open water. That
shouldn't take more than a minute or two, once we're

in the boat. Your grandson is going to be cold and he may be wet, and he's definitely going to be traumatized. Do not leave us waiting."

Yelena's eyes never changed. "I hear you," she said.

"And you'll do it."

"I'll make sure she does," David said.

Somehow, that didn't make Jonathan feel any better.

Len Shaw checked his watch for the thousandth time. The transfer trucks were due anytime now. Against his wishes, Dmitri had dictated that the shipments be made all at once, rather than piecemeal, which would have been Len's preference. Dmitri's feeling was that it was better to open the doors one time and monitor the exchange of materials in one continuous flow.

Len understood the logic of that—in fact he had difficulty articulating an argument against it—but he was concerned about the appearances of it all.

Saint Stephen's Island lived largely unmolested, as its own entity in the middle of the Canadian capital. Police rarely ventured out here, and when they did, it was always during the day, and it was more out of curiosity than any professional concern.

Now, Dmitri was committing them to long motorcades of traffic with dozens of voices all rising past the limits of the walls to bounce across the water to raise people's curiosity. Len worried that curiosity would lead to concern, which would lead to a telephone call to the police, which would in turn vastly complicate everything. Dmitri wouldn't hesitate an instant to engage the police in a gun battle. In Dmitri's mind—the mind that was so poisoned by Soviet indoctrination and so encouraged by the new power grabs by the Russian leadership—hurting Canada was the same as hurting the United States.

Dmitri had reached that point in his life when he just wanted to hurt people. It was unfortunate that at that precise moment, Len had reached the point in his own life when he treasured peace over war.

And now, on top of all the weapons, he had to deal with celebrity prisoners. That was sheer madness. The stepson of the president of the United States. Rationalize as you wish that the Americans were powerless to react to this affront, but the reality was that Dmitri had poked a stick directly into the most secure hornet's nest on the planet, and it was unreasonable not to expect consequences.

Soon, though, it would end. In less than an hour, the trucks would arrive. Among the trucks would be a van that would spirit the Mishins on to their next station, wherever that was, and come dawn, Len's life would settle back to something that resembled normalcy.

Then, two days later, America would be under attack.

Mother Russia would once again be feared, and her allies—Iran, Syria, Lebanon, China (an ally not yet to be trusted)—would make the moves they'd been waiting for a generation to make, without fear of retribution. NATO and Israel growled like fearless dogs when their American handlers were firmly in their corner, but would they be so bold if the Americans slid into isolationism? Or, as one of Len's favorite Western expressions went, would their asses be able to cash the checks their mouths had written?

He suspected not. Certainly, his handlers in Moscow suspected not.

When it all was done, all Len wanted out of this life was to be able to turn this remarkable island into the tourist attraction it had the capability to become.

CHAPTER TWENTY-EIGHT

Boxers piloted the Chevy around the curve on Ottawa River Parkway, and as he slowed to take the truck and the boat over the curve to head toward the water, he corrected abruptly to the left and continued around the circle to take another pass.

"I had someone on my tail," he explained.

As he made the six-minute detour, Jonathan was struck with a thought that hadn't occurred to him before: When they pulled off to drop the boat, they were going to leave tracks in the snow through the grass. How could they prevent that?

They couldn't.

Shit. See? This was where planning and reality started to separate themselves.

On the second tour around the circle, conditions seemed perfect. Boxers slowed the truck to about fifteen miles per hour as he swung the turn, and then straightened it out to head for the water.

Thirty seconds later, they were at the water's edge. Boxers made a wide U-turn to get the boat's ass facing the shore, and then he carefully backed up to the edge.

"Be careful," Jonathan warned, watching out his side view mirror. "With the ice and snow cover, I don't know where land ends and thin ice begins."

Boxers brought the truck to a halt and threw the transmission into park. He turned in his seat to face the back. "Which one of you two is the next driver?"

Yelena looked at David. "I haven't driven anything in years," she said.

David raised his hand. "I'm the next driver."

"Okay," Boxers said, "but first you're a Sherpa for just one more time."

David looked confused.

Jonathan translated. "We need to move the equipment to the boat."

That took all of three minutes. Maybe less.

Jonathan and Boxers climbed aboard the boat. "Have you ever launched one of these things before?" Jonathan asked David.

"Only about a thousand times."

"Okay, good. Is your radio earpiece in place?"

David and Yelena both touched the buds in their ears.

Jonathan switched his radio to channel three and pressed the transmit button. "Radio check," he said.

David gave a thumbs-up.

"I need you to say it out loud," Jonathan said. "There's a button in the center of your vest. Press it and talk."

Good God, what else don't they know?

David went first. He pressed the button and announced, "I'm here."

Jonathan replied, "No shouting. Conversational tones are fine. You can even whisper and we'll hear you. Yelena?"

She touched her chest. "I hear you."

"And Mother Hen?"

"Right here," she said.

Jonathan cast a glance to Boxers, who gave a thumbs-up. "Big Guy is good too. Remember radio discipline, folks. Don't talk on the air unless you have to. Channel one will be the tactical channel, and under no circumstances do I want to hear either of you on it. Channel three is yours. Mother Hen will be monitoring everything. If you need something from me, tell her, and she'll tell us. I'll be in your ear within a minute. Got that?"

They answered in unison, canceling out each other's signals.

Jonathan pressed the transmit button. "David, get into the car and back us up to the water. I'll tell you when we're afloat. You, too, Yelena."

As they walked back to the car and Jonathan cinched up his collar against the cold, Boxers mumbled, "I remember when we dealt with professionals."

"Boring, wasn't it?" Jonathan replied.

"Yeah," Boxers said. "That was exactly the word I was hunting for."

The boat was a twenty-two-foot Mako with twin Mercury outboards. Jonathan wasn't a water guy, but this looked like a boat that could get out of its own way in a hurry. The motors were tilted up and out of the way as David backed them into place. They wouldn't jam into the ground (or the ice) and ground the mission before it even started.

"I feel like we should be at the water," David said into his ear.

"I'll let you know."

As the words left Jonathan's mouth, the ice gave way with a crack that might have been a pistol shot, and just like that, they were afloat.

"Stop," Jonathan commanded, and the truck jerked to a halt.

Only the driver's door opened, and David walked out, nearly falling when he lost his footing on the first step.

"Be careful," Jonathan said. "I don't know where the land ends and the ice starts."

He watched with night vision as David skillfully released the ratchet on the winch and let the boat unravel its own tether. When there was enough slack, David pulled the boat back in a few feet, and released the tether's hook from the eye in the bow of the boat.

In the last few seconds before he floated away, Jonathan said, "Are we clear on the plan?"

"I am," David said. "I'll see you in Quebec."

"Just leave the trailer," Jonathan said. "It'll be our gift to the people of Canada." He tossed off a nonregulation salute, and then turned to Boxers. "You gonna let me drive, Big Guy?"

Boxers stopped messing with the equipment and moved forward toward the controls at the center console. "Did pigs start to fly?" This boat was designed purely for recreation. The cockpit stood amidships, covered by a flyaway canopy that no doubt provided comfort on a hot summer day, but was less than useless on a cold winter night. The canopy actually posed a hazard to Boxers as he instinctively stooped a little to fit underneath. Other than that canopy, the deck was wide open.

Jonathan moved to the aft end of the boat and rocked the enormous outboards into the icy water of the Ottawa River. According to Venice, he'd spent about forty thousand dollars for this boat—all of it billable to the government—and for that kind of coin, he expected performance.

"I'm ready back here," he told Big Guy, and ten seconds later, the motors belched clouds of white smoke, and they growled to life.

They were maybe three yards away from shore when sudden movement from the darkness behind David made him duck, as both Jonathan and Boxers went for their sidearms.

Yelena Poltanov ran full-out toward shore and launched herself at the boat. In an astonishingly acrobatic move, she timed the leap perfectly, somehow pulling Michael Jordan airtime before landing awkwardly on the open bow of the boat. Her feet slipped out from under her on impact and she landed hard on her back.

"God *damn* it," Boxers cursed, way too loudly as he broke his aim. "Are you out of your mind? I damn near shot you!"

He stole the words from Jonathan's throat. "Stop the boat," he commanded as he holstered his .45.

Boxers throttled down.

Jaw locked, and struggling to control his anger, Jonathan stepped from behind the cockpit, and strode to the bow, where the First Lady was struggling to stand. He grabbed her by her collar and lifted her to her feet. He spun her to face him, then changed his grip to the front of her vest, just beneath her chin.

"Get the hell off my boat," he said.

Even in the darkness, he could see the heat in her eyes. "Only if you throw me overboard."

"Don't tempt me."

Boxers appeared behind him. "Be happy to," he said.

"Stand down, Big Guy," Jonathan said. This was about three seconds from spinning completely out of control. "Keep us close to shore. We're drifting out."

Boxers hovered.

Without looking at him, Jonathan said, "I've got this, Big Guy. Please."

"I don't give a shit who she is," Boxers said. "She gets off this boat, or I will drown her myself."

Jonathan kept his eyes on Yelena. "You heard him."

"I heard big words from a big man," she said, utterly unfazed. "But I remain the First Lady of the United States, and there are some laws that even you fear."

Truer words had never been spoken. Jonathan changed tacks. "Mrs. Darmond, you can't be here. I cannot allow you to be here. Christ, you're the one I was supposed to save in the first place."

"But I didn't need saving," she said. "My son and grandson do. I'm going to be there."

"Ma'am, I swear to God we'll bring them to you."

"Suppose you don't?"

"We will."

"But if you *don't*."

Another swell of anger. How could he make her understand this?

"Scorpion, we really don't have time for this," Boxers said as he nudged the throttles forward to hold them as close to the icy shore as possible.

"Ma'am," Jonathan said, "with all respect, this is what we do for a living. This is what we've *always* done for a living. With you along, it's like having a third hostage. Your presence *endangers* your family, and it endangers Big Guy and me. I can't allow it."

"Please let go of me," Yelena said. Her tone was that of a gentle, reasonable request.

Jonathan released his grip. Then he took a step back to be less threatening.

"Thanks to Director Rivers—your Wolverine—and others, you think you know who I am," Yelena said. "In reality, you don't have a clue."

She stopped there, apparently thinking that there were some dots for Jonathan to connect. In reality, there were none. He waited.

Yelena sighed. "Dmitri and his friends have good reason to be angry with me. People sit in prison today for bombs I planted and people I shot. I know my way around a firefight."

Jonathan felt his heart skip, but he made sure his face didn't show it. So she was a murderer.

"I don't know what to say to that," Jonathan said.

"Say whatever you want. Say nothing. I don't care. Just know that I won't step away from a conflict."

"No," Boxers said. "You'll just betray your comrades." He pronounced "comrades" with his best Russian accent.

Yelena kept her eyes on Jonathan. "People change, Mr. Grave. Priorities change. Motivations change. But skills remain. They may dull some with time, but they never go away entirely. I can be an asset to you."

In his ear, Jonathan heard, "Scorpion, Mother Hen. You're not moving. Is there a problem?" Back in Fisherman's Cove, in addition to the SkysEye satellite imagery, she could also track them by their GPS signals.

Jonathan pressed his transmit button. "We're fine. Stand by."

"I go with you, Mr. Grave, or I go in the front door. I will not be relegated to sitting on the opposite shore waiting."

Jonathan tried to think of an alternative that would not involve drowning her or zip-tying her and shoving her in the backseat of the Chevy. If all of this fell apart, he could actually explain that the First Lady was killed in a firefight to rescue her family. Wolverine would even give him cover. But there'd be no explaining away an assault on the First Lady.

He keyed his mike. "Mother Hen, Scorpion. There's been a change in plans."

Behind him, Boxers said, "Ah, shit."

As Jonathan laid out the new plan, Venice wished that she had not allowed Wolverine to listen in on the speaker. She'd piped all the audio and video into the War Room so that they could watch together.

"No," Irene said. Her lips looked pale even as her cheeks flushed. "No, tell him he can't do that."

"But you heard—"

"You tell him," Irene insisted. "Tell him to abort the whole mission if that's what it comes to."

Venice considered arguing, but then realized she didn't need to. "Okay," she said. "But you're really not going to like his answer." She keyed her mike. "Scorpion, Mother Hen."

"Go ahead." She could hear wind and engine noise in the background.

"Wolverine says that you may not include Sidesaddle in the operation. If she will not cooperate, you must abort." Jonathan was the assigner of radio handles, and Sidesaddle was his play on the Secret Service's Cowgirl handle. David and Becky were Rooster and Chickadee, respectively.

A pause. "You know that's not gonna happen, right?"

Irene pointed to a skinny black microphone that extended up out of the workstation in front of her seat at the table. "Is this thing hot?"

Venice pushed a button. "It is now." *This should be really interesting.* "Just push the button at the base to talk, release it to listen."

Irene pushed the button. "Scorpion, this is Wolverine."

"Hey, Wolfie. I appreciate your concern, but it's not happening. She says that if I don't take her with me, she's going in by herself. And I don't think she's bluffing. Maternal instinct and all that."

"Then you have to abort."

"There's an innocent guy and a thirteen-year-old in there. I can see the building. I am not aborting. I don't really even think you want me to. Mother Hen, kill her mike for me, will you? And keep the channel clear unless you've got critical intel. Oh, and give Rooster a call on channel three. He probably needs a pep talk."

Irene's face showed an emotion that hovered somewhere between ire and acrimony. She'd set her jaw and pursed her lips until her mouth had formed a pencil line below her nose. "He hung up on me," she said. Clearly, it had been a long time since anyone had dared to do that. "Who the hell does he think he is?"

"Welcome to my world," Venice said.

"Get him back."

Venice cocked her head and folded her arms. "Come on, Irene," she said. "You heard him." She tapped keys on her computer and pointed to the big screen. "You can see where they are. This mission has already gone hot in Digger's mind, and he's got more urgent things on his burner than an argument with you."

Irene's jaw gaped as she pressed a hand to her forehead. "But what happens if—"

Venice shot up her hand. "Don't say it."

Irene recoiled. "Say what?"

"Anything negative. We don't do that here. Once we're hot, we only anticipate one outcome. Every move we make, every word we say is geared toward making success happen."

Irene looked amazed. Maybe mildly amused. "You're serious?"

"We've never failed," Venice said. "I know you mean well, ma'am, and you're welcome to stay. But please don't get in my way."

Venus was not ordinarily a confrontational person, but that felt good.

Right away, she felt guilty for thinking such a thing.

"Rooster, this is Mother Hen."

David was still staring out at the water in utter disbelief as the boat disappeared into the night, leaving him stranded and alone on the shore. The sound of Venice's voice in his ear made him jump.

"Shit." He fumbled to find the transmit button on his chest by feel. He pressed it. "What?"

The voice came back soothing. Motherly, even. "I know that was a bit of a surprise to you. Scorpion wanted me to make contact. Thought you might be upset."

"Ya think?"

"You still need to stay focused," she went on. "If every other part of the operation goes perfectly, it's still a failure if they can't get home. You understand that, right?"

He heard a click and assumed it was his turn to talk. "They just left me. Over."

"You don't have to say over. And they didn't leave you. They started the mission."

"But Mrs. Dar—Sidesaddle wasn't supposed to be there. She was supposed to be with me."

"You've got to adapt."

David's heart hammered fast enough to make him dizzy. He didn't know why this suddenly seemed so much more daunting a task as a single than it was when he had company. What he should have done was listen to Becky. Who the hell did he think he was, playing soldier in the middle of the night?

"Rooster, are you there?"

"Yeah, I'm here. I'm busy adapting."

"Good for you. Adapt faster."

Once they were in open water, Boxers idled the motors. He and Jonathan met in the middle of the craft to open up the duffels and divide the equipment. By natural selection—because of his size—Boxers carried more than Jonathan, by a significant margin. Call it one hundred fifty pounds versus one hundred pounds.

But that was before weapons and ammo. Jonathan had left his M27 back with Striker in the chopper. He expected this op to be mostly CQB—close quarters battle—and the length of the M27's barrel made it difficult to maneuver in tight spaces. Instead, he promoted his H&K MP7 to be his primary weapon, wearing it battle-slung across his chest, fitted with a suppressor.

A pistol-grip Mossberg 500 12-gauge hung from a bungee under his left arm, fitted with a breacher muzzle, and loaded with five breacher cartridges, whose special-purpose projectiles could concentrate nearly 1,500 foot pounds on energy on an area the size of a quarter. If the Mishins' cell door was made of wood, neither its lock nor its hinges were likely to survive an assault like that.

He'd shifted his Colt to a thigh rig holster on his right, and just in case every other weapon had run dry, he had his last-resort five-shot Detective Special in a pouch pocket near his right ankle. The pouches of his ballistic vest were crammed with ten spare forty-round mags for his MP7, and four spares for the Colt. Other pouches contained two flash-bang grenades and two fragmentation grenades.

Big Guy had likewise selected a suppressed MP7 as his primary weapon—it looked like a derringer in his hands—but he'd also slung his 7.62 millimeter H&K 417, just in case they needed a bigger bullet for something. With his ruck on his shoulders, the long handles of heavy-duty bolt cutters gave him the silhouette of a giant insect.

"Hey, Sidesaddle," Jonathan said. "Come over here."

She hesitated.

"I'm not going to throw you overboard. I promise."

"I don't like the name Sidesaddle," she said as she approached.

"We're not really going to compare notes on what we don't like now, are we?" Boxers said.

Jonathan beckoned her closer still. "How many spare mags did I give you back there?"

"Ten, I think."

"It'd be a good thing to know."

She squeezed the pouches on her vest. "Ten."

"Good."

"You ready, Boss?" Boxers asked.

"Let's go," Jonathan said. He blinked against the cold. The wind, even as light as it was, carried ice crystals that felt like as many needles against his exposed flesh. "Just take it slow, and keep the approach wide."

The boat ran blacked out. He'd intentionally chosen a boat that would not stand out in a crowd of boats, but since it was winter, cold as hell, they were the only boat on the water, and that made them potentially easy to see. The plan was to stay as dark and silent as possible.

Saint Stephen's Island was likewise dark, except for the lights in the buildings' windows. If the moon and the stars hadn't been so bright, it would be the perfect conditions for an assault.

"There's an eye in the door," Joey said. He knew that Dad had fallen asleep, but he didn't want to be alone. After the sun had gone down, their tiny cell had filled with the kind of cold that left you feeling weak. At one point during the afternoon, the heavy blanket had become too heavy. Now it might as well have been a sheet. Even with the heavy sweat suit, he might as well have been naked.

Dad stirred, but he didn't wake entirely. Joey poked him with an elbow.

Dad jumped, startled and maybe a little frightened. "What? What's wrong?"

"I'm sorry," Joey said. "I just changed positions. I didn't mean to wake you."

They sat on the floor together, their bodies touching for extra warmth, with double layers of blankets separating their butts from the floor, as well as covering them all over. It was like the world's smallest tent.

"That's okay," Dad said. "I didn't know I'd fallen asleep."

"Isn't it dangerous to fall asleep in the cold? I thought I read that somewhere. Maybe I saw it on the Discovery Channel."

"Hmm. I don't think it's that cold."

"There's an eye in the door," Joey said again.

Moon and starlight seeped into the room, keeping it from being completely black.

"I don't understand what you mean."

"Look at the door. At the peephole." He pointed with his forehead because he didn't want to expose an arm. "It's got an eye around it."

Dad squinted, and then said, "Ah. I see it. Back in the old days, punishment had religious overtones. I imagine that that was supposed to make people think of the eye of God watching them."

Joey stewed on that for a few seconds, but the thought

troubled him. "Shouldn't they have put it on the ceiling? That's where heaven is."

Dad smiled. "That would make more sense, wouldn't it?"

They fell into silence again. There'd been a lot of that. Not that there was anything to talk about.

Conversation took some of the edge off his fear, but the only thing he could think to talk about was how afraid he was.

"Did I tell you that Jimmy Feeny got expelled from school?"

Dad rocked back with surprise. "Big Jimmy? The one who used to paint his mohawk? Why does that not surprise me?"

Joey nodded. Jimmy was one of the cool kids—a member of the class that Joey himself could only aspire to—even though teachers and parents didn't like him very much. Or maybe *because* teachers and parents didn't like him very much.

Joey explained. "In the cafeteria, Norman Kwitniesky walked past him and dumped a thing of chocolate milk on his head, and Jimmy broke his face."

"Why would he do that?"

"Because Norman dumped milk on him."

"But why would Norman dump the milk?"

"I don't know."

"Jimmy's a big kid. Sounds like Norman has a death wish. Did he get expelled, too?"

"No, and that's what pisses everybody off. He *started* the fight, and he only got like a few days' suspension."

"Huh."

And then the silence returned.

Joey shivered, and his dad pulled him tighter. That's when the tears came. They heaved up out of nowhere, burning his eyes and tightening his throat. It was a flood of emotion, and he didn't know how to stop it. A squeaking sound escaped his throat, and after that, they were followed by sobs.

He buried his face in Dad's shirt, and felt fingers gently rubbing the back of his head, the way Dad used to do it.

"I'm so scared," he said, but the words might have been lost in the cough of a sob.

"I swear to you this will be okay," Dad said. "I won't let them hurt you."

CHAPTER TWENTY-NINE

The release on the trailer hitch didn't want to let go. The latch had frozen shut, and no matter how hard David pulled, he couldn't get the lever to lift. "Unbelievable." *Will anything go right tonight?*

He pressed his transmit button. "Hey, Mother Hen."

"Go ahead."

"You're not going to believe this. The trailer hitch is frozen. I can't release it."

A pause.

"And before you ask, I don't have a hammer, and as far as I can tell, this truck doesn't have any tools on board. Everything that was heavy and solid is out there on the boat."

When Mother Hen's voice returned to his ear, he could hear a smile in it. "Wolverine wants to know how full your bladder is."

What the hell kind of stupid question—

Then he got it. Pee on the latch. Not the most dignified solution, but there was a certain elegance to it. Plus there was the whole thing of killing two birds with one stone.

And it worked. The hitch was still steaming when he used his gloved hand to release the latch. *Memo to file: throw the gloves away.* That done, the trailer lifted easily off the ball. He gave it a little shove to impart momentum, and then watched as it drifted into the water . . . and stopped two feet from shore.

Screw it. He keyed his mike. "I'm free of the trailer. Now I'm on my way to save the day."

As he walked carefully through the snow to the front of the truck, he wondered if there'd be DNA or something in the yellow snow that would connect him to this night.

Then he realized it was silly to worry. He'd probably be dead before dawn.

The vest he wore over his coat was as bulky and uncomfortable in the front seat as it had been in the back, but he kept it on. The imagery that Scorpion had conjured as he explained the ballistic trenches that bullets carved through human flesh still lingered vividly in his mind.

The seat was as far back as it could go to accommodate Big Guy, and with the vest in place, David couldn't reach to the floor between his legs to get to the adjustment bar. Muttering a curse, he climbed back outside to make the adjustment from a spot next to the door. When he was done, the seat was probably still going to be too far back, but he'd find a way to deal with it.

Finally settled into his seat, grateful that they'd let the engine and its heater continue to run, he pulled the transmission lever into drive and stepped on the gas.

Nothing happened. The engine whined louder and the tachometer climbed, but the truck itself didn't move.

"You have to be friggin' kidding me." He was stuck in the snow.

Don't panic. You've been stuck before.

He pulled the transmission lever all the way to the right, to low, and tried to be more gentle on the gas. With the slightest application of torque, the rear wheel spun as if it were . . . well, as if it were on ice.

With a flash of inspiration, he searched for the lever that would engage the four-wheel drive. There was none.

"Are you shitting me?" he yelled to the car's interior. He pressed the radio button. "Hey Mother Hen. You there?"

"Go ahead."

"Who's the genius that ordered up a rear-wheel-drive truck?"

Silence. Then: "Please tell me you're kidding."

"Yeah," David said. "I'm friggin' kidding you because that's what I do when I'm about to get caught in the middle of a shit storm. No, I'm not kidding! When we came out here, we were about a thousand pounds heavier than I am now. The bed of the truck is empty, the tires are on ice, and this puppy isn't moving. And please don't tell me to take a shit in the snow, because I really don't see how that could help."

"Stand by."

"Yeah, okay," he said off the air. "I'll stand by. Because, you know, there's no other goddamn option!" He slammed the steering wheel with his hand. He tried the gas again, pressing a little harder this time. The result was to move sideways and drift closer to the water. He took his foot off entirely.

"Shit."

* * *

Boxers had just cut the throttles to coast into the shore when Venice delivered the news that the truck was stuck in Ottawa and would not be able to make the rendezvous in Quebec. The news knotted Jonathan's gut.

He looked to Big Guy. "I say we're in too deep to abort now," he whispered.

"You're damn right we're not aborting," Yelena said. Under the circumstances, Jonathan had granted permission to join them on channel one.

"Hush," Jonathan said. "You don't get a vote, and keep your voice down."

Boxers said, "I think it's tonight or it's not at all."

Jonathan acknowledged with a nod. "Mother Hen, Scorpion. Y'all need to get us an exfil alternative, and you need to do it quickly. Wake up Striker and get him back in the game. If nothing else works, he'll be able to pluck us out of the boat in the river."

Jonathan let up on the transmit button and looked to Boxers. "Are you ready?"

"I'm always ready to make noise."

Jonathan keyed his mike. "We're going hot."

Jonathan turned to Yelena. "Your job is to do exactly what I tell you, exactly when I tell you to do it. You don't shoot at anything unless it shoots at you first, understand?"

She nodded. At last, that hard emotionless mask had started to crack. There might actually have been some fear in her eyes. Jonathan was happy to see it.

"I need you to say it," he pressed.

"I understand."

Jonathan continued. "If all else fails, stay low. Big

Guy and I have night vision, you don't. If you go completely blind, say something and we'll stop. Do not turn on a light unless I tell you to. Got it?"

"Yes."

He gave her a harder look, testing those eyes, then decided she was as stable as she was going to be.

"Okay, Big Guy, let's go."

Barely moving the throttles an inch, Boxers drove the boat up to the edge of the ice line, and then surged the engines once to run the bow aground. He kept the throttles engaged as Jonathan moved around the cockpit to the bow, where he grabbed the once-coiled thirty-foot line and stepped gingerly out onto the ice. With all the crap he was wearing, if he fell through, he would become the anchor.

The ice held. Jonathan suspected that the ice was really just snow-covered ground, which meant that they were lucky not to have broken off the motors' propellers. Waddling across the snow at a crouch, he made his way to a young but sturdy-looking tree, and tied the rope around its trunk. Behind him, the engines cut off.

By the time he turned around, Boxers was helping the First Lady out of the boat and onto the ground. Ever the grouch, he was likewise always the gentleman.

Their designated entry point into the walled compound was the main entrance, an iron gate in the middle of the north-south wall, a hike of about a hundred yards. They moved along the western coast of the island, where the gentle slope down to the water gave them complete defilade from anyone who was not standing on the roof of the building. And after scanning the roofline carefully with a digital monocular, Jonathan determined that no one was.

When his GPS told him that he was directly across from the main gate, he beckoned for Boxers to follow him. "You stay there," he said to Yelena.

Adjusting their equipment to stay out of the way, Jonathan and Boxers moved in unison to drop to their bellies and crawl the last fifty feet or so of the incline. Even the most bored, inattentive of sentries would be attracted to a pair of black silhouettes moving against the horizon.

They lifted their NVGs out of the way so they could survey the area more closely with their monoculars. The amount of ambient light, reflected as it was off the snow, gave them a pretty clear view.

River Road lay between them and the gate, and the far edge of the road passed within fifteen feet of the outermost wall. The front gates were not nearly as imposing as Jonathan had expected, consisting of wrought-iron spikes that rose not quite to the height of the twelve-foot stone walls. And they were wide open. A courtyard lay beyond the gate, measuring sixty feet wide by thirty feet deep. Two massive doors blocked entrance to the main building—building Foxtrot—on the far side of the courtyard.

"You suppose those big doors are locked?" Boxers whispered.

"Nothing a GPC can't handle," Jonathan said. A GPC—general purpose charge—was a block of C4 explosive with a det cord tail. Jonathan liked to think of them as skeleton keys. They guaranteed entry to any-place he wanted to go.

"I count two sentries," Jonathan said. Both stood inside the courtyard, flanking the big doors. They stomped their feet as if they'd been standing in the cold for a long time. "I see AKs—no surprise there—but no sign of body armor. You concur?"

"I concur."

The other sentries they'd seen in the satellite photos patrolled areas inside the compound walls.

"Then let's go to work," Jonathan said. He flipped the NVGs back down and brought the extended stock of the MP7 tight against his shoulder. He'd outfitted the weapon with an infrared laser sight, the beam from which would be invisible to anyone who did not have night vision. At this range, the sight guaranteed a kill.

"You take the guy on the left," Jonathan whispered. "I've got the guy on the right."

"Rog."

"In three, two, one."

The weapons fired in unison, one shot each, emitting a pop that sounded more like a firecracker than a gunshot, and launching a tiny 4.6 millimeter bullet at 2,300 feet per second. The targets died in unison. They were already falling before the sound of the gunshots made it halfway across the road.

"Let's go," Jonathan said. He turned to beckon Yelena forward, but she had clearly heard him and was already on her way. When she joined them, Jonathan said, "Think of yourself as my shadow. Do what I do, but don't shoot unless I tell you to."

This time, he didn't wait for an answer.

Boxers moved out first, just as far as the near edge of the road, where he took a knee, and, with his weapon to his shoulder, he scanned an arc from left to right. "Clear," he said.

Jonathan moved next. He grabbed Yelena by her vest to get her going, but then let go as he led her past Boxers and then all the way across the road to the left-hand edge of the gate wall. "Stay," he said to Yelena, and then he pivoted into the courtyard to scan for any threats they night have missed. Seeing none, he keyed his mike. "Clear." He motioned Yelena to come closer.

Five seconds later, Boxers was back with them. "I hate it when things start easy," he said. Call it warriors' pessimism, but this was a classic way to pull your opponent into a trap. You give them all the encouragement they need to keep moving forward, and then you let them have it when they're in too deeply to retreat.

Jonathan turned to address Yelena and saw that she was staring at the dead sentry who lay at her feet. The sentry seemed to stare back at her. Jonathan rapped on her helmet to get her attention and she jumped. "If you see somebody with a weapon, you say 'gun to the right' or wherever they are, and Big Guy and I will take him out. Your weapon is too loud. Got it?"

"Yes."

"And to think that I actually had to train for years to master this shit," Boxers grumbled.

Jonathan brought his weapon back to his shoulder and nodded to the six-inch ring that served as the knob for the enormous door. "Just how easy is it?"

The ring turned and the door floated open. "Too," Big Guy said.

"Yelena, stay till we call for you." To Boxers, "You call it."

"Three, two, one." Boxers pushed the door open all the way. Following their long-standing protocol, Jonathan went in low and turned to the left while Boxers went in high and turned to the right.

The doors opened onto a wide stone vestibule that Jonathan guessed might have been a processing area back in the day, or maybe a waiting room for visiting relatives. More a part of the structure of the wall than of the prison it surrounded, the vestibule was devoid of furniture and was dimly lit by only a single bulb that dangled from the ceiling. The prominent feature of the room was another door on the far side, directly across from the one they'd just entered.

Jonathan turned back toward the courtyard, where the First Lady stood in the doorway. "Yelena, come in."

As she stepped inside, her eyes never stopped scanning. It was as if she was trying to memorize everything she saw.

When she cleared the jamb, Jonathan and Boxers moved around her to drag the dead sentries inside. With luck, if they were noted to be missing, no one would see the blood slicks. They laid the bodies side by side in the middle of the room, and Jonathan went back to shut the doors. With the panel closed, Jonathan could see the locking mechanism that was clearly designed to keep people out rather than in. Foot-long steel bars slid into matching keepers on the opposite panel— four of them in total, at eye, chest, belt, and knee level. Boxers started to push one of them home, but Jonathan stopped him.

"I'm not sure that's a great idea," he said. "I think we want stuff to look as normal as possible for as long as it can."

"You mean, except for the corpses?"

"Maybe we should move them off to the side,"

Jonathan conceded. They each chose a body and dragged it from the middle of the floor to the corner where the southern and eastern walls met.

Yelena watched in silence. In the yellow glow of the incandescent light, the massive head wounds stood out in clear relief.

"Don't freak out on us now," Boxers said. "This is what you signed on for."

"I'm not freaking out about anything," she said. "I've seen bodies before."

Big Guy drew his KA-BAR knife from its sheath on his shoulder, and used it as extension of his arm to kill the overhead lightbulb with a single swipe, drenching them in darkness.

Jonathan flipped down his NVGs, turning the darkness into green daylight. "Just stay close to us, Mrs. Darmond," he said. "Keep a hand on my back if you have to. We can see everything just fine."

"I can see shadows," she said.

If their intel was right—and so far, it had been holding up pretty well—the door ahead led to a hallway. A turn to the left would take them to the chapel, and a turn to the right would take them to the oldest portion of the jail, which they believed to be empty. Going straight would take them out to the prison yard, and the cluster of buildings that comprised the cell blocks and barracks. If things went according to plan, they could be out of here and on their way home in ten minutes. Fifteen, max.

They moved to the next door, and paused to repeat the same entry maneuver. "Ma'am, remember that you are always the last one through a door, okay? Going in or coming out, you're last."

A radio broke squelch behind them.

Jonathan pivoted and reflexively pushed Yelena to the floor. He planted a knee on her back to keep her out of any field of fire. "Ow!" she protested, but he didn't care.

"Guard units report in," a voice said in a Russian-accented English. It came from one of the dead sentries.

"Unit One is on post and cold."

"Unit Two's okay."

Silence.

In unison, Jonathan and Boxers said, "Uh-oh." Jonathan stood and helped Yelena to her feet.

"Unit Three? Are you there?" the Russian voice said.

"This is trouble," Boxers grumbled.

"What is it?" Yelena asked.

"Unit Three, report."

"Some kind of situation check. Making sure the guards are awake and on station."

"Unit Four?"

No response.

"Ladies and gentlemen," Boxers said, gesturing to the bodies, "allow me to introduce Units Three and Four. We need to get moving."

Jonathan moved to one of the bodies and found his radio. "Might help to know what they're up to," he said.

He joined Boxers at the door, checked to make sure that Yelena was out of harm's way, then nodded to Big Guy. "Let's go."

* * *

Becky hadn't realized she'd fallen asleep until somebody rattled her shoulder. She awoke with a start and a hammering heart, and the utter conviction that she should be running away from something.

"All right, Chickadee, it's time to go to work." It was Striker, and his eyes looked even more intense than usual.

Apparently, she'd been pretty deeply into REM sleep because none of this resonated with her. "I don't understand."

"Scorpion needs our help," he said. "Looks like we get to join the shooting war."

Becky felt a chill. "I still don't understand."

"Of course you don't. Get your pretty little ass up and I'll fill you in."

As wakefulness bloomed larger, Becky became aware of the cold. She'd been sitting in the cargo area of the helicopter as she waited for the others to return from their mission, and at some point, she'd apparently drifted off. Now, as she sat back up, she became aware of the breeze that poured through the aircraft. A few seconds later, she realized that Striker had modified things significantly.

"What happened to the doors?" she asked.

"I'm sorry to say that they had to be sacrificed. Small price to pay, though."

"I don't understand."

"That's because you haven't got your ass up yet."

Becky rolled to her feet and stood. It turned out to be even colder than she'd expected.

"Put your vest back on," Striker said. "We're going into the shit, and I don't want your guts messing up the back of my helicopter."

The vest lay on the floor, where she'd dropped it. Becky stooped and picked it up, then shrugged herself into it. "I still don't know what you're talking about," she said.

"Close all the fasteners," Striker said. "If it's worth doing, it's worth doing all the way."

She worked the Velcro straps. "Tell me again where the doors went?"

"I had to take them off so that you can be my door gunner." Striker said that as if it were the most obvious thing in the world; as if she should have figured it out for herself.

"Your *what*?"

He held out a harness, loops made of three-inch-wide strips of nylon. "Put this on."

"No. Why?"

"So you don't fall to your death out of the open doors."

Okay, that made sense, she supposed. She took a step closer. "How do I . . ."

"Put your legs in here," Striker said. The harness looked a lot like a parachute without the parachute. Becky stepped into the leg openings first, and then allowed him to thread her arms through what was essentially a pair of suspenders. Then Striker clipped it all together into a square plate just below her breasts.

"This is the DFWI button," Striker said, pointing to a round spot on the plate.

"Don't fuck with it," Becky translated. "Like the selector switch on the rifle."

"Right. Press that and the whole harness falls away. You only use it if we, like, fall into the water and you're being dragged down by the sinking aircraft."

"Oh my God."

He waved at the air. "No, I don't mean to spook you. We're not going to spend a lot of time over water."

"Where *are* we going to spend a lot of time?" she asked. "I still don't know what you're talking about."

Striker nodded to the two rifles that lay on the floor. One was the one Scorpion had given her, and the other was one that Scorpion had left behind. To her eye, they both looked the same.

"Were you any good with those?"

Something in the way he asked the question rang a warning bell. "I'm not shooting at anyone," she said.

"I get that," Striker said. "And the only people you'll need to shoot at are the ones who shoot at you first." As he spoke, he stretched out a bungee cord from a spot between her shoulder blades and hooked it into a wire that she'd not noticed, which ran the width of the helicopter, from door to door. "We're open on both sides because I don't know where the enemy will be. You'll be our only defense, though, so try to shoot straight when the time comes."

Becky felt as if she'd entered a show in the middle of the third act. Worse, it was a show she didn't like. "I'm not shooting at anyone," she said. "I've already told you that."

"I respect that," Striker said as he lifted one of the rifles from the floor. He arranged the loop in the strap so that she could slip her right arm into it.

She complied.

"Here's the thing," Striker continued. "I got a call from Mother Hen that the team is in trouble and they need us to pluck them out of it. This chopper is your ride home, and I'm going. Your choices are to stay behind and find your own way back to wherever you come from, or you can roger up and save a few lives."

"I don't believe in killing," Becky said. Why couldn't these people understand such a simple concept?

"Then you're just flat-out in the wrong damn place," Striker said.

Becky opened her mouth to respond, but shut it when she realized that she had no idea what to say.

Striker inhaled deeply, and then planted his fists on his hips, his head cocked to the side. "Look, Miss. Becky, is it?"

She nodded.

"Look, Becky. With all respect, you're in exactly the same position as every soldier who's gone to war for the first time. You're scared shitless. Thing is, you don't know if you're more scared of killing or being killed. That's fine. All I know is there's a bunch of people out there who are taking a lot of risk to separate good guys from bad guys. I'm going out there to help them, and all of us have a lot better chance of coming home alive if I've got a gunner in the door. If you say no, the answer is no, and you get to live the rest of your life wondering how things would have been different if you answered the call. Call it a shitty deal if you want, but it's the facts. Tell me what you want to do."

What she wanted to do was set the clock back and tell David to eff off when he asked her for help.

"I'm not going to shoot," she said.

"Put the safety on, then," Striker said.

She placed her thumb on the lever and pressed. The switch was already in the right place.

Striker twitched his head in an approving nod. "All

right, then," he said. "That lanyard should hold you. If we get into some wild gyrations, though, you might should hang on to keep from rolling out of the door. Worst case, though, you can't fall out." He smiled. "You good?"

The only appropriate answer was a lie. "I'm fine," she said.

Striker's smile became a grin. "Cool. Let's go save us a couple of lives."

"Rooster, Mother Hen. We have instructions for you. You need to leave the vehicle. You're too close to a main highway to risk being seen by police."

It was an outcome that David hadn't even considered. He hadn't seen any traffic, but that was more a function of the hour than the location. Plus, there were tire tracks leading from the roadway to this spot. It wouldn't be unreasonable for a passing cop car to assume that someone had driven off the road into danger.

He'd already pulled the door handle and was sliding back out into the cold when he said, "Where do you want me to go?"

"Are you armed?"

"I can be."

"No. Leave all weapons behind and just start walking east. Keep the river on your left. Walk toward the downtown. If Scorpion gave you a ballistic vest, leave that behind, too. You need to look like a guy out for a walk."

"I want to be very clear," David said. "I do not want to be stranded here."

"Understood. But there's no more surefire way to get stranded than to get yourself arrested."

It was a very good point. He stripped off the vest with its pouches of ammunition and tossed it onto the Chevy's front seat. For good measure, he leaned back inside and turned off the ignition and removed the key. He slipped it into his pants pocket. He was about to close and lock the door when he remembered that the radio was attached to the vest. He pulled it out of its pouch, disconnected the remote transmit connection and slipped the radio into his coat pocket. From now on, he'd have to bring the unit to his mouth to speak.

Wanting to avoid the highway, he turned left and headed down toward the water, where a ring of trees along the shoreline would give him a little cover.

He pressed the mike button. "What do I tell a cop if I do run into one? And how am I getting out of here?"

A long silence.

"Mother Hen?"

"Rooster, right now, I don't know how anybody's getting out of there. Do your best to stay safe and I'll get back to you. Keep the channel clear."

There was an edge to Mother Hen's voice that he hadn't heard before, and in a rush, he realized how many people he'd just let down. Here he was, trying to extract himself from danger at the very moment when everybody else was walking headlong into it. A terrible weight appeared in his gut. It felt like cowardice.

It felt like shame.

But what choice did he have? He wasn't the one who'd abandoned anyone on the shore. The others had abandoned *him*.

The slope toward the river steepened as he approached the tree line, and he forced himself to take smaller steps.

Why did he feel so guilty about all of this? He was a victim, for God's sake. He only came along because it felt like a grand adventure. That, and because if the mission failed, he'd have nothing to live for back home anyway.

He came along because a perfect stranger saved him from certain death, and it seemed like the right thing to do. The decent thing to do.

Now those perfect strangers were heading into hell to save him again. And he was walking away.

He wished he'd jumped on the boat with the First Lady. Except he couldn't have, because then they'd have no way of getting away.

Which they still didn't because he'd stranded the goddamn truck.

The air among the trees was noticeably warmer than the air directly at water's edge, but the footing became progressively more treacherous.

He hadn't walked very far—maybe a hundred yards—when he saw a line of headlights approaching. It looked like a clutch of six, maybe eight trucks, neither huge nor small, heading right for him down the Ottawa River Parkway. At the last minute, just before they would have passed closest to him, the first vehicle swung a hard right onto River Road, the approach that led exclusively to Saint Stephen's Island. The second truck in the line followed, and then the third and the fourth. The others, too. They all bore the markings of various moving and storage companies.

David pulled his radio from his pocket and keyed

his mike. "Yo, Mother Hen, is your satellite picture picking up the parade of trucks that's headed right toward our team?"

The last truck in the line—there turned out to be nine of them in all—stopped just after making the turn, maybe twenty, thirty yards away from David. A man dressed in a puffy blue ski jacket climbed out of the driver's seat and walked around to the back of the truck.

Mother Hen's voice chirped loudly, "Do you have traffic for me?"

The noise might as well have been a cymbal crash, it was so loud against the silence of the night. David moved quickly to press the radio against his chest to muffle the sound, but it was too late.

Blue Coat stopped abruptly and turned. He looked in David's general direction, but not straight at him. And he had a pistol in his hand.

Shit, shit, shit . . .

If Mother Hen tried to contact him again, they guy would hear it for sure. David reached with his other hand and turned the button he thought was the volume control until it clicked. He'd either turned it off or changed the channel. He hoped that either one would buy him invisibility.

Blue Coat didn't move for a long time. In the wash of the taillights, David could see him squinting into the night. After what must have been two solid minutes, he holstered his gun—his *weapon*—and slid open the roll-up panel in the back of the truck. He removed what looked to be planks and saw horse supports.

In fact, that's exactly what they turned out to be. Blue Coat assembled them at the turn and positioned them in such a way as to block off the entire roadway. Battery-powered yellow lights flashed to alert people that from that point north, River Road was closed.

Blue Coat didn't bother to close the back of the truck before heading back to his driver's seat. As he mounted the vehicle, he pulled something from the side door panel and swung it around to point back toward David.

The beam of a powerful flashlight nearly blinded him. He froze, certain that he'd been seen, and, because he could no longer see the driver, equally certain that he would be shot dead within seconds.

Then the light moved. The driver was scanning the tree line, one last look to convince himself that he hadn't heard what he in fact had. Apparently satisfied, he turned off his light and climbed into his seat. Ten seconds later, he was on his way to join his friends.

His heart hammering and his hands trembling to the point of convulsion, David turned his radio back on.

". . . Hen. Respond, please."

"Rooster here. But barely."

"Be advised that there's a line of trucks heading right for you."

"No kidding," he said. "You be advised that I am not walking into town. It's wrong and I'm not doing it."

"What are you doing?"

"I don't know, but I'm not running. Now I'm going to keep the channel clear." He turned the volume down to nearly nothing and put the radio back into his pocket.

He'd spoken the truth about not knowing what he was going to do. But one thing was certain: Bad things were about to happen to people to whom he owed a lot.

If they needed him, he was going to be as close as he could be—not as far away.

If it came to that, though, he was going to need firepower.

He spun on his heel and ran as fast as the snow would allow back toward the stranded Chevy.

CHAPTER THIRTY

Len Shaw's spirits lifted when the watchman told him that the trucks were on the bridge. At Dmitri's insistence, he'd answered the call on speaker. It was already after 1:00 A.M., which put them nearly an hour behind schedule, but there was still plenty of nighttime left to get them loaded up and off the major roads before the morning commuters started to clog the highways.

"Tell the sentries at the gate to line the trucks up the length of the front wall," Len said. "I want them loaded one at a time. When one is filled, it can be on its way, and the next can pull up to take its place."

"Will do," the watchman said. "Once I can find the gate sentries."

Dmitri's face darkened. He stood and leaned close to the phone. "You can't find them? Where did they go?"

"I don't know, sir." The watchman's tone became more formal—more fearful—when he heard Dmitri's distinctive voice. "All I know is I couldn't raise them on the radio."

"Did you send anyone to look for them?"

"Well, sir . . . no."

"Don't you think that might be a good idea?" Len asked.

"I suppose it would, yes. I'll get right to it."

"Thank you." Len pushed the disconnect button. He walked to his window and tried to look down to see the sentries, but couldn't. Even if he opened the window, the bars over the opening would keep him from being able to look straight down.

"Do you see them?" Dmitri asked.

"The angles are wrong," Len answered.

Dmitri walked to the window for his own look. "I don't like this," he said. "I don't like the timing."

"I'm sure the watchman will tell us—"

His phone rang again and he pressed the button to connect. "Have you found the sentries?"

"Not yet, sir, but I've sent someone to find them. This comes from one of the drivers. He just radioed to tell me that he thought there might have some people lurking at the far end of the bridge. He thought he heard a radio."

Len felt something dissolve in his chest. One anomaly could be coincidence. A second almost certainly spelled trouble. "Wake everybody up," he commanded. "Turn on the yard lights, and send a five-man team to the end of the bridge. I want that area scoured. I want to talk personally to whoever they find."

"Suppose it's the police?"

Dmitri said, "If it's the police—"

Len raised his hand to silence him. "If it's the police, then we are done here, and we do all the damage we can do." He hung up.

"I'm proud of you," Dmitri said.

Len smiled and donned the coat that had been draping the back of his chair. "I told you dozens of times, my friend. Growing old and tired does not make me less committed to our cause."

On the wall opposite Len's desk, a gun rack held three AK47s and two American M16s. Len walked to the rack and grabbed an AK and a bandolier of spare magazines. He gave it to Dmitri. "Speed is now of the essence," he said. "We need to get the trucks loaded and back on the road as soon as possible. It could be that this is nothing, or it could be that we are under attack. Either way, the sooner we get the trucks rolling, the better off we're going to be."

Dmitri racked the bolt to chamber a round. "And you?"

Len gestured to the bank of computer screens on his desk. "I'm going to organize the defense. Let's get this done."

The door on the far side of the vestibule opened onto a dimly lit hallway. Probably enough light for Yelena to see where she was going, but not enough to flare out the NVGs.

"Clear," Jonathan said of his view down the left-hand side of the hallway.

"Clear," Boxers said of the right.

"Sidesaddle," Jonathan said at a loud whisper. "On me. Now."

He never looked to confirm—instead keeping his eyes trained continuously on his segment of the kill zone—but he heard her footsteps as she cleared the jamb. Directly across from the vestibule door was the secured passageway that led to a cross hall that led to the cell blocks, the second largest one of which, designated Building Bravo, had reportedly been converted to barracks for the folks who minded the store here.

Jonathan told Yelena to close the vestibule door behind her and put her hand on his rucksack.

The door latched. Yelena said, "I can see all right."

"You're arguing," Jonathan said. "It's not about what you can see. It's about not shooting you because you get in the way. If your hand is on my ruck, I know where you are."

He felt the tug in his shoulders as she grabbed on. "Moving left," he said. He led the way, his weapon at his shoulder, knowing that Boxers was moving as his shadow, in reverse, as they made their way past a heavily reinforced door on the right that led to the northwest quadrant of the yard. This main hallway served in the old days as the primary conduit from the north end of the prison to the south end. Since it was an administrative area, it lacked the internal security walls and gates that blocked free passage through the cell blocks themselves.

Jonathan was still ten feet from the closed chapel door when he caught the first hint of the aroma of explosives. He'd heard others describe the smell as that of almonds, but that never resonated with him. As far as he was concerned, it was a chemical smell unique to itself. For the odor to escape the size of the door he was looking at, there had to be a shitload of them. In the slice of time it took to snap a finger, he'd begun to second-guess his own plan. It was one thing to create a diversion. It was something else to blow up a chunk of Canada.

"I'm at the door," Jonathan announced. He found

the knob—actually, another ring—and he turned it. This time, while the lock turned, the deadbolt clearly had been set. The deadbolt actually looked new. "Hey, Big Guy. Take a look."

Boxers bent at the waist to get closer to the lock. Then he stood tall and looked at the hinge side of the jamb. "If you're asking my opinion, I think the Mossberg is a waste of time on this."

"I agree. But a GPC—"

"—is a bad idea. There's a shitload of boom-boom in there. For all we know it's stored right up against the door. I vote we use the irons."

"All right. Yelena, look at me."

She did.

"Watch both ends of the hallway. If you see anyone, shoot them. And I mean anyone who's not Big Guy or me."

She looked terrified.

"You said you've done it before," Jonathan reminded. As he spoke, he shrugged out of his ruck and laid it on the floor. "You go to hell for the first one. After that, the others don't count. Can you do it?"

"Of course."

Jonathan was learning that one of the most surefire ways to motivate Yelena was to imply that she was somehow soft. "Safety off, finger off the trigger till you need it, and don't point that muzzle anywhere close to me."

Point made, Jonathan unstrapped the irons kit from the outside of his ruck. "Irons" was the collective name for a mini-Halligan bar, a five-pound sledgehammer. and a K-tool, a nifty device that resembled a stylized letter *K*, and was specifically designed to pull the cylinders out of deadbolts. It worked by sliding the K-tool to the edge of the lock's keyway, and then seating it with a few sharp hits from the hammer. Once it was seated, you inserted the flat end of the Halligan into a slot on the K-tool and through pure leverage, you stripped the cylinder from the lock. After that, the rest was normally easy.

The thickness of the door translated to the need for a lot of leverage. Jonathan's first attempt proved to be light.

"Get out of the way, little man," Boxers said.

"Bite me." On the next try, Jonathan all but jumped on the end of the Halligan. It budged, but didn't clear. The third try took care of it. The cylinder cleared the lock casing and launched across the hall with a metallic clang. With the mechanism exposed, the next step was some quick work with a pick, and the door floated open.

"There you go," Jonathan said. "Now, it's your turn."

As Jonathan reassembled the irons, Big Guy scooted past with a huge grin on his face. Truly, Boxers was at his happiest when he got to blow shit up. "I'll only be a few minutes," he said.

Boxers' slice in the hierarchy of assault team assignments was the deployment of heavy weapons, the piloting of vehicles, and the placement of explosives. Big Guy was a true artist when it came to breaking things. He could fashion a shaped charge out of C4 if he wanted to poke a hole in steel, or he could turn a flat spot into a crater if shock and awe were the orders of the day.

Tonight's mission was all about using a small explosive to detonate a lot of explosives. There wasn't much elegance to it, but it was astonishing what a few blocks of C4 connected by a few feet of detonating cord could do. Det cord was Jonathan's greatest friend. Essentially a plastic tube stuffed with PETN, known to chemists as pentaerythritol tetranitrate, detonating cord could transmit an explosion from one charge to another at a velocity of about four miles per second.

Jonathan stayed in the hallway with Yelena, watching the darkness.

The dead sentry's radio rasped in his pocket, "Central, the trucks are arriving."

The now-familiar Russian-accented voice said, "Unit One, go check on Units Three and Four. I can't raise them on the radio."

Yelena's eyes grew huge. "This is bad."

"As good a word for it as I can think of," Jonathan said. He keyed his mike. "Big Guy, we're in trouble. Step it up."

"Never rush an artist." It didn't sound like it, but that was Boxers-speak for "okay."

Thank God for satellite maps. Jonathan had already figured out the routes from one place to another, and unless he was woefully mistaken, the quickest way for the yard guards to access the front gate was to pass through the door that was just fifteen feet from the spot where he was standing.

He used his arm to sweep the First Lady from the hallway into the chapel. "I need you to join Big Guy for a minute," he said. Alone now in the hallway, Jonathan squatted to a rice paddy prone position, leveled his MP7 at the door from the yard, and waited. It didn't take long.

Unit One showed no sense of urgency as he pushed

the big panel open and stepped inside. He pushed the door shut again, and as he looked up, he saw Jonathan and froze.

Jonathan triple-tapped him, two to the chest and one to the forehead, in the space of a heartbeat. The target fell straight back, arms outward, and he flung his AK high. Jonathan cringed as it crashed to the thick wooden floor, half expecting it to discharge on impact. It didn't.

A second or two later, every light in the world turned on, igniting the yard in brilliant yellow, which flooded the hallway through the windows. In the distance, an alarm bell rang. It sounded like one of those rotary jobs that he used to hear in school.

Into his radio, Jonathan said, "Now would be a really good time to announce that you're finished."

Big Guy materialized out of the darkness behind him. Scared the shit out of him. "What the hell just happened?" He glanced down the hall and saw the body. "Oh, you shot a guy. Cool. You know, there's a lot of shit in that chapel. They've got Stingers, mines, grenades, rifles. Some pretty advanced shit. All of it US military. Even saw a couple of mortar rounds, though I didn't see any tubes. KFB, baby." KFB was ka-fucking-boom.

"How big a charge did you place?"

"Big enough. Daisy-chained a couple of GPCs in all the right places. You wanted a crater, right?"

Jonathan thought he heard a hint of teasing in Boxers' voice, but there was no way to be sure. Big Guy was a professional, first and last, and even his lust for big bangs wouldn't cause him to create more havoc than was necessary.

"Where's Yelena?"

"Stuck in the doorway," she said. There was a tremor in her voice that matched the one in her hands.

Boxers moved aside to let her pass. "Oops," he said.

Jonathan pulled her close. "Same drill as before. Hand on my back. Big Guy, I've got point, you make a lady sandwich."

"Yup."

Jonathan more sensed than saw a lot of new movement in the compound. The bad guys had sounded the alarm. That blew the element of surprise, but only one part of it. They still didn't know what was going on. Given the fact that the transfer of explosives was clearly being made tonight, they probably thought that was the focus. The wild card was how nervous would that make the Mishins' guards. Nervous guards either shot too early or ran away too early. There seemed to be no middle ground. Jonathan was going with ran away, if only because it better served his priorities.

Jonathan led the way to the door that would take them down the passageway to the cell blocks. The entry door was unlocked. It made sense, he supposed, that the internal doors would be unlocked. After all, Saint Stephen's wasn't a prison anymore. Soon, it would be hotel rooms and cocktail lounges, if the owners had their way.

Jonathan predicted that the value of the real estate was about to drop precipitously.

By Jonathan's estimation, the greatest hazard lay directly ahead, at the end of this passageway. To go straight would be to take them directly to the cell block that served as the barracks. That meant that everyone who had just been rousted would be heading straight at them. Two and a half against many became far more daunting odds when the confrontation came head-to-head out in the open.

With his NVGs flipped up and out of the way to accommodate for the wash of light, Jonathan noted in his peripheral vision just what terrible shape this place was in. The once whitewashed walls now looked cancerous with peeling paint, and the stone walls radiated cold.

"I'm picking up the pace," Jonathan said. He accelerated. If he could get to the end of the passageway and turn to the right, then they'd have a chance at remaining invisible. If they couldn't—if they got caught here in the middle of the complex, they would have to fight for every step.

Jonathan called over his shoulder, "Seriously, Big Guy, how far away do we need to be before you push the button?"

"Farther than this," Boxers said. The problem with pressure waves was that they didn't give much of a damn about twists and turns and hallways. Physics was all about straight lines, and despite the fact that they'd covered an easy hundred yards on foot, they were still only twenty-five yards from ground zero when they initiated the charge.

Jonathan and his team were still twenty-five feet from the end of the hallway when the door on the opposite end burst open to reveal would-be warriors stumbling out of bed and into action. A few were mostly dressed, but most were still assembling themselves. In Jonathan's mind, somebody was beating these guys to quarters, but they were still thirty seconds from being fully awake.

And every one of them was armed with a rifle. It

was an offense that carried the death penalty. In a dynamic assault like this one, when the good guys were so vastly outnumbered by bad guys, there was no time to tell bad guys to drop their weapons and zip-cuff them into submission. The secret to survival lay in convincing the OpFor—opposing force—that the benefit of surrendering outweighed the benefit of fighting. It was a lesson hard learned by every first wave of defenders.

The first group of three or four hadn't even seen their enemy when Jonathan mowed them down. He flipped the selector to full-auto with his thumb and one-handed the MP7 as if it were a pistol, launching a full forty-round mag into the open door. Blood and tissue flew and people fell, and he felt another piece of his soul peel away. Intent notwithstanding, he'd just murdered those men. He told himself that given the chance, they'd have done the same for him.

But they hadn't. They didn't even know they were in danger when they died. Jonathan fingered the mag release and even as the empty was hitting the floor, he had a fresh one in and a round chambered.

As the bodies stacked at the doorway, panic spread to those behind. Jonathan recognized the ripple of fear and confusion as an opportunity to buy real time. The most terrified person in the world was the first survivor behind a line of people who had been killed. Splashed by blood, and maybe even cut by splintering bone, the will to fight evaporated. The effect is contagious, but the returns diminish as the line builds.

That meant that Jonathan faced a unique opportunity to freeze these assholes in their tracks.

"Yelena, get on the floor."

She dropped.

The first man to die had blocked the door open, and through that open door, some brave souls were laying out a steady volume of fire. It was random and un-aimed, but supersonic projectiles were supersonic projectiles. Even the ones that didn't directly impact flesh fragmented when they impacted the stone walls, and those tiny bits of shrapnel could be every bit as deadly as the bullets that sponsored them.

Rather than shout above the din, Jonathan keyed his mike. "I'm going to frag them," he said. "Cover me when I open the door all the way."

"Got it," Boxers said. Covering fire had less to do with hitting targets than it did with making them take cover and say a prayer before looking up again.

Jonathan half-carried, half-dragged Yelena to the end of the passageway, and slung her to the right, into the cross hall and out of the line of fire.

The incoming fire had died significantly as Jonathan approached the door. He didn't know if they'd lost their nerve, or if they were just changing out mags, but now they would pay for whatever caused their delay. As he pulled an M67 fragmentation hand grenade from its pouch, he hurried to the half-open door and hit it hard with his shoulder to bounce off anyone who might have been poised on the other side.

He looked back to Boxers, who'd taken a textbook standing shooter's position. He'd deployed his H&K 417, their portable cannon. "Just stay low," Big Guy said.

Jonathan crouched and pulled the safety pin on the grenade. He pulled on the door, and as it opened, Boxers let loose with one long, sustained string of 7.62 millimeter bullets. When Boxers paused, Jonathan heaved the grenade into the crowd, pushed the door shut again, and whirled to press his back against the door as he saw Boxers flinging himself to the ground.

The explosion was bright and sharp, and immediately followed by the sickening high-pitched screaming of terrified, wounded men. It was their cue to move.

"Hand on my ruck," Jonathan said.

Yelena stood there, staring at the smoking stairway and the bodies on the floor. "Oh my God," she said. "How many people did you just kill?"

"The hell do you care?" Boxers countered. "Move." He nudged her forward.

She resisted. "Oh my God."

Jonathan grabbed her by the front of her vest, under her chin, and pulled her close. "This is what you signed on for," he said. He intentionally infused his tone with a hefty dose of menace. "Inside these walls, there's only good guys and bad guys. Think of Nicholas and Josef and let's finish what we started."

In that moment, Jonathan lost patience with the First Lady. Who was this confessed terrorist, no matter how reformed by time and privilege, to pass judgment on him for doing the job that she'd asked him to do? She wasn't his precious cargo anymore. She'd surrendered that role the instant she chose to jump onto the boat and join a fight where she wasn't welcome.

"Just keep up," he said. "And consider yourself at weapons free. Take your safety off, keep your finger off the trigger, and shoot at anybody you don't recognize."

A panicked voice rasped from Jonathan's pocket.

"We have intruders in the compound! Oh my God, I don't know how many they've killed. They're in area four, headed south. I think they're heading for the prisoners."

"Hey, Boss," Boxers said, "how about we talk less and move more?"

CHAPTER THIRTY-ONE

David sat in the woods on a fallen tree, waiting. For what, he wasn't sure, but his chest heaved from the effort to run back to the truck, and then back to the water's edge, this time with his body armor and rifle. He'd moved from the spot where he'd been seen the last time, but he was still in the same strip of trees. Saint Stephen's Island lay less than a half mile away, across frigid water and an elevated roadway, and while it was so very, very close, it might as well have been on Mars. He'd never felt so isolated.

The caravan of trucks now looked like a string of red lights in the distance, lined up in single file along the front of the prison complex. This had to be for the transfer of the weapons. The timing was too perfect for it to be anything else.

He wished he'd checked his watch when the boat pulled away. He had no idea how much time had passed, but it felt like it had been way too long. Where was the explosion of the storage building? If it didn't happen soon, the trucks would start leaving. And then what?

Well, he had a rifle, didn't he? These people were trying to kill him; shouldn't he be trying to kill them right back? If a truck got past him, who would be left to stop them before the weapons slipped into the United States? Sure, they could alert the authorities to look for moving and storage trucks, but who said the materials would stay in the trucks?

If these guys were smart—and as organized as they were, there was every reason to believe they were smart— they'd have cars staged all over the place into which they could transfer the weapons and explosives. Maybe some of them would get caught, but others wouldn't.

He made up his mind right then that he would stop any trucks that tried to get past him. It was the right thing to do. It was a way for him to participate in the fight that had so much to do with his own survival.

If he didn't freeze to death first. He was so desperately cold—not so much his torso because his coat and his vest took care of that—but his hands and feet ached with the cold, despite the gloves and boots. He'd lost feeling in his lips ages ago. Sitting on a snow-covered tree trunk didn't help much.

He waited, staring out across the road and water at the behemoth of a building, wondering how many other benign buildings in North America—hell, around the world—harbored such evil secrets. If terrorists could gather en masse in the middle of a metropolis, what hope was there of ever stopping them?

He knew from his reporting that the FBI and the other alphabet agencies around the world did their best to track the organizations they knew about, but what about the ones they didn't know about? Anybody with a cause and a knife could become a small-time terrorist. Anybody with a cause and connections could become the next Al Qaeda. These nut-jobs were like weeds, growing without limit, wherever they decided to take root.

David thought back to the cheering and political posturing that always attended the death of a high-profile terrorist, or the takedown of a known stronghold. He'd read the reports in his own newspaper extolling the success of American power over that of the bad guys, and the implication was that as the FBI or CIA rolled up that group or the other group, we were making progress against terror in the world, yet apparently, no one even *knew* about this group. How many others didn't people know about?

These thoughts took him to a dark place in his gut. It was a hopeless place, one he'd never visited before, and definitely didn't like. As a reporter, he understood that people needed to know about such things, but he also knew that they wouldn't want to. For sure, Charlie Baroli wouldn't print such a story. He'd want the proof, the evidence. But that was just the point: there *was* no proof or evidence for the unknown threat that we nonetheless know is present.

Jesus, how stupid can we be? In popular culture, we were so protective of our perceived security that we didn't want to burst the bubble with a dose of reality. We were so concerned about hurting someone's feelings that we won't suspect obvious intent until the intent becomes reality. As a reporter, he felt terrible for having been a tool of that complacency.

It all felt like too much to process. It all made him feel ill.

He damn near fell off his log when every light in the prison came on at the same instant.

As he squinted through the cold to figure out what was going on, he realized that those weren't the only lights added to the darkness. A vehicle was screaming through the night, headed right for him. It wasn't one of the moving and storage trucks, but rather something smaller. Maybe a pickup or an SUV?

He wondered if Scorpion had already scared them into running. The thought amused him, though it begged the question of what he should do about it. It was one thing to shoot at a truck that he knew was loaded with explosives destined to kill innocent people, but absent that, wouldn't shooting into a fleeing vehicle just be murder?

As he thought these things, he kept the safety engaged on his rifle. The last thing he wanted or needed was to fire off a shot accidentally.

The vehicle slowed as it approached, leading him to believe that they truly were fleeing, reducing speed to make the turn onto the Ottawa Parkway.

As it passed him, David saw that it was indeed an SUV, and it had more the one person inside. A whole group was running away.

Only they continued to slow. Finally, they stopped at the spot where David had been standing when he encountered the truck driver.

They were looking for him.

Len heard the unmistakable hammering of automatic weapons, and a moment later, the urgency of the tone on the radio confirmed his worst fears. "We have intruders in the compound! Good God, I don't know how many they've killed." In the background, he could hear the cries of the wounded.

Dmitri's voice appeared on the radio just a moment later. "Two sentries have been shot. Their bodies are in the reception area."

Len scanned his surveillance screens, looking for some indication of what was happening, but everything looked entirely normal.

Oh no. He felt his face flush. The reception hall showed normal. Area Four showed normal. Good God, this was a nightmare. Someone had hijacked their video feed. He was blind.

He felt the early signs of panic boiling up inside him. Too many thoughts swam through his head to process them quickly enough. That meant he needed to prioritize. He needed to think not just about the words he was hearing, but about their meaning. He inhaled deeply to calm himself, and then modulated his voice to be as calm as he could make it.

He brought his radio to his lips. "I understand two bodies in the reception area. Unit reporting intruders. Who are you?"

"Gregory Jones."

Len recognized it as a cover name, but he didn't remember who it was covering for. "Okay, Gregory, how many intruders are there?"

"I don't know," he said. The horrible cacophony of wailing men echoed in the background. "I didn't get to see, but there must be many."

A large and talented attack force could only mean the police, perhaps with the assistance of the military.

"Thomas to Central," someone said. "What do you want me to do with all these trucks?"

"Central" was the radio designation for the watch commander, but Len spoke up before he had a chance. "This is Len," he said. "I am taking command. Dmitri, what do you see?" By now, he'd had plenty of time to get to the door of the chapel.

"I don't see anyone," Dmitri replied. "There's another body in the hallway outside the chapel, and I smell smoke coming from Area Four, but I see no signs of intruders."

How could that be?

Wait. Of course! This wasn't about the weapons in the chapel. This was about the Mishins. That explains why they were in Area Four. That was the innermost part of the complex. Only the cell blocks lay within. That had to be where they were headed.

He switched to Russian for better radio security. (If his enemy could tap his security cameras, they could certainly listen in on his communication.) "Thomas, tell the drivers to start loading right away. Gregory, gather those who are capable, and all of you meet me at the base of the barracks stairs in three minutes."

Grabbing an AK and a bandolier of ammunition, Len headed for his office door. He moved quickly down the spiral stone steps to what would have been a lovely reception area in the hotel that would now never exist. The stairway door, which would normally be dead bolted, lay open, no doubt because Dmitri had been in a hurry.

The front doors opened as he passed them, admitting three men dressed as anyone might be for the cold weather. Two of them wheeled hand trucks, but it was the third one who spoke. "Where—"

Len pointed. "Through those doors and then left," he said.

The truck crew took a few steps, and then stopped as they all saw the dead sentries at the same time.

"Don't worry about them," Len said. "Just do your job, and do it quickly."

"But what happened to them?"

"They didn't do their jobs quickly enough," Len said.

"What's with the Russian on the radio all of a sudden?" Boxers asked.

"I think that means we're made," Jonathan said.

Yelena translated, "He told the trucks to start loading. Then he told people to wait at the base of the sleeping quarters for him."

"Like I said," Jonathan said. "I think we're made"

They were hustling through a honeycomb of stone and steel. Jonathan had always found jails to be terrible, soul-stealing places, but this one was particularly bleak with its peeling paint and low ceilings. He recognized their location from the satellite photos as the oldest part of the prison—the original part. Building Delta sat at the end of this corridor, and somewhere in there sat their PCs.

"I don't like that they're loading the trucks," Jonathan said.

"I've got the detonator right here," Boxers said. "Say the word and I'll ruin their whole day."

Thanks to layer upon layer of stone walls, Jonathan was confident that they were far enough away from the explosion that it wouldn't impact them, but he worried about the timing. For diversions to work their magic, the choreography had to go just right. They hadn't even located the PCs yet. Did he want to blow stuff up now to buy more time to locate them, or did he want to wait until he had the Mishins in his custody and play his trump card during the exfil?

The deciding factor for him was the arrival of the trucks. If people started pulling stuff out of the chapel, there was a reasonable chance that they'd either discover or disconnect the charges they'd set.

"Go ahead," Jonathan said.

Boxers grinned. "I love this part."

"Why did they turn the lights on?" Josef asked with a start.

Nicholas thought the boy had been sleeping. Hoped he had. There was a certain irony, he supposed, to the fact that the only way to escape a living nightmare was to close your eyes and risk a sleeping nightmare. On a night like this, it was hard to tell the difference.

"I don't know," Nicholas said. "Maybe they have nighttime chores to do. Try to go back to sleep."

The boy dug at his eyes with the backs of his hands. "It's too bright."

"That's just because it was so dark before. It won't look so bright in a few minutes."

"I hear a bell, too," the boy said. "Do you hear a bell?"

Nicholas pulled him closer. "We'll be fine." Nicholas had never felt so helpless. Josef had done *nothing* wrong.

In his heart, Nicholas knew that all of this had something to do with Tony Darmond. Whether he'd ordered them to be kidnapped—a wild stretch, even in the midst of panic—or they'd been kidnapped to hurt him, the president of the United States was at the heart of the Mishin family's misery. Nicholas remembered the endless screaming matches between his mom and Tony back when he was a nobody and she was still trying to perfect her English and make something of herself.

He'd been young when they first found each other—maybe two or three years old—and he was five when they married. Never once—not for a single day—did Tony treat him as anything but the bastard stepchild that he was. Punishment regimens that were designed as household chores, whether painting fences or mowing the yard or bagging up dog shit in the back yard. Tony made sure that Nicholas would have no real friends because there was never time to hang out with them. As he got older, the chores morphed into jobs that were couched as opportunities to teach him responsibility.

Thinking these thoughts now reminded him of the single time he'd tried to voice them to his mother. The tasks all seemed so normal at their face—so character-building—that it was impossible to get others to realize the malevolence behind them. Nicholas could see it behind the bastard's eyes when he gave the assignments, and he was confident that his mother saw it, too.

Yet she never intervened. Not once. It was always Tony's way or the highway. Nicholas had always suspected that at one level, she was afraid of Tony. And the more power he gained, the more frightened she became.

So Nicholas had taken it upon himself to get even for a childhood full of nastiness. Nothing like a presidential candidacy to give a disgruntled stepson a bully pulpit for payback.

So, maybe this was payback for his payback. What better way to shut up the enemy than to pluck them out of their sleep and ship them off to someplace anonymous?

Sitting in the cold darkness—and now in the cold light—anger at Tony Darmond continued to be his most vicious inner demon. Worse, even, than his anger toward his jailers. At least they hadn't hurt him yet, unless you counted the initial bruises, and in the warped logic of the moment, he was willing to write off those bruises as necessity.

The other dark demon was simply the unknown. Suppose the plan was to just leave them here—wherever here was—to starve to death or freeze? Suppose—

The unmistakable staccato beat of a machine gun made Nicholas and Josef jump in unison.

"Someone's shooting," Josef whined. He turned to look at his father. "Who's shooting? What's happening?"

Nicholas kissed the top of his son's head. "I love you, Joey."

The SUV disgorged five men, all armed with rifles affixed with flashlights. They rolled out of the vehicle quickly, and snapped their rifles up to their shoulders, ready to shoot anyone they saw. The formed a line, with maybe five feet separating each of them from the next nearest shooter, and rushed the tree line in a move that looked practiced.

David took advantage of the noise and dropped to the ground. Branches stabbed him on impact and snow jammed his mouth, but he wanted to make as small a silhouette as possible while still being able to see what they were up to.

Clearly, the driver had seen him, or had been spooked enough to sound an alarm. The spot to which they charged was precisely the one where he'd been standing when his radio had betrayed him. They scoured the area thoroughly, speaking in urgent, animated tones. He couldn't hear the words, but the clipped syntax and the jerky movements of the muzzle lights made their meaning clear.

David pressed himself tighter to the ground and tried to maneuver his rifle for greatest mobility and flexibility, but he'd managed to tangle the sling as he fell, and between the tangle and the underbrush, he wasn't sure he'd be able to aim at a target from his belly.

What was Scorpion's phrase for that? Oh, yeah. Spray and slay. Or, in his case, spray and pray.

One member of the group apparently saw something that interested him. In the flare of the other muzzle lights, David watched the guy point to the ground, and then the lights all moved in unison. They'd found his tracks in the snow.

David's heart jumped. If they followed the tracks, they'd find the truck. If they found the truck, they'd find the trailer and through the trailer, they'd know that someone was coming at them by boat. If that happened, they'd know everything, and then all of this will have been for nothing.

The group started moving away, following exactly the path that David had worried about. There was something frightening—nearly unnatural—about the way they moved as one organism, not quite in lockstep, but certainly in unison, and with each step, they disappeared farther into the tangle of tree limbs and winter scrub. Two of them were already gone from view.

If David was going to do something to stop them, he had to do it now. It was time to either grow a pair or surrender the set he'd brought with him.

He stood to his full height, untangled himself from the sling, and snapped his rifle to his shoulder. Without looking, his thumb moved the selector from safe to single-shot. He settled the red dot that only he could see on the silhouette of the last person in the line and he squeezed the trigger.

The muzzle flash was at least as bright as the gunshot was loud. It blinded him before he could see if his target dropped, but that didn't matter. Hitting the guy would have been nice, but marksmanship was secondary at this point. The real point of the shot was to divert their attention.

And divert it he had.

As he dove for cover, the woods erupted in muzzle flashes, hundreds of lethal fireflies unleashing a swarm of projectiles that shredded the undergrowth.

In a flash of inspiration that might have been madness, David rationalized that the shooters were likewise blinded by their muzzle flashes, so he decided to capitalize on it. He threw himself on the ground and scrambled like a lizard on his stomach to displace himself by as far as possible from the spot where they'd last seen him. That meant arcing around to their left, his right, more or less following the shoreline.

He couldn't imagine the number of shots they'd fired—it had to be hundreds—but by the time they ceased firing, David was easily forty feet away from where they imagined the kill zone to be. When the shooting stopped, so did David. In a stroke of great good fortune, he found himself at the base of a substantial tree, its trunk easily thick enough to conceal him from view.

The chatter among the men who were hunting him had morphed to shouting, and while he still couldn't make out words, he didn't think they were speaking English anymore. They sounded angry, and at least one voice among them sounded anguished. Did that mean his shot had hit its mark?

Instinctively, he knew it had, and intuitively he knew that he should feel terrible about it. But he didn't. Instead, he felt fulfilled—satisfied that no matter what else happened in the next few minutes, the murder of a good cop and decent man named DeShawn Lincoln had been avenged.

Until that moment—until that thought floated through his mind—David hadn't realized how important revenge was. DeShawn had been killed for doing the job he'd been hired to do. They'd murdered him because he was a good cop, and they'd tried to murder David because the good cop had a friend. The guy David had shot might not be the same man, but he was part of the same team, and for now, that was good enough.

David hid with his back pressed tightly against the tree, his legs stretched out straight, so as to be an invisible silhouette against the white background. It felt like the safest position for about five seconds, until he realized that he couldn't see what was going on.

The chatter died suddenly, as if a switch had been flipped. In the silence that followed, he could hear movement in the dry and crunchy underbrush. They were coming for him. More precisely, they were searching for his body.

And when they didn't find it, they would start hunting him again.

Since he'd shot one of theirs, they were as intent on retribution as he was, and with focused intent came focused effort. If he couldn't see where they were and what they were doing, he was defenseless. If he merely hid in the shadows until they finally stumbled upon him, he'd be defenseless. That weird hive vibe meant that it would be many against him, and he'd die. Merely hiding was not a viable option.

They wouldn't stop searching until they found him.

He needed to stack some odds in his favor. Drawing his legs up to achieve a kind of squat, he pushed himself to a standing position, his back never leaving the scouring surface of the tree trunk. He kept his rifle in front, parallel to the lines of his body, within its shadow. When he was fully standing, he rolled slowly to his left, at first exposing only his right eye to the downrange threat.

The hunters moved cautiously, two at a time, advancing from tree to tree. Two moved ahead and took cover, and then the two behind them moved ahead farther and took cover. There were indeed only four of them now. Their movement brought to mind a human inchworm that advanced maybe ten feet with each flex.

As David watched, they were thirty feet away, and each of them presented their left profiles as they looked entirely in the wrong direction.

David moved slowly to bring his rifle horizontal and pressed the stock into his shoulder. He watched two of them advance and followed them with his sight. They were still merely black splotches against a white background, but the angles could not have been more perfect. When they took cover, they presented unobstructed profiles. As two of them waited for their teammates to leapfrog past, their heads were only a two-inch pivot for David's sights.

He practiced the pivot twice, then decided to go for it. He settled himself with a deep breath. The first shot was taken with care, but the second one was all muscle memory and hope.

When the second bullet was away, he dove again for the ground. It took a few seconds for them to react, but when they did, it was just like the previous fusillade, their bullets tearing up the forest.

CHAPTER THIRTY-TWO

The carnage at the base of the barracks stairway was unlike anything Len had ever seen. There had to be seven or eight men dead, twice that many wounded, some of them seriously.

Gregory met him in the hallway, on this side of the carnage. His hands and his shirt and the front of his pants were slick and shiny with blood. Dazed and frightened men gathered behind him, all of them armed with rifles and most of them still in underwear from having been rousted from bed.

"Are you hurt?" Len asked.

"No," he replied. "But so many are. What is happening?"

"We are under attack," Len explained. "But it is not for the weapons. It is for—"

He saw the shutter flash of light first, followed an instant later by the pulse of air pressure that fractured the stone walls and floor and knocked him to his knees. The sound of the explosion registered more as a vacuum of silence than noise as the pressure wave—alternately reduced and magnified by outside and inside corners—hammered his eardrums.

In that instant, he knew that they'd lost everything. Anyone who was standing in the hallway outside the chapel was dead. That meant Dmitri. Whoever had been standing inside the chapel had been reduced to vapor.

Nothing would be left of the Movement after tonight. There'd be no humiliation of America, no return to Soviet principles based upon his heroic deeds. The hopes and plans of two decades had been destroyed in ten minutes. All that was left for Len was vengeance.

That alone was something to live for.

The terrible irony—so clear to him now—was that the weapons had never been the focus of the invaders. He didn't know how he was so certain but he knew without doubt that the explosion was merely a diversion to allow the invaders to liberate the prisoners in cell block six, the ones who never should have been brought here in the first place.

The Americans had discovered the whereabouts of the Mishins, and they had mobilized their Navy SEAL teams or their Delta Force. This was an unconscionable violation of his agreement with the White House, yet he'd understood, as he could never make Dmitri understand, that there were some lines in life that should never be crossed.

He could not let the Americans escape the island alive. To stop them, though, he needed to move quickly to stem the panic that the explosion had solidified among his troops.

"Listen to me!" he shouted in Russian. "Stop shouting! Get ahold of yourselves!"

Others in the crowd took up the request for him, and soon silence washed over the men like a wave.

"Our mission is in crisis," Len said. "We have been crippled by American soldiers who want to humiliate us. We must stop them. If this must be our final battle, let us make it a costly one for the invaders. If we must die, let us die for the dream that is so much larger than any one of us."

He watched the faces of the men as they processed his words. These men were not weaklings—far from it—but many of them paled at their impending mortality. For a moment, Len feared that he would lose them entirely. Had it not been for the smallest man in the crowd, that might have happened.

Geoffrey stepped forward. At five-five, maybe one hundred twenty pounds, Geoffrey looked more like a boy than a man, but had always held sway over the others. "Let's go," he said. His AK looked comically large in his hands, but he handled the weapon as if it weighed nothing. "We're all with you."

Somehow, that sealed it. As Len led the procession down the Area Four corridor, he counted at least fifteen people behind him. Whatever the final number was, he hoped he wasn't hopelessly outnumbered.

Joey screamed. That's the only way to describe the terrible sound that launched from his throat and his gut. A brilliant white light came first, followed just an instant later by a sharp explosion that seemed to make the stones move—to make the whole building move.

And the sound continued to rumble on and on. He'd never heard anything so loud, and his scream escaped before he could stifle it.

Now that it had started, he didn't know if he could stop it. It was as if his fear had sharp claws and was trying to tear itself out of his body. He felt his dad reach for him, but Joey wanted none of that. He didn't need any more *I'll make it betters* or *I won't let them hurt yous*. People were shooting and blowing things up, and there was nothing Dad or anybody but God almighty could do to stop it. Most terrifying of all, God had seemed to be really distracted these past couple of days.

They were going to die here. And Joey would never even know why.

The initial flash turned the night to day. David's eyes happened to be focused at exactly the right point in space to see one of his hunters as clearly as if it were stop-action photography. The image persisted on his retinas long enough for him to shoot at the lingering outline, but the sound of his shot was completely lost in the roar of the explosion. The fact that he'd been expecting the explosion didn't take anything away from the gut fear that it invoked.

The enormous boom seemed to split the world, as if it sucked all the air out of the atmosphere, and then reinjected with the gain turned up full. The noise hit with a physical force, like a hammer blow to his chest that knocked him off balance.

The hunters first jumped, then scattered in the seconds that followed. In the space of a blink, they seemed to realize together that the explosion was a distant event, separate and apart from their confrontation with the single person who was tearing them up with gunfire. In the confusion, and blessed with the infusion of new light, David took a bead on one of the attackers—there were still three of them, so clearly one of his bullets had missed—and squeezed off a shot. He watched the target's head erupt in mist.

Down to two. And they were truly, deeply pissed. They opened fire again, spraying wildly, apparently still with no strong notion of where he was.

Using the noise of the gunfire as cover, David lurched out of his hiding place and dropped to one knee. He chose one of the remaining silhouettes and fired eight or nine bullets in that direction. Someone yelled out in pain, and then someone unleashed what had to be a full magazine of ammunition in his direction. These shots landed much nearer than any of the others. The surviving guy was beginning to adapt.

Now it was down to one on one.

"Holy shit," Jonathan said. "How much C4 did you use?" They'd just been knocked to the floor by the force of the pressure wave.

"Told you there was a lot of shit in there," Big Guy said with a grin. "I think we might have forced them back a few notches in their terrorist dreams."

"Are you okay, Yelena?"

She nodded. Her eyes seemed bigger than her face.

"Yeah, I'm good, too, Boss," Boxers said.

Jonathan stayed focused on the First Lady. "Ma'am,

things are going to move quickly now. You've got to keep up."

He didn't wait for a response. With his rifle at his shoulder, Jonathan led the team to the end of the hall-way, where he encountered a locked heavy wooden door, the hinges for which were on his side. Letting his MP7 fall against its sling, he raised the Mossberg from under his armpit and racked a round into the chamber. "Going hot," he said. "Yelena, look away." In her haste to jump onto the boat, she hadn't donned eye protec-tion.

He pressed the vented muzzle against the top hinge and pulled the trigger. The Mossberg boomed and the hinge disintegrated. He shucked the forestock to cham-ber a new round, pressed the muzzle against the bottom hinge, and fired. The door hung awkwardly from its lock now, and Jonathan used his shoulder to crash it open.

The door gave, but not all the way, hanging up against the bolt that extended deeply into the jamb on the other side. "Big Guy, give me a hand."

Boxers grabbed the back of his ruck, pulled him out of the way, and demonstrated Newton's Second Law of Motion: force equals mass times acceleration. He put everything he had into the shoulder-blow to open the door. The door never had a chance. It swung open and half-collapsed, still hung up on its bolt, but with enough space for people to slip through.

With the Mossberg back at rest, and his MP7 back against his shoulder, Jonathan led the way. He squirted through the opening and took a couple of steps to leave room for the rest of the team. Then he took a knee and surveyed the interior of the cell block. He faced an interior alley with at least twenty cells on a side, for a total of at least forty cells on this floor. Looking up, he saw a ceiling constructed of iron grating that served as the hallway floor for the rank of cells above, and so it continued upward for another three floors.

"Nicholas Mishin!" Jonathan yelled. "Josef Mishin! Shout out! We're here to bring you home."

A burst of gunfire from behind made Jonathan jump and whirl. He saw Boxers with his H&K 417 at his shoulder, firing down the length of hallway they'd just traveled.

"They're on us," Big Guy said, and he fired another long burst.

This was bad. There were too many moving parts between now and all they needed to do to have OpFor nipping at their heels. Jonathan said over the net, "Take out every light you see and go to night vision." He started things off by shooting the five bare lightbulbs that illuminated the first floor of the cell block. Though suppressed, the sharp pops of the MP7 still rattled the senses inside this stone canyon.

The darkness was refreshing, but far from complete as light from the floors above still shone down through the metal floors, creating a spiderweb of shadows. It would have been nice to kill those lights as well, but there was no clean shot through the steel grates.

Behind and to his left, he heard Boxers firing single rounds, and when that hallway went dark, they regained some measure of advantage.

"Yelena," Jonathan said. In the green hue of the NVGs, he saw that she'd drifted somewhere in her head. He took a step closer and smacked her helmet to get her attention. "Yelena!"

She jumped, nearly brought her rifle to bear on him.

He caught the barrel with his palm. "Get your head in the game, ma'am. Be scared and distracted on your own time."

Boxers fired another burst, this one shorter. "Hey!" he shouted. "Can we get some work done here?"

Jonathan said, "Yelena, go find your family. Floor to floor, door to door. When you find them, get on the radio and tell us where they are. We'll be there as soon as we can. You just wait."

She looked horrified. "Where will you be?"

"Buying time," he said. "Go. And once you go up a level do not come down again for any reason, understand? You can move up and out, but never down. Got it?"

She nodded.

"Say it."

"Once up, never come down."

Boxers unleashed again.

"Go. We're almost to the goal line. Don't drop the ball."

Jonathan turned his back on the First Lady and joined Boxers. He put a hand on his shoulder to get his attention. "I'll take over here," he said. "Set some charges we can hold the stairs with."

Big Guy smiled. "Roger that." He peeled away, and Jonathan slipped into his spot in the gap in the door. Peering down the corridor, he counted three bodies on the floor, all of them clustered at the far end. Jonathan scanned for targets with his infrared laser. For the time being, the attackers were all hidden away. He'd like to think that they had run away, but that kind of luck ran counter to what they'd been experiencing.

A more reasonable conclusion was that they'd been spooked. Or they'd found another way.

Shit. They'd found another way.

Josef's eyes grew huge at the sound of their names being called. Nicholas didn't know whether to be elated or terrified. The extended burst of machine gun fire that came immediately after tilted things more toward terror.

"Are they coming for us?" Josef asked.

They'd shed their blankets and stood, instinctively moving farther away from the door. "I think so," Nicholas said.

"Do they want to save us or hurt us?"

Now, that was the million-dollar question. Nicholas tried to make sense of it. If Tony Darmond had had them kidnapped in the first place, what was the likelihood that he would authorize a mission to rescue them? But someone was clearly attacking this place—whatever this place was—and who else but the American military would have the resources to do that?

We're here to take you home.

That's what the voice had said. That could be a trap, he supposed, but wouldn't their enemies—presumably the ones who had brought them here in the first place—know where they'd put them? Why would they need to shout their names to confirm their location?

More gunfire.

Nicholas sank to one knee and took his son's shoulders in his hands. "Look at me," he said.

In the light that spilled into their cell from the high window, the eyes that looked back at him were wet, with irises so brown as to be black. They were the eyes of a boy who would become a handsome man if he ever got the chance.

"I don't know what's about to happen," Nicholas said, "but I think it's going to be big. I need you to be brave."

"Are we going to die?"

Nicholas started to answer with a reflexive no, but stopped himself. "I don't know," he said. "But if we are, let's both die bravely."

There were in fact two entrances to every floor to Building Delta. That meant two additional levels from Building Echo whose corridor he was now covering, and three from Building Charlie on the east side.

Jonathan keyed his mike even as he started to move. "Big Guy, set and arm your charge with a motion fuse and mark it with an IR chem light. I think they're also coming at us from Charlie." He sprinted toward the east end of the hallway. "Set and mark charges at the west end of every level. I'll set them on the east ends."

In the old days, when they did this kind of work for Uncle Sam, they worked in teams of two dozen operators, with support from hundreds of logisticians and planners, with reinforcements only a radio call away. Every contingency was planned for and every bet was hedged. If Jonathan had had the benefit of additional trained manpower, he would have had all of the stairways and entrances covered, just as he would have had individual operators assigned to breaching duties and PC rescue duties. Tonight, they'd rolled the dice on going undetected until the diversion of blowing up the chapel gave them an edge.

As it was, the edge still existed, but the enemy was adapting. He needed to cover the eastern side of the building as well as the western side.

The arrangement of the doorway and the stairs on the east end was the mirror image of the one on the west. While the bad guys had probably gotten a head start, they had to travel two sides of a large square to get there, while Jonathan could travel from point to point in a straight line.

"First charge set and marked," Boxers' voice said in his ear. A few seconds later, a new layer of darkness fell as Big Guy shot out the lights on the second floor.

Above him and seemingly from everywhere, Yelena called out for Nicholas and Josef.

"Is that Babushka?" Josef's voice cracked with excitement. He looked up at Nicholas. "That sounds like Babushka."

And damned if it didn't. Was that possible? How could Tony Darmond's wife—the First Lady of the United States—possibly break free to come and rescue them? How could she even know that they had been taken?

When she called a second time there was no denying the identity of the voice.

Josef ran to the door and pounded on it. "Babushka! We're here! Babushka!"

The boy seemed oblivious to the additional gunfire.

Jonathan unslung his ruck while he ran. He glanced quickly to his left to see that the door from Building Charlie was still intact, then cut the turn to the stairway. The stairs themselves were surrounded by a sheath of metal mesh. Ten steps led to a landing, at which point the stairs turned one hundred eighty degrees to the right and then spiraled up to the next floor.

Jonathan climbed to the first landing, took a knee, and placed his ruck on the floor next to him. Without looking, his hand moved to the right-hand exterior pocket to find the thick rectangular curve that he knew to be a claymore mine. As he lifted it from its pocket, his other hand found the detonators that he carried in the left-hand pocket. Working from muscle memory, he inserted a detonator into its designated spot on the back of the mine.

He didn't have time to run a trip wire, and a timer fuse was inappropriate. He chose instead to use what he called a motion fuse. It was an unforgiving initiator that was tied to a motion sensor. He set the arming timer to thirty seconds to give himself time to get out of the way before the sensor went active. Once it did, there'd be no turning back, and no disarming the device. If a person or an animal moved within the range of the sensor, one and one-third pounds of C4 would detonate, launching seven hundred steel balls in a sixty-degree arc straight at the enemy.

Just to be on the safe side, Jonathan inserted a second detonator, this one tied to a radio receiver so that he could shoot it manually if he wanted to. The last step before setting the arming timer was to pull an infrared chem light from its elastic mount on his vest. When he snapped the tube and shook it, the chem light emitted a green glow that was visible only to those wearing night vision. He laid it next to the claymore so that he'd know where it was. Then he punched in the thirty-second delay and he got the hell out of there.

Hefting his ruck with his left hand, he was halfway up the next flight of stairs when the radio popped to life in his right ear. "I found them!" Yelena shouted. He could have heard her without the radio. "They're on the fourth floor. I'm standing outside their cell."

"Roger that," Jonathan said. "Don't move. We're on our way. Just need to place one more claymore."

An instant later, the command net popped to life in his left ear. "Scorpion, Mother Hen. The Ottawa police and fire services are dispatching the world to your location."

CHAPTER THIRTY-THREE

The sound of sirens grew in the night as David pressed himself against the snow. The last surviving attacker was apparently as freaked out as David was. The guy fired his machine gun randomly into the woods, close enough to David's general direction to keep his head down, but nowhere near close enough to pose a real hazard.

David didn't know what to do. What had started as a random encounter had settled into a one-on-one hunt to the death. And the sound of sirens was growing in the distance. David would welcome any reinforcements he could get. But even as that thought formed, it amended itself. Who said that the reinforcements would be on his side?

Out of nowhere, he remembered that he hadn't turned his radio back on. He made sure that the bud was seated securely in his ear and he pressed the transmit button. "Mother Hen?"

"Good God, Rooster, where have you been?" Mother Hen sounded both angry and relieved.

He whispered, "Those trucks. They saw me. They sent five guys to come for me, but I've killed four. The fifth one is nearby, but I can't stick my head up to find him without the risk of getting it shot off. Can you help? Can you tell me where the other guy is?"

"Negative. Our satellite refresh rate is every four minutes, and the last update was two minutes ago. From that last photo, I can see six images, but I don't know which one is you."

His heart hammering, David tried to think it through. There had to be a way. "Mother Hen, I haven't moved in the last two minutes, and I won't move in the next two. That will mean that the image that does move will be the one who's trying to shoot me."

A pause. During the silence, David listened for signs of movement. Hearing none, he wondered if the other guy was even more frightened than he. In the distance, the sound of sirens continued to crescendo, as did the sound of an approaching helicopter. Not surprisingly, the sound from the air increased more quickly than that from the ground.

"Rooster, do you have a flashlight on you?" Mother Hen asked.

"Yes," David answered. *What the hell kind of question is that?*

"Get it ready," she said. "When I tell you, I want you to flash it three times toward the sky, and repeat it three times for a total of nine flashes. Acknowledge."

"Why?"

"Three times three. Do you understand? And switch your radio to channel one."

"I understand, but why am I doing that?"

"Because Striker is going to land his helicopter and save you."

Becky was terrified. They flew at an altitude of four feet at four thousand miles an hour. In the green wash of the instrument panel, she could see that Striker wore binocular thingies over his face—she presumed them to be night vision goggles—but to her, the world outside was a blur of rushing cityscape.

A minute ago, Striker had told her over the radio headset, "Our first save is going to be your friend, Rooster. I need you in the door on the port side of the aircraft to look for three flashes from a flashlight. That will be Rooster. He's going to do it three times. I'll look for it, too, but I'm gonna be a little busy flying the aircraft. If neither of us sees it, we need to circle around. Do not guess. If you see it, say so. If you don't, don't bullshit me to save your boyfriend."

Something in the way he delivered that last sentence offended her, but she didn't mention it. "Which side is the port side?"

"Left," he said. "Sorry."

Becky rose from her kneeling squat on the floor and moved to the open door on the left side. The temperature inside had dropped to something south of frigid. It felt good to stand just to get blood moving in her legs again. Maybe by sometime next week, she'd be able to feel her toes again.

"I'll tell you when to start looking for the light," Striker said. "Meanwhile, what's the status of your weapon's safety switch?"

"It's on."

"When you're in the doorway, take it off. Don't point the weapon at me, and don't point it at the aircraft. Other than that, if you see anybody who didn't flash a light at you, I want you to shoot at him. I don't care if you hit him—though it would be nice if you did. I just need you to keep their heads down long enough for us to pull Rooster aboard. After that, we'll draw for another mission."

Becky didn't understand half of what she'd just been told, but the important parts got through. They were going to rescue David from wherever he was, and her job was simply to shoot anyone she saw who was not David. Frankly, she didn't know that she was capable. Who was she to be the arbiter of who should live and who should die? Who gave her that power?

"I want you to remember that you're here of your own volition," Striker said, as if reading her thoughts. "When you volunteer for a mission, the least you need to do is show up. Now keep your eyes peeled for that light."

"Flash your light now," Mother Hen said over the radio on channel one. "Now, now, now."

This was a mistake. David knew it in the depths of his soul even as he pointed the flashlight to the sky and thumbed the button. Once, twice, three times.

The ripple of gunfire came almost immediately, with the bullets impacting so close that his opponent must have been looking directly at him when he flashed the light.

David rolled three rotations to his right and switched his selector to full auto to rake what he thought was the other guy's position. He fired till his magazine ran dry, and then he rolled to his back and executed a mag change that Big Guy would have been proud of. He slapped the bolt closed and released another long burst toward his opponent, hoping to keep his head down as he raised his light toward the heavens and flashed it another three times.

This time, when his opponent opened fire, the bullets didn't come anywhere close to him. Instead, they were all directed toward the approaching helicopter.

Tink, tink, tink, tink. The noise, which had the cadence of a card shuffle, sounded like the one you'd get from hitting an empty soup can with a wooden stick. The floor of the helicopter pulsed with each impact.

"Shoot back!" Striker shouted in Becky's ear. "What the hell are you waiting for?"

"What do I shoot at?" Becky yelled back. "Everything I see is a flashing light."

"Don't worry about muzzle flashes," Striker said. "The bright light you saw was Rooster. Sparkly flashes from that location are him shooting back at the bad guy. Other flashes are the bad guy shooting at him."

It was all too much to process.

"You can save his life, or you can cost him his life," Striker said over the intercom. "Choose."

The radio in David's ear said, "The chopper is landing for you. You need to make it there to get out."

A second voice that sounded like Director Rivers added, "Set your rifle to full-auto and let the rounds rip while you run. That'll keep their heads down.

A thousand questions and ten thousand objections formed in David's head, but he voiced none of them. If this chopper was his ride to safety, he didn't want to say anything to queer the deal.

The hum of the chopper's rotors continued to increase in volume, and a few seconds later, he could actually see the outline of the helicopter flaring to land. His ride had arrived. But how was he going to run to it without getting shot?

As if the helicopter had heard his question, someone in the doorway started shooting back. Long bursts of automatic fire raked the area where the final shooter had been lying low.

Striker's voice scratched from David's radio. "Rooster, Striker. Now would be the time for you to start running." His tone was light, almost amused.

This was a mistake. He was going to get out in the open, and he was going to get shot. With dozens of rounds being fired in both directions, it would only take one to kill him.

But staying here wasn't an option, either.

Screw it. He found his feet and he took off, running as fast as he could with all the gear dangling from him. The gunner in the door must have seen him—good God, was that Becky?—because she opened fire again on the woods. The hammering of her rifle was so loud that he didn't think he'd be able to tell if the other guy was shooting back.

Between the slippery footing and the heavy gear, he felt like he was running at a walker's pace, but finally, he could feel the wash of the rotors, and three steps later, he flung himself at the open door. He'd barely landed on the floor before he sensed the lift and he knew they were airborne.

As the ground fell away, he was amazed by the number of emergency vehicles that were approaching Saint Stephen's Island from every road and from miles away.

Len Shaw knew that he needed to settle down. It had been a mistake to follow the attackers down that corridor into a kill zone. It was always a mistake to follow your enemy's tracks. Saint Stephen's was his home territory. He knew every nook, crease, and chip as well as he knew the face he saw in the mirror every morning. There was no need to chase the intruders and walk into their traps. Not when he could set a trap of his own.

He'd put the Mishin family on the fourth floor because it was the warmest. From it, there was no escape but to come down the stairs and exit to ground level. Even if they chose to exit through other cell blocks, they would have to climb down to the third floor or below. And that's where he would set up his teams to ambush them, one team each on the east and west stairwells. The instant either one came face-to-face with the enemy, they would engage, and the other team would move in to reinforce them.

As a hedge against the possibility that the attacking team left security details in the hallways to guard the stairwells—thus splitting their forces—Len decided that he had to split his as well. Four men each would enter the southern wing from the second and third floors from both the east and west. He had to assume that the attackers had taken the radio from the murdered sentries and they therefore could monitor his communication, so before he split the teams, he synchronized everyone's timepieces and they established a precise moment when they would move into their stairwells.

As he addressed his troops, he looked each of them in the eye, assessing their commitment to the cause. With Dmitri dead, Len was the sole leader of the Movement, and the men would look to him for confidence and resolve. What he got in return concerned him. The deaths of their comrades at the base of the barracks stairs, followed by the deaths in the corridor, had unnerved them. He tried to spin them up with the glory of avenging their fallen friends, and while they nodded and said the right things, he sensed that they were ready to run.

Finally, he said, "Listen out there, comrades. Do you hear the sirens? We are ruined here. Our mission is over. Now, our choices are only two: we die in prison, or we die in the glory of our cause. If there is a third path, I'm willing to listen to anyone who knows what it might be."

Their faces had shown sadness and anger—anger at him, he imagined, and anger at the loss of so much when victory had been so close. But Len's instincts told him that that comment—the choice between death in prison or death in battle—had been what cemented their resolve. His troops were informed, motivated, and ready to go.

As commander, he'd chosen to be a part of the team on the east side third floor, the one in his estimation most likely to encounter the enemy. It had been his plan to lead the team until Geoffrey said that he was insulted. He used the distinctly American phrase "glory hound" to describe Len's effort to lead the final assault, and Len had stepped aside. It was the will of his team, in fact, that as commander, he should be the last man in.

It was a statement of commitment not only to the cause, but to him as a leader.

As the clock ticked down the final ten seconds, Len said, "Remember. Enter slowly. We remain silent unless we encounter the enemy, and we engage any enemy we see."

They all nodded.

"Five seconds," Geoffrey said.

The men pressed their weapons to their shoulders.

"Three . . . two . . ."

The final digits went unspoken. Two seconds later, Geoffrey turned the lock and slid through the opening into the stairwell. They moved like a single organism around the corner and into the danger zone. First man, second man, third man.

Len was just about to make the final turn when an explosion ripped the night apart.

Jonathan hit the top step to the fourth floor just as Boxers was taking out the hallway lights. He backed down a couple of steps to protect himself from ricochets or fragments. After the shooting was done and the fourth floor was as dark as they could make it, he reentered the corridor and jogged to the spot where Yelena stood outside a cell, her hands pressed against the door, as if to touch the occupants on the other side.

He heard her say, "I'm coming, sweetheart. We're going to get you out."

The cell was nearly in the middle of the northern wall, slightly closer to the east than the west. Despite Boxers' head start, the two men arrived more or less together. "Yelena," Jonathan said, "Watch the west hallway. If you see anyone who's not us—and I mean *anyone*—kill them. Don't challenge them, don't tell them to drop their weapon. Just shoot. I'll cover the east end."

It was not uncommon for Jonathan to involve PCs in the mechanics of their own rescue, and experience taught that the concept of the quick kill was an elusive one among civilians raised with bullshit TV honor codes where every enemy had to be given a chance, and it was cowardly to shoot a bad guy in the back.

"Nicholas Mishin!" Jonathan yelled. "Are you inside?"

"Who are you?"

"I'm one of the guys who's here to take you home. Josef, are you there, too?"

"What happened to Babushka?" a young voice answered. From the way it cracked, Jonathan knew that puberty had not arrived, but was on its way.

"I'm right here!" Yelena yelled.

As Boxers unslung his ruck and put it on the floor, Jonathan said, "Listen to me. I need you to—"

The building shook with four explosions in such rapid succession that an inexperienced ear might have heard them as a single blast.

Jonathan jumped at the sound and the PCs yelled.

"Oh my God, what was that?" Yelena said. She ducked to a low stoop to protect herself.

"That's the sound of evener odds," Boxers said. "I bet it's a mess down there."

"What does he mean?" Yelena asked.

"Never mind," Jonathan said. "Keep an eye on your door."

If nothing else, he thought, there was a lot less chance of her having to shoot anyone.

Nicholas had never felt this level of fear. He worried that his heart might bruise itself against the bones of his chest. The explosions, the shooting, the screaming of wounded men. These were the sounds of the Apocalypse, a conclusion that seemed borne out by the dancing white and yellow light of fires burning out of control.

He worried that Josef would never be right after this. That last explosion seemed to take him to a place that was literally out of his mind. He dropped to the floor in a crouch, pressed his hands against the sides of his head, and screamed.

Nicholas dropped with him and gathered him into his arms, rocking him. "We'll be okay," he whispered. "We'll be okay, we'll be okay. Babushka is here to rescue us." He spoke as if that actually made sense. As if the First Lady of the United States routinely engaged in warfare. A distant part of him wondered if maybe he was the one who had lost his mind, and that none of this was happening at all.

"Nicholas, listen to me," yelled the voice from the other side of the door. "Are you there?"

Josef had stopped screaming, but he continued to cry, his hands still pressed to his face.

"I'm here!" Nicholas yelled. "We're both here."

"We're going to open the door with an explosive charge," the voice said. "I need you to get as far away as you can, against the back wall. Lie on the floor with your backs to the door. Plug your ears, close your eyes, and don't open them until I tell you."

"Is that safe?" Nicholas asked.

"Safer than leaving you inside."

He heard a smile in the man's voice with that last line, and he realized how stupid a question he'd just asked.

"We're in a time crunch here, Nicholas, so keep your head in the game. Repeat back what I just told you."

Nicholas repeated it, and was pleased to see that Josef was already getting himself into position.

"Just a few more seconds now," the voice said.

CHAPTER THIRTY-FOUR

Len Shaw had never seen bodies so mangled. They'd been torn apart by the blast, bits of flesh and internal organs embedded into the stone of the walls, ceiling, and floor. There were no survivors. There were no corpses complete enough to identify. His stomach churned at the sight and the stench of the carnage, the combined stink of explosive, burned hair, and shit.

Len had survived only because he had yet to turn the corner when the bomb exploded. Had he been in the lead—had he been in the position he'd wanted—he would be among this carnage.

As the dust settled and the smoke thinned, he saw what he had feared. This scene was replicated at the far end of the hallway. These Americans—these animals— had set dual traps.

No, it was even worse. As he looked down through the metal floor, he saw the same devastation yet again, directly below.

They'd booby-trapped every level, a brilliant move that guaranteed that no one could interfere with what they were doing—or at least that there would be an unspeakable price to be paid by anyone who tried.

Len knew now that he was alone. His comrades were mostly dead, and of those who remained alive, none would be willing to risk such violence again. They were spent.

But Len would not give up. Nothing remained of any of the plans that he had made or the dreams that he had entertained. All he had left now was revenge against those who had wrought this violence upon him and upon the Movement.

As his ears cleared from the explosion, he heard voices shouting from above, and then there was another explosion, this one not a fraction of what caused the slaughter that surrounded him, but the instant he heard it, he knew exactly what it was. The invaders had just blown open the Mishins' cell door.

The Americans were going to win unless he stopped them.

Resolute in the certainty that one way or the other he was going to die tonight, he started up the final flight of stairs.

Boxers' GPC had shredded the wooden door at the lock, but had wedged the hardware into the jamb, requiring Big Guy to kick the door four times to get it open.

The Mishins were exactly where they were supposed to be, in the back of the cell, cowering against the floor. Jonathan pulled a visible-light chem light from his vest, broke it open, and shook it. It glowed a green that everyone could see. As Yelena darted into the room to be with them, Jonathan pressed his hand against the center of her vest. "No," he said. "You hold the hallway. Shoot anything that you see."

"But I don't see anything. It's dark."

"Then shoot anything that you hear moving. We're almost done."

Jonathan closed the distance to the PCs in three strides and put his hand on Nicholas's back to roll him over. "You okay?"

He looked terrified. "I'm fine."

"How about you, Josef?"

"Joey," the boy said. "Who are you?"

Jonathan heard strength in the kid's voice. He liked that. "Listen up," he said. "We're in a hurry."

The man with the gun looked like a four-eyed monster. Joey knew that was ridiculous, and he told himself to listen to the words he was hearing, not the ones that were screaming in his head. He knew they weren't eyes, but that's what they looked like. He'd seen night vision eye things on the History Channel before, but they were always just two. He figured that the four ones were better.

"Listen up, we're in a hurry," the man said. "My name is Scorpion. My big friend is Big Guy. I think you know the lady over there."

Babushka stood in the doorway. She was dressed like the men, but without the four eyes. She wore a black outfit and she carried a rifle. "Hello, Joey," she said. She held out her arms for a hug, but before he could move, the man who called himself Scorpion stopped him.

"The hallway, Yelena!" the man yelled. Then he turned to Joey. "Put this on," he said. He'd pulled a helmet out of the backpack he'd put on the floor. "This is bulletproof," he said, settling on his head and adjusted the chin strap. "Don't even touch it if you don't have to. These things'll keep you alive if someone shoots at you."

Joey cast a glance over to his father for confirmation, and saw in the weird green light that a huge man who looked just like Scorpion was giving a helmet to Dad.

"What if they shoot someplace other than my head?" Joey asked.

He thought he saw Scorpion smile. "Bad guys don't shoot at legs," he said. "And if they tried, they'd have to go through me."

As Scorpion stood, he grasped Joey's shoulders and moved him toward the door. The guy was a lot stronger than he looked. But rather than put him out in the hall, he pushed him to the corner near the open door. A few seconds later, his dad was next to him, and the men gathered under the window to talk about things.

"I told you we'd get out of here," Dad said.

Len Shaw moved with agonizing slowness up the eastern stairs into the darkness, putting out of his mind the carnage that he'd literally crawled through. He was terrified of being caught and shot like a dog, but he was equally terrified of pressing his hand on an unseen trip wire and inadvertently blasting himself to vapor. These monsters who'd invaded Saint Stephen's killed without hesitation and without granting dignity to other brave soldiers.

The Americans had the audacity to label him and the Movement as terrorists, yet they unleashed this brand of wholesale murder. It was unspeakable.

Soon, he was able to hear voices over the pounding of his heart, and as he approached the top step to the fourth floor, he could just barely see a silhouette in the dim light of the fires outside, combined with an otherworldly green glow emanating from the interior of the cell, which had clearly been opened. The silhouette was that of a soldier, but a small one. He imagined it to be a woman, commensurate with the Americans' decision to finally allow women to do their duty for their nation's defense. Where there was one, there had to be many more. The others must be stationed in shadowy corners that he could not see.

Len had a clear kill shot on the woman if he'd wanted to take it, but it made no sense to kill only one when they had killed so many. He would wait. Sooner or later, they would all have to enter into the hallway, toward one of the two stairs. Either direction they chose, he would have unobstructed access to them.

He could show patience when he needed to.

The view from the air showed destruction of a scale that David had never seen before. Through the left-hand door of the cargo area, where a harness kept him from falling out, and from which he was supposed to shoot people if it came to that, he could see that an enormous hole had been blown open on the north end of the complex, along the western wall. Scale was hard to judge from this far away, but he guessed that it was every bit of sixty or seventy feet square. What wasn't blown open had collapsed in on itself, and that whole part of the complex was on fire.

Two trucks were burning as well—two of the very trucks that had passed him on the way in. One of them lay on its side, as if the blast of the explosion had toppled it. Somehow, the lights in the compound had remained on, and in their glow, David saw maybe two dozen people moving around on the ground, and half that number sprawled in crimson-stained snow. The ones who were still alive seemed to be organizing themselves, clustering in groups on the southern end of the compound, as if to greet the incoming emergency vehicles. They all appeared to be armed.

Striker had given him a headset to wear after he climbed aboard the helicopter, and through it, he heard the pilot's voice say, "Scorpion, Striker's on station at eight hundred feet. Rooster and Chickadee are both on board, and I'm awaiting instruction."

Scorpion's reply was immediate: "Good evening, Striker. Welcome to the party. Give me a sit rep from up there."

"It isn't pretty. You made a hell of a dent—" He paused. "Break. Mother Hen, are you still on the net?"

"Affirmative."

"Contact the Ottawa authorities and tell them that the police and fire units responding to Saint Stephen's are driving straight into a firefight. The bad guys are lined up, and it looks like the fire trucks will be hit first. Break. Okay, Scorpion, you're pretty much screwed."

The helicopter nosed down and banked hard to the

left as they dropped a couple hundred feet and headed toward the north end of the shoreline. Down below, the ground was strewn with burning debris.

"Your primary exfil site is inaccessible from the western side of the compound," Striker said over the radio. "No way to get to the boat, and way, way too many people with guns. Secondary exfil is now filled with skirmishers lining up to do battle with emergency responders. If I set down there, we'll never have a chance. We need a third option."

"Stand by," Scorpion said.

As they turned to go south, David saw the flicker of muzzle flashes among one of the clusters of people with guns. "They're shooting!" he shouted.

"So I see," Striker said. "Let's give them something to think about. Both of you move to the starboard—*right-hand*—door."

As David moved across the cabin, dragging his safety line along the wire that ran the width of the ceiling, the chopper gained altitude again, and flew out over the river a ways before pivoting on its own axis and heading back toward the compound at a million miles an hour.

Striker's voice sounded excited as he said, "Put your weapons on full-auto. When I say 'shoot,' point the muzzles down forty-five degrees below the horizon and just pull the trigger till I say to stop. In three, two, one, *shoot*!"

David had expected more warning. He'd barely switched the lever to full-auto when the order came. He didn't aim the gun so much as he pointed it, pulled the trigger, and let fly. His bullets raked the line of shooters, all of whom appeared to be facing the other direction. His magazine went dry the instant before Striker said, "Cease fire."

David looked over to Becky. In the dim, deflected light, she looked pale.

"Sounds like Striker pretty much hit the nail on the head," Boxers said in a low tone. "We're screwed. We need a way to get to the roof."

Jonathan smiled. It's funny how sometimes it's the simplest things that bring clarity to your mind. "I've got six GPCs left," he said. "What about you?"

Big Guy shrugged. "I used them all in the chapel. I've still got probably twenty feet of det cord, though. What are you thinking?"

"Well, this room's pretty tight," Jonathan thought aloud. He pretended not to hear the increased rate of fire from outside. He hated the thought of the local police getting caught up in all of this and dying for a cause they didn't even understand. "And this stone, while it's strong, it's probably pretty brittle, too. If we can combine the charges, wrap them in the det cord, and then place them up against the wall—"

"We can get enough overpressure to make a door," Boxers said, finishing the thought for him.

"Bingo."

Jonathan turned to the Mishins. "Nicholas, you and Josef go into the hallway." Next, Jonathan started stripping his kit of GPCs and handing them to Boxers. "Yelena!"

"Yes!"

"Take your family to a cell at the end of the hall, at

least three doors down, and go inside and close the door. We're going to set off explosives, so don't peek out until you hear the boom."

When she didn't respond, he turned to see a reunion in action, the three of them in an embrace.

"Now, Yelena."

"Which way?"

"You tell me."

An indecisive pause. "I'll move east," she said.

"Fine," Jonathan replied. "Get there quickly, and don't come out until I say."

Len recognized the outlines of the boy and his father as they exited the cell, but the greeting they received in the hallway startled him. This was not the body language of a hostage meeting his rescuer. There was genuine affection. Could it possibly be that—

Hearing her speak removed all doubt. That was Anna Darmond, the former Yelena Poltanov. Good Lord in Heaven, could revenge be any sweeter?

He raised his rifle to his shoulder and slipped his finger into the trigger guard. He could take them all with one long burst. He could shred them just as certainly as they had shredded is brave soldiers.

And they were walking directly toward him. His finger tightened.

Between the PETN in the det cord and Jonathan's six GPCs, he figured they had eight or nine pounds of explosives to work with. Absent the luxury of the time necessary to form it all into its optimal shape, Boxers molded the C4 into an eight-inch-long white brick and gave it to Jonathan to hold. Then he unspooled the det cord and folded the tube of explosive back and forth against itself, the way you would fold an extension cord for storage. That bundle was maybe fifteen inches long and six inches thick when he was done. With his left hand, he pressed the finished bundle into the angle where the outside wall met the western cell wall, while with his right, he picked up the brick of C4 and then molded it to hold the det cord in place.

Their plan was simple and inelegant. The C4 had a detonation velocity of 26,400 feet per second, the det cord 27,000 feet per second. In the first few milliseconds after detonation, the charge would direct a peak pressure wave of well over one hundred thousand pounds per square inch through the stone, shattering it. At the same instant, the explosion would overpressure the interior of the cell, with the result—they hoped—of collapsing the exterior wall and part of the roof it supported.

Boxers fished two OFF detonators out of his ruck— old-fashioned fuse—and pressed the first one into the end of the det cord, and the second one into the body of the C4. "Keep your fingers crossed."

Fact was, this was their only shot. If it didn't work, they wouldn't have direct access to the outside, and they'd have used up all of their resources except firearms. If the hole in the roof didn't happen, they had a long and bloody firefight ahead of them.

Boxers drew his Randall knife from its scabbard. "You figure thirty seconds?"

"Perfect," Jonathan said.

Boxers cut away half the length of the fuse, then fished a lighter from his trouser pocket. "Ready?"

Jonathan keyed the mike for the troop net. "Striker, Scorpion. I think you want to put some distance between us. We're about to make another mess."

"Roger that. I'll be waiting for the fireworks."

Jonathan nodded to Boxers. "Ready," he said.

Nicholas followed his mother's shadow through the darkness as she led the way down the corridor, keeping their hands on the left-hand wall as a point of reference. Josef clung tightly to his father's shirt, his feet shuffling in short quick steps to keep up.

They were to enter the third cell. As his hand passed along the door to the second cell, he wondered how they could be sure that the doors were even unlocked. This was a prison, after all. Yet it was unoccupied. He supposed they'd just have to take their chances. It wasn't as if there were a lot of alternatives.

"Howya doing, Joey?" he whispered.

"What's that horrible smell?" the boy asked. "Smells like somebody took a shit in here."

That was exactly what it smelled like, but with the addition of burned hair. It was nauseating. Terrifying.

"We're here," Yelena said, and as she pushed open the door, he was grateful to see the wash of some light, even if it clearly came from the fires that raged out there in the night. She led the way, and Nicholas ushered Josef in next.

As Nicholas stepped across the threshold, something hit him hard from behind, and a hot pain engulfed him like a searing girdle, an agonizing jolt that exploded back to front. It buckled his knees and as he sank to the wooden floor, he more felt than saw a man step past him, deeper into the cell.

A rifle dangled from the man's shoulder, and a knife blade gleamed from his fist. As Nicholas clutched at the agony in his back, he felt the wetness of his own blood, and he knew that he'd been stabbed.

The man went right for Josef, grabbing him from behind and hoisting him with an arm wrapped around the boy's shoulder and throat.

Yelena whirled with her gun up and ready to shoot, but it was too late. He'd lifted Joey high enough that in the limited light, there was no way to shoot the man without shooting the boy.

"Put the rifle down, Yelena," the man said. He brandished his knife blade and pressed it against Joey's throat.

Yelena's eyes widened as her jaw dropped open. "Alexei," she said.

"It's been a very long time. The gun, Yelena. Put it down. I won't hesitate to kill him. You know that."

Nicholas tried to find his feet to rush this man, but every move was excruciating, each flex of a muscle another jolt of searing pain.

"Please don't do this," she said.

"You should not have come," Alexei said.

"You took my children."

"And that one," Alexei said, tossing his head toward Nicholas. "He looks so like his father." He pressed the knife point deeper into the soft flesh under Joey's chin.

"Ow!" Joey cried. "Ow, please."

"Your choice, Yelena. Do you really want a little boy to die for you?"

Yelena lifted the sling from around her shoulder and lowered her rifle to the ground.

"Why?" she said as she stood. "Why my family?"

"Because it was easy," Alexei said. "Their father still loves them so."

"Their father is dead," Yelena said, but through his pain, Nicholas detected something wrong in her tone.

"We both know that that's not true, don't we, Yelena?"

"I've done what you asked," Yelena said. "Let Josef go."

"How many others are there?" Alexei asked. "How many Secret Service or soldiers?"

"Ten," she said, but again, her eyes betrayed the lie.

Alexei squeezed Josef tighter. "How about you tell me, Josef Nikolayevich? How many attackers are here?"

With his feet dangling just off the floor, Josef had to hang onto Alexei's forearms with both hands to keep from strangling. Tears streaked his face in the yellow light of the fires.

"Must I cut your throat?" Alexei asked softly.

"Ten." His voice squeaked.

Alexei gave a dramatic sigh. "It's such a shame—"

Josef shrieked, "Scorpion! Help!"

"Fire in the hole," Big Guy said, and he touched the lighter to the fuse. "Now, let's get the hell—"

The boy's scream for help echoed through the prison.

Jonathan and Boxers pivoted in unison, weapons up, and headed for the door.

Nicholas had never seen anyone move as fast as his mother did after Josef screamed. She lowered her head and charged Alexei like a bull, driving both the man and the boy into the stone wall. They hit hard, and in the impact, Alexei lost his grip on Joey, who fell to the floor and scrambled out of the way to join his father.

It was hard to see the details in the dim light, but Yelena seemed to be in a rage that was beyond anger. After the initial impact, she drove her forehead into the bridge of Alexei's nose. His knees sagged and he dropped his knife. As he slid to the floor, Yelena gripped his hair or maybe his ears and drove the back of his head over and over again into the stone. The vibrations of the impact reverberated through the floor.

She was going to kill him. And Nicholas was fine with that.

With his NVGs down and in place, Jonathan slid the turn into the cell with his weapon up and ready to shoot. It took a few seconds to process what he saw. PCs One and Two were together on the floor near the door, while Yelena struggled with a man in the far corner. Her rifle lay on the floor five feet away as she smashed the guy's head repeatedly against the wall. Even if Jonathan had had a shot, there'd be no need to take it.

"Yelena!" he yelled. "Stop!"

She was beyond listening to instruction. She'd entered the realm of murderous frenzy.

"Hey!" He yelled it louder this time, but she still didn't respond. Jonathan crossed the cell in three long strides, and pulled her away from the unconscious man by the collar of her vest.

Yelena whirled on him, spun up to do battle with whomever she saw. She threw a punch, but he blocked it and grabbed her shoulders. "Stop," he said. "He's out cold. No need to kill him."

"Bullshit! He tried to kill me. To kill us."

Jonathan glanced over to Nicholas and the blood he saw on the floor near him, and put that picture together with the knife that lay on the floor. *Well, shit.* At least they were still alive.

Big Guy was already stepping over everybody, with a zip tie in his hands for the guy Yelena had been beating up on.

"We'll take him with us," Jonathan said. "We'll squeeze him for intel, and then Wolverine can do with him whatever she wants. For now, plug your ears and—"

The explosion was epic.

CHAPTER THIRTY-FIVE

Becky was horrified. She was looking right at the prison compound when a chunk of the building erupted in a blast of flame and flying debris.

"Holy shit!" David yelled over the intercom. "Did you see that?"

"Looks like the boys just cut themselves an exit door," Striker said. As he spoke, the nose of the helicopter dipped, and the engine noise crescendoed. "Yee-hah."

He said that last part—"Yee-hah"—in a normal conversational tone, and if she read his body language correctly, he was laughing. *Laughing!* What was wrong with these people? They pretended that this was somehow fun. It was a sickness. People were dying, and they were laughing about it.

The helicopter dropped quickly, like a roller coaster. As they closed to within a hundred feet of the hole in the stone, and then fifty and then ten feet, Becky saw the details of the wound that had been avulsed from the building. At first, the view was dominated by smoke. Or maybe it was dust. An opaque cloud that rendered details undetectable. As it cleared, she saw that the entire wall was gone, and that the roof had collapsed on an angle.

Tink. Tink-tink.

"We can't stay here," Striker said over the intercom. "Rooster, take that bag of rope on the floor there and get out on the roof and help them out."

"What?" David looked terrified. "You mean outside?"

"Yep. And quickly. Before we get shot down."

Tink-tink.

"Now! Chickadee and I are going to fly cover for you."

David looked to Becky for advice. "No," she said. "It's crazy."

He nodded. Then he unclasped his harness, grabbed the bag, and jumped.

The instant David cleared the skid, Striker poured on the power and tore away from the building. "We can't just leave them!" Becky yelled.

"We're not leaving anybody. Now do me a favor and shoot back."

She looked out the door at the ground. It was chaos, a mass of people running and shooting. "I don't know who to shoot at," she said.

"It's easy," Striker said. "If they're on the ground and they're not next to a cop car, shoot them."

The blast launched the cell door across the hall with such force that the heavy wooden door was reduced to shards and splinters.

"Listen up," Jonathan said. "This is the last step in

the mission. If we screw it up, we're dead." He paused for a beat to make sure they were all listening. "Follow me, do precisely what you're told, and we'll have you out of here in the next couple of minutes. Give me a thumbs-up if you understand that."

It was important that hostages were actually dialed into what was going on, and there was no better way than to elicit an affirmative action like a thumbs-up. He got three of them. Perfect.

"Big Guy, leave the rucks," Jonathan instructed as he shrugged out of his own. There was nothing in them that couldn't be replaced, and perhaps more important, there was nothing in there that would trace back to them. "How many claymores did you set?"

Boxers held up two fingers.

With Jonathan's two, that made four, and he'd definitely heard four explosions, so they were good to go. If that were not the case, since the next people to pass in front of the motion triggers would likely be good guys, he'd have had to manually trigger them before they left.

Without waiting for instruction, Boxers lifted Nicholas into a one-shoulder fireman's carry on one side, and held Josef's hand with his other as he led the way to the ruined cell. Yelena followed, leaving Jonathan to carry the still-unconscious Alexei.

Shattered stone and wood littered the corridor, making footing treacherous. It didn't help having to negotiate the route with an unconscious man on your back. Lingering smoke and dust stung his eyes.

Jonathan turned the corner into the blasted cell and saw that the explosion had done its job and then some. The wall was gone, but so was half the floor, creating a chasm that dropped to the level below. The roof had partially collapsed as well, creating a cantilevered section of timber that tilted into the cell and presented a kind of ramp that started six feet off the floor and sloped at a steep angle to the roof. Beyond that, they had a clear view of the night sky, marred as it was by flames and roiling smoke.

He laid Alexei onto the floor.

"Now what do we do?" Yelena asked.

Outside, the shooting continued. Rounds weren't impacting close to him or his team, so Jonathan ignored them.

"We've got to get up there," Jonathan said.

"On the *roof*?"

"Then Striker will bring the chopper around and we'll climb aboard."

Yelena looked at the distance to the edge of the cantilevered ramp, then shook her head. "I can't reach that."

"That's where having Big Guy along becomes a big advant—"

Movement on the roof caught Jonathan's attention. It was a face, and Jonathan reacted instantly, pushing Yelena away and stepping in front of her as he shouldered his MP7.

"Jesus, no!" the face yelled. "It's me. David. Christ, don't shoot."

"How the hell did you get on the roof?" Jonathan yelled in anger. David would never know how close he came to having his head blown off.

"Striker dropped me off. I've got rope." He displayed a hundred-fifty-foot drop bag of climbing rope.

"There's a tail of rope sticking out of the end of that bag," Jonathan said. "See it?"

David looked, then nodded. "Got it."

"Okay, hang onto that tail and drop the bag down here."

David dropped the bag, and a length of rope unspooled as it crashed to the shattered wooden floor.

"If I remember my sat photo right," Jonathan said, "there's a chimney coming through the roof about a hundred feet behind you."

David craned his neck and then nodded. "Yes."

"Take the end of that rope—take as much rope as you need—and tie it around the chimney. Then come back and tell me you've done that."

"I don't know knots."

"I don't care. I give not a shit. Any knot will do."

David disappeared from view, and the rope continued to unspool. If it came to the point where the end of the rope emerged from the bag, Jonathan would grab it and pull. Otherwise, they only needed enough to climb ten feet.

He figured it couldn't take more than a few minutes.

Becky didn't realize that Striker was intentionally trying to draw gunfire away from the roof of the prison until five or six bullets pierced the floor of the helicopter within eighteen inches of her foot.

"You need to shoot back," Striker told her through the intercom. "Otherwise, we're just a target in a shooting gallery. Make 'em pay for that shit."

Becky pointed her rifle out the door and pulled the trigger, launching a string of bullets that may or may not have hit anything. Striker said to shoot, and so she shot. That didn't mean that she had to intentionally kill. Those people down there were every bit as frightened as she was. From their perspective, they were defending themselves from an attack. And from their perspective, she was the attacker.

Who was she to pass judgment on their lives from three hundred feet above their heads?

Her magazine went dry and she dropped it out, replacing it just as she'd been taught. This one, too, would be sprayed into the night. She couldn't imagine living with the knowledge that she'd taken another person's life. Think of the children they'd never have. Of the grandchild—

A bullet passed within an inch of her head, shattering the earphone on her left side. It was a bone-jarring noise, loud enough that it might have deafened her. And as luck would have it, she'd seen the muzzle flash of the gun that had sent it her way.

Using all the lessons she'd been taught from Big Guy, she settled her sights on the spot where that shot had come from, and she emptied a thirty-round magazine into that space.

The monster of a man—they called him Big Guy— lifted Joey under the arms and put him onto the slanting bit of roof that he said led to safety. "Just go to the top," the man said, "then lie flat against the roof until someone tells you that it's safe to move."

Big Guy said that as if it were easy as pie. In reality, there was nothing to hang on to. Big Guy lifted him onto this sagging slab of roof, but after that, it was all about not losing your grip as you did a lizard crawl up to the point where the roof flattened out.

Joey forced himself not to think about the cold or about the noise or about the fires that burned all around him. He forced himself not to think about the stink of what he knew had to be dead bodies.

The men who came to save him had apparently killed a lot of people to deliver him from danger. He decided not to think about that, either, but to concentrate on the fact that he was *this close* to being out of this terrible place.

He belly-crawled up the incline of the collapsed roof until it flattened out. When he got to that point, a guy he hadn't seen before put a hand on his shoulder.

"Hi," the guy said. "I'm David. You're almost home."

Within a few seconds, Josef's grandmother was next to him on the roof. She reached out with both arms to embrace him in a hug. "Josef," she said. "Don't be afraid. We'll be safe in a few minutes."

God, I hope that's true, Joey thought. Because for right now, everything pretty much sucked.

"You're next," Jonathan said to Boxers.

The next step was an engineering challenge. Even though Boxers could easily carry Nicholas on his back to make the climb, there was no guarantee that Nicholas would have the strength to hang on. And the penalty for losing his grip was death.

"You make your way to the top," Jonathan said, "and I'll tie the PC into a rescue knot. Once you're in position, haul him up and send the rope back down for our Russian friend. I'll bring up the rear."

Big Guy didn't respond, but rather eased Nicholas onto the floor and started to climb toward the roof. From a distant part in his brain, Jonathan wondered if the cantilevered roof flap had the strength to hold Boxers, but he realized it didn't matter. They'd all know at the same time in just a minute or so.

He stooped to go eye to eye with Nicholas. "How are you doing?" he asked.

"I'm hurt," Nicholas said. "Badly. I think he might have gotten a kidney."

Jonathan gathered the rope. "Don't worry too much," he said. "You've got two. That's a hundred percent overkill." He'd meant it as a joke, but Nicholas was either not in the mood, or in too much pain. Maybe just plain scared.

The rescue knot is a complex bit of ropesmanship, starting with a bowline on a bite for the legs, and then evolving into an elaborate knot around the chest. It took time, and that was the one commodity of which they were quickly running out. He aborted fancy in favor of simple.

"Listen up, Nicholas," Jonathan said. "I'm going to slip a rope over your head and under your arms, and then Big Guy is going to lift you to the roof. Do you have the strength to keep your arms crossed under the knot so you don't slip out?"

"Sounds like I don't have a choice."

"Oh, you have a choice," Jonathan said with a smile. "But the alternatives all suck." It was nowhere near as secure as the correct knot, but sometimes you just had to take chances. Jonathan tied a simple slipknot into the end of the rope and he slipped it into place around Nicholas's body. A glance toward the roof delivered a thumbs-up from Boxers, and it was time to go. Within seconds, Nicholas was airborne, his feet dangling as he was hoisted up.

Thirty seconds later, Boxers said, "Heads up," and the looped end of the rope landed back on the ground next to Jonathan.

Alexei was awake by now, but he wasn't yet dialed back into reality. His eyes were unfocused, and blood poured at a pretty good clip over his face from a wound somewhere under his hair.

Jonathan slipped the loop over Alexei's head and shoulders, and then tugged it all the way to the man's waist to accommodate the hands that were tied behind his back. That done, he cinched the knot, and exchanged another thumbs-up with Big Guy, and watched as Alexei levitated away.

In his ear, he heard Boxer's voice say, "Striker, Big Guy. We're ready for dust-off whenever you are."

And now it was Jonathan's turn. He didn't trust his ability to execute the kind of pull-up that would be necessary to follow the path of the others with all his gear in place, so he opted to scale the broken stair-stepped bricks of the broken outer wall. Never a fan of heights, he stayed focused on the view above, and avoided looking at the spot down below where he'd leave a grease spot if he fell.

While he was poised there on the ledge between success and death, his spine launched a chill as he saw the chopper turn on its nose and head back into the maelstrom to do its job. Helicopter pilots continued to be the great unsung heroes of nearly every Special Forces op that Jonathan had ever been on. They rarely took the shot at the HVT—high-value target—and they rarely put their hands on a PC, but without them, thousands of brave operators would have died.

Striker came in fast and hot, his door gunner spraying a shield of lead that kept the bad guys' heads down.

Jonathan had been in enough firefights and bloodbaths to know that the tales of glory in combat were all bullshit, but there was something strikingly beautiful about the living portrait of people risking death for others. It was an image that transcended cynicism, and triggered yet again his sense of pride that the things he and his team accomplished were bigger than who they were, whether individually or collectively.

He was jarred from his reverie by the glancing blow of a bullet against the front of his body armor. It didn't hit him so much as it took out a half a rack of magazines that he had stored there. He started climbing again.

He got to the top of the roof just as the chopper skidded in to accept them.

"You first!" Jonathan yelled to Boxers. "Give us cover fire." Becky was doing as good a job as she knew how, but with Boxers' finger on the trigger, bad guys would start falling down for good.

Striker never actually touched down on the roof. Instead, he hovered with the starboard skid just three inches off the surface.

Boxers hoisted himself in first, and charged directly to the far side to start pouring more firepower into the people on the ground. Within seconds, the incoming fire decreased by ninety percent. Jonathan heaved Alexei in first, and then lifted Nicholas into the doorway. The first glimpse of the blood smear on his back showed a critical injury. Joey was next, though he pretty much scaled the skid by himself, and then Yelena brought up the rear.

Jonathan checked one more time to make sure that he hadn't left anyone, and that there were no immediate threats that could hang off the side of the chopper, and then he heaved himself onto the deck.

"Go, go, go!" he yelled to Striker, and then to the others, "Keep your heads down. Lie flat on the floor." As the words left his mouth, he took up a position next to Boxers in the doorway and he opened up on to ground on full auto. The MP7 sounded positively anemic next to the pounding pulse of Boxers' HK 417.

Striker pulled pitch, and they climbed like a rocket, pivoting out of harm's way, and then dropping again like a stone to treetop level when they were out of range.

Jonathan felt someone pounding on his shoulder, and he turned to see David, extending a headset to him. "It's Striker," David yelled. "He wants to talk to you."

With the doors off, there'd be no direct communication with this much power poured into the engines. Jonathan slipped the headset over his ears. "Scorpion here," he said.

"I'm making a dash straight back to Vermont," Striker said. "I'm abandoning everything we left at the staging area. You okay with that?"

This was exactly why it was important never to leave fingerprints or DNA behind. "Roger that," Jonathan said. "Let's go home."

In Striker's world, treetop flying meant the actual collection of treetop material in the skids of the helicopter. He flew at full throttle, and as Jonathan watched the world pass inches below him, he envied those who had no goggles and therefore could fly without stress.

The Mishin family had found itself in the darkness. They sat clustered together amidships at the aft end of the aircraft. Boxers, one of the best combat medics Jonathan had ever known, had done his best to treat Nicholas's wound, but the fact was that the man needed a trauma surgeon right now, and they were not in the position to provide him with one.

"Thirty seconds to the US border," Striker said over the radio.

Jonathan knew he should breathe a sigh of relief, but thirty seconds could be an eternity when things were running against you. Still, there was something about being back on American soil, where contacts had influence, that made life easier.

"Ladies and gentlemen, I welcome you back to the United States of America," Striker said over the intercom.

Jonathan yelled to the PCs over the engine noise, "We're almost home."

If they cheered, he couldn't hear it.

"Hey Scorpion, we have a problem," Striker said over the intercom. "Take a look at eleven o'clock high."

Jonathan moved to the door, with Boxers right behind. Looking up and above the left-hand side of the helicopter, he saw the well-defined outline of a Blackhawk helicopter, fully lit.

"He's got a friend at six o'clock level, and he's squawking on one twenty one point five megahertz for us to put down immediately."

Jonathan's heart sank.

"You know my rule on incarceration," Boxers said. It was a simple one: he'd die first, but he wouldn't die alone.

"He just threatened to shoot us down," Striker said.

Jonathan's mind screamed. With the NVGs in place, he looked over to Yelena and her family. The blood from Nicholas's back showed white in the infrared glare. This guy needed help a half hour ago. In another hour, he might be beyond hope.

"Tell you what," Jonathan said over the intercom. "Let's make a deal with them."

While Striker bargained to keep them from being shot out of the sky, Jonathan worked through Wolverine to make a few phone calls. There'd no doubt be a lot of guns when they touched down, but if everyone stuck to the script, none of them would be fired. The whole process took less than fifteen minutes.

Jonathan stood conspicuously unarmed in the starboard doorway as they flared to land on the heliport of the trauma center at Fletcher Allen Hospital in Burlington, and Boxers occupied the other door. Striker settled the chopper with such ease that there wasn't even a bump.

"I hope you know what you're doing," Striker said over the radio.

"Me, too," Boxers added.

Well, Jonathan thought, *we're all about to see together.*

Striker shut the engine down, but the rotors were still turning as a dozen cops approached in SWAT gear, their weapons drawn and at the ready. This was a twitchy group that needed to be handled carefully.

Keeping his hands visible, Jonathan pivoted to the side and said, "Okay, Mrs. Darmond, you're on."

The First Lady of the United States made her appearance in the doorway just as the floodlights erupted to illuminate the scene. The crowd of police and medical personnel had been told to prepare themselves for her, but from what Jonathan could see through the glare, they were nonetheless shocked by her presence. She even waved, and in that moment, Jonathan realized that he'd seen that very wave from the steps of Air Force One.

"I need you to help my son!" she called to the crowd. "He's been stabbed."

They'd been prepared for that, too, and as her words rolled into the night, a trauma team moved forward, pushing a cot that was loaded with all kinds of high-tech gear.

"You!" one of the cops yelled to Jonathan. "You in the doorway! Step out and keep your hands where I can see them." Behind him, on the other side of the aircraft, he could hear similar orders being delivered to Boxers. Because of his size, Big Guy would have to be particularly careful not to spook these guys.

As the doctors piled into the helicopter, Jonathan climbed out, first to the skid, and then down to the pad. "I'm unarmed," he said to the first man who approached him.

"But only recently, as I understand it," the cop said. He was approaching fifty, and he wore parallel bars on his collar that would have indicated a captain in the army, but could have many meanings in the civilian world. By any meaning, though, the bars meant rank, and rank meant seniority.

As he got even closer to Jonathan, the cop—Jonathan could see now that his name tag read Amen—said, "I'm Deputy Chief Eric Amen. My boss says I'm supposed to treat you like a prisoner, but like a VIP one. I'm not sure what that means, but I know it includes handcuffs, at least until we can figure out all of the details."

"I'm fine with that," Jonathan said, moving his hands behind his back, "but if my friend objects, try to reason with him, okay?"

As it turned out, Boxers readily got with the program. As Nicholas Mishin was ushered down to surgery, Scorpion and Big Guy were escorted to a parking garage. True to the stated spirit of things, Amen removed the handcuffs before he ushered his prisoners into the backseat of a cruiser. Boxers had to sit mostly sideways to accommodate his legs.

Once they were settled in, and the cruiser was moving, Amen asked, "So who do you have to be to get the director of the FBI to put in a courtesy call for you?"

The Chittenden Regional Correctional Facility in South Burlington covered a footprint that Jonathan estimated to be about thirty thousand square feet. Deputy Chief Amen escorted Boxers and him into the reception area of the jail, and then sat with them while they chatted about nothing. They accepted coffee when it was offered, and no one got overly stressed when first Boxers and then Jonathan asked to use the restroom, which itself was built like a prison cell, with concrete walls, a heavy door, and no windows.

All things considered, Jonathan was getting tired of concrete walls. When this was over, he thought he owed himself a trip to an island. He was equally tired of being cold.

Overall, the atmosphere of the meeting—if that's what you could call it—was cordial yet weird. Amen had clearly been instructed not to ask questions about what he'd just witnessed at the hospital, but it was equally clear that he ached to disobey his orders. For Jonathan's part, he'd have been happy to have been left alone for a nap.

After nearly two hours, a couple of high-and-tight guys in suits arrived and identified themselves as FBI agents. "Thanks for taking care of things, Chief," one of the agents said. "We'll pick it up from here."

They all said some cursory good-byes, and then the Fibbies escorted Scorpion and Big Guy out to a waiting Suburban in the parking lot. As they approached the vehicle, the agent who did the talking inside said, "Mr. Scorpion, and Mr. Big Guy, I am Agent Able and this is Agent Baker. I have been instructed by Wolverine to ask you to come with us. You are not under arrest and you may refuse if you wish."

Able made no effort to camouflage that as anything but the memorized speech that it was. The code names lent convincing credibility to the words. "What do you say, Big Guy?" Jonathan asked.

"It's been so much fun so far," Boxers said. "I wouldn't miss another minute."

The Suburban drove them to the airport, where an unmarked Gulfstream jet awaited them, all gassed up and ready to go. Able drove them right up to the aircraft's ramp, and as he approached, he said something into his radio that Jonathan couldn't decipher.

A few second later, Jonathan's cell phone buzzed. Caller ID read J. Edgar.

"Scorpion here," he said.

"Nice job tonight," Irene said. "The Bureau is supplying you with a nice ride home. I believe you'll find some surprises in the plane."

"How is PC One?" Jonathan asked.

"Still in surgery, but the last report I got was that he'll pull through. Might lose the kidney, might not, but my people tell me that it's not a huge deal."

"And Sidesaddle?"

"Not my problem anymore. The Secret Service took jurisdiction over her safety as soon as we crossed the threshold into the hospital."

"But what about—" Jonathan stopped himself, aware of the additional ears.

"Some things we might never know," Irene said. "I'm fairly sure that there's much that ultimately won't be shared with you at all. Nothing personal, you understand. Just need to know."

Jonathan's ears turned hot. He deserved better than this. "You're a tease, Wolfie."

"You won the big one tonight, Scorpion. There are a lot of powerful people indebted to you. Put a check in the win column and go to bed."

"And what about Alexei?" Jonathan pressed. They hadn't given the Russian a code name, so he had to default to the real one.

"Good night, Scorpion." She clicked off.

Sometimes Jonathan forgot that Irene Rivers was

the ultimate professional. He in fact did not have a need to know the details. All that was important from where she sat was that Jonathan did his job and that the mission was accomplished. As in the past, his was not to reason why.

Still, it sucked.

Climbing into the plane, he had to laugh when he saw the surprise Irene had spoken of. All of their gear had been delivered to the plane and stacked neatly along the last row of seats. In the forward part of the passenger cabin, someone had placed a bottle of Lagavulin scotch for Jonathan and a six-pack of Sam Adams beer for Boxers.

As they squared themselves away, a female voice said over the intercom, "Welcome aboard. Please make yourselves comfortable, sit back, and enjoy the flight."

CHAPTER THIRTY-SIX

Jonathan understood that there could be no White House reception or formal declaration of a job well done, but after two weeks, would a thank-you note have been out of the question? Even the Army had issued him citations for jobs exceptionally well done, though most of them were highly classified and could never be spoken of.

Reading the paper every day—he'd taken a special interest in the stories reported by the *Washington Enquirer*—it pleased him to read that the Canadian government had thwarted a terrorist plot against the United States. It seems that units of their military had received a tip from a confidential informant that the renovation of Saint Stephen's Reformatory in Ottawa had in fact been a cover for a Russian dissident group that had been plotting for years to create havoc in America. Unfortunately, during the raid, the explosives were detonated and all of the terrorists were killed.

That last part intrigued Jonathan most, because he knew for a fact that a number of bad guys were still alive when Striker flew away. He wondered if the others were actually killed, or if they were just spirited away for some quality time with CIA interrogators.

Most important from Jonathan's perspective, there were no reports of a helicopter being forced down that night, nor of VIPs being admitted to any hospitals in Vermont. Apparently when the administration actually cared about controlling leaks, secrets could be kept.

Jonathan was hunkered down in his office with a fire roaring against the blistering chill of the air outside, wading through the accumulated administrative crap that made business ownership such a pain in the ass. JoeDog was as close to the fire as she could be without actually igniting, and all but the most ambitious workers had gone home for the night. Jonathan had to kick Venice out of the place, telling her that she was not allowed to return until tomorrow at 10:00 A.M. Yes, she had a lot of responsibility, and yes, she had a lot of work to do, but sooner or later, she'd burn out if she didn't step away for a while.

Besides, with her gone, the Cave was exceptionally silent, which meant that he could concentrate without interruption.

A gust of wind rattled the building at the same instant that his cell phone buzzed. J. Edgar.

Shit. He considered ignoring it, but Wolverine wasn't the type to bother him for chitchat. He answered after the second ring. "Evening, ma'am," he said.

"I see your light is on. Can you leave your desk long enough to let us in? It's cold outside."

Jonathan resisted the urge to look out the window. It would have been too . . . predictable. "Us?" he said. "Who's 'us'?"

"You'll have to look to see," she said. "But I'd rather talk in your residence than in your office."

He sighed. The reality was that he welcomed any opportunity to so something other than the stuff he was doing. "Two minutes."

Jonathan stood from his chair, triggering JoeDog to scramble to her feet, tail wagging, ready and anxious to find another place to lie down and sleep.

"Come on, Beast," he said. "Come attack a government official." They walked together to the office door, but upon opening it, he let JoeDog go first. It was better than being run over from behind.

He said good night to the guards and walked down to the residence. He pressed the code, and then he was home. He turned lights on as walked down one more flight to the main level, then across the living area to the foyer. He slid the latches and pulled open the door.

Irene Rivers stood wrapped in mink, the collar pulled tight under her chin, with a fuzzy fur hat down low over her ears. David Kirk stood next to her in a ski jacket, smiling from ear to ear. "Bet you didn't think you'd see us again," David said. On the other side of him stood Becky Beckeman in a poufy down coat that hadn't been in style in Becky's lifetime.

"Truer words," Jonathan said. He stepped aside and ushered them in. "Have a seat. Get warm." They entered and Jonathan scanned the area outside. "Where's your detail?"

Irene peeled off her coat. "In the car," she said. "And don't feel too sorry for them. It's a nice car." JoeDog examined the visitors long enough to determine that they had no treats for her, and then she retreated to watch from under the coffee table.

Irene blew into her hands and rubbed them together. "I heard a rumor that you have an excellent collection of single malts."

"Excellent is such a relative term," Jonathan said. "But I think we could all agree on 'fairly comprehensive.' What do you like?"

"Glenmorangie," she said.

"Can I get in on this?" David asked.

"You're not going to ask me to put ginger ale or Coke in it, are you?"

"No, I like mine neat and peaty. Got any Talisker?"

Jonathan smiled. "I might learn to like you after all, kid. Becky?"

"I'll take the ginger ale."

As his guests took their seats, Jonathan walked to the bookcase that housed the bar and poured three drinks of two fingers each, and a tall glass of ginger ale. His own glass, of course, contained Lagavulin. He served them with an apology. "I don't have a freezer in the bar. Would you like me to get ice from the kitchen?"

Becky smiled. "No, this is fine."

"I confess you've piqued my interest," Jonathan said, lowering himself into a lush green leather reading chair. Irene sat to his right in another lounge chair, and David and Becky had taken spots on the sofa to Jonathan's left.

Irene started. Sort of. "Mr. Kirk and Ms. Beckeman have something to tell you."

The hairs on Jonathan's neck moved. "Oh, yeah?"

David took a sip as he nodded. "Yeah. I wanted to tell you about the story we're never going to write. It turns out that Nicholas and Josef Mishin have the wrong last names."

Jonathan crossed his legs and took a sip of his own. This was going to be interesting.

"By DNA testing, their real last name should be Winters."

Jonathan nearly choked. "You mean as in Douglas Winters? As in the president's chief of staff?"

"Yep."

Jonathan scowled and glanced at Irene for confirmation. She answered with her eyebrows.

"How can you know this?"

"During our research, we found out that Winters has been joined at the hip with Tony Darmond since the Mesozoic era—since before Darmond was even in Congress. And you know how everybody says that Nicholas is the image of his mother, with the light hair and the blue eyes? That given the president's coloration, Nicholas got every recessive gene?"

Jonathan rocketed back to his first meeting with Winters in Arc Flash's barn. The hair was going gray, but he had blue eyes and the complexion that suggested that he might have been a blond in his youth. "And because Winters has similar coloring, you're suggesting—"

"We're not suggesting anything," Becky said, hijacking the narrative. "We've got proof. When the rest of us were left behind at the hospital, we got to talking with Joey Mishin—a nice kid, but man is he gonna need some counseling. Actually, he was afraid of David, but he talked to me. He told stories that he'd heard from his dad that Tony Darmond was never nice to him when he was growing up. He said he felt like—and this was the phrase he quoted—a redheaded stepchild. That's when the lightbulb went on over my head."

Jonathan scoffed, "But that's hardly—"

"Jesus, are you going to let us finish or not?" David snapped. "We have a confidential source inside the White House who was able to bring me a soda can that Winters had drunk out of. We sent it, along with a sample of Nicholas's blood that I got off my pants that night." He paused for effect.

"It's a match?"

"Perfect."

Jonathan gaped, and then he chuckled and took a longer sip of scotch. "Holy shit. So why are you both here?" He looked to Irene for the answer to that one.

"Because you've got enough skin in this game to get really pissed off, and I wanted you to know that restraint is the key to everything."

"I don't follow."

She explained. "David showed the courtesy of running this past me. Frankly, it's not a suspicion that had ever occurred to the Bureau or anywhere else that I know of. We took it to Alexei—he actually prefers to be called Len—and he seemed shocked as hell that we knew. That had been the Movement's trump card."

"The Movement?" Jonathan asked.

"Sounds like the shits, doesn't it?" David said with a laugh.

"That's what the Russian expats called themselves. They found out about the truth of Nicholas's paternity through Pavel Mishin, the man who was supposed to have been the kid's father. Apparently, they've been sitting on it for a while, waiting for the best moment to hurt the president."

Jonathan scowled again. "Nobody cares about bastard children anymore."

"President Darmond didn't know," Irene said. "The president had always assumed that Mishin was the father, which was why he and the First Lady never got along, and why Nicholas the Younger was never treated well. Only Winters and Yelena knew the real truth—and Mishin—and Winters understood that if word leaked, he'd be toast in the administration."

"Is he also involved with this terrorist stuff?" Jonathan asked.

"Yes," Irene said. Her scotch was gone now, and she motioned for another. This time, Jonathan set the bottle next to her. "Apparently, Winters really loved the kid, and by extension, I guess he really loved Yelena, too."

"Did he know about the witness protection stuff?"

"He does now, but he didn't when they had their affair. He says he didn't know until a guy named Dmitri Boykin approached him with that, and the knowledge of the true paternity. He was devastated and the bad guys knew it. That's when they started applying the screws. They promised to hurt Nicholas if Winters didn't pull strings to grant the Movement access to weapons."

Jonathan recoiled. "Can a chief of staff do that?"

"A chief of staff can do anything he wants to. As a practical matter, he is surrogate president, so long as nothing has to be signed into law. That's what chiefs of staff do. In Winters's case, it meant alerting Alexei or Dmitri to the movement of materiel. Apparently, that's a pretty simple matter."

"So that explains all the US military munitions at Saint Stephen's," Jonathan said, connecting the dots.

Irene poured another two fingers.

"So, when are you arresting Winters?" Jonathan asked.

Irene's answer came without hesitation. "We're not." It clearly was the money shot that she'd been preparing for.

"You can't be serious," Jonathan said.

Irene said, "What would be the point? All that stuff we told you on the first meeting—the fragility of the world economy, and the devastation that a crisis of confidence could do—that's all real, Dig. The threat of further damage went away when the cache of weapons was destroyed. In the opinion of the attorney general, more harm than good would be done by prosecuting Winters."

"What about the victims at O'Hare? Their blood is on his hands."

"Only if you look ridiculously closely," Becky said.

"Come again?" Jonathan had sort of forgotten that she was even there.

"He was acting to protect his only child," she said.

Hot blood rose in Jonathan's face. "He murdered over a hundred people."

"No, he didn't," David said. "The Movement did that. I guarantee you that's the editorial slant the *Enquirer* would give it. Sure, there'd be a clamoring for Winters's head, and he'd get fired, but at the end of the day, the editorial board of the *Enquirer* and every network would see this as a human interest story, and Winters as a benevolent scapegoat."

"Even as the financial markets tumbled," Irene added. "This isn't without consequence," she continued. "Tomorrow, Doug Winters will announce his retirement from the Darmond administration."

"No doubt to 'spend more time with his family'," Jonathan mocked.

"Or something like that," Irene confirmed.

"And then he'll pull in a million-five a year on K Street," Jonathan said, referring to the home of the major lobbyists.

"Or something like that." Irene paused for the words to sink in. "You know, Digger, justice isn't always about the individual. Sometimes, it really is about the commonweal. If a threat is eliminated, it's not necessary to find someone to blame it on. It's not as if he were personally ordering the murder of individual people."

Jonathan thought through everything that had been told to him, and he marveled at how limited his options were. They'd constructed a box around him. "Why are you telling me this?" he asked.

"Because you'll find out, one way or the other," Irene explained. "You're that inquisitive, and you're that good. I drove all the way down here with David and Becky to make sure all of you understand the consequence of individual retaliation. It is not to happen."

Jonathan regarded his longtime friend with a cocked head. "Have you been drinking the Darmond Kool-Aid, Wolverine?"

"Don't you dare go there with me," she said. "My oath is to the Constitution, not to petty politics. I swore to protect this country from all enemies, foreign and domestic. I'm not happy with the twist that phrase has taken over the past few years, but I'm not going to oversee a global collapse based on a high-horse 'gotcha.' Not on my watch."

"So he walks on a murder charge," Jonathan said. The words tasted like acid.

"Is that *really* the line that you of all people are going to walk?" Irene fired back.

Under a strict interpretation of the laws of the land, Jonathan had committed multiple murders on his own. "I do what I do in service to the innocent," he said. Even as the words left his mouth, he realized that they sounded like they came from a Superman movie poster.

"Then do it again," Irene said. "Let this go."

Jonathan turned to the others in the room. "How are you guys doing?"

"I killed people," Becky said.

"They were all bad guys," Jonathan replied.

"But they were *people*. I need to find my way on that." She looked at her lap. "I'll get there."

"I don't think I can continue to do journalism," David said. "I like the investigation, but I don't like the politics."

"So, what's the alternative?" Jonathan asked.

"There's always a spot for you at the FBI academy," Irene said.

Jonathan laughed. "No politics there."

"That's an interesting option," David said. "But I've also been thinking about becoming a private investigator."

Jonathan smiled and took a sip. "Is that so?" he said.

"Yeah, that's so. In fact, between you and Wolverine, I'd like to set up a bidding war. Who wants to go first?"

At eight-thirty the next morning, a jogger in Burke Lake Park saw a shadow behind a tree. As she moved closer to investigate, she saw the blood and she screamed. A panicked 911 call brought the Fairfax County Police and Fire and Rescue Departments in force.

It took the White House two hours to make the formal announcement that Douglas Winters, chief of staff to the president, had committed suicide by firing a single bullet into his brain.

ACKNOWLEDGMENTS

My beloved bride Joy continues to be a source of strength, inspiration and sanity, making every day worth waking up to.

Thank you, Chris, for being who you are. I couldn't be more proud.

David Kirk did a brave thing through his generous donation to the Recycling Research Foundation and therefore earning his fictional namesake, as did Becky Beckeman with her donation to Living Word Lutheran School in Rochester, Michigan. I'm not sure either realizes how rarely stories end up well for characters whose names are so earned, but in this case they lucked out. I assure everyone who reads these words that the David and Becky who appear in this book are truly works of fiction, and bear no similarity to their namesakes.

My Canadian buddy and single malt sensei, Len Shaw, is neither a terrorist nor a former resident of the Soviet Union. Instead, he is a respected colleague whom I am honored to call my friend. He, too, shares no traits with his fictional namesake.

I owe a great thanks to Michelle Gagnon and John Ramsey Miller for reading an early draft of *High Treason* and giving me some excellent advice. If there are any mistakes in the book, blame them because they should have told me. Thanks also to The Rumpi—Art Taylor, Ellen Crosby, Donna Andrews, and Alan Orloff—for their ongoing advice and enduring friendship.

The team at Kensington Publishing continues to amaze me with their overwhelming support and guidance. Special thanks go to my editor, Michaela Hamilton, production editor Arthur Maisel, and my publisher, Laurie Parkin, and the guy who runs the whole shebang, Steve Zacharius. Adeola Saul is the best publicist in the business, and Alexandra Nicolajsen is my mistress of the Internet. Thanks to all.

But none of it would happen without my good friend and agent, Anne Hawkins.

Special Bonus

Turn the page to enjoy an exclusive short story that provides surprising insights into the character of hostage rescue specialist Jonathan Grave . . .

First time in print!

DISCIPLINE

Dr. Marvin Eugene Applewaite, Ed.D., had no idea what drew him to open his eyes in the middle of the night, but when he did, and he saw the child's battered face staring at him, he screamed. His body jerked like a grounded fish as he struggled to flip from his stomach to his back to defend himself. His legs tangled in the covers, rendering him momentarily defenseless.

His reaction startled the ten-year-old, who reflexively stepped backward.

Marvin sputtered, "Who . . . what do you mean . . . good God."

He'd seen this boy before. He was a student. Because of the adrenaline coursing through his system, he couldn't remember his name. In fact, just this afternoon—

"Headmaster, my father says he would like to speak to you," the boy said.

"Jon Gravenow?" The name popped into his head at the same moment when he realized that the boy had turned on the bedside lamp. "Get out of my house. Who do you think you are?"

The boy looked down and shoved his hands into the pockets of his jeans. Denim jeans and a T-shirt to visit the headmaster's house. This was exactly the kind of disrespectful behavior that made the boy a perpetual discipline problem at Northern Neck Academy.

"He, um, said he wanted to see you *now*."

As the adrenaline drained and awareness returned, Marvin sat taller in his bed. He adjusted his pajama blouse to make the buttons align.

"He did, did he? Well, it must be very urgent if he sends his son to burglarize my house. Do you know that you can go to prison for this? Do you know that you can be *expelled*?" That last point was a certainty, Marvin thought.

The boy continued to stare at his sneakers.

"Look at me, young man," Marvin commanded. His head was completely clear now. If there was one thing that an experienced educator knew, it was how to project authority over a child.

Jon Gravenow did as he was told. His left eye was still swollen from this afternoon, and it appeared that someone had applied a new butterfly bandage to his lip.

"Get out of my house at this moment, or I will call the police. Tell your father that if he wants to see me, he can call for an appointment."

Jon's face showed nothing. The rebuke triggered neither anger nor fear. "We'll be waiting in the living room," the boy said. He turned on his heel and left through the open door to the hallway. Sure enough, the far end was illuminated in the wash of light from the parlor downstairs.

The temerity! Marvin felt his blood boiling as he

rolled to his side and lifted the telephone from its cradle. Just who did these people think they were? Maybe a chat with the local police would set them on the right—

No dial tone.

The fear returned, fueled by a new rush of adrenaline. He realized for the first time that this was more than some childish prank; that he might truly be in danger. They'd cut the phone line, for heaven's sake, and now a man he'd never even met sat perched in his living room.

Marvin ran his options. The first was to flee, but he dismissed that out of hand. He was forty-six years old, not in the best of shape, and on the second floor of a home that boasted twelve-foot ceilings. As if that weren't bad enough, a leap from either of his bedroom windows would send him into a nest of wrought-iron patio furniture. Even if he survived the fall, he would likely wish that he hadn't.

He could dash down the stairs and try to make it to the front door, but that path would take him directly through the living room where his uninvited guests sat waiting.

He could try hiding, but then what? Would he just wait for them to become bored and leave on their own?

No, he thought, the only reasonable option was to face them. He would summon as much dignity as the occasion allowed, and he would hear what they had to say. After all, if their main desire had been to do him harm, they could have hurt him in his bed.

Come to think of it, the very fact that a man sent a child to deliver his message was a sort of peace offering in its own right.

His options, then, boiled down to only one: He would hear what his visitors had to say, and when their conversation was over, he would take the necessary actions to ensure that the adult went to prison, and the boy never again set foot in Northern Neck Academy.

Marvin took his time getting dressed. There was no time to shower, but he could certainly comb his hair and brush his teeth. That done, he donned the navy blue suit he had laid out for today. White shirt, yellow tie, black socks and matching shoes, shined to a high gloss. When he was buttoned and cinched, he tucked the loops of his wire-rimmed glasses behind his ears and headed for the stairs.

The man he saw waiting for him could have been his brother—better yet, his business partner. He, too, wore a suit—a slightly outdated gray three-piece, complete with a watch chain that stretched from pocket to pocket in his vest. He stood as Marvin entered the room, and beckoned for his son to likewise rise from his perch on the sofa.

"Doctor Applewaite," the man said, extending his hand. "Simon Gravenow. Forgive the intrusion. It's very nice of you to meet with us."

Marvin made no move to accept the gesture of friendship. "I will not forgive the intrusion," he said. "How dare you invade my home in the middle of the night—"

"Doctor," Gravenow interrupted. "Shake my hand."

Marvin felt a chill. The man's voice remained soft, and his tone reasonable, but his eyes projected danger. As if working on its own accord, Marvin's hand allowed itself to be folded into that of his guest.

"Please take a seat," Gravenow said, nodding to the

only remaining piece of furniture in the small room—a wooden chair with a padded seat which in Marvin's previous assignment had been part of a dining room set. "You, too, son," he added, nodding to the spot on the sofa that still bore the boy's impression. Simon kept Marvin's leather reading chair for himself.

Marvin felt heat rising in his ears. This seemed to be an effort to embarrass him in front of one of his students. "Might I ask—"

"No, you mightn't. Just sit. Listen and answer." Simon smiled as if he'd just told a joke at the dinner table.

Marvin sat. He'd long considered himself to be a good judge of character, one whose first impressions rarely were wrong, and Simon Gravenow was projecting a level of danger that he'd never witnessed before.

"You remember my son, don't you?" Simon asked.

"I do indeed. He's the one who frightened me out of a very sound sleep."

Gravenow nodded. "Is that all you remember him for?"

Marvin sighed. "Clearly, you're here for a specific reason. Perhaps if you could share what that is—"

"Listen and answer," Gravenow said again. "Do you remember his name, for example? As headmaster, I'd think that would be simple enough."

"His name is Jonathan," Marvin said.

The visitor smiled. "Very good. Thank you. And does he look at all different to you right now?" To the boy, he said, "Look at the headmaster, Jon."

"Clearly he's been in an altercation," Marvin said. "But surely you don't think that I had anything to do with those bruises on his face."

Gravenow's eyes turned even darker. "If I thought that, I'd be driving your teeth into your skull with a hammer."

A fist gripped Marvin's intestines. He knew without question that the man was speaking the truth, absent exaggeration.

"Tell me what you *do* know about his bruises."

"Your son was in a fight on the playground today."

"Over what?"

"Oh, for heaven's sake. Children fight all the time."

"But in this particular case, Jon told you specifically what the fight was about."

The fist in Marvin's gut grew tighter. Certainly, there had been an explanation, just as there was *always* an explanation when boys fought. But the explanations were never more than empty excuses. "Northern Neck Academy has very strict rules that prohibit fighting for any reason."

Gravenow pounded the arm of his chair with his fist. "Listen!" he boomed. Then, more softly, "And answer."

Marvin glanced at the front door. Was there any way, he wondered, to get past this lunatic and run for his safety? "Someone had allegedly taken something from him."

"*Allegedly?*"

Marvin saw the trap right away, and reconsidered. "Someone had taken his property," he said, correcting himself.

"That someone would be a boy named Raymond Carnes, right?"

Marvin's mind raced ahead to this same scene being played out in the Carnes household.

"That's okay," Gravenow said. "I understand your

hesitancy to speak of the other boy. Particularly under the circumstances. But to refresh your memory, the Carnes boy had stolen a Saint Christopher's medal that was given to Jon by his mother before she died. Jon told you this, did he not, the day before yesterday—the day when it was stolen?"

Marvin rolled his head on his shoulders. "His teacher did mention it to me, but when we asked the other party, he denied it ever happened. Without corroborating witnesses, we had no choice but to let the matter drop."

"So, the thief went free."

"The *alleged* thief. What else could we do?"

Gravenow leaned forward in his chair. "Let me tell you what I did," he said. "I told my son to get the medal back, and beat the shit out of the kid who'd taken it."

Marvin couldn't believe that he'd heard correctly. "Then you must be very proud," he said. "The other boy—"

"A broken nose, two broken teeth, and a sprained wrist," Gravenow finished for him. Indeed, he was proud. He fairly glowed with pride, in fact. "And after you pulled the parties apart, what did you find in little Raymond's pocket?"

Marvin rolled his eyes. He'd seen this coming. "The medal," he said. "But in a civilized society—"

"My son's medal," Gravenow clarified. "In the pocket of the boy who *claimed* he had not taken it."

"Mr. Gravenow, surely you're not suggesting that the kind of violence your son delivered can be justified under any circumstance. It was only a *thing*. An object. Apparently an object of high sentimental value, but no reasonable person hurts someone for the sake of things."

Gravenow smiled. "Because we live in a civilized society?"

"Exactly."

"I see." He turned to his son. "Jon?"

Marvin watched as the boy shifted his position on the sofa and reached behind the cushions to pull something out. When he saw what it was, Marvin thought he might cry.

Gravenow held out his hand, and Jon handed him a fifteen-inch wooden paddle, varnished to a high gloss and emblazoned with the Official Seal of Northern Neck Academy. "This look familiar to you, Headmaster?"

"Please don't," Marvin begged.

"Don't what?" Gravenow said.

"Please."

Gravenow stood. "Come now, Headmaster. Don't get all shy on me now. Please don't what? Hit you?"

Marvin felt tears on his cheeks. It was all he could do not to cower. He'd used that very paddle on Jonathan this afternoon. Fighting could not be tolerated.

"What, you think it would hurt to get hit with this little bit of wood?" Gravenow walked to Marvin's three-month-old 27-inch television and took out the screen with a golf swing. Something flashed inside the box as the glass shattered. "Whoa, that's got some heft to it. What do you use it for?"

Gravenow walked past Marvin into the dining room, where he took out the glass of the breakfront with three overhead chopping strokes.

"For God's sake!" Marvin yelled. "Please stop!"

"They're only *things*," Gravenow mocked. Somehow, he zeroed right in on the china that had once belonged to Marvin's great grandmother, and he reduced them to shards. "We don't worry about *objects*, remember? What do you want me to take out next, Jon?"

The boy looked like he wanted to dissolve into the fabric of the sofa.

Gravenow poked Marvin's shoulder with the rounded edge of the paddle. "You were going to tell me what you use this for," he said.

Marvin wanted to hide. He wanted to run. He was in the presence of a madman. Whatever he said, nothing would be understood. "Discipline," he said. Might as well spit it out and get it over with.

As Marvin tried to avoid his attacker's eyes, Simon Gravenow kept moving his head so that they could lock gazes. "Do I frighten you, Headmaster?"

Marvin was crying openly now. "Please don't do this."

"Listen and answer! Do I frighten you?"

"Yes," he mumbled.

"I'm sorry, I couldn't hear you."

"Yes!" He shouted it.

"But I haven't even hit you," Gravenow said. "I'm not even bigger than you. Imagine what it must be like to be a child when someone twice your size beats you with this." He made a show of holding the paddle like a baseball bat and took a few practice swings.

"We don't *beat* the children," Marvin said through a sob. "The paddle is a tool, not a weapon."

Gravenow took out the dining room chandelier with a full swing. "And what a fine tool it is. Share the procedure with me, *Doctor* Applewaite. How exactly do you use this tool?"

Marvin thought he might throw up. He'd never in his

life felt so terrified, so helpless. "We paddle the students' backsides when violations of policy are particularly egregious."

Gravenow nodded dramatically, as if finally understanding a great discovery. "You paddle their backsides." He spoke the words as if they tasted like vinegar. "Jon, stand up."

"Please," the boy said. "I don't want to."

"Now, boy. Show the good doctor the souvenir he left for you."

Slowly and hesitantly, Jonathan Gravenow turned his back to them. His hands trembled as he lowered his jeans and underpants just far enough to show the purple bruises. Just a quick flash, and then he hiked them up again and retreated back to the sofa, where he began to cry.

"So, tell me, Doc. When does paddling a backside become the *kind of violence that can't be justified under any circumstance*?" He leaned on the words that had come from Marvin's own mouth.

Marvin was shocked. He had no idea he'd hit the boy that hard. Sure, he'd been angry, and the ambulance had just taken the Carnes boy to the hospital, but never in a million years did he think—

His chest exploded in pain as Gravenow landed a full-force swing in the center of his breastbone.

"That, for example," Gravenow said. "Would you call that a paddling or a beating?"

Marvin struggled to catch his breath. "Please don't kill me."

"Tell me how it works, Jon. Where do you have to stand while he beats you?" After a moment of silence: "Answer me, son."

"At his desk," the boy said.

"Uh-huh. Well, the dining room table will do. On your feet, Headmaster."

"Please don't do this," Marvin begged.

"Up to you, Doc, I'll beat your ass with this thing, or your face. Decide now."

This was so disproportional. Gravenow had it all wrong. This was so much more violent than any punishment meted out in his office.

"Face it is, then," Gravenow said, and he set up for his swing.

"No!" Marvin yelled. He scrambled to his feet, despite the screaming pain in his chest, and darted to the dining room table. He faced it.

"Is this right, Jon?" Gravenow asked.

"His pants have to be down," Jonathan mumbled.

"You heard the boy."

His face burning with humiliation, Marvin undid his belt and pants and let them slide to his ankles. Now the world knew that he wore black Jockey briefs.

"He has to rest his forehead on his hands," Jonathan instructed, and as Marvin did just that, he heard the boy giggle though his tears.

"See, Doc, it's more about humiliation than pain, isn't it?" Gravenow asked. "Take a look at him, son. Put that image in your mind, and you'll never be afraid of him again."

A camera flashed. Marvin raised his head, but Gravenow pushed it back down. "If you want a copy, I'll get it to you," he said, close enough that he could feel the hot breath on the back of his neck. The paddle rested on his ass and he jumped.

"My son took back what belonged to him," Gravenow

said. "And you beat him for it. You humiliated him. You tried to break his spirit."

Marvin's panicked, choking sobs filled a brief silence.

"Listen very, very closely to me, Headmaster. Touch my boy again, and your next beating will come with a baseball bat and a ball-peen hammer. It will last for hours. You'll get a lesson in discipline that you will never, *ever* forget. Do you understand what I'm saying?"

Marvin nodded, trying in vain to keep his snot from leaking onto the table. "I understand," he said.

"I know you'll be tempted to report our little chat to the police," Gravenow went on. "I caution you that that would be a mistake. Of the many people in my employ, I assure you that I am among the most reasonable. Now, do you plan any further discipline against my boy?"

Marvin's terror swelled like a foul balloon, all but squeezing out his ability to breathe. "No," he choked.

"No what?"

"No sir."

"Because he's a nice boy, don't you think, Headmaster?"

Marvin wanted to turn and look—wanted to demonstrate how truly committed he was to treating Jonathan Gravenow with the care of fragile china. "Absolutely," he said. "I've always thought he was a nice child. And I swear to God that from now on, I'll never—"

The front door closed.

They'd taken the paddle with them.

Don't miss John Gilstrap's next breathtaking thriller
starring Jonathan Grave

SOFT TARGETS

An e-book exclusive novella coming from
Pinnacle in 2013!

CHAPTER ONE

Special Agent Irene Rivers gaped at the man who sat across the conference table from her. "You can't be serious."

"I am," Stephen Greenberg said. "We're dropping the charges."

Irene's heart raced. This couldn't be happening. "But he's a murderer," she said. "He kidnapped two children."

"Did he?" Greenberg folded his hands and leaned closer. "I'm not sure what version of the Constitution you read, *Special* Agent Rivers, but the one on my wall presumes innocence until proven guilty. If I can't prove my case, then by definition, Barney Jennings is innocent."

Irene felt anger rising in her cheeks. It was Greenberg's self-righteous smirk more than anything else. She, too, leaned closer. "What's with the smile, counselor? Whose side are you on?"

Greenberg threw back his head and launched a guffaw that was too big by half. "Oh, is that your strategy?" he boomed. "You're going to mask your own incompetence by impugning my priorities? That's very smart. Very quick." He winked. "It's no wonder that you're Assistant Director Frankel's favorite rising star. You've got the politics thing down pat."

She became all too aware of the pistol on her hip, and how easy it would be to snuff this asshole.

"You screwed up, Irene." Greenberg used his fingers to count off the transgressions. "You didn't have a warrant to enter Jennings's house, and you didn't Mirandize him before putting on the cuffs, and you beat a confession out of him."

Irene hadn't done any of those things—she hadn't even been on the raid—but two of her subordinates had. She didn't bother to correct the record because she knew where the buck stopped, and her shoulders were plenty broad enough to handle the burden.

Greenberg wasn't done. "As for the kidnappings, I don't remember you presenting any napped kids. I'll stipulate that we haven't been able to find the Harrelson boys, but in the eyes of the law, there's a giant step between being missing and being kidnapped."

"He confessed, Steve."

"While he was handcuffed and bleeding from the nose. Doesn't count."

"They're still missing," Irene pressed. "Doesn't that bother you at all?"

"A lot of things bother me. World hunger bothers me. The fact that the Menendez brothers needed a second trial bothers me. But I try to save myself for the stuff I can control."

"If we continue to lean on Jennings, we can squeeze him to reveal the location of the kids."

Greenberg retreated from the table and cocked his

head to the side. "Come on, Irene. Let's be adults here. We all know that those boys are in a shallow grave somewhere. Found or not found, dead is dead."

Right there, in clear relief, lay the difference between Irene's brand of lawyering and Greenberg's brand of career protection. "I'm not sure what version of justice you subscribe to, *Counselor* Greenberg, but in my world, we continue to operate on the assumption that people are alive until they are proven to be dead."

"That was clever," Greenberg taunted. "The way you used my sentence structure against me. That was very Harvard-like."

Her face went hot.

"Come off it, Irene. Be honest. In your experience with the Federal Bureau of Investigation, how many live, thriving victims have you found after, say, forty-eight hours?"

"It happens," Irene said. "And as long as it's possible—"

"You'll battle the Loch Ness monster and Satan himself to deliver the darlings from their danger. I get that. I even admire that. It's just a damn shame that your folks broke all the rules."

"But you could *try*," Irene said. "Even if you think you're looking at a mistrial down the road, if you filed the charges, we could at least make Jennings sweat."

Greenberg held his hands out to the side, a gesture of helplessness. Of surrender. "Do you know what Judge O'Brian would do to me if I brought this dog to him in open court? He'd eat me alive. He'd chew on the tender parts for a while, and then he'd feed on my guts. I'm not walking into that propeller, Irene. You can call me all the names you want and stick a hundred pins into your Steve Greenberg doll, but I'm not burning up my reputation on a ridiculous roll of the dice."

Greenberg checked his watch. "In three hours, maybe less, Barney Jennings will be a free man." When he looked up and made eye contact, his demeanor softened. "I know this is a tough moment for you, Irene. I wish it could be otherwise." He stood, pushing his wooden chair away from the table with the back of his knees. "This is going to sound patronizing as hell, but consider it a learning moment. We have rules for a reason, Agent Rivers."

Irene kept her head down, her eyes focused on a pale water ring that had bleached the dark surface of the cheap table. When she heard the door latch, and she knew she was alone, she considered succumbing to the pressure that built behind her eyes, but she pushed the emotion away.

This was just another case. You win some and you lose some, and if you let cases get inside the wall that was integral to every emergency responder's survival, you vastly increased the chances of ending your life with a pistol in your mouth. Irene was an expert at building and maintaining protective walls, but something about the Jennings case had cracked her foundations. Maybe it was the volume of blood on the walls, or the forensics that showed the obvious pleasure Jennings had taken from the slow torture of Julian and Samantha Harrelson.

She understood the passion that drove the investigating agents to act spontaneously. They had been tracking this monster for more than two months, and at the time they'd crashed the door without a warrant, they'd had reason to believe that the Harrelson boys were still inside Jennings's apartment. One fewer moment of torment had to be worth a lecture from your supervisor, right? Especially when kids were involved.

Except the boys weren't there. The investigating agents tore through the apartment, turning the place upside down looking for any evidence that would support what they already knew. They threw Jennings on the floor, ratcheted him into handcuffs tightly enough to draw blood, and they kicked him until he confessed to having watched the Harrelson boys walking to and from school, and of harboring sexual desires for them. Later, after Jennings had been hauled off to jail, investigators found a pair of boy's underpants that matched the size and the style of name-brand underwear that they'd found in the Harrelson home. The underpants had been crammed into a drawer in Jennings's bedroom that also held a variety of sadomasochistic sex toys.

Yet that haul of evidence had been deemed by the office of the United States attorney to be fruit from a poisoned tree and inadmissible in court. All because two well-meaning, hardworking public servants had failed to knock on a murderer's door.

Irene felt numb as she walked out of the federal courthouse onto Washington Street in Alexandria, Virginia, on as beautiful a day as the Washington, DC, suburb could conjure in early April. The bright sun took the edge off the chilly air, and as she walked down the sidewalk to rescue her car from the lot, she cast an impatient glance at the towering statue of the Confederate soldier that blocked the intersection with Prince

Street, the soldier's back perpetually turned on the north. "You freaking lost," she mumbled under her breath. "Get over it."

Irene's anguish wouldn't go away. Her boss made sure of that.

Barney Jennings held a press conference on the day he was released of all charges, lambasting the FBI for what he called their "overreach" in persecuting the innocent instead of prosecuting the guilty.

Later that same day, Irene's boss, Peter Frankel, publicly chastised her and her staff for unprofessional behavior, and Judge O'Brian sent a letter for her jacket that expressed his personal displeasure over the way she conducted herself in the Jennings investigation. "Justice and bullying are not the same things," he wrote. "They are not in the same league. As an officer of this court, your first responsibility—your primary responsibility—must always be to protect the rights of the innocent."

As if she needed a lecture on justice.

And then there was the final humiliation. She summoned the two agents involved—Tony Mayo and Amanda Whitney—into her office to deliver the verdict from the Office of Professional Responsibility, the FBI's version of the police department's Internal Affairs Division, held in equally high esteem.

Though they were both in their mid-thirties, they looked somehow much younger as they walked in step into the nondescript bland space that doubled for Irene's office. They stood at attention, their hands at their sides, by all measures prepared to take their medicine.

"Have a seat," Irene said.

They hesitated.

"Both of you." She used the tone that people wisely interpreted as leaving no room for negotiation.

They sat. In unison.

Irene wanted to tell them to relax, that this really was just a bit of posturing that would quickly blow over, but this was no time to lie. "It's bad," she said.

At the sound of Irene's words, color drained from around Amanda's mouth, even as Tony sat a little taller. "How bad?" Tony asked. His Latin heritage clearly reflected in his coloring. Tony Mayo had a chiseled, athletic look about him. If he hadn't chosen the FBI, he could have chosen to model clothes.

Irene sighed. She'd learned that the most merciful way to deliver awful news was to shrug away all the weasel words and drill straight between the eyes. "On the one-to-ten scale of badness, it's about an eleven," she said. "The letters going in your file are crippling. They hold you accountable for Barney Jennings being reinflicted onto the American public."

Amanda said, "Maybe if Assistant Director Frankel hadn't made such a big deal out of the arrest—"

"You screwed up," Irene said, cutting her off. "That's the bottom line here. Don't make the mistake of assuming that your role was anything short of causal."

Tony's face reddened. "You're suggesting that we should have just ignored the potential suffering that was going on behind that door?"

Irene felt her cheek twitch. It was her anger tell. One of the major traits that separated new agents from veterans was the ability to embrace one's role in a Golf Foxtrot—a goat fuck. "You made a call," she said. "In a perfect world, that would be admirable simply on the basis of the courage it took. Unfortunately, we live in the world created by his royal eminence J. Edgar Hoover, and the anticipation is that everybody will not only have the courage to make the call but the clairvoyance to know that it is the right one. You missed on the clairvoyance part."

"With all respect, ma'am, you weren't there," Amanda said.

"I didn't have to be," Irene snapped. "We have rules, and the rules are based upon the Constitution of the United States. None of us has the authority to circumvent them. That's why we emphasize them so heavily in the Academy and retrain you on them so frequently. You two broke the rules."

Mayo screwed his face into a scowl. "Excuse me, Irene, but this is an entirely different tune than the one you sang before you met with the AUSA. Back then, you seemed to understand."

"Back then I thought I had a valid argument on your behalf," Irene said. The words tasted like acid. "It turns out that I did not."

"So we're just your sacrifice to the career gods."

Irene felt something break inside her gut, taking with it her sympathy for her team. She felt her face redden and she deliberately fought the urge to yell. Rather, she lowered her voice to barely a whisper. "It's time for you to be quiet, Agent Mayo," she said.

Mayo's eyes flashed fear at the sound of her voice. He looked like he might want to apologize, but he wisely chose to desist.

"A career in the FBI is a lot like a poker game," Irene said. "The safest move is to walk away and watch a movie instead. Once you give in to the temptation, though, the game is on and every hand is high stakes. Taking a big chance can bring great reward, or it can bring ruin."

Amanda interrupted with "I don't think—" But that was as far as she got before Irene cut her off with a glare.

"It's time for you to shut up, too. Let's forget about the good intentions and the gut feelings and settle in on the facts of what you did. You entered a targeted home without a warrant, and you beat a suspected felon in order to extract a confession. I confess that it's been some time since I was in the Academy, but wasn't there a class or two about the evils of invoking Gestapo tactics?"

The reality of their situation hit both of the young agents simultaneously. Mayo's jaw slackened. "Are we being fired?"

"No," Irene said. The next part would hurt most. "You're being encouraged to resign." She looked away from the tears that rimmed his eyes.

"This is all I've wanted to do," Mayo said. "It's all I know. It's all I've trained for."

"And you can stay," Irene said. "For as long as you can tolerate the worst postings on the planet and a career of scut work." She looked up at them and sighed as she leaned closer to the edge of her desk, her elbows on her thighs. "You're fundamentally good agents," she said. "You've developed some solid cases and made some good arrests. No one disputes that. But the Bureau is a political place and you committed the unpardonable sin: you embarrassed the assistant director. As Peter Frankel himself has said countless times, 'One *oh shit* wipes out a lifetime of *attaboys*.' We can complain that it's unfair and old school and fundamentally wrong, but that doesn't change the nature of the Bureau."

"I've got a family," Amanda said.

"As do we all," Irene replied. She leaned back and struck a more positive tone. "Come on, people. You've both got law degrees from top ten schools and you're both young. You can make this a speed bump in your larger career, or you can make it the end. That's up to you. But the fact remains that with your file burdened with a letter like you received from OPR, your careers are over. You're the equivalent of a duty officer in the Navy who's on watch when the ship runs aground. It's over."

"What if I choose not to resign?" Amanda asked. "What if I decide that scut work is a fair price to pay for my government retirement?"

"Don't," Mayo said, standing. Anger had displaced sadness in his eyes, and Irene was glad to see it. "Don't give her the satisfaction." He focused on Irene and leveled his forefinger at her. "I just got it. Our careers have to end so that yours can flourish. Throw us on the sacrificial fire and gods of bureaucracy are satisfied."

Irene took care to keep her face impassive as she listened to the truth. "You may go now," she said. "Good luck."

CHAPTER TWO

Irene sat in a booth near the front window of the Cracker Barrel restaurant in Massaponax, Virginia, just a few hundred yards from the perpetual motion of Interstate 95. She kept one foot tucked under her to make the seat slightly more comfortable, and she bided her time playing the golf tee triangle game that came with the table. The trick was to leapfrog golf tees across the board until only one remained. Thus far, the best she'd managed was three, and that pissed her off. She knew she was better than that.

She was so engrossed in the game that when her guest finally arrived at tableside, she jumped.

"I'm sorry to startle you," the man said. He wore his perpetual smile, and his mere presence made Irene relax. He also wore a black suit and a clerical collar.

She stood. "Dom," she said. "Thank you so much for coming." She'd known Dominic D'Angelo since he was a teenager. Tall and lean with a thick mane of black hair, he'd always been a handsome kid, and now he was a gorgeous man, perhaps rendered more attractive by the fact that his vows made him unapproachable.

He drew her into an embrace. "Irene," he said. "It's been a long time. The tone of your message scared me. Are you all right?"

As she pulled away, she gestured to the booth. "Please," she said. "Have a seat."

Father Dom slid into the space across from her. "Do I need my stole?" He asked the question with a smile, but she understood that beneath the banter lay a genuine offer.

"No," she said. "I don't need to confess so much as I need to vent."

"First things first," Dom said. "How are the girls?" In addition to his doctor of divinity, he also carried a PhD in psychology. He knew how to wield both specialties to great effect.

Irene felt herself lighten as she smiled. "They're both fine," she said. "Ashley is destined to be the freshman soccer superstar of her high school, and Kelly is twelve going on thirty-five. Ashley is on her way to an invitation-only soccer tournament as we speak, in fact. She's that good."

Dom smiled. "I'm impressed. But good lord. Fifteen and twelve? How is that possible?"

"Fourteen and twelve," Irene corrected. "Don't make it worse than it is."

"Still. It seems just yesterday that they were toddlers."

Irene laughed. "Okay, let's not go there. I can nearly say the same about you. How are you, by the way?"

"I've been well," he said. "I could complain, but no one would listen."

A moment of silence passed. "You know, I missed you during your Army years. You just fell off the face of the earth."

Dom shrugged with one shoulder. "I didn't fall. I wandered. For whatever reason, it was important for me to disappear for a while." He forced a smile. "If nothing else, Uncle Sam helped me realize what my true calling was."

"And it wasn't killing people."

He held up his hand. "Not fair. Some of the finest people I've ever met, I met in the Army. It's not the cliché."

Irene blushed. She had no idea why she'd taken a cheap shot. "I know that," she said. "I meant no offense."

"And I took none."

Irene let a moment pass to reset the conversation. "So, you're in Montross, Virgina, now?"

Before he could answer, a pretty blond thing named Gabby stopped at their table. It turned out that she would be taking care of them this afternoon, and she wanted to know if they were ready to order. It was barely two in the afternoon and Irene was anything but hungry, but it would have been rude to take up space without paying at least a little rent. She ordered a cheeseburger and Dom ordered a waffle. Once the waters and coffee were poured, Gabby left them alone again.

"I'm not in Montross," Dom corrected. "I'm near Montross, in a little place called Fisherman's Cove. It's a delightful town filled with wonderful people."

"And you're the pastor of a church there?"

"I am. Saint Kate's—Saint Katherine's. It's a wonderful old place that sits on a hill. Just a perfect setting."

Irene heard her bullshit bell ring. Sometimes she wished that she could stop being a trained investigator. "I mean no offense, Dom, but aren't you a little young for pastorhood?"

He smiled. "Yes," he said, "but that's a story for a different time." He folded his arms across his chest. "You called me here for a reason."

And so the pleasantries ended. She held nothing back as she revealed the details of the Barney Jennings debacle, pausing only long enough to accept delivery of their meals and to assure Gabby that they needed nothing else for now.

Dom listened, the furrows in his brow deepening with every passing detail. When she finished, he looked as if he wanted more. "Is that all of it?" he asked.

"A murderer went free, Father. And two fine careers were ruined in the process. Isn't that enough?"

Dom cocked his head and offered a smile. "I'm always on your side, Irene," he said. "Never think for a moment that I'm not."

"But?" She didn't get why he wasn't frothing with ire over her circumstance.

"No but," he said. "You made a mistake. It comes with that human package you wear. We all do that from time to time. You need to cut yourself a break."

Irene's ears went hot. "A man and a woman are *dead*, Father. Two boys are missing. For all I know, they're dead, too. Worse, for all I know, they're in someone's basement being tortured every day. I allowed that to happen."

Dom had cut his waffle into precise quadrants, which he reduced to triangles before detaching a corner and slipping it into his mouth without syrup. He took his time chewing while Irene positively vibrated in her seat awaiting his answer.

He took a sip of coffee and said, "You don't impress me as a whiner. Why are you whining?"

Anger bloomed. "Excuse me?"

"You're whining. You're showing righteous indignation. Throwing yourself a pity party. If I understand the details correctly, if the ball hadn't been fumbled, we would know for a certainty that this Barney Jennings fellow had killed people. Now you only suspect that—or maybe you know it in your heart. Whatever. Explain to me where you could have prevented the deaths or the kidnappings in the first place."

"I don't understand your point."

"Sure you do. You're beating yourself up as if you'd somehow pulled the trigger on the crime itself. You didn't. The Jennings guy did. Now there's been a screwup and he's free, but that's where your fault—if that's even the right word—begins and ends. There is no blood on your hands, Irene."

How could he not understand something so obvious? "But Dom, it's my job to keep bad guys off the street. If he moves on from this and hurts someone else—"

"Then you'll be there to catch him. Or you won't. But that isn't what we were talking about. Don't change the discussion in midstream."

Irene felt a stab of anger. This wasn't how the conversation was supposed to go. She was supposed to vent and Dom was supposed to understand.

Dom's expression softened. "I sense I'm making it worse," he said. "I don't mean to sound harsh. In fact, I mean to sound the opposite of harsh. I just don't want you beating yourself up more than is reasonable."

"I understand. I don't know what to do with the anger."

Through a mouthful of waffle, Dom said, "I imagine a couple of extra hours on the shooting range might help."

Irene chuckled. "They don't let you put up pictures of suspects and shoot at them."

"But only you and God will know what's in your heart while you're wasting a silhouette." They shared a laugh. "Isn't there some place in FBI Land where you can talk through these things with people who have been there?"

"Absolutely there are," Irene said. "And to go there is to mark the first day of the end of your career. The spirit of J. Edgar Hoover still wanders the halls. Any and all weaknesses are seen as deal breakers."

"Precisely the attitude that keeps psychologists in business," Dom said.

"But you don't cost anything," Irene said with a smile.

"I see. I am merely value added for your membership in the Catholic Church."

Irene reached across the table and grasped his hand. "Do me a favor, Father. Never use the word *merely* in any sentence that refers to you. You're a very special man."

He blushed, considered saying something, then put another wad of waffle into his mouth.

"What you're telling me is that I should put on my big-girl panties and get over it," Irene said.

"Do yourself a favor," Dom said, grinning. "Never use the word *panties* in a conversation with a priest. It makes us uncomfortable."

Irene had burned a few hours of personal time for her meeting with Dom, and rather than driving all the way back into the District to return to work for a couple of hours, she headed home to King's Park, a bastion of suburbia in Fairfax County, just outside the Beltway. Constructed in the early sixties, the homes here were all built like fortresses on quarter-acre parcels of land. Her model—a Duchess located on Thames Street— was the only home she'd ever seen where the sole access to the backyard was to go upstairs. That's what happens when you build a house into the side of a hill.

She and the girls had moved here after the divorce, and over the intervening three years Irene had come to think of the place as a real home. Getting rid of the avocado appliances had helped.

Upon entering through the front door, Irene dropped her purse on the bench that sat in the foyer and crossed over to the kitchen, where she unholstered her SIG Sauer P228 pistol and deposited it into the cupboard over the refrigerator. Back when the kids were little, she'd taken the extra precaution of locking the weapon in a box, but now that they were older and accomplished shooters themselves, that no longer made sense.

With her weapon put away, she removed a Diet Coke

from the fridge, popped the top, and wandered over to the answering machine on the counter next to the stove. The flashing light told her that she'd missed five phone calls today. Actually, if recent past was precedent, Ashley had missed four phone calls and Irene had missed one. Now that her naturally athletic daughter had sprouted breasts, the boys had begun to swarm.

Irene pressed the replay button. "Um, hi, Mrs. Rivers. This is Bruce Parker, coach of the War Hawks, Ashley's team for the Northern Virginia Invitational League. Ashley was supposed to report to the gym by eight-thirty, but now it's eight forty-five, and I was wondering if there was a problem. Give me a call, please, one way or another. If she's not going to be able to make the game, I'm going to have to make arrangements very quickly." He then gave a call-back number.

Irene's stomach knotted. Ashley had been looking forward to this tournament for weeks. It was all she could talk about this morning as she left the house to walk to the school bus stop. How on earth would she—

The machine moved on to its second message. Same voice as before. "Mrs. Rivers, Bruce Parker again. It's nine-fifteen, and we need to get on the road. I cannot tell you how disappointed I am in Ashley—and, frankly, in you—for not having the courtesy of informing the team that Ashley had other plans." Then a click as the call terminated.

Irene looked at the clock on the wall. It was four-twenty. What the hell was going on? Where was Ashley? For that matter, where was Kelly? She should have been home by now, too. A talker by nature, Kelly prattled constantly about her adolescent schedules and concerns, but as Irene scoured her brain for any snippet of conversation they might have had that would explain her absence, she came up with nothing.

The third message: "Hello, Mrs. Rivers. This is Roberta Ingersoll at Lake Braddock High School. Ashley didn't make it into school today, and I'm just calling to make sure that you are aware, and to ask you to verify that her absence is excused. Please call me at . . ."

Irene made no note of the number. Clearly, something was wrong. Her children were missing. *No,* she chided herself. *There has to be some reasonable—*

Next message. "Um, yo, Mrs. Rivers. This is Charlie Binks, and I was wondering if Ashley could call me when she gets home—"

Irene pushed the dump button. She had no idea who Charlie Binks was, but he was clearly young, and he was one of the honey-sniffing bees.

Message five. "Hello, Irene," a voice said. "When you get a chance, check under the welcome mat outside your front door. This should be fun." Click.

The caller's voice had a gravelly quality that made Irene wonder if the voice was being faked. The tone was all menace. Taken in context with the rest, the message made Irene's heart rate triple. Her family was under attack. Moving quickly now, her hands trembling, she pulled her firearm back out of the cupboard and slid it back into her holster, high on her right hip. Normally, she went to considerable lengths to hide the weapon from sight, but now she didn't care. In fact, she wanted the neighbors to be fully aware of the fact that she was willing and able to gun down anyone who got in her way.

Irene forced herself to move slowly as she approached the front door. Frightened and jumpy, she recognized this as the time when she would be most likely to make a bad judgment. Panic was the number-one killer among law enforcement personnel. Adrenaline rushed, hands shook, and the first casualty was situational awareness. She'd seen it happen countless times, both in the heat of a firefight, and in the evidence that followed such firefights.

She walked to the front door and pulled it open, standing there for a moment, scanning for anything out of the ordinary. More specifically, for any*one* out of the ordinary. The world seemed stable. Glancing at the stoop, she saw where the mat lay askew. *Welcome to the Rivers's.* The girls had bought her that for her birthday last year and she remembered suppressing the urge to correct the placement of the apostrophe.

Never taking her eyes away from the horizon for more than a few seconds at a time, Irene squatted low and lifted the corner of the mat with her left hand. The right stayed free for the SIG, just in case.

She thought the envelope was small for its color. Generally, manila envelopes were big things—eight and a half by eleven, minimum, designed to mail documents flat—but this one was actually smaller than a white envelope you'd use for the mail. Even as she lifted it, she knew that she was breaking the most basic rules of evidence gathering. She was contaminating what might otherwise be a trove of trace, but to the depths of her soul, she didn't care. Ashley and Kelly were *missing*. The weight of that word, and all that it implied, made her knees sag.

The envelope bore no markings on the outside. What was she expecting, a return address? Stupid criminals had done stupider things. As she pinched open the butterfly clip at the top of the back side of the envelope, she made note of the fact that the glue on the flap hadn't been moistened. That meant that the guy who was responsible—Jennings—had been smart enough not to leave any DNA evidence. And if he'd been smart enough to do that, then he'd no doubt been smart enough to wear gloves and some kind of outer garment that would keep fibers and hair from settling onto whatever the envelope brought.

She told herself that that meant there was no harm in ignoring the evidentiary procedures. As she pulled the contents out, she noted the details. White printer paper, folded in half, words in, not out. That told her that Jennings had a gift for drama. Hide the reveal until the last possible moment.

Her mind screamed for her to stop and call the CSU—crime scene unit. This document needed to be processed. It needed to be evaluated for all manner of trace evidence. The ink on the paper could be traced, and the grammar could be evaluated for ethnic patterns. All of it could be pristine only once, and here she was ruining that moment.

Ashley and Kelly are missing.

Opening the paper, she noted that the words were printed in a standard typeface—she thought it was called Times New Roman, but her own printer was new enough that she just used what the machine prescribed, so how could she know? She did see, however, that the print was fancy, not the work of the upscale dot matrix printer that she'd paid a fortune for. Did that mean that Jennings was rich, or did it mean merely that he had access to a good printer, one of those ink-jet jobs that she'd seen in the director's office?

Her hands shook.

I have them. If you contact your colleagues, I
will know and I will kill them. That would be
such a sad end for two such beautiful little girls.
As long as you suffer in the knowledge that they
are gone, they needn't suffer at all. One day, if
you behave, I'll give them back to you. If you
talk to the police, you'll get them back one part
at a time. If you just play the game, you'll get
them back whole, older, wiser, and very street
smart.

Irene's vision blurred as she read the words. The air became too thick to breathe. Honest to God, if this monster so much as touched her girls—

What? What would she do? What *could* she do? He'd *already* touched them, for Christ's sake. How else would he have shoved them into a car, or done whatever he'd done to snatch them off the street? Her anger melded with her fear, and the resultant stew of emotion was a toxic one. Irene felt overwhelmed by the need to kill someone. To kill Barney Jennings. Could it be that simple?

Her stomach seized as she thought about that smirk in his press conference. It was his way—well established via the Harrelson boys—to completely hide those he took. If Irene killed Jennings, then she would never know where her girls were.

Her head ached as thousands of thoughts flooded her brain all at once, as if they were trying to expand the volume of her skull. Maybe this is what panic felt like. Panic: the emotion that everyone promised was the big killer in an emergency. It occurred to her in a bitter haze just how easy it was to think of panic as a weakness when it's considered in the third person, yet is so organic in the first.

A monster had taken her *children*. She saw their innocent faces, smiling under their helmets of blond hair, and then she saw those angelic faces morphing into masks of terror. Of pain. She saw them wondering when their mother was going to come and rescue them.

The only rational course was for her to call her office and get the Bureau involved. This was precisely the kind of case that would galvanize every agent in the Bureau to avenge the harm that had befallen one of their own.

I will know and I will kill them.

The words terrified her. Instinctively, intuitively, she knew that the kidnapper was bluffing—how could he possibly know what was going on inside the closed sphere that defined the law enforcement community?—but Jennings had shown a disturbing level of cunning and cleverness. Would he state something so dogmatically if it were not true? She sensed not.

Irene tried to corral her thoughts, bring order to the blooming panic. It was obvious what she *should* do, what she would tell the person on the other end of a phone call to do. But this was real. This was *first person*, and deep in her soul, she knew that Jennings—the author of the note—was telling the truth.

So, what was she supposed to do with that? Was she supposed to just trust this asshole with the lives of her daughters? That was as nonstarting as any nonstarter could be. Was she supposed to pretend that none of this had happened and pray that it would come to a happy ending? Surely Jennings would know that that would never happen.

Maybe he was expecting her to go to the police, and as soon as she did, he would use that as an excuse to kill Ashley and Kelley. She had to assume that was the case.

Irene stepped back into the foyer and pushed the door closed. When she was confident that she was invisible to the outside world, she sat down on the patch of tile floor and read the note again. And again. It was all too much to process. What was that monster—?

No. She couldn't go there. That was a trip from which there could be no happy return. Once you started to imagine the harm that *could* befall a loved one, no scenario but the worst could possibly resonate.

She needed to remain positive. Or if not positive, then optimistic. Not pessimistic. There was a way to solve this.

But how?

Irene needed help, but all of the standard avenues for assistance—the ones who carried badges and guns—were out of the question, at least for the time being.

I will know and I will kill them.

Jesus.

Jesus. Exactly. In that moment, in that single rush of clarity, she knew exactly what she needed to do.